RETURN TO ISLE OF THE DEAD

AND OTHER TALES OF ALHAZRED

RETURN TO ISLE OF THE DEAD

AND OTHER TALES OF ALHAZRED

DONALD TYSON

WEIRD HOUSE

First Edition Paperback

ISBN: 978-1-957121-12-3

Text © 2022 by Donal Tyson

Editor and Publisher, Joe Morey

Cover art © 2022 by Cyrus Wraith Walker
Cover and interior design by Cyrusfiction Productions

Weird House Press
Central Point, OR 97502
www.weirdhousepress.com

Contents

Return to Isle of the Dead

1.

"There is no island listed on my *chart* for this part of the Red Sea."

An edge of belligerence crept into the voice of Captain Hassan of the trading galley *Eastern Star* that I had not heard him use before. The glaring black eyes in his sun-darkened face and his uncommon height gave him an intimidating aspect as he stood leaning over me. I am a tall man. Very few other men lean over me.

I took my time as I surveyed the southern horizon across the galley's rail. The sky was a cloudless blue and the water a deeper color that was almost purple. We were far enough off the Arabian coast that no land of any kind was visible.

"Isn't that the point of this expedition?" I replied casually.

He swallowed his frustration and spoke as an adult who reasons with a child.

"I am here because my Caliph, Moawiya ibn Yazid, has ordered me to convey his soldiers wherever you tell me to take them, but I do not believe that such a thing as a floating island exists, or ever has existed."

"I never told you it floated, Captain. For all I know, it comes into being for a time, and then simply disappears."

Harsh laughter revealed his stained teeth. He was fond of chewing betel nut, which he obtained through eastern trade. The stimulating red juice of the nut made his teeth appear rotten.

"That is even more ridiculous."

"Nevertheless, you have been well paid to take us where we want to go."

"But not for eternity," he objected. "I have a ship filled with cargo destined for various ports along the Arabian coast. Bales of cotton, bolts of silk, tea, sugar, amphorae of wine, vinegar, aqua fortis."

"The ship will remain under my command until I tell you otherwise," I said with an edge in my tone. "Continue to follow the shipping lane south."

His beard bristled and his dark eyes widened, but he thought better of his answer, and instead silently turned on the heel of his boot and climbed to the elevated rear deck.

Altrus had been watching the exchange. He came over and leaned on the rail beside me.

"The crew is starting to talk."

"What could they possibly say that would interest me?" I asked, my eyes on the horizon.

"They say this voyage is cursed, and that you are a necromancer who will lead them down into the maelstrom of hell."

"How did they learn I was a necromancer?"

"Probably our good captain told his first mate. There is no place on this ship where you can speak and not be overheard."

This statement could not be argued. There was no spot on the deck that was unoccupied by cargo or men. In many places men lay across the cargo, eating or sleeping.

I looked at the battle-scarred face of the mercenary. Apart from

Martala, the young Egyptian girl who kept my house at Damascus and accompanied me on my excursions away from the city, he was the nearest thing I had to a friend. The red sear mark on his cheek above his beard gave him a piratical aspect. He met my gaze with quiet confidence.

"It would be embarrassing to return to Moawiya without even locating the island, given that I am the person who encouraged him to back this expedition with his private funds," I murmured.

"Someone needed to propose it. The devilish creatures on that ensorcelled island are not of this world, and they are building a walled fortress city. It can only mean that they plan an invasion."

"I agree, someone had to do something." I returned my eyes to the horizon. "But why by the Old Ones did it have to be us?"

He laughed. "Because there is no one else. We three are the only ones to have seen the island and lived."

"I should be at home in Damascus," I grumbled. "I hate the water."

"As do I, Alhazred. How much longer should we search?"

"I don't know." I pondered the matter. "Three days. If we don't locate the island in three more days, I'll let that oaf of a captain deliver his wares and we'll return home."

Martala approached the rail on my other side. As was her usual custom when we ventured far from the gates of Damascus, she was disguised as a young man. She had bound her breasts to flatten her chest, and wore her long, dark hair coiled up beneath her head scarf, the corner of which she kept across her mouth and nose. I had told the captain that she was my scribe. No doubt the crew believed her to be my boy lover. Better that than have them realize her sex. It was considered by superstitious seamen a misfortune for any ship to sail with a woman aboard.

We all had adopted the loose trousers and tunics best suited to a sea-faring existence, but out of cautious habit I had ordered my companions to retain their stout leather boots. It was the custom of seamen to go barefoot on ship, but bare feet were a poor way to cross desert sands, as I had learned from bitter experience. I wanted us prepared to face any mishap that might arise.

As was my usual custom, I had elected to travel with a shaved chin and no head covering. It was a personal choice influenced by my virtual immunity from the rays of the sun. There was a rumour in my native village that my mother had lain with a djinn, and that I was the result of this coupling. I had reason to believe the truth of it, and attributed my pale skin and near-immunity to the solar rays to my inhuman father's blood.

As always, the polished white skull of a ghoul hung from my belt. Most people, upon seeing it for the first time, assumed it to be some kind of trophy, but it was a tribute to Gor, the leader of the Black Spring Clan, who during my exile in the Empty Space had taken me into his clan and taught me the ways of ghouls that had allowed me to survive in the most hostile desert in the world. I wore it always to remind myself that I was more ghoul than man.

"Every time we come to sea, I swear to myself I'll never get on another ship. Yet here I am," Martala said.

"You can't be seasick," I told her. "The sea is as quiet as a lily pond."

"It's the smells. They turn my stomach."

I tilted back my head and scented the air. Salt, tar, wet wood with a trace of rot, urine. It was not any worse than the marketplace at Damascus.

"How are the Caliph's guardsmen?"

"Quiet," she said. "Relaxed. They are treating this as a leave of duty from the palace."

"They haven't started to mutter amongst themselves?"

"They aren't as superstitious as the ship's crew."

I had noticed that the captain of the soldiers, a serious man named Bassir, kept them under a tight discipline. Every morning he drilled them on the open deck, and in the afternoons he had them maintain their weapons and armour with goose grease so they would not rust in the salt spray. Busy hands are the best remedy for idle talk.

"Three more days," I said, watching a pair of dolphins sport in the curling white wave from the ship's bow. "Then we'll go home."

2.

When the ship beached itself upon the sand, the impact was so gentle it did not even wake me from sleep. It was the beautiful human face of Sashi, the lesser desert djinn who inhabits my body, that drew me from my dream by floating upon the darkness of my closed eyelids.

Something has happened, my love.

What is wrong? I asked her in my mind even as I was passing from sleep to wakefulness.

There was a tremble that ran through the ship, and now the crew is stirring.

I heard their voices raised in alarm and the pounding of their bare heels through the planks above my head. Sliding from my bunk, I felt over the surface of the little table that stood near for my tinder box, and began to strike sparks.

My activities woke Altrus in the bunk above mine. Martala, who slept on the floor, did not stir.

"What's wrong?"

"The ship has struck something, I think. Wake the girl."

We dressed quickly, if awkwardly, by the light of a single candle. The captain had given us his own cabin as a courtesy. It was the best accommodation on the galley, but cramped quarters for three people. The deck beams were low enough that Altrus and I needed to duck our heads to avoid hitting them.

"Alhazred, your face," Martala reminded me as I was about to leave the cabin.

No matter how often I applied the spell of glamour that hid my mutilated features from the world, at times I still forgot. The glamour gave me back the face I would have had, before King Huban of Yemen ordered my ears and nose cut off and my cheeks slashed open in punishment for getting his daughter, the princess Narissa, with child. It also restored the illusion of my missing manhood, which Huban's torturers had severed from my body, but the spell only endured for a span of hours. I was forced to renew it two or three times a day. It was a clever mask, but still no more than a mask. When I forgot to apply it, those who saw me ran screaming.

The waxing moon had already dropped below the horizon, and even the light from the stars was obscured by a haze in the heavens. On deck, we found a kind of organized chaos. Men ran back and forth, dim shadows in the ship's lanterns. The crew did not seem greatly alarmed, which reassured me, but the galley slaves chained to the oars in the hold were yelling through the open hatches and waving their arms for attention. The same thing was in all of their minds – the fear of drowning in irons as the ship dragged them to the bottom.

As Bassir hurried past, I grabbed his elbow. He glared at me, and I thought for a moment he was going to raise his fist, but he held his annoyance.

"The ship grounded on a sandbar," he said. "The hull does not appear to be breached, thank Allah, but some of its planks may have sprung." He hurried away before I could reply.

A familiar scent touched the remnant of my nose. It was not the smell of wet sand, but of black mud.

"I think we may have found what we searched for," I told my companions. "Or rather, it may have found us."

The first pale glow of dawn confirmed my surmise. We had grounded, not on a sandbar, but on the beach of an island. All around us were upthrusting rocks, but by some miracle of fortune the ship had threaded its way between them and lodged its keel in the soft sand.

Captain Hassan came to me, his bristling face at war between wonder and confusion.

"There is no island in this part of the sea. My charts are good charts. They show only deep water here."

"Calm yourself. This is the isle we sought."

With an effort he mastered his emotions.

"Forgive me, Alhazred. When you spoke of an island that moved, an island of the walking dead, I did not believe you."

"But you believe me now."

"By Allah, I do. What would you have of me?"

I thought for a moment as I surveyed the shore.

"Your task and that of your crew must be to refloat the *Eastern Star* and insure that no serious damage was done to her hull."

He nodded. This was something he understood.

"We can do that at the next high tide. But I will need more men."

"When is the high tide?"

He glanced at the sun, which was just rising above the sea.

"Another seven or eight hours."

"How many soldiers do you need?"

"If Bassir would give me twenty of his strongest men, I believe we could succeed."

This the captain of the royal guard was willing to do. He also assigned twenty more of his soldiers to stand ready on the beach with war bows, to guard the ship and her crew while the rest worked to loosen her from the sand.

The remaining twenty guardsmen followed us as we made our way into the morning shadows beneath the tall trees. They were unlike any trees I had ever seen before. Not strange enough to draw attention to themselves from a distance, but subtly different from ordinary trees. Instead of cracked bark on their trunks, they had a kind of wrinkled covering that was almost like elephant hide.

"A strange forest," Bassir said. "There are no birds."

"And no beasts," Altrus said.

We stood for a moment to listen. The silence was unnatural.

Altrus slapped his neck. "But no shortage of biting flies."

Around mid-morning, after several hours were wasted forcing our way through dense undergrowth, we came upon the road that led across the island to the walled city of the dead at its center. The last time I and my companions had followed it, we had been accompanied by walking corpses from the shipwreck that stranded us on the island, but this time there were no drowned seamen for the island's strange sorcery to return to a false semblance of life.

"Tell me again about the monsters who rule this place," Bassir ordered in a tone that was too much like a command for my liking. I let it pass.

"They are as I already described them to you, in appearance somewhat like the insect known as the preying mantis, but black all over and taller than a man. They talk to each other in a language made up of clicking sounds and hisses."

"Their weapon is a kind of web," Altrus said. "They cast it like a net. It is too strong to break, but its strands can be cut with a knife or sword."

"That is the only weapon we have seen," I pointed out. "They very likely have others we have not seen."

"Tell me again what they do with the tubes that hang down from their mouths."

"They insert liquids into the stomachs of their slaves. I think they must feed them that way. But they have other uses for the tubes. They did the same thing to my companions and myself to render us unconscious."

A soldier near enough to hear, who thought I could not see him from the corner of my eye mocked a face of disgust. The man beside him started to laugh, but managed to control himself by coughing into his hand.

Altrus looked at me. I shook my head. No point in arousing hostility by noticing fools.

"Forgive me, Alhazred, but my men have never heard such a story before," Bassir said with a slight smile of apology.

"Before we are finished here they will have stories of their own to tell," I said.

"Those who survive," Martala added under her breath.

3.

We emerged from the forest and stood at the edge of the lake. It was as I remembered it. The walled citadel of the monsters occupied an island in the midst of the brackish water, and a causeway extended from the road to its gates, which were shut.

"They rebuilt the gates," Altrus murmured.

We had managed to destroy the gates just prior to leaving the island, but there was no sign of this damage. The new gates looked stronger than the old. They were reinforced by straps of iron.

"We'll have to build a scaling ladder from the trees," Bassir said. "Are you certain we are not being observed?"

"The creatures conceal themselves during the day, and the walking dead care nothing for the living," I told him.

He dispatched squads of soldiers with axes to cut poles. At this task they were surprisingly efficient. A scaling ladder took rapid shape.

I saw the dead watching us from the wall, their rotting heads projecting above the parapet. Their eyes were empty, but the very fact that they looked at us was out of keeping with their behaviour the previous time we had visited this accursed island.

"Something doesn't feel right," Martala said to me as we stood watching the industrious, woodsman-like activities of the soldiers.

"What is wrong?"

She shook her head, squinting at the citadel. "The sounds are wrong."

I listened for a long while before I realized what she was talking about. On our previous visit, the air had rung with the noises of hammers and chisels on stone, saws cutting wood, the squeak of pulleys hoisting heavy loads. The dead had been building the city.

Today, there was no sound apart from those the soldiers made. This lack of construction noise from the other side of the wall made me feel a chill of apprehension. I approached Bassir, who was occupied overseeing the final bindings on the rungs of the ladder.

"Captain, maybe it would be best to return to the forest and observe the gates for a day or two from beneath the concealment of the trees."

He glared at me with a mixture of impatience and contempt.

"Nonsense. I'll send some of my men over the wall with axes. They'll soon have the gates open for us."

Four soldiers picked up the ladder and carried it across the causeway on their shoulders while the rest trailed casually after them. My companions and I followed, but we hung back behind the last of the armoured men.

The first volley of crossbow bolts caught the soldiers by surprise. The second rained down on them while they were milling in confusion, trying to help the fallen. The third volley struck the backs of those who were slowest when they fled along the causeway. Their steel helmets and studded leather tunics offered no protection against the hard-driven bolts.

The gates of the citadel boomed. I paused on the edge of the forest to look back, with the crossbow bolts falling around my feet like slanting raindrops. Through the gateway came a kind of cavalry of the dead. They held short spears in their hands and were mounted on things that resembled giant ants. At any rate, the creatures they rode possessed six legs, and were black and hairless. Their large heads hung close to the ground, and elongated antennae extending from their heads twitched and waved in the air as they came skittering along the causeway.

I realized Martala was pulling on my hand.

"Come to cover, you fool, before you get skewered by a bolt."

Her sharp words reminded me of my danger. We ran along the road into the forest where Altrus awaited us with his sword in his hand. He did not speak, but turned and ran with us.

I glanced at the trees on either side of the road. They grew so densely together at its edge that they were almost impenetrable. If we tried to flee into the forest, we would be heard forcing our way through the brush, and we would leave an obvious trail that would betray our passage.

The cavalry of the dead were not as fast as they would have been mounted on Arabian horses, but they were quick enough to press us along the twisting road. Each time I glanced back, I caught a glimpse of their lead riders.

At length we caught up with the Caliph's guardsmen who could not run very fast due to the weight of their armour. They jogged along two-by-two in a ragged formation with their captain running beside them. I counted them as we followed at the end of the line of men. Thirteen guardsmen remained, and half of them had been wounded by the crossbows.

I ran to Bassir's side.

"We need to stand and fight."

He glared at me.

"If we can reach the ship, we will have more bowmen to oppose them."

"This road doesn't lead to the ship," I reminded him. "The dead will cut us down from behind while we are forcing our way through the underbrush."

"We'll follow the beach."

I shook my head, but he did not respond. It was clear to me that he was at the limit of his strength, as were his men.

As so often happens in matters of war, the decision was forced upon him. The dead riders caught up with us before we reached the beach. They began to impale the guardsmen in the backs with their lances while Altrus and I cut at them with our swords from opposite sides of the road, all the while running to keep pace with the soldiers. The girl had no sword, but she did her best with the little dagger she always carried.

I discovered that the bodies of the beasts bearing the dead were covered with a kind of hard black shell that resisted the slashes of our weapons. The same was not true of the decaying corpses that rode them, but the legs of the dead were armoured with plates of steel strapped on with leather thongs.

Seeing several of his men stabbed through the back from behind, Bassir ordered them to stand and fight. Even though they were exhausted, they gave a good account of themselves. When the antennae of the six-legged monsters were hacked off, the creatures ran in circles, exposing their riders to the sword. But the dead showed no sign of fear or weakness. Their greater numbers began to control the battle, which I realized could have only one outcome.

"Throw down your swords," I cried as loudly as my voice allowed. "We must surrender."

"Throw ourselves on the mercy of the dead?" Bassir growled. "You must be mad."

He was cut above the eye and on his shoulder, but the fury of battle was upon him.

"If we don't, they will kill us all."

Putting action to words, I waved my arms to get the attention of our foes, then cast my sword on the ground and lowered myself to one knee. Altrus did the same beside me.

The dead did not kill us, but turned their attention on the soldiers. Seeing this, the soldiers began to discard their swords and kneel in imitation of us.

"Pick up your weapons, you useless bastards," Bassir roared.

Before he could say more, a thrust lance skewered him through the throat and emerged from the back of his neck. His eyes bulged from their sockets and blood erupted between his parted lips and ran into his beard. When the lance was jerked away, he collapsed.

Seeing this, his men quickly threw away their swords and knelt. We all waited for the killing thrusts of the dead knights. They never came. The armoured corpses seemed to listen to something only they could hear. They began to prod us to our feet and herded us together with their blood-stained lances.

Then something happened that chilled my heart. The dead guardsmen began to stir and stand upon their feet. They looked around with blank eyes that seemed to see nothing, but they gathered up their weapons where they had fallen.

We living were forced to give up our daggers, except for Martala, whose little dagger had already disappeared somewhere within her clothing. She had a way of hiding it so that no search would ever discover it. I passed over my curved dagger with reluctance, but inwardly I was relieved that no attempt was made to strip me of the ghoul's skull that hung at my belt. It was my most prized possession.

Dead Bassir stared at me with lifeless eyes that held no trace of recognition. He made a gesture with his sword for me to walk back along the road. Several of his men who still lived began to weep loudly on their knees, unable to control their terror. They sounded like women newly informed of the deaths of their husbands. They hid their blubbering faces in their arms until they were beaten to their feet by the flats of the blades of their dead comrades.

We were forced to walk back to the city at the head of the mounted column, surrounded by the revived corpses of men we had known in life only minutes before. Not a single word was spoken.

4.

The gates of the citadel opened, and the dead prodded us through with lances and swords. I saw that the work of building the habitations inside the walls had been completed in the months since I had been there. The dead, who then had carried hammers and saws, now held swords and bows. The smell was the same, however. The stench of decay hung thick in the air and made the surviving guardsmen gag.

We were compelled to walk through the courtyard which, during my previous visit, had contained the strange black sphere that served the city's masters as a portal between our world and theirs. The sphere was gone. What this portended I could not fathom, but it worried me.

One of the dead men in a better state of preservation than the rest glared at me with lifeless eyes. It made me uneasy. How much awareness did these damned souls have of their former lives? Did they retain an echo of the emotions they knew in life? As their brains and livers rotted, who knew what foul convulsions they might suffer in their fading, twisted recollections? Truly, no hell conceived by men could be worse.

"Where are all the monsters?" Marla muttered beside me.

"Asleep, or in whatever state they occupy during daylight. Remember, we only saw them active at night."

"Do you think they are inside these houses right now?" she asked.

I studied the buildings, with their windows too high for a man to look out, and their odd doors. It was a chilling thought. If the citadel was fully occupied, there might be thousands of the monsters asleep inside these walls, waiting for sundown to wake and stir and come into the dark streets to feed their dead slaves.

The city of the dead did not boast a jail. We were thrust into a long room with stone walls and high windows too narrow to crawl through. From the cut lumber and sacks of sand piled against one wall, I took it to be a storage room.

The cowed guardsmen milled about, their eyes darting fearfully from side to side. Without their captain they had no purpose. Many had suffered ugly wounds. Several appeared to be dying from blood loss. One man began to bang on the door with his clenched fist and demand that they be given water to wash their wounds, and clean bandages to bind them. The dead outside ignored his noise.

"I should have stayed in Damascus," Altrus mused. He sat on the floor with his back to the wall, and clasped his hands with his forearms resting on his knees.

I looked around, and sat on the end of a nearby lumber pile.

The girl perched herself beside me.

"You miss Nealayna," she told him.

He nodded, his scarred face moody.

"I should never have left her alone."

Nealayna was a Persian widow with whom Altrus had recently fallen in love. She was at my house in Damascus, acting as house mistress while Martala was away. How long the mercenary's affair would last, or how serious the affections of the woman might be, were matters I did not trouble my mind over. There is a fatalistic saying among ghouls – what is to be will be. Altrus was happy. In his own quiet way he was happier than I had ever known him.

"She's safe enough in my house," I said.

"That's not what I mean. There are many temptations in Damascus, many deceivers. Many other men."

"Don't you trust her? Martala asked.

"I do trust her," he said. "I would not have left her had I not trusted her. But who can know what will happen in the future? Fortune can be a black-hearted bitch, and Fate plays many tricks."

I cast my gaze around at the walls of our makeshift prison.

"Indeed."

The monsters came to us not long after the sun set. The rattle of the bar across the door alerted us. I stood up, and heard the others standing, those who could stand. It was black as pitch inside the storeroom. Two guardsmen had died, and two others were on the brink of death. For the past several hours their wet coughing had been the only sound, as the light dimmed to gray and finally to an impenetrable blackness.

The door opened. Three monsters entered, only three. This in itself was a bad sign. It suggested complete confidence in their ability to control us.

Two of the towering insect-like beings held short silver rods which they extended in a threatening way. Glowing crystals on chains around their necks gave a reddish illumination to the storeroom. The third, who carried no rod and wore no crystal, appeared to be their leader. They reminded me of a praying mantis elevated on its long hind legs, as their small heads swivelled from side to side to study us, but their naked limbs were black and their bodies more upright than that of an insect. The smallest of the three stood head and shoulders above us.

It was their towering stature that intimidated the guardsmen as much as their horrific forms. The men cowered with their backs against the wall and whimpered like infants. They made no attempt to stop the two monsters who wore the red crystals from touching their sceptres against the dying guardsmen who lay upon the floor. The men died instantly. They simply ceased to breathe.

The monsters made clicking, chittering noises as they looked over the rest of the Caliph's guardsmen. They bent their backs and thrust their swivelling, twitching little heads close to the terrified faces of the men, with their complex mouth parts clicking and moving from side to side. Antennae on the tops of their heads waved back and forth, brushing the sweating cheeks of the soldiers, who stood like marble statues, frozen by fear.

The differing garb of my companions and I from that of the terrified guardsmen seemed to excite their interest. They chittered and clicked amongst themselves, then gestured for us to move aside from the soldiers. I wondered if they recognized us from our previous visit to the citadel? My stomach rolled as I remembered the tube from the mouthparts of one of the things extending itself down my throat, and the slime it injected into me that caused almost immediate sleep.

One of the guardsmen was pulled forward, seemingly at random, and the very thing I dreaded in my mind was done to him while his fellow soldiers watched in horror. His arms were held by the two monsters with the crystals, and his jaw was forced wide as the tallest monster bent its head to insert a black tube into his throat. I saw his throat bulge wide in the light of the crystal lamps.

He did not fall unconscious, as I expected, but became still. The others released his arms and he slowly lowered them to his sides.

"Why came you to this place?" the tall monster asked in hissing Arabic that was distorted, yet clear enough to understand. The voice came from a hole in its chest.

Martala and Altrus looked at me in surprise. I shrugged and shook my head. On our last visit to the citadel, they had not spoken to us, or so we had believed. I wondered if they had done so while all three of us were under the influence of whatever potent drug they had injected into our stomachs? Could it be that they had questioned us, and we had answered, without remembering?

Like most soldiers, the man knew almost nothing of his mission. He was scarcely more than a boy, short of stature and slender. He spoke in a slow voice and told everything he knew, which was only that he had been ordered to leave his usual duties in the palace of the Caliph at Damascus, and ride south with the military column to the port of Ayla, at the head of the Gulf of Aqaba, there to board the *Eastern Star*.

The tallest of the creatures, who seemed to be superior in rank to the others, pointed at me with its upper limb and hissed in Arabic.

"What know you about this one?"

The eyes of the guardsman rolled to look at me. His face was as white as parchment.

"They say he is Abdul Alhazred, a mighty necromancer who has bespelled the wits of the Caliph."

"Why is he come here?"

"He guided us to this island. They say he was here once before, with the two who always travel with him."

The three monsters conversed in their own clicking language for a time, before the tall one asked his next question.

"What is necromancer?"

"A man of great wisdom," the youth said. "A worker of wonders. A speaker to the dead."

This final comment seemed to excite them. They spend several minutes conversing between themselves in their own language while facing inward with their antennae touching. Communication with the dead held some special meaning for them, which was not surprising in view of their use of corpses for slaves. In a sense, their entire race could be called necromancers.

From the corner of my eye I saw the door to the storage room open a crack to reveal the glaring eye of the same corpse I had noticed earlier. This was interesting, since none of the walking dead were animated during the night. Then he did something even more startling – he winked at me.

Some kind of silent communication passed between the monsters. As we stood and watched, the two who held the metal rods killed all the guardsmen with nothing more than light touches to their heads or breasts. So broken with terror were the guardsmen that none of them even made an attempt to resist.

"I'll kill the tallest one," Altrus said in a murmur close to my ear.

"Wait. Do not attack until I do."

He raised an eyebrow, and reluctantly nodded.

The man with the glaring eyes thrust wide the door and entered the storeroom with his sword raised. Nine other armed men followed.

"Strike now," he cried in a rasping voice that sounded like a dry hinge.

They hacked and hewed at the monsters, who stood for a moment like statues, unable to comprehend this sudden change of circumstances. When at last they started to defend themselves, they demonstrated how lethal their silver rods could be. One after another, their attackers began to drop to the ground.

"Now we strike," I said to Altrus and Martala.

They needed no urging. The girl produced her tiny blade and the mercenary snatched up a sword and threw it to me, then got another for himself.

One of the subordinate monsters who wore a red crystal began to shriek from a little hole just below its neck. It sounded eerily like a woman's scream. I cut off its head while the glaring man attacked the other who wielded a metal rod.

When I started toward the tallest monster, he grabbed my arm and pulled me back.

"Not that one," he said with a fierce grin. "We need it alive."

As quickly as it began, the battle was over. The tallest monster stood in the midst of a circle of swords. It was impossible to guess its emotion, but it made no movement and emitted no sound.

The fierce-eyed man I had taken for a corpse sheathed his sword. The other walking dead who had fought with him gave him a ragged cheer, but he motioned with his hand for their silence. Nine had entered with him. Of those nine, four lay lifeless at his feet. They would become undead, and rise and walk again at dawn.

Altrus started toward one of the metal rods, but the fierce-eyed man barred his path.

"Don't pick it up," he warned the mercenary. "It's merest touch is death for us, though it does these creatures no harm."

"You're uncommonly lively for a dead man," I said to him.

He laughed.

"My name is Aziz," he said, voice rasping from long disuse. "Forgive the deception, Alhazred. It was necessary."

Martala approached him uncertainly.

"Are you truly alive?"

The ghost of a self-mocking smile passed over his dry lips. "I am of the dead, but my body yet lives."

"What are you doing in this place?"

At the compassion in her voice, some of the bitterness faded from his expression.

"I was the captain of a trading ship that ran onto the reefs that so artfully surround this accursed moving island. Most of my crew and my passengers perished on the grinding rocks. My wife and three children were on board. They died in the waves before the storm abated. When I crawled onto the beach at dawn, I found them standing together. At first I thought they were still alive, but their wounds were horrifying. My eldest son had a broken arm and half his skull was crushed. The throat of my wife was ripped open, but no blood came from the wound. I realized they were all dead.

"I gathered together those of my crew who had survived the wreck. You see them here with me, the few that are left. When the dead began to walk into the forest, we followed them. We entered the gates of this hellish city behind them. I told my men to pretend to be dead. I needed time to understand what had happened to my family and my crew."

"How did you avoid the monsters?" I asked.

His savage grin was like that of a wolf.

"It is not difficult when you know their habits. They are predictable creatures. We kept to the background, and hid during the nights. When I realized they could not detect that I was alive, I became more bold and began to serve them so that I could get closer to them and learn their ways. They call themselves the *Tic'qoc*." He made a kind of clicking noise with his tongue in the back of his mouth when he spoke the name.

"Why have they come to our world?"

"They mean to conquer it. This island is their first outpost. They travel from their own world by means of floating black spheres."

"We have seen the spheres," Altrus said.

"Why did you not escape?" Martala asked. There was pain in her voice. The horror of Aziz's loss had touched her deeply. "You could have warned the world about the island."

"Do you think they would have believed us?" He shook his head. "I had another purpose. I decided to destroy them all."

"Is that even possible?" I asked.

"I don't know. But if a way exists, I will find it."

The controlled rage in his voice left no doubt that he meant what he said.

"How have you lived so long?" Altrus asked. "There is no food." His eyes widened. "Unless you ..."

Aziz chuckled dryly.

"Rats. The bowels of this island are infested by rats."

"Where did you get water?" I asked.

"Come with me. I will show you."

5.

We formed a procession with the tall monster at its head, so that it appeared my companions and I were being led captive through the streets. Aziz went just behind the monster, his sword ready to thrust into its back. The monster understood the peril of its position and made no attempt to resist. In this way we crossed the central plaza of the citadel.

Red lights glowed on tall poles. All around us the monsters filled the open space, going and coming on whatever unimaginable business occupied their waking hours. There were hundreds of them around us. They ignored us completely, or watched us pass in silence. Some were feeding their somnolent slaves by holding their decaying bodies tight and extruding liquid down mouth tubes into their bellies.

It was a scene from nightmare, more than enough to drive the average man raving mad, but I had seen many strange things since my expulsion from the palace of King Huban at Sana'a. I laid my hand across Gor's skull and rubbed its smooth bone with a meditative gesture that had become habitual. In my heart I was still a ghoul, and always would be a ghoul. It was a source of strength in trying times.

Aziz led us through a maze of narrow, winding lanes between high brick walls. Several times he stopped, and we hid, but what we were hiding from was not obvious to me. I judged we were moving toward the center of the citadel. At last we entered a tall, narrow door and descended several flights of steep stairs, the steps of which were unnaturally high for human legs.

We came at length to a place of humming machines. Crystals

set in the metal walls provided red light. The machines were enormous. I felt like a mouse in a blacksmith's forge. Great pistons thrust from side to side, and metal gears revolved one inside another. The warm air was moist and laden with the smells of metal and oil.

"What is this place?" Altrus asked.

"I believe this is what propels the island when it moves," Aziz said. "It may also be what keeps it above the waves."

"Something must sustain it," I said. "It is far too heavy to float on the surface of the sea."

"Do all these great machines run by themselves?" Martala asked in wonder. She held her palms pressed over her ears. The noise of the pistons was painful.

"From time to time the dead slaves come to service them, but they do not come often."

He led us yet deeper into the bowels of the city, where the noise was less. I wondered how far the island extended under the water, and how close we were to its bottom.

"Here is our water," he said with pride. "It took us almost a week to find it. Those were days when I thought we would surely die."

Several of his crew murmured agreement.

The water fell in a thin stream from the darkness far above. I put out my hand and let it patter on my fingers, then lifted them to my parched lips. It was warm and without taste.

"Where does it come from?" Altrus asked.

"I don't know, but it has done us no harm over the past three months."

We all drank from the stream. Discretely, I renewed the glamour that concealed my disfigured face from others. I had no wish to offend Aziz, although I doubted anything he saw for the remainder of his days would horrify him.

"Why have you not destroyed the machines?" I asked him.

"How? A sword makes no impression on them."

"It's a pity we didn't bring any amphorae of aqua fortis with us," I murmured.

"We don't know that it would hurt the metal of the machines," Martala said.

"Come with me," Aziz said. "I have one more mystery to show you."

We went still lower, and reached a passageway where the air hummed and was lit with a strange glow. When the monster realized where it was being taken, it made frantic stifled sounds in its chest and tried to tear itself away. Altrus beat it into submission but it remained terrified. It crouched and shuffled along in a craven posture I had never seen any of the alien creatures adopt. I wondered what filled it with so much fear?

At the end of the passage we came upon a massive door of a gray metal that looked like steel. Painted upon it was the symbol of three crossed lances and some writing in a script I had never seen before. The sharp points of the lances seemed to threaten the hand of any who might reach toward them.

When the *tic'qoc* saw the door with the three crossed lances, it redoubled its effort to twist its body away from our grasp. Although tall, it was not powerful. We held it fast between us and forced it to approach the door.

"What lies beyond the door?" Altrus asked.

"That I know not," Aziz admitted. "But I believe it to be the beating heart of the island, and the source of its power."

I tried the massive metal latch. It was locked by some locking mechanism that was strange to me.

"I cannot open it," Aziz said.

"If it had a keyhole, I might be able to pick it open," Martala said. It was no idle boast – the girl was good with locks.

Altrus tried the point of his sword on it and snapped off the tip of his blade.

"The steel, if it is steel, is too hard and thick to break," he said to me.

"We have spent months looking for a way through this door, or around it," Aziz said. "There is no hatchway, no vent, no passage, that I have not sounded. This is the only way in."

Laying the palms of my hands against the door, I pressed my ear hole to its surface. The humming was louder. I felt it through the bones of my skull and at the roots of my teeth. The door was also warm to the touch.

"We cannot open it," I said at length, straightening up. "But we know who can."

"Yes," Aziz said. "The *tic'qoc* must be able to open it."

The reason for the capture of the tall monster became obvious.

"Open it," I commanded.

"You not understand, necromancer" it said. "Great danger here."

"What kind of danger?"

It struggled to find words in our language.

"Fire unseen burns in the air and sickens living things, and there is a power that crushes our shells."

I had no patience for this enigmatic response. If there was a door, I reasoned, it meant that the room beyond it was entered, and if it could only be opened by the monsters, it meant that they entered it. Drawing my dagger, I struck off one of the upper appendages that served as one of its hands. Its thin womanly scream was gratifying to hear.

"Open the door."

Trembling all over its body like a leaf in the wind, it pressed a small panel in the door, and the panel popped open. Behind it was a kind of grid of unmarked squares. In rapid succession it pressed six of the squares on the grid with the tip of its other appendage. The door clanked loudly and swung outward. The humming became much louder.

We had to almost carry the monster over the threshold and into the dimly lighted room beyond.

It was a round chamber with a domed ceiling and a matching depression in the metal floor. Between ceiling and floor floated a large black sphere. The surface of the sphere was like black velvet. It resembled the one my companions and I had encountered in the plaza of the city on our previous visit. That had served as a kind of portal between our world and the world of the monsters. This sphere was larger, and was penetrated by enormous shafts of crystal that extended out of the walls of the chamber and passed into the sphere. I counted the crystal shafts. They were twelve in number and penetrated the sphere at equal intervals over its surface. Its overall structure was similar to the geometric figure known to the Greeks as the dodecahedron.

On the wall between two of the crystal shafts stood a metal cabinet with dials and buttons on its surface.

"It is hot in here," Aziz said.

I felt something tingle all over my skin, like a thousand ants crawling on me, but ignored it. The air shimmered with heat that radiated from the black sphere.

"What do these crystals do?" I asked the monster.

It cowered down and tried to cover its head with its upper limbs. I took my dagger and cut off one of its flailing antennae. This caused it to shriek in agony. Even so, it would not speak until I removed several more of its appendages.

"Your language no words for this," it said.

I raised my dagger.

"They keep black sphere safe," it said quickly.

"What would happen if they were broken?"

"You would die. You would all die."

"What would happen to the island?"

"The island would die. Everything would die."

I wondered if it meant everything on the island would die, or did it really mean everything? That was a chilling thought. When I tried to force the creature to refine its answer, it curled up on the metal plates of the floor and refused to give any response. Nothing I did would make it speak again.

Martala stepped forward with her dagger and severed its neck, removing its head from its body.

"Why did you do that?" I demanded.

"The thing was not going to answer." She glared defiantly at me. "Anyway, it had suffered enough."

"We need more information."

"Have you no pity?" she demanded.

"Pity? For a monster that intended to torture, and then kill us?"

"Pity for a living thing," she said.

I gazed into her eyes and wondered how I had upset her.

"I have no pity for anyone. You already know that."

"What does it matter?" Altrus said in disgust. "It's dead."

With this wisdom I could find no dispute.

"The *tic'qoc* said the island would die if the crystals are broken," Aziz said. "That is enough to know."

"If we break the crystals, we will all die with the island," Martala pointed out.

We stood looking at each other with the dead monster at our feet.

"I have no intention of sacrificing myself," Altrus told me.

"Nor do I."

"One of us will need to stay behind to break the crystals," Martala said.

"I will stay," Aziz said quickly. The fierceness returned to his face. "I am dead inside already. It is a small price to pay to avenge my wife and children."

Several members of his crew volunteered to stay with him, but he cursed them and told them they were fools. He wanted no other to die at his side.

We did not argue with him, but searched the level until we found a heavy metal rod some two cubits in length with a bulbous end. I had no idea what its purpose might be, but knew it would serve as a hammer.

I laid my hands on Aziz's thin shoulders.

"The Caliph will hear of your life story."

"Is he a generous man?" Aziz asked.

"He is, and a fair one."

"I ask nothing for myself, for what good would it do me? But I ask for the village in which I was born." He named a village in Egypt.

"I will convey your request, you have my word on it."

We left him standing over the dead monster, gazing at the black sphere with the metal rod in his hands.

6.

It took us hours to find our way out of the maze of passages and chambers beneath the citadel. Perhaps it was just as well, for day was dawning as we emerged under the open sky. All of the alien citizens of the city had retired to sleep, leaving only their walking-dead guardians, who expressed no interest in us.

"How long will Aziz wait before destroying the crystals?" Martala asked. The girl had a gift for asking questions that could not be answered.

"His hatred is great," Altrus pointed out. "He will not wait longer than he thinks necessary."

"We must move quickly. We've already wasted too much time."

We located rope and climbed the stairs to the top of the citadel wall in an unoccupied corner. The walking dead who passed us continued to ignore us, but we had no way to know what action might trigger their hostility.

They did not try to prevent us from sliding down the rope to the ground below, but when we started across the causeway that linked the small island on which the citadel stood with the larger island, they began to loose crossbow bolts at our backs. We ran, and by some miracle all of us avoided the darts.

"They are going to ride us down, as they did before," Altrus said.

We ran along the road. Nothing pursued us. I thought at first the mercenary might be wrong, but he kept looking over his shoulder.

"Here they come," he said.

Around a score of the dead warriors rode after us on their six-legged steeds. I did not intend to repeat the mistake of Bassir.

"Into the trees," I said. "They may not follow through the undergrowth."

It was frustrating to have to fight our way through the dense forest, but the dead knights did not attempt to leave the road.

"We are losing more time," Altrus pointed out.

I looked through a gap in the trees above my head and found the sun. It had reached its noon height and was beginning its descent. How long would Aziz allow for our escape? How could he even tell the passage of the hours with any accuracy?

At length we emerged onto a rocky beach.

"What way is the ship?" Altrus asked.

"That way, I think."

No one contradicted me. It was difficult to run across the loose stones, which rolled beneath our boots, and harder still for Aziz's men, most of whom had bare feet.

"Here come the dead," the girl said.

Behind us they rode, slowed by the loose stones, but they were closing the distance.

"They must have followed the road to the sea, then came after us along the coastline," I told her.

We rounded a headland and saw the galley floating at anchor not far off the sandy shore. My relief was great. I had worried that it had been attacked by the dead knights and destroyed. As we drew nearer, we waded into the water. The slope of the sand was not steep. The water came no higher than our armpits when we reached the galley and were pulled up over its low sides, with the thrown lances and crossbow bolts of the mounted dead soldiers raining into the water all around us.

"We did not expect you to return," Captain Hassan said cheerfully. "But I decided to wait a little longer."

"Your generosity shall be rewarded," I promised him. "Now have your rowers get us away from the island."

The guardsmen who had stayed with the galley to help float it off the beach fired on the dead with their bows, but arrows made little impression on the dead soldiers. Fortunately for us, their ant-like steeds had no liking for the sea. They tried to force the beasts into the waves, but they resisted and threw off their riders, until at last the leader of the dead ceased the effort. They sat their strange mounts and watched us move rapidly away from the shore by the power of the galley's rowers. The square sail was useless, as there was not a breath of wind to fill it.

As the distance between ship and shore widened, I forced myself to relax, at least in part. I still had no notion of what the destruction of the crystal rods would accomplish, other than that it would be very disastrous for the island. If the effect extended beyond the island, there was nothing I could do to stop it, so worry was pointless. Even so, a part of me continued to worry.

When we were far enough from the island to eliminate any concern that we would be attacked, I had the captain still his rowers. We drifted on the placid sea. The sky was a cloudless vault from horizon to horizon. We were far enough from the Arabian shore that we could not see land, but I knew it lay no great distance to the east.

"What are we waiting for, Alhazred?" Hassan asked.

"That, I do not know," I told him.

"Then how long shall we wait?"

I smiled at his impatience. It was a miracle he has waited for us to return to the ship. The presence of the guardsmen probably had something to do with it. Before I could answer, the island vanished.

It did not gradually fade from view, or glide below the horizon into the distance. It simply vanished, leaving a basin-shaped depression in the sea where it had floated. It happened in an instant as I watched, and was followed by an intense flash of white light that blinded me, and several seconds after that, a boom in the air that was like thunder.

The crew began to babble in confusion and dread. Hassan had not been watching the island. He blinked from the flash of light and looked past me.

"Where is the island?" he said wonderingly.

"The island is gone," I told him, rubbing my eyes to clear them. "As to where it has gone, I have no idea. Captain, regard the sea."

"By the Prophet," he said in a weak voice, then hollered down the open hatch to his oarsmen, "Row, you dogs! Row!"

The water of the sea had begun to rush in to fill the hollow where the island had floated. It drew the ship back with it. As I watched in alarm, the water crashed together and rose into a kind of mountain peak, before falling with another crash. A great wave capped with white foam spread outward across the surface of the sea in all directions.

"Steer away from it," Hassan shouted at his steersman.

The nose of the galley slowly turned until it pointed directly away from the rushing wave, which was almost as high as the ship's mast. I saw Martala hug the base of the mast with both arms.

"Grab something," I shouted at Altrus, who scarcely needed my advice on self-preservation. He wrapped his arm around the rail of the galley.

The wave struck the galley on its stern and propelled it forward the way a small boy pushes a model ship with his hand. The mast snapped midway down its length as the rear of the galley lifted higher and higher, until the galley stood on its bow. Soldiers and seamen fell into the sea, their screams faint below the roar of the water.

Slowly, the stern of the galley fell as the wave passed under us. Hassan ran back and forth, shouting at his crew until he restored order, then stopped his ship and began to search for those who had fallen overboard. Several were picked up, but when the final count was taken, thirty-seven of the sixty guardsmen had been lost to the wave, and thirteen of the crew.

"If we ever get back to Damascus, I will never set foot on another ship," Altrus said.

"I have heard you make the same oath before."

"This time I mean it."

The girl's headdress had fallen off. She hunted for it and quickly covered herself, but not before a sharp-eyed member of the crew noticed her long hair. I saw him whisper to another seaman and point at her as she came over to where we stood.

"The Caliph should be pleased," she said cheerfully. "The island is no more."

"So it would appear," I agreed.

But I turned to look back at the roiling sea, and wondered.

Red Tide of Vengeance

1.

The air inside the captain's cabin of the trading galley *Eastern Star* was hot despite the early morning hour. It could scarcely have been otherwise, with both of the small portholes shuttered and the door closed. The only light came from an oil lamp that swung from the ceiling on three brass chains.

Captain Hassan stood with his back bent and his head lowered beneath the low-hanging beams that supported the upper deck of the galley. Whoever had built his ship had not designed it for the comfort of tall men. His fierce, bearded face bore an expression that was almost pleading.

"All I ask of you is that you keep the girl hidden inside this cabin until the voyage is concluded."

He spoke to me, but it was Martala who answered.

"Can't you feel how stifling it is in here? I'd be dead in three days."

I sat in the chair before his small writing desk. My traveling companions Altrus and Martala perched awkwardly on the edge of the lower bed that was built into the wall of the cabin. The rail of the bed above it pressed against their hunched shoulders.

A bedroll took up much of the open floor. Martala preferred to sleep on the floor, rather than in the narrow bed beside me. It was cooler, she said. Where she slept was a matter of indifference to me. I have never been greatly troubled by the heat, although I had grown accustomed to her lying beside me over the past year.

"Are you so certain this is necessary?" I ask Hassan. "I have seen no mutinous tendencies among the crew."

"That is because they are terrified of you. They whisper that you are a great necromancer, and that you used your magic to make an entire island disappear, and that you raised the wave that almost capsized my ship."

"I can understand why they might fear me, but why do they wish to kill the girl?"

He shook his head at my simple-mindedness.

"All seamen are superstitious. It is universally believed by them that a woman on board a ship brings ill fortune. They blame her for all our troubles. Trust me, Alhazred, I have seen this kind of thing before. They will not rest until they have cast her into the sea."

"They can try it," she said, grinning at him with her teeth set edge on edge.

"It's unfortunate your head scarf came off when the wave struck the ship," I told her. "You would have continued to pass as a young man."

"I'm tired of binding up my breasts and hiding my hair. Why should I pretend to be what I'm not for these fools?"

"Because these fools have knives, and will kill you," Altrus reminded her.

"It's too late for pretending," Hassan said. "The men are at the breaking point. They get little sleep, working day and night to repair the ship. When we ran aground on the island, several planks in her bottom were sprung. The wave snapped off our mast. The Caliph's guardsmen use buckets both day and night to bail the water from the hold and keep us afloat, but many of them were injured by the wave. Without our sail I must rely on my rowers, but the wave killed a third of them. Some of my crew are taking their turns at the oars even though it is no fit occupation for free men."

"The seamen we rescued from the island must be of some help."

"They are good men, but there are too few of them."

I looked at Martala. I had seen that determined pout on her face many times. It meant that she would not listen to reason.

"I'm sure we can arrive at a compromise. Suppose the girl keeps the door barred, but opens the ports?"

"They will try to look in at her. It will madden them."

"She needs fresh air. At night when most of the crew are asleep, I will escort her around the deck."

"They will fall on you from behind and cut your throat, then rape the girl and cast her body into the sea."

"No they won't," Altrus said. "I will guard their backs."

This fascinating conversation might have continued much longer, but a cry came from the lookout on the makeshift mast the crew had succeeded in erecting on the stump of the original timber.

"A sail has been sighted," Hassan said. "I must examine it."

"I will accompany you." I was glad for any excuse to escape the airless cabin.

"And I," Altrus said.

Before the girl could speak, I held up my hand. She scowled at me but kept her tongue.

We were progressing along the Red Sea in a northward direction, staying a safe distance off the Arabian coast, where the prevailing winds were better adapted for our purposes and we were less likely to encounter pirates. Contrary to popular belief, it is safer for a ship in distress to keep its distance from the coastline. The coast presents too many dangers in the form of reefs and sandbars.

The sail of the other vessel projected just above the horizon to the northeast.

"I don't like this sail," Hassan said, leaning on the starboard rail of the rear deck above the cabin, which we had ascended for a better view. "It bears toward Africa."

"Why is that bad?" Altrus asked.

"There are few trading ports of any importance along this part of the African coast. A galley of that size has no honest reason to go there."

The mercenary stroked his beard and stared at the sail with greater interest.

"A pirate vessel?"

"That is not unlikely."

"Can we outrun it?" I asked.

Hassan laughed.

"Look around you."

A line of men stripped to the waist were lifting wooden buckets from an open hatch and emptying them over the side. There was wreckage from the shattered mast and torn sail in piles around the deck, and a chaos of ropes and timber which the ship's carpenter was using to rig a smaller emergency sail to the awkward spar he had strapped to the stump of the mast.

"Without a sail, and with a shortage of fit rowers, we cannot possibly escape this galley, should it decide to pursue us."

"We could run for the Arabian coast," I suggested.

"We are too far from any port where we could find safety."

Altrus had his hand against his forehead to shade his eyes from the sun.

"What is that design painted on the sail?"

I squinted and shielded my eyes.

"I can't make it out."

"I may be able to tell you," Hassan said. "My eyesight is good. It looks like —"

He stopped speaking for so long, I turned to look at him.

"It is the *Eye of Allah*," Hassan said in a voice of lead.

His face had lost its healthy sun-browned color and taken on a gray hue. There was despair in his dark eyes.

"We are all dead men. This ship is doomed."

"What does it mean?" I demanded.

"It is the emblem of a man they call One-eye. He is Greek by birth, a ruthless pirate who burns ships and puts entire crews to the sword. All attempts to hunt him down have failed. They say he is without honour or mercy."

I shielded my eyes with both hands for a better look at the symbol. It was the stylized eye I had seen carved into ancient monuments in Egypt, painted in red on the white linen of the galley's square sail. Some called it the eye of Horus, who was a war god of Egypt.

Hassan grabbed my arm and squeezed with enough force to cause pain. "If you are truly a great necromancer, is there nothing you can do to save my ship?"

I gently removed my arm from his hooked fingers and shook my head.

"I have no materials, no tools, no time for preparation."

"But can't you hurl fireballs at them?"

The impulse to smile at his simplicity arose within me but did not reach my lips.

"Hurling fireballs is not among my necromantic skills. Without time to construct the necessary wards and occult barriers, anything I call forth from the other side would be more likely to destroy this ship than the ship that pursues us."

He frowned in thought for several moments, and nodded.

"Then you are less than worthless to me. Stay out of my way until this is over, or I may remember that it was you who ordered this accursed voyage."

Without another word he pushed past me and began to rally his crew.

"I always assumed our lives would end badly," Altrus said. "I hoped it would be on dry land."

"Does it really matter?"

"No. But I wish I had been able to speak a few words to Nealayna."

This was the young Persian widow Altrus had recently fallen in love with, and brought to dwell in my house in the Lane of Scholars.

"She will be taken care of," I assured him.

He looked at me in surprise.

"You've seen to that already?"

"Before we left Damascus. It seemed a prudent precaution, in view of the precarious nature of our quest."

He gripped my upper arm and squeezed it. For Altrus, it was an unusually effusive display of gratitude. Unfortunately, he chose to grasp the same place where Hassan had dug in his fingers. I pretended to ignore the pain of my bruised muscles. In an hour such minor considerations were apt to be of no consequence.

2.

Our vessel turned and fled due west so that the pirate galley could not intersect our northerly course. The captive rowers below the deck gave their best exertions while the carpenter and his helpers struggled to get some kind of sail raised that would catch the wind, but it was futile. I saw that the approaching pirate ship was much faster than the *Eastern Star* had ever been. Even had we been undamaged, they would have overtaken us.

"They will try to board us," Hassan said to his assembled crew. "We must keep them off the ship. Our lives depend on it."

His courage had rallied the men during his attempt to outrun the pirate galley. I saw that he was determined to sell his life for a high price.

The slaves at the oars continued to row, and the guardsmen continued to bail, but the crew gave up its efforts to rig a sail and took up boat hooks and pikes and any other long poles they could use to push the pirate vessel away and knock boarders into the sea. Some of the guardsmen, who were not working the buckets, readied themselves with their bows.

The pirate galley was narrower of beam than the *Eastern Star* but floated higher in the water, perhaps because it was not laden with cargo. It loomed over us when its captain brought its bow just to port of our stern and had his rowers ship their oars. The wind in its sail carried it to a grinding union with our hull as the oars our rowers were slow to retract snapped off one by one, like so many toothpicks. A dolorous wailing arose from the slaves chained below our feet.

The pirates were seasoned veterans in the art of boarding a hostile ship. They swept over us like locusts. Both seamen and soldiers fought with courage, but there could only be one outcome. I saw Captain Hassan killed in the first wave of the attack.

Altrus and I fought shoulder to shoulder with our swords, but we were driven back to the cabin just as Martala emerged with her dagger in her hand and fire flashing in her clear grey eyes. Her dark hair hung over her shoulders and the bulge of her firm breasts was obvious beneath her tunic. We pushed her back into the cabin and stood on either side of the open doorway.

I fully expected to be killed at any instant. Oddly enough, I was not troubled by this prospect. There was a fierce joy in standing beside my trusted companion in the brightness and heat of the sun with blades flashing all around our heads and the clash of steel ringing in our ears.

I have always loved you, Alhazred, Sashi said in my mind.

The smiling, beautiful face of the djinn who dwelled inside my body formed itself for an instant in my field of vision. It was not Sashi's true face, but the face she used as my lover. Her true face had nothing human about it.

And I, you, I told her with my thoughts.

The next instant, I split the bald head of a leering man with a gold piece dangling from his ear, and he collapsed in front of me.

Blood made the deck slick beneath my boots. My heel slipped and sent me to one knee, but Altrus kept me alive by catching on his sword a blade that flashed toward the back of my neck.

"Enough," roared a deep voice.

I scrambled to my feet and blinked the blood from my eyes. Only then did I realize the fighting was over. We stood surrounded by a semicircle of pirates, their swords held threateningly toward us. The rest of the galley had already been pacified. Both soldiers and crew had cast down their weapons. The bailers had ceased to bail, and the chained oarsmen no longer rowed.

A man stepped forward. He was as tall as I, but much broader in the chest. He had the kind of skin that reddens in the sun and salt-spray instead of tanning. A full golden beard shot with orange highlights where the rays of the sun struck it hung over the front of his black silk shirt. He wore matching black silk pantaloons that flared wide above his high boots, and a black turban upon his head. The broad leather belt around his waist was cinched tight by a massive buckle of gleaming silver. But his most striking feature was the leather patch that covered his left eye. Upon the outer surface of the leather was impressed in red the same stylized Egyptian eye that adorned his sail.

With a sword that still dripped blood he motioned for his men to part so he could approach us. I laid a gentle hand on the sword arm of Altrus.

"You are not seamen or soldiers," the yellow-beard said in a powerful voice that boomed across the deck. "What are you?" His accent was Greek.

"Valuable hostages for ransom," I said quickly. "I am on this ship at the order of the Caliph, who will pay handsomely for my safe release, and the release of my two companions."

He smiled at me with his lips, but there was no smile in his single living eye. It remained grey and cold.

"And where is your other companion hiding?"

"Martala," I called behind me. "Come forth. Unarmed."

The girl stepped out of the cabin and stood between us. She wore nothing on her head, and her hair hung down her back. A murmur of appreciation arose from the pirates, along with scattered laughter. The yellow-beard looked at her with an admiration he made no effort to conceal.

"Take their weapons. Lock the woman in my cabin."

"What of the men?" a lean seaman asked.

"Don't kill them, yet. I will question them later."

I watched two of his crew swing Martala across to the higher deck of the pirate galley on ropes. Captain One-eye divided the men of the *Eastern Star* into two groups, the fit and the injured. He had all those who bore wounds put to the sword. The guardsmen uninjured in the battle he took as replacements for his rowers. The fit crew of the *Eastern Star* he used to augment the diminished ranks of his own crew. The exhausted slaves chained to the oars he ignored.

When he learned the condition of the galley's hull, he laughed.

"We won't need to scuttle this scow. She'll scuttle herself," I heard him say.

With increasing haste, as the *Eastern Star* listed and sank lower in the water, the pirate crew grabbed anything of significant value from the trade goods. By the time they remembered to swing Altrus and I across to the other vessel on ropes, waves were lapping over the lower deck and the screams of the galley slaves had ceased. As we watched from the pirate galley, the pathetic jury-rigged mast the carpenter had worked so hard to erect sank slowly and disappeared into the deep.

Altrus let his emotionless dark eyes survey the deck of the pirate galley from bow to stern.

"The captain went into his cabin a quarter hour ago," he murmured. "You know what he is doing now."

"I expect he is raping Martala. I hope she has the good sense not to murder him. These men have no discipline but his – they would tear us apart."

"There must be something we can do to get her out of there."

I thought about our options.

"No. Let him have his way with her. He may be more amenable to reasoned discourse afterwards."

He stared at me with a strange expression.

"Whenever I think I am coming to understand your ways, you say something that makes me realize I know nothing about you."

"You want to rescue the girl. That it admirable, but unnecessary. Did Martala ever tell you that her father raped her when she was nine years old?"

He blinked. "No."

"She killed him for it. Cut his throat with his own knife. Then she fled down the Nile to Bubastis and lived for years with the king of thieves of that city, performing whatever services he told her to perform. She is no virginal unplucked rose. Satisfying the sexual needs of the captain is far from the worst thing she's had to do in her life."

I turned toward the sea and took a moment to renew the glamour that concealed the mutilated condition of my face from the world. It was a simple matter of a few muttered words and a gesture of the hand. I had done it so many times since my expulsion from Yemen that it was almost a reflex. If the pirates glimpsed my true face, which was missing its ears and nose, and covered in scars, they were apt to assume I was a djinn and cast me overboard. Which I found to be mildly amusing, given that I actually was half-djinn by blood. Or so the village rumours about my mother had informed me during my boyhood.

"I will kill this One-eye for what he is doing to Martala," Altrus said.

"Of course you will. But that is another time, another place. We must be patient."

A female cry of pain issued from the open portals of the captain's cabin. Several seamen glanced slyly at each other and laughed. I found that my fists were clenched and made a conscious effort to relax my fingers.

I laid one hand on the ghoul's skull that hung from my belt and stroked its smooth, white surface with my thumb. A ghoul would be patient, and wait for the moment of vengeance. In my heart I was more ghoul than man, having lived and eaten with the Black Spring Clan of desert ghouls for months during my exile in the Empty Space.

"We must be patient," I repeated. "The time for vengeance will come."

3.

After more than an hour, to judge by the movement of the sun across the heavens, we were escorted into the captain's cabin. It was a lavish affair compared with the cramped quarters Hassan had occupied on the *Eastern Star*. The curved ceiling was high enough that a tall man could stand upright beneath the beams. Ample light came through four large window screens set in the stern. The box bed built into one corner was large enough for a married couple, and the desk that was presently strewn with charts of the African coast was full-sized, not the tiny portable thing Hassan had used.

Martala sat on a padded divan. She wore a dress of emerald green silk that was of a Persian cut, and Persian slippers with upturned toes on her feet. Her long, dark hair hung over her left shoulder.

She was watching me as I entered. I saw that the corner of her mouth was cut, and there was a bruise on her forehead. The low neck of the dress revealed another larger bruise above her right breast, and the red impress of teeth on the side of her neck. It appeared that One-eye was a vigorous lover.

I raised my eyebrows. She shook her head.

We were familiar enough with each other to be able to communicate in this way. I had asked if she was injured. She had denied it.

The captain sat at his desk, naked to the waist. Beneath his spreading beard, his hairy torso was impressively muscled. He glared at us.

"Martala has informed me that you are both close friends of the Caliph in Damascus. For this reason I have decided not to kill you. We will hold you for ransom until the Caliph chooses to send the amount of gold I shall demand for you. In the meantime there is no reason why you cannot work this ship as members of her crew."

"What about Martala?" I asked.

He looked at her, and the corners of his mouth twitched.

"She and I have made other arrangements."

The low growl in Altrus's throat should have warned me, but he moved too quickly for me to react. In a single leap he was stretched across the desk with his hands fastened around One-eye's thick throat. The pirate gave forth a strangled roar of fury and stood up. The muscles of his bare arms bulged, but he could not break the grip that throttled him.

The two seamen who had escorted us to the cabin got over their momentary surprise and advanced with their swords drawn. I saw Martala from the corner of my eye rush low at the seamen nearest to her and stab him in the stomach repeatedly with her dagger. This attack distracted the other man long enough for me to grab his dagger from his belt. I stepped inside the sweep of his sword and sank the blade sideways between his ribs over his heart. As he died he learned an age-old lesson – the sword is a poor weapon for combat in a confined space.

Our victory celebration was brief. Four other crewmen rushed in with daggers. At the same instant One-eye threw Altrus aside and drew his own dagger.

"Stop," he roared. "Don't kill them. I want to savour their deaths."

I saw that Martala's blade had already vanished into its mysterious hiding place, which the girl would never reveal to me no matter how many times I asked her. I threw down my dagger in disgust. The mercenary's rashness had not profited our situation.

"I could have ransomed you two for a heavy chest of coins," One-eye said, breathing hard from his exertions. "It doesn't matter – I have enough gold."

"What will you do with the girl?" I demanded.

"I will do nothing with her. She is my property and will continue to serve me."

Martala met my eyes, and smiled. In his fury the bearded man had not noticed her little knife. If he continued to rape her, at some point she would show it to him. This was good to know. I smiled in return.

They led us out of the cabin onto the deck. The Captain took a brass key from his belt and locked the door to his cabin. As he did so, the lookout perched on top of the mast gave a long cry and shouted down to us at he pointed northwest.

"The *Black Horse*."

The reaction of the crew was extraordinary. They all stopped their work and stared at the captain, frozen in their positions like marble statues. Apart from the creak of hemp rope and the slap of waves against the bow, the galley was silent for a heartbeat.

"What are you waiting for, fools?" One-eye roared. "Give chase."

Altrus and I were forgotten. We stood and watched the frantic exertions of the crew to turn the ship and trim the sail.

"We'll get him this time," One-eye said to a lean man I took to be his first mate. There was a wildness in his look, almost a madness.

The mate nodded. "The new sail should make a difference."

"We've got the wind at our backs. He won't be able to vanish as he has in the past."

Altrus and I looked at each other. What could we do? We were both unarmed. It would be suicide to jump overboard. We could try to capture the captain and use him to control his crew, but as I gazed over their fierce faces, I doubted they cared very much whether One-eye lived or died. I decided the best thing at present would be to just stay out of the way. The crew did not yet know that One-eye had decided to kill us.

Banging sounded on the inside of the door of the captain's cabin.

"Let me out," Martala called through the panels.

"The door is locked," I told her. "The Captain probably did it to keep you safe from the crew."

"You're safer where you are, girl," Altrus said gruffly.

"Altrus, what you just did, it was stupid."

"I know."

"Your love for Nealayna has softened your heart."

He grunted dismissively. Privately, I thought the girl was correct. His love for the Persian widow had made him more protective.

We began to slowly overtake the fleeing galley, which appeared to be much the same size as the *Eye of Allah*. Its square black sail was painted with a curious elongated symbol in white. As it drew nearer, I realized that it must represent the bleached skull of a horse viewed from the front.

I mentioned this to the girl – we had remained close to the door of the cabin in case any of the crew tried to take advantage of the confusion to break in and rape her.

"It must be the *Black Horse*, the galley of his twin brother, Xanthippos. Xanthos told me he was going to capture the ship and kill his brother."

"Xanthos? Is that One-eye's true name?"

"Yes."

"What else did he say about his brother?"

"Only that he is insane. He sees visions of war and pestilence, and talks to Death, who comes to him riding up out of the earth on a black horse. He believes he is Death's chosen warrior. When they were boys, living in Athens, he pricked out Xanthos's eye with a dagger so that no one would ever mistake Xanthos for him."

"I'm glad Xanthos confided these things to you," I told her through the door. "It means he has some regard for you."

"He is a pig," she said, disgust in her voice.

"I'm sorry I could not protect you from him."

"There is nothing you could have done. It doesn't matter. I'm not some trembling flower."

All the long day and into the evening we followed the death's-head sail. The *Black Horse* fled toward the African coast, and with the wind at our stern, the *Eye of Allah* swiftly closed the distance. Then the black sail turned due south, and the wind came from our port side. The crew trimmed the square sail as much as was possible, but it no longer drove the big galley through the waves as swiftly, and the *Black Horse* came no nearer. We would surely have lost it in the twilight gloom had it not been a few days before the phase of the full moon. The shining lunar orb, rising behind us in the east, made the death's-head emblem on the black sail glow with silver fire.

I saw Xanthos and his first mate standing together and moved closer behind them so that I could listen to their talk. I have been trained as a ghoul – no human can hear me when I approach with stealth.

"He is going to ground," Xanthos said with an exultation that cracked his voice. "Somewhere on the African coast there is an inlet. He will lower his sail at the last instant and try to dart in, hoping in this way to throw us off his track."

"How can you know this?" the mate asked with a note of superstitious fear in his voice.

"We are twin brothers. We think alike. I always know what he will do before he does it, just as he knows the same of me."

"What shall we do?"

"Get your sharpest-eyed lookout and put him on the mast. Tell him never to take his eyes off the black sail."

They separated and I drew back before I was seen.

Events transpired as Xanthos had foreseen. As the *Black Horse* neared the African coast, it dropped its sail and relied entirely on its rowers. It was almost invisible against the dark hills that rose behind it. Several times, as I strained my eyes at the rail, I thought it had vanished, only to see a faint outline of the hull rising above the crests of the waves.

At last there came a shout from the man at the top of the mast. "The galley is gone."

"Mark the place on the coast where it disappeared!" Xanthos shouted. "Do not take your eyes away from it for an instant, or you are a dead man."

He had the lookout point the direction with his arm, and ordered the steersman to keep the ship surging ahead in that direction. In this way he almost drove his ship up on the rocks, but the sound of the breakers in the still night alerted him of the danger in time. He had the sail dropped and cut back the pace of the oars, so that the galley glided forward at no more than a fast walking pace.

As we rounded a headland, I saw that behind it an inlet opened between two steep hills. There was no trace of the *Black Horse*, but it could scarcely have gone anywhere else without running up on the rocks.

4.

A crewman was set in the bow to drop the lead and sound the bottom, but as we entered the channel the water remained reassuringly deep. It was narrow, however – so much so that in places the oars had to be shipped to allow the galley to glide forward between the vertical walls.

Behind us, as we glided along, I heard the rattle of iron chains against the rocks. It was difficult to see in the moonlight, but when I peered back I thought I could make out, stretched across the entrance, what resembled a spider web. I realized that winches on top of the twin buttresses had raised a web of iron chains from the bottom of the channel, blocking its entrance. We were caught as effectively as any fly.

High above us on either side, burning lights began to appear. When they came raining down onto the galley, thudding into the deck all around us, we realized they were flaming arrows. The crew ran around with buckets of water, putting them out as they fell.

"It was a trap," Xanthos roared. "Rowers, full speed."

Fortunately, the channel had widened enough to allow the oars to be extended. The galley surged forward like a hunting hound released from its leash.

Above our heads, a rumble sounded that at first I mistook for thunder, but I soon realized my mistake when stones began to shower upon us like hail.

"Row, you dogs," Xanthos screamed down the open hatchway. With his golden beard flying in the wind and spittle spraying from his lips, the Greek barbarian looked raving mad.

Whips cracked as they were applied to the backs of the weary rowers, and the thud of the drum that gave the rowers their rhythm doubled its pace.

Several large stones broke through the planks of the deck. Altrus and I pressed our backs against the wall of the cabin and hoped that the slight overhang of the upper deck would protect our heads. Fortune smiled on us, but not on a score of the crew, who had their skulls crushed or suffered broken bones from the rocks that thundered down the length of the galley.

As quickly as they came, they ceased. The tempest of stone had lasted no more than a dozen seconds, yet it was only luck that the hull was not breached. The largest stones had been pushed from the cliffs too late, and had fallen into the water behind our stern. None of the rocks broke through the sturdy rear deck that served the captain's cabin as a roof.

The channel opened into a small bay. On its far side stood a city, its low stone buildings painted with moonlight. I recognized the lotus and papyrus columns that lined the colonnade leading up from the beach, and wondered what an Egyptian city was doing here. This part of Africa was ruled by black tribes. I knew of no Egyptian outpost so far south.

The *Black Horse* was in the process of making a slow circle of the bay to confront us bow to bow. Its captain may not have expected the swiftness of our exit from the channel. We shot into the bay like an arrow. Xanthos made no attempt at subtlety. He was insane with his lust for vengeance. He sent the armoured bow of the *Eye of Allah* directly into the side of the *Black Horse*, before the other galley could complete its turn. The planks on the side of galley burst inward like the staves of a wooden bucket when struck by a hammer.

The sail above us was ablaze from the rain of fire arrows. The ropes supporting it at the top of the mast burned through, and as it came free from its yard, the wind blew it across the crowded deck of the *Black Horse*. Dozens of men were trapped beneath it. Their screams rose above the din of battle as the two pirate crews clashed. The battle spread to the decks of both galleys, and they began to burn furiously.

"We need to get Martala out of the cabin and onto the shore," I shouted at Altrus. He nodded to show that he had heard my words.

I followed him along a narrow walkway at the side of the cabin to the stern of the ship, where there was also enough of a walkway to stand upon. He climbed the stern and kicked in one of the window screens. In the heat of the chase and the ensuing confusion, no one had thought to close and bar the shutters of the rear windows. The girl climbed quickly forth like a little monkey. She had taken off the Persian dress and put back on her travel tunic and pantaloons, along with her boots.

The dead and dying lay everywhere around the deck. We were ignored for the moment because we posed no threat. The fighting was too savage for those caught up in it to waste time on us. Altrus and I gathered swords and daggers from the corpses and withdrew to the rail. The rocky beach that separated the city from the bay was no more than a hundred cubits away, but the water looked black in the moonlight.

"Can we swim in these boots with the weight of our weapons?" Altrus asked. He was not an accomplished swimmer.

"We must try. If you get into difficulty, kick off your boots before you let your blades fall to the bottom."

Suddenly, the rail was swarmed by gleaming black men, who came up from the sea with daggers between their teeth. Apart from bits of cloth bound around their loins, they were naked. I realized they had swum to the galley from the beach. They transferred their daggers to their hands as they clambered onto the deck, glaring fiercely at us. There was at least a score of them, too many for the three of us to fight.

Altrus started to draw his sword as they silently approached us. I held his arm.

"We are valuable hostages, in ransom to the Caliph at Damascus for much gold. Your captain, Xanthippos, will be angry with you if you kill us." These words had become almost a litany for me.

Their leader understood enough Arabic to stop the others with his widespread arms.

"You are hostages?" he asked in a deep voice.

"Yes. We are worth very much gold to your master."

At the last word he drew himself up to his full height and looked at me with scorn.

"We have no masters here."

"I meant your leader," I said quickly. "The one who rules this city."

"The Goddess Nepthys rules the city of Apep," he said, bristling with anger.

This was more complexity than I wished to deal with.

"Do not kill us, we are worth much gold," I repeated, and threw down my sword and dagger. After a moment of hesitation, Altrus did the same.

Both galleys were now a conjoined inferno. Roaring flames undulated into the night sky like dancing salamanders. The blacks lifted us over the rail and dropped us into the sea, than fell in all around us, and guided us toward the shore.

The beach was littered with armour and weapons that weary fighters had cast down in disgust after swimming from the interlocked galleys, which began to slowly drift away from the city and into the bay. I gathered from the threatening postures of some and the bowed heads of others that the brother known as Xanthippos had prevailed, though it was what the Greek historians sometimes called a Pyrrhic Victory. The greater number of both sides had perished in the flames or at the point of a sword.

Xanthos stood glaring at his brother. Four men held his arms behind his back. He strained and raged against them, his curses and mad bellows rising above the roar of the burning galleys. His brother stood looking at him in a meditative way with his arms crossed on his chest. It was astonishing how much alike they looked. One might have been the mirror image of the other, but while one raged the other remained calm.

"Bring him," Xanthippos said, and his deep voice even sounded like his brother's.

5.

We were taken along a broad, paved colonnade of papyrus and lotus columns and up the broad steps of an Egyptian temple, which occupied the center of the city. The cut stone blocks that made up its foundations were large, but even larger was the lintel stone that spanned its entrance. It was as massive as anything I had seen in the ancient temples at Thebes and Memphis.

Inside the temple, torches burned along the walls. We were pushed down a long hall, at the far end of which was a raised platform where rested what I at first took to be a painted statue of a black woman seated on a golden throne. Her hair was cut and styled in the Egyptian fashion, encircled by a gold cobra that reared above her forehead. She wore a green dress patterned to give the illusion of scales, and many gold chains around her neck that hung partly over her bare breasts. It was only when she raised her right hand that I realized she was not a statue.

"Bring him to me," she said in perfect Arabic. "I wish to look at your brother."

Two black men armed with spears started forward from either side of her throne but she motioned them aside. Xanthos was dragged forward by those who held his arms. He stared all around him with an expression of rage and did not seem to know where he was.

"So this is your mad brother, Xanthos," she said after examining his features at length. "He does look very much like you."

"It could not be otherwise," Xanthippos said. "We are twins. I was born no more than two minutes before him."

She pointed at the leather eye patch. "What is wrong with his eye?"

"He attacked me and tried to kill me when we were boys still living at our father's house. In the struggle his eye was put out."

Xanthos laughed harshly. "Liar! You put out my eye while I slept, like the coward you are."

"He has always hated me," Xanthippos said with sadness in his voice. "I fled the Mediterranean to avoid confronting him. For seven years he pursued me up and down the length of the Red Sea. His lust for fratricide knows no bounds."

"A pity," the woman who called herself Nepthys said. "I had hoped he could be brought to reason, and that both your galleys would raid the shipping lanes for me; but instead of two galleys I find myself with none."

"His mad lust for blood could have but one ending. Give him a sword and let me kill him, as I should have done long ago."

"No!"

The sharpness in her voice irritated him, but he concealed it well, through long practice no doubt – but not before I noticed.

"He will be sacrificed to Apep along with the others. His courage will honour the serpent god of chaos."

Fearing that these words might mark the close of our audience with this black goddess incarnate, I took the risk of stepping forward.

"Great Nepthys, I bring greetings to you from the Caliph, Moawiya ibn Yazid, as his emissary."

She regarded me with mingled scorn and amusement.

"What is the Caliph at Damascus to me?"

"A friend, if you wish it."

"Why should I believe that you are his emissary, or that you even know him?"

A very good question, I thought.

"When we were taken prisoner by One-eye, this man you know as Xanthos, we were on a mission of great importance entrusted to us by the Caliph himself." In a few words I told her of our quest to find and destroy the floating island, and of its outcome. "The crew members who still survive from the *Eastern Star* will verify what I have told you."

"We have a second Scheherazade with us," she said, looking around her throne room. Her black guard and the pirates alike roared with laughter.

I waited for the laughter to die with a placid expression on my mask of a face.

"Let me write a letter to the Caliph and have your men carry it to Damascus by their fastest boat. Within six weeks you will have enough gold to replace the two galleys you lost to fire."

"You have a persuasive manner ... what is your name?"

"Abdul Alhazred."

"Very smooth, very convincing, but I do not believe you. To prolong your life you would say anything."

"Alhazred spoke the truth," Altrus said.

She waved her hand in a negligent gesture.

"Lock them up," she told Xanthippos. "We will sacrifice them to Apep after we give him your brother."

Along with the pirates, we were shut up in a large pen made of sticks woven together. It was of much cruder construction than the stone buildings of the city, and appeared to have been designed to keep wild animals. Without swords or axes to hack a hole through the wall, it was sturdy enough to hold us. Besides, we were under constant watch from outside. Any attempt to escape would have been met with a rain of spears.

Xanthos had fallen into a moody silence. He ignored the three of us. Without an order from their captain, the other pirates left us alone. I counted them. Including their captain there were thirty-nine, some of whom were wounded with minor slashes that had ceased to bleed. It was a significant force, but without weapons against the crew of the *Black Horse*, who were twice its number, it had no chance. The armed blacks I had seen in the city were even more numerous than Xanthippos's men.

I approached Xanthos. He ignored me, even when I stood directly in front of him.

"We need to plan our escape from this place."

He raised his golden head to regard me, and laughed bitterly.

"Can you count, necromancer?"

"How do you know I am a necromancer?"

"I interviewed the first mate of the *Eastern Star*. He was quite talkative before he died."

"That is true," Martala said behind me. "I saw him torture the man."

"It didn't take much torture to make him talk," Xanthos said, chuckling at the memory.

"To answer your question, our numbers are irrelevant. They must suffice."

He spat in the sand at his feet.

"We will wait to see what fate offers us."

As a ghoul of the Black Spring Clan, I could appreciate his

fatalism, but as a man it irritated me.

While I considered how I could prick him into some form of action that would not get us all killed, the door of the pen opened and four blacks armed with spears entered. Their leader pointed at me and made a gesture. I did not resist.

"Where are you taking me?"

"The Goddess Nepthys demands your presence."

Altrus started forward, but I motioned him back. This was not the time to show resistance. I allowed them to prod me out of the pen and along the streets to the temple. Night had fallen. We entered it through a different doorway and descended to a lower level.

I found myself in the private living quarters of a woman of wealth. Cloth of gold shimmered on the walls in the lamplight. Persian carpets adorned the stone floor. On one wall was mounted a huge oval mirror of solid silver that had been so carefully polished, it looked like a window into another room. I did not neglect to notice a large bed covered with silk sheets and pillows. Transparent silk curtains of pink and blue hung down on all sides of it from a golden frame.

She was seated on a low divan of Egyptian design, with rolled bolsters at both ends and a padded seat.

"Sit beside me," she commanded. "I wish to talk with you."

The black guards released me, but remained in the chamber beside the door. I approached her the way a mongoose approaches a cobra.

"Sit," she said again.

I sat on the edge of the divan, half-turned to face her.

"Is what you said about your relationship with the Caliph true?"

"It is true."

"I have been told you are a necromancer."

"That is also true."

She studied my face with her head tilted to the side, a slight smile on her lips. She was astonishingly beautiful. Had Cleopatra been Nubian instead of Greek, she might have looked like this.

"It is a great pity I cannot hold you for ransom."

"May I ask what prevents you?"

"You should know the answer already, if you are as clever as you look. I cannot afford to have the Caliph learn of the existence of this city. He would regard it as nothing more than a port for pirates and order its destruction."

"I could tell him to leave your city unmolested."

"But would you, once you were safe in Damascus? And would the Caliph listen to you? No, I cannot take such a chance, and it saddens me." She laid her hand on the side of my face. "You are such a comely young Arab. Your eyes are quite beautiful."

"I have my father's eyes. I have been told that he was a djinn."

"Really?" She laughed. "How delightful. It makes you even more fascinating."

I reached out slowly and touched her cheek. The guards started forward, but she motioned them back with an impatient gesture.

"You are also of mixed blood, unless I am mistaken."

"My blood is as much Egyptian as it is Nubian. I am descended from a line of goddesses who have ruled this city for three centuries."

"This city was built by the Egyptians."

"Of course. They built it because the well of Apep is located here. Three centuries ago their black slaves rebelled against them and slew them all, except for the ruling family, with whom the leaders of the uprising mingled their blood. My family has protected the purity of its blood for the past three centuries by breeding in the same fashion as the Pharaohs of old, brother with sister, father with daughter, mother with son."

I betrayed no reaction to this confession. The strange customs of the world had long since ceased to outrage my moral sensibilities.

"I assumed you were wed to Xanthippos."

She laughed again, but this time her laughter held an edge.

"I provide for him a safe haven for his ship and his crew.

In return he gives me what spoils I wish to take of his raiding expeditions. He is not my master. I am Nepthys, a goddess of the Two Lands. I have no master."

She took my hand and drew me to my feet, then led me to the bed.

"Take off your clothes."

I looked at the four guards who watched alertly.

"I'm not a trained dog in the marketplace."

"You Arabs have such false modesty," she said with a shake of her head, then spoke to the guards. "Turn your backs to us and face the wall."

Their leader frowned and hesitated, then ordered his men to do as ordered before imitating them.

"Won't they turn to look if you cry out in pleasure?"

"You have a high opinion of yourself, Alhazred. No, they will not turn until they receive my explicit order to do so."

This assurance was welcome news. It might give me the chance to throttle her. Of course the guards would kill me as soon as they realized what I had done. But I could think of no other action. When Nepthys realized that my manhood was no more than a glamour, she would be outraged and would surely have me put to death. The glamour that made my disfigured face appear normal also concealed the absence of my prick and balls, but it was not quite potent enough to deceive a woman during lovemaking. Better I kill her before she had me executed.

Wait, Alhazred, said Sashi in my mind. *There may be another way.*

She spoke to me silently in my thoughts. When she finished, I had to prevent myself from nodding. It might work.

I disrobed while Nepthys slid out of her dress and undergarments and lay on top of the silk sheets in the middle of the bed. She admired my erect manhood with a smile. The thought of lying with her was enough to cause the spell of glamour to feign my arousal. I crawled between the silk curtains and between her open legs.

I felt a flowing sensation within my body as Sashi focused her substance between my thighs. She was by nature a lesser djinn of the darkness, and possessed little substance in her body, but when she chose she could concentrate herself for a brief time in a confined space and simulate solidity. I hoped she would be able to hold her concentration long enough to satisfy the needs of Nepthys, who was no doubt accustomed to the skills of a large number of men.

Leaning forward on my arms, I pressed my hips against hers. She groaned in pleasure. I kissed her lips, her throat, her nipples, all the while continuing to move against her. My pace increased. She began to rake her fingernails across my back but I ignored the pain. Before my mutilation and castration, I had managed to amass a considerable practical knowledge of sexual technique in company with the ladies of King Huban's court at Sana'a. I brought those happy memories to the fore of my mind and concentrated on replicating them.

She arched her back and cried out in a kind of dying scream of pleasure, held her posture, then fell limp upon the bed. I looked at the guards as I lay on her. Not one of them turned his head. From this I surmised it was not the first time they had stood facing the wall. I slowly pretended to withdraw myself from between her thighs, and felt Sashi's concentrated substance begin to melt away as she flowed back into the rest of my body.

You did well, I told the djinn in my thoughts.

All for you, my love.

"You were very good for me," Nepthys said, rolling off the bed. She picked up her underclothes and began to slide into them with a sinuousness that was almost serpentine. "It is a pity that I must sacrifice you to Apep. I will have tears in my eyes as I watch you die."

6.

The well of Apep was a round opening in the ground bordered by large blocks of stone. The blocks were different from the sandstone that formed the temple and city buildings. A dark green color, the stones had almost a glassy smoothness as they reflected the vertical rays of the sun. The sacrifice was timed to begin at noon, with the sun at the zenith. The stones of the well were rounded on the corners, suggesting that the well was much older than the city that had been built around it.

A small amphitheatre encircled the well. The near-naked citizens of the city with their sweating bodies shining like polished ebony, and the pirates from the *Black Horse* dressed in their colourful silks, occupied the lower tiers of benches, but they did not even half-fill the amphitheatre. When it was ruled by the Egyptians, the city must have held a much larger population. That the city was in decline was obvious from its state of neglect. Damage to its stonework had not been repaired. The roofs of many of the dwellings had fallen in. In a few more generations it was likely that the blacks who presently inhabited it would drift away, and it would return to the dust from which it had been raised so many centuries ago.

The goddess sat upon a portable throne of carved rosewood, which was positioned in such a way on a raised platform to give her the best view of the proceedings. She wore royal robes of shimmering gold threads and a golden crown upon her head. In her right hand she carried a golden sceptre with a head in the shape of two rearing serpents that faced in opposite directions. The shaft of the sceptre was formed of their entwined bodies.

Those of us to be sacrificed were herded into a kind of holding pen with a low wall of wickerwork. Guards stood around it, spears at the ready. The pirates had accepted their deaths. Their heads hung down and their shoulders drooped. Only Xanthos glared in defiance.

I stood some distance apart from the other captives with Altrus and Martala beside me, and wondered if Nepthys knew her city was doomed. Why were there no other members of the royal family to view the sacrifices? Were they all so deformed by generations of inbreeding that they did not dare to show themselves, or was Nepthys the last of her royal line? These thoughts and others passed quickly through my mind like fluttering birds caught in a great wind.

Xanthos was dragged struggling and cursing from the ranks of his crew to the lip of the well, where an iron chain was fixed around his left ankle. There was enough slack in the chain to allow him to walk several paces from the well, but no further.

Nepthys stood from her throne and pointed at Xanthippos, who sat among his crew on the lower tiers of benches. Black guards quickly surrounded him and forced him away from his confused and protesting men.

"What is this outrage?" he demanded as he was dragged beneath Nepthys' throne.

"I have decided that you should join your brother, as the first sacrifices to Apep."

"Are you mad?"

"I tolerated you and your crew in my city because you were of use to me. Without a galley, you are no longer of any use."

"You traitorous bitch. You told me we would rule this city together."

A line of black musicians gathered in a crescent behind the well and began to play upon drums and bone flutes. The rhythm of the drums was curiously irregular. I realized that it was intended to simulate the swaying head of a cobra.

Xanthippos was chained like his brother. He bent and jerked the black iron links, testing their strength, then gave up. Xanthos watched his efforts with enjoyment, laughing heartily at his curses.

"Fate has united us at last, my brother, as I always knew it would."

The elder of the twins glared across the amphitheatre at his men.

"Fight, you fools."

His men had quietly been surrounded by black warriors while their captain was dragged to the well. Some stood up with their hands on their sword hilts, but when they looked around themselves they lost heart and sat down again.

I realized that our only chance of escape was if the pirates of the *Black Horse* and those of the *Eye of Allah* rose up together and fought side by side, as a single crew, but the two groups of men appeared as disunited as their captains.

A large drum was swung over the well on ropes. A elderly black man with hair white as snow approached the side of the well with caution, a long stick in his hand. Leaning forward, he began to beat the big drum with the rounded end of the stick. The booms of the drum echoed down the shaft of the well. From the curved tiers of benches in the amphitheatre, black women and men began to chant in a language unknown to me.

"You were born first," Xanthos roared at his brother above the din of the music. "It is only fitting that you die first."

He rushed forward and fastened his hands around his brother's thick neck. Xanthippos put his own hands on his younger brother's throat. They stood locked in this posture, swaying with effort, their faces reddening as the blood was trapped in their heads. With their bristling beards, ruddy cheeks and bulging eyes, they looked like twin demons.

I glanced up at the stone prominence that supported the rosewood throne of Nepthys, and saw her laughing with delight as she watched the brothers battle. It was obvious that this had always been her plan, why else chain them so close together?

Beneath my boots, the stones began to vibrate. Altrus caught hold of the girl and looked at me. I ran over to the remnants of Xanthos's crew.

"Fight for your lives," I yelled at them. "Fight with the crew of the *Black Horse*. Unite, or you will all be sacrificed."

"He's right," one of them cried. "Alone, we don't have enough men, but together we might stand a chance."

They overwhelmed the guards at the gate of the pen and surged toward the rows of benches where the crew of the *Black Horse* stood staring down at their captain. The warriors assigned to guard the men of the *Black Horse* were caught by surprise as the crew of the *Eye of Allah* came at them from the side. They were knocked down and their spears torn from their hands. This act of defiance aroused the survival instinct of the other crew, and with a cry of fury they turned their swords and daggers on their black guards.

As this was happening, the vibrations in the ground continued to strengthen. A tremendous roar turned every face toward the well. A serpent white as alabaster emerged and rose up into the sunlight, but such a serpent as has not been seen crawling free on the surface of the world for aeons. Its ridged body continued to slide higher and higher, until it towered above us like the pillar of some lost temple of giants.

Suddenly, it split apart and peeled downward into half a hundred milk-white worms, each as thick through as my waist. They writhed about in different directions like the hair of a gorgon, questing on the air, and I realized they were blind. But I was mistaken, for when they began to open their mouths, which were lined with razor-sharp teeth, I saw that each had a large black eye set in the back of its throat.

The gaping head of one worm dropped down and engulfed Xanthippos in its maw, closing its jaws around his knees. Almost simultaneously, another did the same to Xanthos. When they rose up again, there was a severed foot and ankle in each of the loops of the iron chains, but nothing more remained of the brothers, who carried their mutual hatred into the gullets of the monster, and from there no doubt into hell.

The serpent called Apep continued to writhe back and forth, its many mouths tasting the wind for blood, eagerly awaiting the next sacrifice. But no sacrifice came. All the men of the city were engaged in battle with the pirates, who despite their lesser number fought with the fierceness of men who knew they were fighting for their very lives.

"Now is our chance," I told Martala. We left the pen by its broken gate.

Altrus was already battling two black warriors with a sword. I did not ask where he had found the weapon, but snatched up a spear as he killed one of his foes and thrust its point through the belly of the other.

"Where do we go?" Altrus shouted above the din of battle.

"The fishing boats pulled up on the beach."

As we raced from the amphitheatre, I risked one lingering look behind. Nepthys sat serene on her throne, gazing forward with no expression on her face as the many swaying heads of the giant serpent snatched up mouthful after mouthful of her warriors and cut their bodies into two with their teeth. The pirates were also caught up by the monster as they tried to flee.

The living goddess appeared to be in a trance as the final death of her city played itself out at her feet. As I watched, two white serpents took her up, one by the head and shoulders and the other by the legs. She was ripped apart in a fountain of blood drops that glowed like a stream of rubies in the sunlight.

The beach was undefended. Everyone in the city had flocked to the well to be entertained by the sacrifices. With some difficulty, the three of us managed to push one of the fishing boats off the pebbles and climb over its sides as it slid into the water. It was the kind of vessel common on the Nile. I had been a passenger in such boats several times and thought I could solve the riddle of its triangular sail, given time. For now, I used the steering oar to move the boat across the bay toward the narrow channel that led to the Red Sea.

"At least we are provisioned with water and flatbread," Martala said cheerfully, holding up a clay jug and a package wrapped in woven grass.

"I hope the iron chains are not still across the channel," Altrus said.

"How can ill fortune touch us, when your thoughts are always so harmonious and positive?"

"If the chains are still up, we will find a way to lower them," I said, breathing heavily from the labour of working the steering oar.

The multiple roars of the monster in the well and the screams of the dying reached us faintly across the placid water as the fitful breeze changed direction.

"Then it is back to Damascus," Altrus said. "And never, ever, ever will I set foot on a ship again."

"Don't make promises you can't keep," I cautioned. "It annoys the gods."

The spider web of iron chains was not across the mouth of the channel. We raised the sail and I pointed the bow of the little boat northward.

THE WELL OF WADD

1.

When my companions and I sailed our stolen boat into the tranquil port of Ayla, at the head of the eastern gulf of the Red Sea, our drinking water and most of our food was gone. We had lived for days on raw fish. The previous owner of the boat had been thoughtful enough to leave his fishing lines and hooks tucked away in a leather pouch under the sail.

"I never thought I could be so sickened by the taste of raw fish," Altrus murmured as we watched the wooden dock approach our gliding craft.

I lowered the triangular sail and tied it fast, then found a mooring rope and prepared to leap onto the dock.

"My throat is so dry I can barely swallow," Martala said. "I just want a drink of water."

More than anything else, I wanted a bath. The local administrator at Ayla had been given orders from the Caliph to assist me in any way he could. I had carried those orders to him myself upon our arrival at the port overland from Petra on the old Roman road, with sixty of the Caliph's best mounted guardsmen. Alas, the guardsmen were all dead along with their captain, but there was no reason why the orders themselves should not still stand.

I left Martala and Altrus drinking and washing themselves at a public well in the city and went up the hill to the administrator's palace, a modest affair of white stone and red tiles. Fortunately, the guards at the gate remembered my face, or what they took to be my face. My real face, mutilated by King Huban of Sana'a in Yemen, few others than my close acquaintances would ever see. My mask of glamour was firmly in place.

Uzair ibn Khalid received me with a broad smile of enthusiasm that lit up his chubby features. He was not a corpulent man, but the padding of fat beneath his soft skin coupled with his shortness of stature made him appear so. Like so many minor officials of the Caliphate, he overdressed himself in fine silks and gold braids. His short beard was waxed and trimmed to perfection, with not a single whisker out of place.

He escorted me into his audience room and sent a servant scurrying away to bring
glasses of sweet fruit juice and cakes. When I informed him that all of the Caliph's guardsmen were dead, he stared at me with an expression of perplexity like that of a dog who has just been given a strange command.

"All dead? Do you mean, all of them?"

"I do."

"But what am I to tell the Caliph?"

"Put your mind at ease. I will inform the Caliph as soon as my companions and I arrive in Damascus. That is why I am here. I need from you three good horses and a pack mule for the journey along the road to Damascus."

"Yes, of course, you may have whatever you wish." He paused and blinked at me.

"Is there something else?" I asked mildly, sipping my sherbet. The drink was too sweet.

"A letter arrived from Damascus three days ago. It is from the

Caliph and addressed to you."

He motioned a servant over and whispered a few words into the man's ear, then we waited for his return. I recognized Moawiya's bold handwriting on the front of the letter, which was parchment and addressed to me. Turning it over, I snapped the royal wax seal into fragments and unfolded it.

My friend Alhazred,

If this letter reaches you before you depart from Ayla for Damascus, I have another task for you to fulfill. I want you to ride with my guardsmen eastward to the city of Dumatul Jandal and investigate the rumour that there has been a revival of pagan idol worship among its citizens. It is an ancient but obscure habitation located some two days west from Sakakah, at the northern edge of the Nafud desert.

The locals are a perplexing mix of Christians, Jews and formerly pagan tribesmen who were converted to Islam by Khalid ibn al-Walid, who was sent there by the Prophet himself some fifty-two years ago to pacify the city and destroy its pagan idol, an abomination of stone that bore the name Wadd. Khalid fulfilled his task with zeal, by smashing the idol to fragments, razing its temple to its foundation stones, and killing any of its worshippers who resisted his soldiers. These worshippers were chiefly of the Banu Amir al Ajdar and Banu Abd-Wadd tribes, and by all accounts fierce warriors.

About this Wadd I can tell you little. He is a god of the moon, and the serpent is sacred to him. He is mentioned in the Koran as a god worshipped at the time of Noah. The name signifies love and friendship in our language, but it is said by sages that this god is the same as a god of the moon named Sin that was worshipped at Babylon before the fall of that great city. Concerning the attributes and qualities of this Babylonian god, I know nothing other than his appellations, among which are "father of the gods" and "creator of all."

Find your way to the city, investigate the religious observances of the tribes mentioned, and if they have reverted to idol worship, use my guardsmen to punish them.

You may wonder at my religious rigor, given my tolerance for other faiths here at Damascus. All I can tell you is that it is a political matter, and that I am compelled to show the edge of the sword. Among the Imams there is great concern that if any revival of pagan worship is allowed to exist, it may trigger a general revision of the barbarous tribes of the Al Jawf region to the old gods.

I know you will execute this task with the same enthusiasm and efficiency you used in the matter of the floating island of the dead, to which I trust there was a successful conclusion. We will discuss these matters when you return to Damascus.

Your Caliph and friend in this life,
Moawiya the Second

For several minutes I sat in silence, turning over in my mind the significance of the letter. What annoyed me the most was its tone. Although respectful and coached in familiar terms, it was written more as a command than as a request. It is true, I had performed a number of tasks for Moawiya during the past year, but always as a courtesy, in response to his requests. It vexed me that he might be growing so comfortable with our relationship that he felt he could order me about like a servant.

I was of half a mind to continue home to Damascus, and deny to Moawiya that I had ever seen his letter. Martala and Altrus would come with me wherever I led them, but the three of us were tired.

"Has some great calamity befallen?" Uzair asked nervously. "Forgive me, Alhazred, but your face is so grim."

Forcing a smile, I shook my head.

"The Caliph wishes me to perform a service for him at Dumatul Jandal. I will need camels for myself and my two companions, as well as travel garments more suitable to the desert than what we are wearing, weapons, sleeping rolls, water skins, provisions, a small purse of gold coins, and one other thing."

"Yes? What is the other thing?" he asked brightly.

"A bath, filled with hot water."

"Naturally. I will arrange it at once. I will assign a slave to scrub your back."

"That won't be necessary. I have someone who will perform that service."

He cleared his throat, nodded, and avoided meeting my gaze. I realized he assumed that Martala, who went disguised as a young man, was my male lover, and that I wanted her in the bath with me. How would he react, I wondered, if he knew that she was a fifteen-year-old Egyptian girl?

"Shall I order three baths?"

"No. My traveling companions can use my bath water after I have finished with it, if they are so inclined."

2.

Dumatul Jandal was an ancient city with pagan roots that extended further back than the Romans, who had used it as part of their *limes Arabicus*, or Arabian limits, the furthest extent of the Roman Empire into Arabia. Indeed, it was the extreme eastern outpost of the Roman *limes*. Dumatha, as the Romans called it, was incorporated into the *limes* under the Emperor Trajan, and remained a part of the empire for four centuries.

The city was much older than the Roman occupation. The Assyrians knew it as Adummatu, and wrote in their histories that it was the center of an Arab kingdom named Qedar. Sages claim the kingdom was named Qedar after the second son of Ishmael, and that the city is called Dumah after the sixth son of Ishmael. The name in Arabian signifies "Dumah of the stone," something I found quite interesting, for the question naturally arose, what stone?

It was an easy matter to explain away the name as "Dumah of the stones" or "Dumah of the stone blocks" meaning the stone city of Dumah, but what if the name intended only a single stone, perhaps the carved stone of a pagan idol? That would throw a completely different light of meaning on the name. It suggested that the entire city had at one time been devoted to the idol.

"What are you reading?" Altrus asked with just a hint of irritation in his voice.

I smiled and said nothing. We had been riding along a winding road eastward for several days, and each day I took out the little book I had found in Uzair's library and read it, but this was the first time he had been unable to resist the impulse to ask me about it.

"It's a history of some kind," the girl said sourly. She was sore from the ceaseless rocking of her camel.

"How would you know that?" I asked her.

"I took it out of your pack while you were sleeping and read part of it."

"Once a thief, always a thief," I chided her without passion.

"Says one who should know the truth of it," she responded.

"I stole to survive, I was never a thief by profession."

"That is a fine distinction that the judges and executioners care nothing about."

"There is truth in what you say. We live in judgmental times, when the act itself is more regarded than the intention."

It was not long after this exchange of words that we came upon the city. It was, indeed, a city built of stone. Standing over it like a stern father was a great stone fortress with tall towers at its corners that I knew from my little book was called Marid. As we rode closer, it became evident that the fortress had suffered damage from assault or neglect. Some of its walls were crumbling down in places and none of the crowns of the towers were intact.

We rode through the open gate unchallenged. The people in the streets were a varied lot. White-robed Christian priests. Jewish merchants in tall black hats. Bedouin women with their naked faces tattooed with tribal markings. There were even some followers of the Prophet, although they appeared to be a minority.

I looked around for the largest and most opulent dwelling in the city and pointed the nose of my camel in that direction. In this way I located the house of the mayor. I sent word by one of his guards that I was on an official expedition for the Caliph, and was admitted into the courtyard, but my companions were left outside despite my request that they be allowed to accompany me.

When I saw Iman ibn Heydar, the reason he had not come to the door of his house to greet me became apparent. He was an old man with a long white beard, and both his legs were missing from the knees down. He sat in a padded chair beneath a ceiling fan that was worked by a small black slave boy. As I entered the room, he motioned me to sit opposite him. For a full minute he did nothing but study my face with a shrewd expression. I waited for him to speak.

"So the young Caliph at Damascus has finally seen fit to notice the existence of Dumatul Jandal. I am honoured, so very honoured."

He did not sound honoured, he sounded angry.

"As to my mission here –" I began.

"What is your name again?" He feigned a smile and touched his temple. "An old head forgets so easily."

"Abdul Alhazred."

"A very curious name."

"So I have been told."

"Go on, what does the Caliph want with me and my city?"

I explained my mission, and as I talked his face became harder and colder. Before I finished speaking, he could not contain himself any longer.

"Has the Caliphate still not done with punishing this city? Well do I remember fifty-two years ago, when the Sword came and slaughtered its finest and bravest young men. That's what they called Khalid ibn al-Walid, did you know that? They called him the Sword of Allah. A bitter edge he bared to the people of Dumatul Jandal."

"Surely that is a matter of history, not an issue for present debate."

"You think so, do you? I was a young man of nineteen years when the soldiers of Mohammed came — twice they came in successive years, but the second time they caused the greatest hurt."

"That was when the idol of Wadd was smashed and his temple thrown down, was it not?"

"It was indeed. We tried to be good followers of the Prophet back then, but the old gods that had watched over this city for countless generations were still strong and had thousands of worshippers. Many men were killed that day, men of the tribes, Christians, even some Jews."

He paused and frowned, looking down at the stumps of his legs, which were wrapped in blue silk.

"I was not one of the god's worshippers, but by a mischance I was among them when they were attacked, and I was tortured with the rest. They made us stand for three days and three nights. When we fell, they beat us until we died, or we managed to get to our feet. I stood the three days, but corruption set itself in my feet because the flow of blood was hindered by the swelling of my legs. A surgeon cut my legs off, and here I am today, alive but less of a man that I should be. Yes, it was half a century ago, Alhazred, but I remember it very well."

"I am not here to torture or to kill, merely to inquire into the rumor that has reached the Caliph that some of the people of this city have returned to their old pagan ways."

"And if you find that they have, what will you do then?"

I thought of the contents of Moawiya's letter. His directives hardly applied, since he thought I would be accompanied by sixty soldiers, and I was here alone other than for my companions.

"If I find pagan worship, it is surely my duty to report it to you, and your duty as the leader of this city is to investigate and suppress it."

"What kind of suppression do you expect me to employ? The same used by the Sword fifty-two years ago?"

"That is a matter for your discretion, bearing in mind that the Caliph wishes any revival of pagan worship eradicated."

He nodded, eyeing me shrewdly from his chair.

"I think we understand each other, Alhazred. Is there any service I can perform for you while you stay in Dumatul Jandal?"

"One trifling service. I need a guide who is familiar with the ancient monuments of the city and its old places of worship, in the days before the Prophet spread his word across the land."

"That is a service I can provide easily enough," he said. "I will tell my eldest child to take you wherever you wish to go."

He motioned for a servant, who bent his head and listened, then vanished through a door. Within a few moments a woman emerged from the same doorway. She was slender and tall, and walked with a swaying grace. A veil covered all but her dark eyes, which studied me with quick intelligence as she entered.

"This is my eldest child, Badriya. She will serve as your guide. She has an extensive knowledge of the old religions of the city, don't you, my child?"

"It has always been an interest of mine," she said. Her voice was low and pleasant.

I nodded at her with a smile of greeting, then looked at the old man.

"We may be climbing over rocks and hills. Perhaps your son –"

"I have no sons."

It was said simply enough, but he could not hide his bitterness.

"No matter. I would be delighted to have your daughter show us the ancient shrines and the places where temples stood before the Prophet enlightened us all."

3.

"This is where the Temple of Wadd stood?" I could not keep the doubt from my voice.

"It was here," Badriya said.

Slowly, I turned a full circle, gazing around at the tumble of broken columns and scattered stones that littered the flat expanse on the top of a low hill. I was able to make out the angle of a single corner of the foundation. The rest of the foundation stones had been torn from the ground. There was not one stone standing upon another.

"I'm surprised no one has built here in the past fifty years," Altrus said.

"No one would dare," Badriya said.

"Is there still such reverence for the god?" Martala asked her.

"It's really more of a superstition these days. They are all afraid of the god's curse."

Martala wore her dark hair long over her shoulder. When she had learned that our guide was to be a woman, she had decided it would be futile to attempt to disguise herself as a youth.

"Curse?"

"Some nonsense that anyone who defiled the dignity of the god would be doomed both in this life and the next."

"You don't believe in the curse?" I asked her.

"No good Muslim is afraid of the old gods."

"Tell me more about the god Wadd."

"I only know what I've read in the chronicles of our city. He is called the god of love and friendship. The serpent is sacred to him. His home is the moon but when his worshippers call to him, he comes into his idols of stone and brass and speaks to them. His worshippers gave him offerings of goat's milk and grain."

"What did the idol look like?"

"There is no description."

"None?" This surprised me.

"None that I could discover."

"Where was the altar located?" the girl asked.

Wordlessly the woman walked across the littered hilltop and pointed at a recumbent black stone some six cubits long and two cubits wide. It was cracked through the middle and one corner was broken raggedly off, as though by the blows of some great hammer.

"The idol of Wadd must have stood just behind it," I mused. There was nothing to show that anything had stood there.

"How big was it?" Altrus asked.

"None of the chronicles states its size," she told him.

"Your chronicles are singularly lacking in useful information," I said.

"It may have been forbidden at the time to describe the idol," she explained. "Only those who saw it with their own eyes could describe it, and they were worshippers who respected the sanctity of the god."

"Khalid ibn al-Walid and his soldiers must have seen it."

"They left no description."

I wandered around the hilltop, wondering what course of inquiry to adopt next. If all traces of Wadd had been erased, and the people of the city continued to maintain their silence, there was little I could do, other than take individuals at random and torture the truth out of them. But with no royal guardsmen to protect us, this would be a perilous course. The hostility of the citizens of Dumatul Jandal was already so great, it could be felt as a palpable blow when they glared at us in the streets. In some way they had discovered our purpose. It could only have been the mayor or his daughter who informed them.

My ruminations were stopped when I noticed the opening of a well. It had a neglected appearance. Not only did it lack a cover, but it was flush with the ground and easy to miss amid the tumbled blocks of stone from the ruined temple. I motioned for Badriya to come over.

"What is this?"

"It is a dry well."

"Are you sure it is dry?"

"It has always been dry, as long as anyone can remember."

I picked up a pebble and dropped it into the darkness. After a moment I heard it tick off the rocks at the bottom.

"Was this well sacred to the worshippers of Wadd?"

Badriya shrugged her shoulders. "It has never been spoken of in that way. It is just a dry well."

A thought occurred to me. "Is it possible fragments of the shattered idol of the god were cast into it by Khalid?"

"I know nothing about what happened to the pieces of the god."

Martala and Altrus were staring down into the well. It was impossible to see the bottom due to the contrast of the glare of sunlight on the stones of its rim against the shadows in its depths.

"Can you climb down a well as expertly as you can climb a tree?" I asked Martala.

She grinned at the memory. While a thief in Bubastis she had often found her way into the houses she robbed by climbing the trees that grew close to them. I had seen her climb. She was as nimble as a monkey.

Without another word she bent her head into the well to look for footholds on its walls, and swung her slender body over the rim. In moments she was lost below in the shadows, but we could hear her heavy breathing and grunts of effort.

"It's not difficult," she called up. "There are handholds and footholds in the sides."

This was common with wells, which needed periodic cleaning. The builders left stairs by which they could be entered at a later time.

"I'm on the bottom," she called up.

"Do you see anything?"

"It's dark down here. I can see a little."

Look at the rocks. Do any of them look like pieces of a statue?

We waited in silence for her to answer.

"No," she said at last. "They're just rocks."

"Climb back up."

Her answer disappointed me, but I tried not to show it in front of Badriya. The question of what had happened to the broken pieces of the idol seemed important to me, but precisely why I could not have said.

4.

We left Badriya at the door of her father's house and made our way in the direction of the inn where Altrus and the girl had earlier rented rooms while I was talking with Iman. Had it been up to me, I would have found more expensive accommodations in a better part of the city, since the Caliph was paying for it. But those two cared little for luxury.

As we passed people in the streets, they glared at us. A few made the sign for warding off the evil eye.

"I've seldom seen a more hostile city," Altrus said.

"It's odd, given the diverse nature of its inhabitants. If Christians can live in contentment next to Jews and Muslims, why should they resent the visit of strangers?"

We might have continued the conversation, but a stone struck me in the back between my shoulder blades. We turned in time to see a young man flee down an alley.

"That's one stone he'll regret," Altrus said grimly, and ran in pursuit.

"Wait, don't follow him," I yelled, but the girl had taken off after the mercenary. There was little I could do but go after them.

As I had feared, the youth led us into a kind of enclosed courtyard with only two entrances. He fled out the other entrance, which was quickly blocked by half a dozen men wearing black head scarves that concealed all but their eyes. I whirled around, but another group of men with their faces concealed was striding purposefully up the alley toward us. All had their swords drawn.

"A trap." I could not keep the bitterness from my voice. "I anticipated as much."

Altrus wasted no words on an apology. "Get behind me," he hissed at the two of us. "Backs against the wall."

The girl and I did not argue. Altrus was the finest swordsmen I had ever seen, and I speak as one who was trained in the art of the sword by King Huban's own sword masters, who taught me as they were teaching his son, Prince Yanni. I could handle a blade as well as the next man, but compared with Altrus I was no more dangerous than a child. The girl and I concentrated on protecting his flanks.

No more than three or four of the assassins could attack him at any one instant, and as they crowded shoulder to shoulder, they interfered with each other. They were eager and blood-thirsty, but not especially skilled. I saw Altrus cut one on the hand, another on the arm, another across the face. Still they kept coming, and would no doubt have overpowered us and killed us all, had not a shout sounded up the alley by which we had entered the courtyard.

"What's going on in there? Lay down your swords, all of you."

Eight members of the city guard rushed in with their swords drawn. The assassins confronted them but had no heart for such even odds. In moments they fled through the other gate, leaving nothing in the courtyard but scattered drops and spatters of fresh blood on the cobblestones.

"Lay down your weapons," the leader of the soldiers commanded us.

Altrus and I sheathed our swords. As for Martala, her hands were already empty. The guardsman frowned at her, but raised no objection.

"What just went on here?" he asked Altrus.

I stepped forward.

"We were attacked by a band of masked assassins. Had you not arrived when you did, they would surely have killed us."

He studied me up and down, and I could see that he was not favorably impressed.

"Why should you be attacked?"

"I know as little of that as you do. Perhaps you should ask the Mayor."

"What has Iman ibn Heydar to do with this?"

"I don't know, but he is the only person who had knowledge of our purpose in Dumatul Jandal."

In a few words I explained our reason for being in his city. He nodded as he listened, eyeing me shrewdly.

"This is an independent city. Until it fell under the sword of the Prophet it was the capital of its own kingdom, with its own laws and its own gods. There are many who still follow the old ways. I have nothing to do with such trash myself, I am a good Muslim, but many here pretend to follow the Prophet, when in reality they listen to older voices and obey more ancient customs."

"Is the Mayor among them?"

He smiled at me. "You have a dangerous tongue."

"Is that your answer?"

His smile became a frown. "I know not if the Mayor worships the old gods. I obey the laws of the Prophet, do my duty as a soldier, and mind my own business."

"So that is the way of things in Dumatul Jandal," Altrus said.

"It is the way of things," the guardsman agreed. He extended his arm to Altrus. "My name is Shahin. You look as though you know how to handle a blade."

"I've done my share of fighting in other men's wars." Altrus gave his name and grasped the man's arm in comradeship.

"I thought as much. I'm not a native of this city, but my wife was born here and her father secured me a position with the city guard. These clumsy fools behind me are my men, some of them."

Altrus introduced me and the girl, but Shahin had little regard for us. We were merely civilians, no more important in his eyes than cattle he was set to watch over. In Altrus he recognized a fellow soldier.

After promising to give an account of the ambush to the Mayor and to do what he could to investigate the matter, he left us on one of the main streets with a warning.

"Take care when you walk abroad in the city, be it by day or by night. Outsiders are looked upon with suspicion and even with hatred. Nothing good ever came to this city from outside. Many men lost their fathers and uncles to the Sword of the Prophet, as Khalid ibn al-Walid was called after the massacre he enacted here. Men still spit when they say his name."

5.

When I was cast naked into the Empty Space by King Huban of Sana'a, a clan of ghouls took me in and made me one of them. They taught me many skills, among them how to move so silently through the darkness that no man, and indeed no dog, could hear my passage.

I left the inn through my bedroom window without waking Martala, who lay on the bed beside me. The night was not as dark as I would have wished. A waning moon rose in the eastern sky, casting the black shadows of rooftops down the empty streets. I stayed in those shadows.

In my mind I had no clear purpose, only the thought that Wadd was a moon god. Surely a moon god would not be worshipped during the day under the sun, but at night beneath the rays of the moon.

My feet took me along the streets as they willed, and I found myself climbing the low hill crowned with the ruins of Wadd's temple. More by instinct than design, I crouched behind some blocks of a fallen pillar and waited.

The wind blew. An owl hooted mournfully. If ever a place was ripe for haunting it was that expanse of broken stones. Perhaps an hour passed. I was beginning to grow restless when I saw the first black silhouette climbing the hillside. It went, not to the ruins of the temple, but to the dry well behind it. As I strained my eyes through the darkness, there was a flash of yellow light and the black shape abruptly vanished.

I was tempted to advance, but kept my place. Others came, alone or by pairs, and all vanished at the mouth of the well. When no more arrived for a long time, I cautiously advanced and peered into the well. I could see a faint line of yellow light in the side near the bottom, but there was nothing to show where it originated. Also, when I bent my head into the opening, I thought I could hear chanting voices.

Climbing down by touch alone was an invigorating experience that I hope never to repeat. When my boots found the bottom, I bent to examine the bar of light and discovered that it shone through the crack in a door at the side of the well that had not been closed properly. I was able to get my fingertips into the crack and force the door inward. It swung wide on a well-greased hinge that made no sound, leaving a gap large enough to crawl through.

On the other side of the door, the tunnel was wider and taller, though not quite high enough to walk upright. I ran along its length toward the light at its far end. It sloped downward, but with how steep an inclination I was unable to judge. When I reached the end I had to catch myself by spreading my hands and pressing against the walls.

The tunnel led into a network of passageways with niches and hollows in the walls, all of them filled with bones. It was a necropolis of some sort, deep beneath the city. This made a kind of sense. Before Muslim rule, Dumatul Jandal had been ruled by Christians. This was how Christian sects sometimes buried their dead.

The necropolis gave way to a series of interconnecting natural caverns. Oil lamps had been lit to show the way, which was well-trodden by centuries of passing feet. The very rock itself was worn smooth. The chanting became clearer as I progressed into the largest cavern. It was the size of a large mosque interior and roughly the same shape, with a high domed ceiling.

About two hundred people were gathered around a stone image, some standing and some kneeling on prayer rugs. Before the image lay a recumbent black stone similar to the broken black stone on the hilltop above, but this was intact and smaller, no more than four cubits in length. On it rested a flat silver basin.

All this I took in from the corners of my eyes, but my attention was fixed on the idol, which was of a shape not entirely unknown to me. It was man-sized, but in the figure of a goat that sat on its haunches with its back legs crossed and its forelegs upraised. Between its sagging, opened thighs stood an erect phallus that would have done the Egyptian god Amun proud. Yet from the torso of this figure there sprouted rows of breasts that appeared swollen with milk. In the center of the chest was a gaping female sex organ. A lamp blazed on top of the goat's head, between its horns. At the ends of its forelegs were human hands. One held a short, thick rod and the other a deep bowl like in shape to a pestle. The strangest feature of the idol was a closed third eye in its forehead.

When I thought about what would happen, should these foolish worshippers ever succeeded in actually evoking this god to visible appearance, the roots of my hair lifted. They might know it as Wadd, god of love and friendship, but I recognized in the form of this stone idol a variation of the Goat with a Thousand Young, otherwise known as Shub-Niggurath, one of the Great Old Ones who had walked the earth before the creation of man.

Contrary to what has been written by fools who should have known better, the Old Ones never really left the earth. They simply withdrew into secret places when the coloration of the stars in the heavens became hostile to their natures. When the stars change again, as they assuredly shall at some future time, the Old Ones will emerge from their concealment and walk the world once more.

It will be merciful if our race does not survive to witness their coming forth.

I wanted to move forward so that I could hear what was being chanted, but there was too much light from lamps in the cavern to insure my concealment. Even so, I crept from one jutting spire of stone to the next, always closer to the altar and the idol.

That it was the original idol of Wadd I had little doubt. At some point it had been shattered into many pieces, and those fragments collected and painstakingly mortared back together. The lines where these joins had been made were visible in the flickering light.

A woman presided over the rite of offering. She wore a long gown of white silk and her face was veiled in the same fabric. Only her arms were exposed. I should have recognized her from her posture and the way she moved, but it was not until she spoke that I realized the high priestess of Wadd was Badriya, daughter of the mayor.

"You have given the lesser offerings of milk and grain to the god," she said in a deep and stirring voice. "Now come and give the greater offering, that the god may descend into his image and be with us, as we celebrate his gifts of life and love."

The worshippers needed no urging. They rushed forward. I saw that they all carried daggers. With frenzied enthusiasm, they bared their forearms and gashed themselves repeatedly, then allowed their blood to drip into the silver basin on the altar stone.

"Now dance the dance of Wadd," Badriya commanded.

Behind the idol, several men and a woman picked up musical instruments and began to play upon them a reedy, nasal kind of music that rose and fell like a swaying serpent. The worshippers, with blood still streaming down their arms, began to dance around the idol and the altar. They undulated their arms above their heads as they rotated their bodies and rocked their hips in time to the music. The effect was strongly sensual. Had I not lacked a prick and stones, I might have been overcome by it, so insidiously did the music wriggle its way into my mind. Even castrated and a eunuch, as I was, I could not help being moved by the sounds and sights before me.

Then Badriya held up a small dagger and cut her own forearm over the basin. Her red blood gushed into it. She took up the basin in her hands and placed it in the lap of the god, just in front of his jutting sex organ. She dipped her hands in the hot blood and laved it over the god's prick, sliding her hands up and down, until it was stained all along its considerable length with scarlet.

The dancers had begun to tear off their robes to dance naked. Many of the women bore tribal tattoos, and danced with the complete abandon of Bedouins. The rhythm of the drums increased its pace. I watched in fascination as Badriya stripped out of her white gown and pulled off her veil. She was a beautiful woman. Removing the basin from the lap of the god, she climbed up onto his knees and slowly lowered herself onto his bloody prick while embracing his torso with her arms.

I had seen this kind of worship before. Wadd was not only a god of friendship and love, but of lust and engendering. It may have been an illusion created by the flickering flames of the lamps, but the polished stone skin of the idol seemed to flush with pink, and its many-breasted chest appeared to rise and fall with gasping breaths. When its third eye suddenly opened, I almost fell off my haunches.

Badriya arched her back until she was bent over backwards, her head inverted, her long black hair spilling around it. Her face bore an expression of pure ecstasy. She swayed her body and rose and fell on the stone phallus to the beat of the drums and the whine of the flutes. All around the idol the naked worshippers began to pair off – man to woman, man to man, and woman to woman. They fell to the floor of the cavern and copulated with sensual abandon. Some of them were scarcely more than children.

Between the horns of the god, the flame of the lamp writhed and twisted upward like a rising pillar of fire, and the god's red third eye seemed to glare at me. I did not know if it could see me, but decided I had seen enough to confront the mayor.

I started to back away, but stepped on a loose piece of stone that rolled under my boot and sent me sprawling to the floor of the cavern. My only thought was how the ghouls of the Black Spring Clan would have laughed to see such unpardonable clumsiness.

6.

"Seize him!" Badriya cried, glaring furiously at me with her face inverted.

It did not take long for the lovers on the floor to disentangle themselves. They rushed at me with their daggers, and would have cut me to pieces had not Badriya stopped them.

"We will offer him to the god, to make amends for his sacrilege."

"But that is the greatest offering," an older man protested, his face awed and fearful. "The greatest offering has not been given for generations."

"We will give it tonight," she told him in a voice that would tolerate no argument.

He fell silent, but continued to look fearfully at me as I was dragged by my arms toward the idol. I saw that its third eye was now closed. Had it ever been opened, or had that only been an illusion created by the dancing lamplight?

"What are you going to do with me?"

They stripped me naked. My glamour was in place, so they saw me as I would have appeared had I not been castrated by King Huban's torturers.

"Rejoice, Alhazred," Badriya said, her dark eyes shining with fanatical zeal. "You are about to experience the greatest honor a man can receive in this life. You will walk among the blessed for eternity in the land of Wadd."

"I was hoping for a more specific answer."

They did not respond to this poor attempt at bravado. The musicians resumed their reedy song, and I was forced toward the idol. Men on either side of me grabbed my legs and spread them as they lifted me up towards the lap of the stone god. Its blood-soaked phallus stood glistening in the lamplight. In length, it was more than the distance from my fingertips to my elbow. I realized that Badriya had only taken the tip of it into her body while making love to the god. A kind of sickness washed through me as I understood what they intended to do.

"This is the greatest offering, which our ancestors gave to Wadd when the wells ran dry and the crops failed and the she-goats ceased to being forth their young. It is fitting that we offer this meddling outsider, who has come to our city seeking to destroy our god and our faith. Truly, he is the enemy of Wadd, but the god is all friendship and all love. Wadd will forgive him in his death embrace. Even this evil outsider will be carried up to the land of Wadd, to enjoy unending bliss among the faithful."

"This is a bad idea," I said to her. "The Caliph knows I am here and what I have come here to do. My companions will search for me when they awaken in the morning and find me gone from my bed."

"Silence," she hissed. "One more word and I will cut off your tongue."

The blood-wet tip of the stone phallus pressed between my naked buttocks as the men on either side lowered me into the lap of Wadd. Now that I was so close, I could see that the lips of the idol bore a kind of smirk of satisfaction. The pressure increased. Tight is the gate called the Eye of the Needle at Jerusalem, but tighter still was the ring of my anus. In the long run, I knew this would not matter. They would continue to force me down until my anus opened to receive the stone rod, and they would not stop until it had ripped its way into my entrails and killed me.

I can render you unconscious, my love, Sashi said to me in my thoughts.

For a moment I considered the offer.

"No. Whatever happens, we will face it together."

It shall be as you will.

Harsh male voices began yelling commands behind me. My arms were suddenly released. I twisted away from the lap of the idol. My naked body was covered in sweat from the effort I had made to avoid being pressed down.

The cavern was a confusion of human beings, some naked and others clothed as soldiers, running back and forth, shouting and screaming. Some of the men of Wadd took up their daggers and tried to fight, but the soldiers cut them down with swords. The others fled through various passageways that led out from the cavern.

My entire body shook with a combination of relief and muscle strain. I crouched by the idol on one knee, hoping no overzealous guardsman would cut me down. The chaos quickly began to subside.

Martala came to me with my discarded clothing in her hands. The white skull of Gor sitting on top of my black desert robes seemed to mock me with its toothy grin. She said nothing while I dressed and strapped the ghoul's skull to my waist. This allowed me a few moments to regain my composure.

"How did you know to come here?"

"I got up to piss and found you missing from the inn. I woke Altrus. We assumed you had gone back to the ruined temple. We found the hill empty, but noticed light shining up from the bottom of the well. Altrus ran back to rouse Shahin and his men from the guardhouse while I stood watch. We descended into the well and found you ... as we found you."

My cheeks flushed with blood.

"You arrived not a moment too soon. Indeed, I wish you had arrived sooner."

"Your virginity is still intact," Altrus said, slapping me on the shoulder. "That's all that matters."

I looked around the cavern. Only a few of the worshippers of the god had been captured. Twice as many lay dead on the floor, but the greater number had escaped down the passages. The guardsmen hesitated to pursue them since the tunnels were dark and the ways unknown. Shahin caught my eye and approached. His sword was stained with blood. He cleaned it on a white handkerchief as we talked.

"What of Badriya?" I asked. "Was she taken?"

"Do you mean the eldest daughter of Iman ibn Heydar? Was she here?"

"Didn't you see her?"

"How would I know?" he said with a shrug as he sheathed his gleaming sword. "Whenever we meet, she is always veiled."

"She must have escaped down one of these tunnels."

"Are you sure it was her?" he asked doubtfully.

"I am sure. I recognized her voice."

"Only her voice?" he said. "That may not be enough to convince her father."

"Don't you think her father knows she is the high priestess of Wadd?"

"I doubt it. He has no love for the Caliph, but he is strict in enforcing the laws of the Prophet."

"We must go to him at once, and inform him about this temple."

"I agree." Shahin said. He looked at the idol. "What should we do with this?"

"That is for the mayor of the city to decide, but if he follows the will of the Caliph, he will have it destroyed a second time."

7.

Iman was irritated as being awakened in the middle of the night, but his annoyance diminished as he listened to our story. We told it in turns; first my part, then Martala, and then Shahin. Altrus was there also, but remained silent.

"So they took up the pieces and put the idol back together again," he said with a slight smile of admiration. "That was clever of them."

His smile fell from his face when I told him of his daughter's role in the idol worship.

"That is ridiculous. Badriya has been in this house all night. She is still in bed as we speak."

"Shall we go to her room and discover the truth of this?" I suggested gently.

He was inclined to refuse, but at last had his servant push his wheeled chair down a hall to the door of his daughter's bedroom.

"Don't knock," I said. "We will surprise her."

I pushed open the door. It was dark within the room, but some light came in from the hallway. A shape lay beneath the sheets in the bed. I wondered if it was made up of pillows, but then it stirred and sat up. Tinder was struck and a lamp lighted. The girl blinked her eyes as if to clear them of sleep. It was a convincing deception.

"What is going on, father? Why have you come to my room?"

"There, do you see?" Iman said with disgust. "So much for your ridiculous and insulting accusation."

"There is one way to be sure," I said. "Have your daughter show us her left forearm."

"My patience is coming to an end, Alhazred –"

"I don't mind," Badriya said in a sleepy voice.

She slid up the sleeves of her nightdress and bared her forearms to the light. Both were unblemished. Not a single cut, not even a scratch, broke their whiteness.

"There, you see?" Iman said. "I knew you must be mistaken. My daughter would never take part in pagan rites."

Badriya met my gaze. There was no hint of anything in her dark eyes to betray her innocence.

"May I go back to sleep now, Father? I'm tired."

We left her to her dreams, whatever forms those might take, and returned to the old man's audience chamber.

"I can vouch for the truth of the rest of Alhazred's story," Shahin said.

"As do we," Altrus said, speaking for the first time, and the girl nodded.

"Very well. I do not doubt you, Shahin. You are a good man. In the morning we will go together to this well and investigate the matter. For now, let us return to our beds for the few hours of darkness that remain."

Early in the morning we assembled at the well on the hill, only to discover that it was completely filled up to its rim with stones and rubble.

Iman sat in a sedan chair carried by four black slaves. He had them bring his chair right to the edge of the well so that he could look down upon it.

"Are you certain this is the well by which you entered the caverns?"

"There is no doubt of it," I said firmly. In my own heart I wondered how it was possible to fill the entire well in the space of only a few hours. Ghouls could have done it, but the townspeople were not ghouls.

"There must be other entrances," Martala pointed out.

"Yes, but where are they?" Shahin asked. "I know every foot of this city and have never found any such tunnels."

"They are hidden," Altrus said.

"Perhaps, but where? What are we to do if we cannot find them?"

"This well can be excavated."

Shahin looked doubtfully at the rubble in the well, then at the mayor.

"It would be a considerable labor."

In the end, Iman ordered the well cleaned out. This took three days, with a crew of nine men working around the clock. When the well was empty, I descended to the bottom and searched for the door, but could not find it. I poked and pressed and kicked every block of stone. None of them moved. None of them rang hollow when tapped with the hilt of a dagger. I took down an iron pry bar, yet still the stones in the sides of the well could not be shifted.

"What are you going to tell the Caliph?" Altrus asked when we chanced to be standing together on the temple hill, some distance from the others.

"The truth. He deserves that much."

"Are you sure we know the truth? That girl's arm was not cut."

I shook my head.

"There are mysteries here I don't pretend to understand. She may have used some glamour to hide the cuts. Or perhaps the power of the god healed her."

"She would have killed you, had we not arrived in time to stop her."

"I know that, and I will remember." My voice was grim and as cold as moonlit desert sands.

"After all, what does it matter to us which god a city worships?" Altrus said moodily, staring at the well. "We are all bound for hell in our own way."

"You speak truth."

Later that day, we mounted our camels and set off for Damascus.

Blood Bond

The library is my favourite room in the house. It is always cooler and quieter than any other room. The quiet comes from the books and scrolls that line its walls. They act as an extra layer of insulation against the sounds from the street, and from the other rooms. I don't know why it is cooler. It must be the way the air flows through the window screens. When I want to think, or just relax without thinking, I will often retire in solitude to the reading desk in the library and simply sit, staring with unfocused eyes at the bookshelves.

I was engaged in this lack of activity, and savouring it in a quiet way, when Altrus's Persian woman, Nealayna, tapped on the closed door and entered with something in her hand. She always seemed nervous in my presence, though I had never done anything to intimidate her or make her feel less than welcome under my roof.

"What have you there, Nealayna?"

"Forgive my intrusion, sir. A messenger came to the door and left this for you."

I leaned forward and took the letter from her hand.

"There's no need to call me sir. As I told you before, we don't use such formalities in this house. You're not a servant, after all, you're a welcome guest."

"Yes, Alhazred. I forgot."

I set the letter down on the table and studied her.

"Are you happy here?"

She blinked in surprise. "Of course."

"Does Altrus beat you?"

She laughed at the absurdity of the question before she could catch herself, then blushed.

"He is the kindest and gentlest man I have ever known."

"I'm delighted to hear it. So you are happy here?"

"Truly, Alhazred, I have never been happier."

"Then you need to start acting like it. This is your home now. You don't need to tip-toe along the halls, or lower your voice when you talk. Let Borka answer the gate bell some of the time. That's why I employ him as my servant. The poor man thinks you are trying to put him out of a job."

The distress on her face was so genuine, I had a hard time resisting the impulse to smile.

"Just relax and enjoy the house, Nealayna. Let the servants be the servants. I know you want to help Martala with the household management but she was doing it alone for many months without difficulty before you came. If she needs help she'll ask for it."

She bowed her head. She was a very beautiful woman, with the dark eyes and heavy dark eyebrows so common to Persian women, a straight nose, a mouth perfectly formed, and lustrous black hair. It was easy to see why Altrus had fallen in love with her.

"I will heed your words, sir ... I mean, Alhazred."

She bowed and left the library with her head lowered.

I watched her close the door and shook my head. At some point she had been bullied, probably by a domineering man, maybe her father, maybe her late husband. It had left an enduring mark on her that would be difficult to erase, but I was determined to set her at ease. At least under my roof she should be able to relax and express her true nature, which I believed to be gentle and kind.

Picking up the letter, I turned it over. It was addressed only with the name "Alhazred" written in that bright scarlet ink from the land of Chin that is known as Dragon's Blood. The seal was curious. It was smaller than the typical letter seal, and the wax was almost black. The symbol impressed into the wax puzzled me for a time. At last I opened the drawer in the reading table and took out a magnifying lens. Through the cloudy glass of the lens I saw that it represented the mythical beast of Persia known as the manticore, which has the body of a lion, the face of a man, and the tail of a dragon that is armed with long, sharp, barbed spikes. The name means "man-eater."

When I snapped the wax seal into two parts, I heard or thought I heard a sound like that of a stone slab falling into place in the earth. It was a kind of dull thud.

I unfolded the sheet of parchment and saw that the letter was written in the same Dragon's Blood ink that had been used to address it.

Alhazred,

I require your help in a matter of some urgency. Your discretion is essential. Tell no one the contents of this letter and come alone. If you agree, allow the servitor that rings your bell to guide you to me.

Your, Father

Before I could read this brief message twice, the red lettering began to glow like the embers of a fire when blown upon, and a moment later the parchment burst into flame. I released it and it fell to my desk, but when the flame died there was not a trace of ash.

I smiled to myself. It was a simple juggler's trick of the kind that could be seen in any marketplace. As for the sender identifying himself as my father, what better way to insure my interest and obedience?

What the sender did not know was that I despised my father. He was an oaf who had been happy to sell me to King Huban in Sana'a at an early age to play the part of court poet. Even as a boy, I had been gifted with the ability to compose songs and poetry on demand. For many years Huban valued my verses more than his court jester or his dwarf. Those had been happy years for me.

My service in his palace came to an abrupt end when I deflowered his daughter and got her with child. For that he mutilated my face, tortured and castrated me, then forced me to eat both the stillborn foetus of my engendering and my severed manhood. I shrugged like a ghoul at the memory. Well, it could have been worse. After all, the meat had been well cooked on a charcoal grill.

Nealayna was in the kitchen, teaching the cook how to properly cut vegetables. The cook cast me a grateful glance when I pulled the Persian into the back hall, where we could talk without being overheard. I wondered how her expression would change were she to see me as I truly was, beneath the mask of glamour that disguised my features.

"The messenger who delivered that letter you brought me, what did he look like?"

She frowned in thought.

"He was a strange little man. Very short, with a bald head and a shaven chin. His skin was unnaturally pale, just as yours –" She stopped herself as she realized what she had said.

"Did you notice anything else?"

"He spoke with an accent I have never heard before."

As I released her, the bell at the street gate rang. Borka was returning to the house by the time I reached the front door.

"A man requests that you accompany him."

"Do I know him?"

"I don't believe so, sir."

"What does he look like?"

Borka frowned in thought and rubbed his beard.

"He is a little bald man, no taller than my shoulder. His face is shaven and he wears strange clothes. His eyes are very black and he speaks in an odd way. I am certain he has never been admitted to the house."

"Very well, Borka, tell him to wait by the gate. I will join him presently."

I was intrigued by this strange little messenger from someone calling himself my father. My father was a drunken lout who had never held onto money long enough to hire a messenger. Besides which, he did not know how to write.

Was it possible the letter had been sent by my other father? That was the insidious little thought that intrigued me. It refused to leave my head.

How can a man have two fathers? Well, one may be a fat, drunken fool who beats you every day until the day he sells you, and the other may be a whispered rumour, a bit of malicious village gossip with which you are tortured by the other children, who will not play with you because you look different. The gossip said that on the day of her unhappy marriage to my earthly father, my mother had lain down with a djinn of the desert, and that I was the fruit of that unholy union.

As wild as the story was, my pale skin that refused to tan and my pale green eyes seemed to support it. At any rate, they were enough reason for the other children of my poor village to shun and abuse me.

Gor's skull already hung from my belt. I seldom removed it. The ghoul's skull was my reminder that after my ordeal in the Empty Space I was no longer human. I might look like a human being with my mask of glamour in place, and I might talk and smile like a human, but inside I was a ghoul of the Black Spring Clan, and always would be. I went upstairs to fetch my sword and dagger. Martala noticed me buckling them into place.

"Do you need me?"

I hesitated. "No. I am only going to meet with someone who claims to be my father. It is probably just an attempt to extort money."

"It is a bold man who would try to extort money from a necromancer. What if you are led into a trap?"

"I will not allow myself to be drawn away from the main streets of Damascus and will not leave the city."

"Why go at all?"

"I am bored. This is something to do. Call it an amusement."

The girl lifted her eyebrows but raised no other objection.

2.

The little man at the gate stared at me with emotionless black eyes. He was as Nealayna had characterized him, strange. His suit of clothing appeared to come from the far east. He wore blue cotton trousers and a gray collarless jacket that buttoned all the way up the front. On his feet were what appeared to be black felt shoes.

Without speaking a word or acknowledging my presence in any way, he turned and began to walk. His pace was astonishingly quick for someone with such short legs. I took long strides behind him but barely managed to keep up. After a while I gave up trying to walk beside him and contented myself with merely keeping him in sight, which I could do without running. His outlandish costume made him easy to spot in the colourful crowd that filled the main streets of Damascus.

We moved to the east for a time, then turned to the north, and then west. I wondered what game he was playing? Was he waiting for confederates to come up behind me and manhandle me into a wagon? I remained alert to those around me but had no sense of being followed.

Now we were moving through a part of Damascus unfamiliar to me. The streets were narrower and twisted to the left and right like cobblestone serpents up and over the crests of low hills. We turned so often, I lost all sense of direction. The languages spoken by those around me were strange to my ears. Damascus is one of the most traveled cities in the world. A resident of the city will hear all tongues spoken in its marketplace at one time or another, but the common language of the street is always Arabic.

There was something else. The odours of the street were strange to me as well. Every city has its own unique blend of stenches that forms a kind of background in the mind. In some way I could not explain, the background smell had changed.

I looked around while keeping the elusive little man in the corners of my eyes, and saw that the very architecture was different from that of Damascus. The roofs of the buildings were steeply pitched and tiled in a dramatic fashion, with great out-thrustings of the eves. Their walls were made of painted wood rather than mud bricks or stone.

"Enough of this," I said under my breath, and stopped in the middle of the street.

The little man vanished around a corner. I ignored him and turned around so that I faced the opposite way. With deliberate steps I began to try to retrace my path. This was a futile effort. Everything looked and sounded and smelled strange.

"Do you know where we are, Sashi?"

The beautiful oval face of the minor desert djinn who shared my body formed itself before my open eyes and seemed to float upon the air.

I am sorry, my love, but everything is strange to me, she said silently in my mind.

"This isn't Damascus," I told her with conviction. She did not contradict me.

Movement across the street caught my eye. It was the bald man, who stood at the mouth of an alley, beckoning to me with his arm. I hurried toward him but he did not wait for me. He vanished into the alley. By the time I reached its mouth he was nowhere in sight. The alley twisted to the left and right a number of times. The walls were featureless and lacked both windows and doors. At its end was a double gate that was not locked.

I pressed through the gate and found myself in the well-tended gardens of a large country house that occupied a low hill. All around the house on the slope of the hill grew dark, narrow cypress trees. The lane that led to the house from the gate crossed a field that had been mowed for hay some few days before.

Following the lane to the front door, I pulled the chain that rang a bell inside. The door opened almost instantly. The little bald man I had followed bowed to me and indicated with his arm for me to enter. I noted that he was not even breathing hard. For my part, I was covered in sweat from my effort to keep up with him. It was uncommon for me to sweat.

"The next time I follow you, I will bring a horse," I said.

He gave no indication that he had understood my words, but led me deeper into the house, to a tiled atrium that was dominated by a central fountain and open to the sky above. The house overhung this space on all sides for some distance, providing protection for the furniture against the rain, and shade from the sun. Small orange trees grew beside the fountain. White doves perched in the branches of the trees. A colourful peacock walked across the large paving stones on the floor.

I had seen such architecture in Alexandria. Everything had a Roman aspect. Indeed, everything about the house and its grounds looked Roman, including the bright frescos painted on the walls. The only sound was the splash of water from the fountain.

A man who lay on his side on a padded divan looked up from his book and regarded me. I had not noticed him until he moved. I looked behind and realized the bald servant had vanished. I wondered if he had ever really existed.

The man slowly stood and gestured for me to come forward. He was impressive without being intimidating. Taller than me and broader in the shoulders, he wore wrapped about his body a Roman robe of white linen of the kind that the senators of Rome wore during the age of the Caesars, and laced sandals on his bare feet. His blond hair was cut short, his face beardless. I found it impossible to judge his age. That he was older than me was obvious from the fine wrinkles at the corners of his jade-green eyes, but how much older I could not hazard to say. His skin seemed to glow with inner health, so that it radiated a kind of golden light.

Without warning, he stepped forward and embraced me. I was startled but allowed him to complete the gesture.

"Welcome to my house, Alhazred. My name is Salaymorlaynah."

"You are a djinn." I made it a statement rather than a question.

He nodded. "I could have brought you here myself, but I wanted you to come of your own free will."

He went to a low table and filled two crystal goblets with red wine, then passed one of them to me.

"They say men should never eat or drink anything offered by the djinn."

He smiled and sipped his wine. After a moment, I put the glass to my lips. Never have I tasted anything so rich and yet so subtle. Its coolness soothed my throat.

"Let us sit and talk," he said.

I took a chair with a cushion on the seat, but had no back that was near the low table, and he sat on the side of the divan where he had been reading.

"Your letter indicates that you are my father." It felt strange to say these words, but he merely nodded.

"I lay with your mother. You are my son, half-human and half-djinn. Or to be more accurate, human with some djinn attributes. Your mother was flesh, so you are predominantly flesh, but half of your blood is mine."

For some reason, I did not doubt his words. Maybe it was his easy manner, which held no trace of guile. Or maybe the fact that his eyes were the same color as my own.

"Why did you never visit me when I was a child?"

He frowned and shook his head.

"That is never a good practice. Humans become fearful so easily. I did not want you and your family to be stoned to death as witches."

He stared at me keenly, but with compassion.

"You were very handsome."

I touched my cheek and realized that the mask of glamour that I use to hide my mutilated face had been stripped away.

"Speak the name of the man who did this to you and he will suffer for it."

"There is no need. King Huban was killed by a falling roof tile that was dislodged by a foreign agent."

"An accident?"

"It was made to look that way."

He nodded. "You are a man of many resources, Alhazred. That is why I asked for your help."

"How can a mere human be of use to a djinn?"

"You have fought the djinn twice before, and won. Is this not true?"

"In a manner of speaking. The first time I turned the power of Allesalasallah, a djinn of the Seventh Circle, against her. The second time I allowed her son, Xhalarhinni, who is half-djinn by blood, to dishonour himself in a duel."

"Xhalarhinni sought to kill you because you killed his mother."

I nodded.

"His mother was a djinn, so he was not a creature of flesh and bone, but of air and fire. I could not possibly have defeated him with a sword, so I chose a contest that would be decided by luck, but he could not believe I would play fairly, so he cheated and was exposed doing it to the Seventh Circle."

"What was the nature of your contest?"

"We played a game of dice."

He laughed in appreciation of my choice of weapons.

"He must hate you very much."

I shrugged. "That is of little importance, since he is bound by

honour not to harm me or anyone in my household. Indeed, all of the Seventh Circle are bound by the same oath."

"So I was informed when I made an inquiry after you. It seems that your name is infamous among the Seventh Circle."

"Which circle are you?"

"I am of the Ninth Circle."

"You must have great powers."

"In some ways, I do, but they are constrained by my ethical creed."

"Who is it that seeks to kill you?"

"Xhalarhinni."

I regarded him with surprise. "Then surely the contest is already over, since you must be much more powerful that a mere half-djinn could ever hope to be."

"That is so, in a way. He cannot attack me directly."

"Therefore, he is attacking someone of importance to you," I finished as understanding dawned.

He nodded. "Unless I do as he asks, he says he will kill my wives. But to do as he asks would dishonour me forever. I would be cast out from the Ninth Circle."

"What exactly is it that you want from me?"

He hesitated before replying, his gaze locked with mine.

"I want you to fight a dual on my behalf with Xhalarhinni."

3.

"You may indeed be my father, as you claim to be, although I have only your word for this."

"Be assured, I am your father."

"But even if this is so, you must realize that I have no reason to help you."

"The ties of blood demand it."

"Do they?" I looked at him narrowly. "Where were you when I needed help in my life?"

He said nothing.

"Where were you when King Huban mutilated my face and castrated me? Where were you when he cast me naked into the Empty Space to die? Where were you when I slept under rocks with scorpions and burrowed into the sand like a lizard to escape the rays of the sun?"

"I gave you existence."

"As harrowing as your five minute ordeal with my mother must have been, it is scarcely reason enough for me to risk my life for you."

"If you do not act as my champion, my wives will die."

"Surely you can get other wives."

"I am fond of those I now possess."

"We must all learn to bear disappointment in life."

He frowned, and all at once the sunlight left his countenance and his eyes filled with storm clouds.

"I am forbidden to harm djinn of a status lower than my own unless attacked by them, but I am not forbidden to harm human beings."

"That's more like it," I said, clapping my hands together slowly. "Now you sound like my father."

"You are a man with a heart of stone."

"I am not a man, I am a ghoul," I patted Gor's skull at my belt. "You would be wise to always remember that."

He stood up, walked to the fountain and back again with his head lowered in brooding.

"If I must, I will threaten to harm the members of your household. Both the djinn of the Seventh Circle and Xhalarhinni have sworn to you never to harm you or your house, but I have not made any such oath."

"You have just made the threat."

"Yes, I suppose I have. What is your answer?"

I took my time to think the matter over. I owed Salaymorlaynah nothing, and even less to his wives. On the other hand Xhalarhinni was my enemy. I suspected that the only reason he had sought out Salaymorlaynah was my blood connection with him. It was his way of striking at me. Sooner or later I would have to deal with Allesalasallah's half-human spawn, so why not now?

Then there was the practical consideration that Salaymorlaynah could erase from the face of the earth my house and all who dwelt in it with a single gesture. To the djinn, particularly those of the higher circles, human beings were looked upon at best as no more than cattle, and at worst, as vermin. I wondered what ever could have possessed Salaymorlaynah to lie with my mother?

"Very well. I will take your place in your duel with Xhalarhinni, and I will fight for your honour."

"I am relieved to hear it. Truly, my son, I have no wish to harm your household."

"What makes you believe I could possibly stand against Xhalarhinni in a real duel for more than a few seconds?"

"I cannot fight him directly, but as my champion I can lend you some of my powers for a brief period."

"Why must it be brief? Your powers would be a great asset to me in my life."

He smiled at me as a father smiles at a foolish child.

"They would burn you to a cinder if they were left within you. Because you are of my own blood, you may be able to withstand their heat for a few minutes, but no mortal could carry them for longer than this. And the more you use them, the hotter they will become."

"How do I find Xhalarhinni?"

"He is waiting for us in one of the realms at a specific time and place chosen for the combat."

"Do you mean he has been just waiting all this time?"

He smiled as me as an adult smiles at a foolish toddler.

"You fail to comprehend. He is not waiting at all in the sense you mean – he *awaits us* at a particular moment in time, and at a specific location in the multitude of dimensions. I will carry you to the place."

"Do I get to choose the weapon, as I did last time?"

"No. Xhalarhinni is not foolish enough to allow you to play the same trick twice. Your weapons shall be the natural weapons of the djinn, which are fire and air."

"I don't know how to use these weapons."

"Let your mind direct them. Think of a blast of wind, and it will appear; think of a ball of fire, and it will come into being."

"What if I were to use the air and fire together?"

"Then you would get lightning."

I remembered the bolt of lightning Allesalasallah had tried to kill me with. I was alive only because I had been able to use the seal of Solomon to reflect it back upon her. Salaymorlaynah was still talking.

"These elements will not only form weapons for you, but shields as well. When you raise your hand in defense, a crystalline shield will manifest. When you point with your finger, the weapon you choose will strike out."

I chuckled quietly to myself.

"What do you find amusing in all this?" he demanded.

"I was just thinking, I'll finally have the kind of magical power the people in the marketplace expect a necromancer to possess – to make balls of fire dance on the air, and to hurl bolts of lightning."

My words meant nothing to the djinn.

"Just remember to use the lightning sparingly. It will heat you up inside."

We stood facing each other beside the bubbling fountain, beneath the open sky, in that odd room without a roof.

"Prepare yourself," he said.

"Wait! I almost forgot. Will these powers harm the *chaklah* who dwells in my body?"

His jade eyes narrowed, and he seemed to look right through me. Then he laughed.

"So you have a pet? No, the air and fire of the djinn-force will not harm the little one inside you. After all, she is herself a djinn, even if only a very minor kind."

He laid his hands on my shoulders. I felt the heat radiating down from them. His eyes turned red and began to glow brighter and brighter, first orange, then yellow, then an intense blue-white. They blinded me to everything else. I felt a kind of lake of fire form inside my lower belly. It turned slowly like a pinwheel. After another moment, he released me and stepped back.

"I dare not give you any more of my djinn-force, or it may consume you. I can only hope it will be enough to confront the half-breed Xhalarhinni."

He opened part of his robe and stepped forward to wrap it around my shoulders.

"Hold tight to my body. We must fly to the place of combat."

I did as he ordered, and felt myself lifted off the floor. We rose through the opening in the roof. As we flew higher, I was able to see the villa and its orchards spread below. Further off was the city I had passed through in coming to the villa.

"What is the name of that place?" I asked.

"That is called Herculaneum."

The name sounded vaguely familiar. I wondered if I had read about it in a book of history or geography.

It soon became evident that we were flying toward a large mountain. Smoke billowed up from its summit. The djinn carried me over the top of the mountain, and began to descend into a kind of crater. It was a gloomy choice for a duel.

To my surprise, we did not land on the floor of the crater, but descended through it into the heart of the mountain, which opened into a great cavern that was filled with a dull red light by rocks that glowed. The heat must have been unbearable, but I was not harmed by it nor did my clothing burst into flame. An aura surrounded my body and protected me.

Xhalarhinni came forward the moment he saw me, almost

dancing on his toes as he walked across the floor of the cavern, which I assumed was where we were to fight. He was dressed as I remembered seeing him last, in a black desert thawb and black turban, with a sword and a dagger hanging from embroidered baldrics that crossed on his chest.

I was struck again by how handsome he looked, with his dark eyes and closely trimmed beard, but I reminded myself that all djinn were handsome unless they wished to be otherwise. They could control their appearance at will. As for myself, I had not even bothered to renew the glamour that concealed my mutilated face. Let the djinn see me as I truly appeared, and to hell with their opinions.

Behind Xhalarhinni, in the shadows, I sensed rather than saw that we were not alone in the cavern. Other djinn had come to watch the duel. Many of them must have been of the Seventh Circle, which hated me for killing their sister Allesalasallah. I wondered if any supporters of Salaymorlaynah were among them.

Stepping away from him, I rubbed Gor's skull for reassurance. If I fought like a man I would lose. If I fought like a djinn I would lose. I must fight like a ghoul.

"I'm surprised you found the courage to face me a second time, Alhazred," Xhalarhinni said. "Surprised, but delighted."

"Why should I not meet you again, when I defeated you so easily the first time?"

He laughed but it sounded forced.

"This time we will not be playing at dice. This time we will fight as djinn."

I looked behind me and realized that my father had faded back into the shadows beyond the ring of glowing rocks.

"There is nowhere for you to flee, no one from whom you can seek help," he gloated. "This time you will surely die."

4.

"Xhalarhinni, I put it to you and to the djinn gathered here that you have violated the spirit, if not the letter, of our agreement that you never seek to harm either me or any member of my house."

"You don't seem to know why we are here, Alhazred," he replied. "Let me make it plain for your understanding. We are not here to debate with words, we are here to watch you die."

Then I knew that the shadowy djinn gathered behind him were quite willing to allow him to violate the spirit of his oath not to harm me or my house, as long as he did not do so directly. To them I was less than an animal, and I had killed their sister. They hated me with a passion that would not cool for a thousand years.

The striking of a brass gong sounded on the air above the low rumblings of the mountain.

"We begin," Xhalarhinni said. "I will let you have the first cast."

I was not quite sure what he meant by this, but he stood some twenty paces away with his arms at his side, waiting.

Well, there's a first time for everything, I said to myself.

Courage, my love, Sashi replied in my mind.

Using the force of my will, I summoned up the anger I felt toward this arrogant, smirking half-djinn and focused it into my tightly clenched right fist. Then I thrust my fist forcefully forward and opened it, as through throwing a stone. A globe of fire that was green at its edge flew at Xhalarhinni. He stepped to the side and raised his hand with his fingers splayed. The fireball bounced off an invisible shield and burst when it struck the cavern wall.

"Now it is my turn," he said, savouring the words.

Raising his hands to his face, he shaped them into a kind of horn and blew with his lips through it. Instinctively I raised a hand in defense. The blast of wind struck my shield like a fist and shattered it. I felt it break into pieces. I was lifted from my feet and flung back at the stone wall behind me. An instant before I struck, I was able to conceive a crystalline sphere around my entire body. This, too, shattered when it struck the rock wall, sending me sprawling face first across the floor.

I stood up. My legs trembled from the effort of supporting

me. Inside my belly, I felt the heat of the djinn-force blaze with increased intensity. It was not yet painful, but I could sense that it soon would be if it continued to get hotter.

Without giving my foe any warning, I put my hands together palm to palm, then thrust them forward and spread them. A bolt of brilliant white lightning flashed out and struck Xhalarhinni in the chest. The lightning caught him by surprise, before he could throw up a shield. He tumbled backwards into the shadows. It was several seconds before he began to stir, and several more before he stood up.

"Not such a child as I thought you were," he said with a brash grin, but I noticed he had a slight limp due to favouring his left hip.

Without warning he unleashed fire on me with both hands. It came, not as a ball, but as a blast such as the jugglers in the marketplace at Damascus use when they spit fire from their lips. The shield I threw up with my right palm did not crack. The orange flame, green at its edges, spread about the shield and flew past me on all sides. I felt the heat of it radiating down on the back of my neck. The heat inside my belly was also more intense.

So the duel went, back and forth. I learned by trial and error that it was easier to deflect his elemental blasts at an angle with my shields rather than trying to stop them head on, and easier still to step to the side if I could anticipate their direction ahead of time. Misdirection was employed to make me think a blast was going to strike me from the left, when it was actually cast from the right. More than once I stepped directly into the blast, but always my shield saved my life.

Xhalarhinni gave no sign of becoming tired, and I tried to present the same jaunty appearance to his eyes, but the truth was, I was growing so exhausted that I could scarcely stand or even see clearly. My vision was beginning to blur from pure exhaustion. Inside, my intestines felt as though they were roasting on a spit, and the heat had begun to creep upward in my chest toward my pounding heart.

"It's a pity I did not think to bring a bed for you to lie down on, Alhazred. You look tired."

"It's the boredom. If you can't hit me any harder, I may fall asleep."

I knew I could not go on like this. In a few minutes, I would be unable to focus my mind to raise a shield, and then I would be dead. My casts seemed to have little or no effect on Xhalarhinni, who seemed to be genuinely enjoying himself and deliberately drawing out the duel to greater length.

"I'm surprised you are so eager to defend the honour of the Seventh Circle," I said to him. "After all, what are you to them? You're not a man, you're not a djinn. You're nothing."

He frowned. "My mother was always loving to me. That is more than you can say about your father."

I looked behind me for an instant, trying to catch a glimpse of Salaymorlaynah from the corner of my eye. This was what he had anticipated. He flung lightning at me with both hands. It would have killed me, but it was thrown with haste and most of it passed me on my left side. Even so, my left arm was numbed and useless. I could not even lift it.

Not waiting for me to respond in turn, he began to pound me with fire, one flaming ball after another. I held them away with my right hand, but my invisible shield began to shatter on impact. I could see its pieces fly off when it was covered with the flame. He forced me back and to one knee, as he strode forward and continued to lash out with ball after ball of fire, so quickly there was almost no pause between them.

When he stood no more than three or four paces away, he stopped and stared down at me with contempt.

"You are nothing. You are not even fit to kill in the manner of a djinn. I will kill you like a man, by taking your head."

He drew his sword. This was what I had waited for. I knew from my last encounter with him that he prided himself on the use of the sword, and that he had been vexed beyond measure when he was denied its use.

Drawing my dagger from its sheath, I raised it to my lips and blew a blast of air between my curled fingers. The dagger flew like an arrow toward his face. At the last instant he batted it away with his sword as though he were swatting a fly.

"A pathetic attempt. I don't know why I ever considered you dangerous." He took a step forward and raised his sword. "Now I will —"

My dagger, carried in an arc around the cavern by the wind, struck him in the back of the head. The point of its blade projected from his left eye socket.

For an instant he continued to stand and stare at me with his remaining eye, as an expression of incomprehension spread across his face. Then a blinding, flickering stroke of lightning blasted through his ruined eye socket from the point of the dagger. It continued to pour forth as he slowly collapsed, turning while he fell. Where it struck the floor of the cavern, the ground was opened, and from below rose a blast of heat and an angry red glow that was brighter than the glow of the rocks.

I felt someone behind me and whirled to defend myself, then saw that it was Salaymorlaynah.

"The cavern is collapsing!" he shouted directly into my face. Even so, I could not hear him. I had to read the words on his lips.

All around us, shadowy shapes were swirling into twisting columns of smoke and vanishing. It was the other djinn who had gathered to watch the duel, fleeing from the upwelling lava beneath our feet. I knew what a salamander must feel like when it walks in the midst of the fire.

He wrapped the corner of his robe about me and pulled me close. I felt us spinning and lifting into the air, while below us the entire mountain erupted, pouring rocks and smoke and black soot into the sky. We rode the blast upward, staying just above its destruction, until suddenly we were in another place and another time.

He released me and drew his robe off my shoulders. I saw that it was night, and recognized my own courtyard at my house in Damascus. We stood beside the fountain amid the statues of Greek gods and goddesses that the previous owner of the house had seen fit to use for decorations.

"You have saved my wives, and the honour of my house. I owe you a great debt."

These were not idle words. When a djinn speaks of a debt, he means it.

"It was something I had to do," I said truthfully. "Xhalarhinni hated me with a passion that was almost madness. Sooner or later he would have contrived to lure me into combat."

"You speak the truth," he said, nodding. "How did you know he would draw his sword?"

"I didn't know it, but when we met the first time, he boasted of his swordsmanship, and seemed greatly frustrated he would not get a chance to use his blade on me, so I hoped that when he became weary of our elemental combat, and I feigned collapse, he might draw his sword as an easy and satisfying way to finish me."

"It was contrary to the rules of the duel, but I doubt the gathered djinn of the Seventh Circle would have raised any objection."

"Once he drew his sword, I was free to use my knife. I knew he would be able to deflect it, so I sent it curling around him on the wind to strike him from behind."

"Clever, so very clever," he said. "Your reputation is well deserved."

I glanced at my front door.

"Will you come into my house and have wine with me? We can sit and talk."

He looked at the door with an expression almost of longing but at last shook his head.

"Another time, Alhazred. I still have enemies. I will not enter your house until I have dealt with them."

"If you need help, send me another letter," I said with a smile.

He reached out and rested his left hand upon my head. The heat in my bowels gently diminished to nothing.

"I will not hesitate to do so," he said.

With a breath of night breeze, he vanished, leaving me alone beside the absurdly ornamental fountain my predecessor had placed in my courtyard, and I had not yet taken the trouble to have removed. I went to it and leaned down to splash cool water in my face. My left arm still tingled, but I could raise it and move my fingers.

When I entered my house, I found Martala sitting on the stairs, waiting for me. She expressed no surprise at seeing me, but said, "What happened to your dagger?"

"I lost it. You'll have to buy another for me at the market tomorrow. What is the hour?"

"Just after midnight."

"I think I will go to bed. I'm feeling a little tired."

She silently took me by the right arm and helped me up the stairs.

"Don't you even want to know what happened?"

"Tonight you will sleep," she said. "Tomorrow you will tell me everything."

And so it was.

Death Stalks Damascus

1.

There is usually scant traffic in the Lane of Scholars at night, or at least little that makes enough noise to be heard, but tonight the winding street was deserted. The citizens of Damascus who did not live there avoided it after dark as a matter of course due to its unhallowed reputation, but tonight even its residents and their servants were locked behind their colourful gates and high walls, hoping to remain unmolested until morning.

Altrus and I were the exceptions. We walked slowly along the street, trying to peer though the gloom as we listened to the night sounds of the sleeping city – the barking of dogs, the yowl of a cat, the scurry of rats across the paving stones.

The abductions had begun just over two months ago. Every night without fail three or four citizens of Damascus simply disappeared. They were never seen again. The abductors had no respect for wealth or authority. Two servant girls had been taken from the Caliph's palace, right from under the palace guard. The abductions always happened under cover of darkness, but there was no pattern that would enable anyone to predict where they would occur next or who would be taken.

When the third servant vanished from the Lane of Scholars; the necromancers, sorcerers, mages and astrologers who dwell along the street met together and formed a citizens' watch. The watches went in pairs. Tonight was my night to walk the street, and I had chosen Altrus to share the task with me. He was an ex-mercenary in my service who lived under my roof. The work he did for me was informal, but when anyone inquired, I generally referred to him as my bodyguard.

"Did Harkanos tell you about the latest outrage?" he murmured at my side.

"No. Who was taken?"

"It was the boy the Hound uses as his seer."

The bald Egyptian necromancer Chigaru el-Masri, more generally known as the Hound, employed a young boy to communicate with the spirits of the dead. The child did this by scrying into polished rock crystals or silver basins of oil, or sometimes into a pool of ink poured in the palm of his left hand.

"Maybe it was a blessing for the child," I said. "You know that Chigaru uses his seers as bum boys?"

"So I have heard. I pay little attention to gossip."

"An admirable quality. I, on the other hand, delight in gossip. It provides such an illuminating window into the secret practices of others."

"I hope you don't intend to talk about our neighbours. I'll go back to the house and send Martala to walk with you."

Martala, the fifteen-year-old Egyptian girl who ran my household, savoured the gossip of the marketplace as much as I did. She was better placed to hear it, thanks to her constant dealings with slaves, servants and tradesmen, but I made the girl tell me every juicy morsel she acquired. Altrus had often heard us talking together, and was disgusted by it.

"I know you want to climb back into bed with Nealayna –"

"Or course. A man would have to be mad not to want that," he said. It was a point I could not argue.

"– but we must continue to patrol the street until midnight, as you well know."

"We've been making these patrols for three weeks, from dusk to midnight, and then two other men from midnight to dawn, and in that time nothing out of the ordinary has been seen by anyone. The night the boy was stolen from the house of the Hound, no one saw anything."

"Your point?"

"Doesn't it strike you as unnatural that these murderers can roam the streets of Damascus every night, yet never once be seen?"

I shrugged. "The streets are largely unilluminated. Maybe they are skilful at moving unnoticed in the darkness."

We came to the end of the street, where the Lane of Scholars was crossed by another street known as the Camel's Way, and stood at the intersection enjoying the cool night breeze. The moon was only half-full and would set by midnight. It hung low between the houses, and the western side of the street was deep in shadow.

From the corner of my eye I saw the faintest shifting of black against black, and at the same time heard the stealthy pad of a bare foot. I grabbed Altrus by the arm and pulled him away from the shadows.

"Stay in the moonlight where you can see," I told him.

"What's going on?" He had already drawn his sword.

They came at us from the shadows, the velvet blackness of their skin almost invisible save where the moonlight lit its edges with silver. There were four of them. They moved with a sureness of intent that chilled my heart. The moonlight gleamed from the black claws on the ends of their outstretched fingers.

"Ghouls!" Altrus said it like a curse.

I drew my sword in one hand and my dagger in the other. A ghoul rushed in close and I caught the sweep of his claws on the back edge of my dagger. By the time I could thrust at him with my sword, he was on my other side, circling to get behind us.

"Back to the wall," Altrus ordered.

I did not argue, but stepped backward until I felt the chill bricks of the wall against my shoulders. In situations such as this I followed Altrus's instructions and kept my mouth shut. He was many times the swordsman I could ever hope to be, and had survived countless clashes of arms during his days as a sword for hire.

The black skin of a ghoul is like velvet to the touch, but tough. It can resist a slash that would lay open a man to the bone. They used their claws to deflect our blades and did so almost with contempt. This was a game they had played often.

Altrus managed to wound two of them, but one wound was little more than a scratch. The other was more serious, and caused the ghoul he had stuck with his point to double over and hold his side.

There is no doubt they would have beaten down the mercenary's sword and been on us with their claws and fangs in a matter of moments. The long teeth and powerful jaws of a ghoul are terrifying weapons. They are designed to crack open bones for their marrow.

Just before they made their rush, a black shape darted into their midst and began to slash at their exposed backs, emitting as it did so a blood-chilling war howl. The four turned in confusion and found themselves confronted by another ghoul.

When he circled into the moonlight I recognized Uto, the leader of the White Skull Clan, which had its warrens just outside the city walls in a graveyard known as the Place of Skulls. Uto and his warriors often had dealings with the necromancers of the Lane of Scholars, who were always in need of fresh corpses for their studies.

There was a striking contrast between Uto's body and those of the other ghouls. Where he was compact and round, they were lean and thin. They stood taller than any ghouls I had ever encountered, and walked with a more upright gait.

Uto's arrival disheartened them. They loped away from him in complete silence and in an instant were gone from view, shadows hidden beneath shadows.

I caught Altrus by the arm as he raised his sword.

"This one is a friend. He is Uto, leader of the White Skull Clan."

Uto and Altrus eyed each other warily. As the ghoul lowered his claws, the mercenary sheathed his sword.

"You arrived at an opportune moment," I told the ghoul. "We are most grateful you happened upon us."

He laughed in the way of ghouls, with a kind of tight cough at the back of his throat, and spoke in a hissing voice.

"I did not happen upon you. I have been wandering the streets of the city every night for the past month, looking for these *su'tuk* so that I could kill them."

I recognized the word. In the language of the ghouls it means scavenger and vermin, but also coward and corpse-fucker.

"They are not of your clan?" Altrus asked.

Uto coughed with laughter.

"The ghouls of my clan do not hunt within the walls of the city and they do not kill humans for food."

"Ghouls can only eat rotting flesh," I explained. "Fresh meat sickens them."

"Then why would these other ghouls try to kill us?" Altrus asked.

"Perhaps they put the humans they kill out in the sun for a day to blacken before feasting on them," Uto told him.

"There is something not right about them," I said.

He nodded vigorously. "So you noticed it also. They are –" He hesitated and searched for the right word. "They are malformed."

"Too tall," I explained to Altrus. "Too thin through the belly. The bellies of ghouls are rounded. And their legs are too long."

"Their heads are too round as well." Uto made a noise of disgust. "They are so ugly."

I looked at the moon, then peered into the mouths of the dark streets that stretched away from us in three directions.

"It's almost midnight – near enough, at any rate. Uto, return with us to my house so that we can talk about this at greater length."

He nodded. We made our way back along the Lane of Scholars to my green gate, all the while taking care to remain alert for any attempt to attack us from behind. None came, but I had a strong sense we were being watched.

2.

Uto perched his naked buttocks on the edge of one of my chairs and squirmed his body around before settling down. Ghouls did not use chairs. Uto was probably the only ghoul in Damascus who knew how to sit in them.

He had become familiar with many human customs through his dealings with the residents of the Lane of Scholars. When the ghouls of the White Skull Clan had more meat than they could eat, they sold the excess to us for our experiments.

We were gathered in my formal sitting room, which I seldom used. I had lit one lamp and shortened its wick so that it gave forth only the ghost of a light. The rest of the house lay asleep upstairs and I did not wish to wake them. Around the small table that held the lamp we sat leaning forward so that we could whisper without having our voices carry up the stairs. It lent our conversation a conspiratorial tone.

"This clan of deformed ghouls came to Damascus some ten weeks ago," Uto said. "It is customary among ghouls for a migrant clan that seeks to hunt in the land of an established clan to ask permission to settle. This they did not do. We only learned of their presence when we saw them skulking around the edges of the Place of Skulls, spying on us. Naturally we drove them off. There is more than enough meat in our graveyard for my own clan, but not enough meat for two clans."

"When did you realize they were hunting the living on the streets of Damascus?"

"The same time you did. We learned of the disappearances and immediately guessed it was the work of the other clan."

"I've never heard of ghouls hunting men inside the walls of a city," Altrus said.

"It is rare, but it happens. Starvation make us take risks we would otherwise never take, and violate customs that we consider sacred."

"Have you ever talked with the leader of this other clan?" I asked Uto.

He snarled and shook his head. "Twice I tried. His ghouls shun us."

"What do you think is wrong with them?"

He rubbed his hand back and forth across his bald head, staring past me into the shadows.

"They have no honour, no customs. They are like wild animals. I don't even know if they speak the ghoul language."

"Maybe they aren't ghouls," Altrus suggested.

"They are not of an ancient bloodline, that much is certain. No established clan would fall into such degeneracy."

It was a curious word to use for the violation of customs, but somehow it seemed appropriate. For ghouls, manners and customs were everything.

"They don't even look like ghouls," Uto said. "They are too tall and thin."

"Maybe they are thin because they are starving," Altrus suggested.

Uto laughed at him, but not unkindly.

"You fought them. Did they seem to be starving to you?"

The mercenary shook his head.

"We know their numbers are few by how many humans they

take each night for meat. They can survive on two a night although sometimes they take as many as four."

Uto caught my eye, then looked behind me at the open door of the sitting room. I heard her bare foot scuff the floor and smelled the subtle scent of her body. It was not something I usually noticed, but being with other ghouls reawakened my ghoul instincts.

"You may as well join us, Martala," I said without turning my head.

The girl came into the room without ceremony and pulled a wooden chair up to the lamp, turned it backwards, and straddled it like a horse. She wore a blue silk robe that tied with a sash at the waist, but nothing else. It was her custom to sleep naked.

"Who can sleep, with all the noise you three were making," she said.

We had made very little noise, but she was a light sleeper.

"Tell me what happened on the street."

Altrus told her of the attack in a few plain words. He credited Uto with saving our lives, which was no more than the truth.

"So there is a clan of strange ghouls hunting people in the streets," she said. "What are we going to do about it?"

"They must be stopped," I said to the ghoul.

"This we both know," he said. "If the people of the city realize it is ghouls, they will hunt us all down and burn us out of our warrens. They will not make a distinction between clans."

"We need to talk with this new clan," I said. "Maybe we can reason with them and send them elsewhere."

"They have no interest in talk."

"We need to try. Do you know where they have their warren?"

He shook his head. "When we follow them, they elude us in the darkness. But it must be close to the walls of the city. It is not near the Place of Skulls. It may be beyond the western wall."

"Have your ghouls search for it, and come to me when it is located. I will try to talk to this clan."

"What if they won't listen?" Martala asked.

We looked at each other for a moment in silence.

"Then we must kill them all," Uto said.

3.

The nightly patrols continued in the Lane of Scholars, but after the attack no other incident occurred. People still went missing – two, three, sometimes four a night, from different parts of Damascus – but the nameless clan of ghouls had learned to leave our street unmolested. This indicated to me that they were not completely lacking in intelligence. They might act and look like wild animals but they had their own low cunning.

Eight nights after the attack, I was sitting late in my library, reading by lamplight, when a faint movement of air caused me to pause and look up. A black form stirred in the darkness that filled the far corner of the room. It came a step forward, and I recognized the outline of Uto's body.

"Dim the lamp. The light hurts my eyes."

I did as he told me, and he moved closer, as silent as a shadow. As much as I prided myself on my ability to move like a ghoul, I could never quite match that level of skill.

"How did you get into my house?"

"The grill in the floor of the cellar."

"Have you found their warren?"

"No. But we captured one of them."

"Excellent." I stood up. "I want to be there when you question him."

"That is why I came. I will guide you to him. But, Alhazred ..."

He hesitated. I met his black gaze and waited.

"This is a matter for ghouls," he said. "It should be handled by ghouls alone. Your friends are not ghouls."

"I have no friends."

"You know who I mean."

"I agree. It is a matter for ghouls alone."

By good fortune I had laid my sword and dagger across a chair when I sat down to read. There was no need to go upstairs to get them. I hung them on my belt beside Gor's skull and followed Uto through the house and down into a particular room in the cellar. The iron grate that was usually set into a corner of the floor lay open. He climbed into the hole down the iron rungs of a ladder that were fixed in the side of the shaft, and I followed.

There was no light in the tunnel. This was the first time I had passed through it. On occasion the ghouls brought corpses, or parts of corpses, through the tunnel to my house. It was not of my making, but had been there when I bought the house from its previous owner, a necromancer named Hapla who had been forced to leave Damascus by order of the old Caliph, Yazid, who had feared and persecuted the residents of the Lane of Scholars. For all I knew, the tunnel entrance had been there in the cellar already when Hapla acquired the house.

Ghouls have an excellent tactile sense of direction. They cannot see in absolute darkness, but they can feel their way by touch along the intricate systems of passages that make up their warrens. Most ghoul clans use warrens. My own clan, the Black Spring Clan of that great desert known as the Empty Space, had used only individual dens dug out of the sand that were not connected, so I did not have much experience in moving through tunnels without light. I followed the scent and body heat of Uto, staying close behind him.

The burrows of the ghouls that ran beneath the foundations of Damascus were there to give the ghouls access to the city, should the need arise, and to allow them to move about under the streets without being detected. There were many miles of them. I don't know how far I crawled and crouched along them, but my back was aching by the time we came to a wooden ladder and climbed it by touch, still in absolute darkness.

The room we emerged into was black as pitch. I could smell the other ghouls, and something fouler that I had smelled once before – the body odour of the nameless clan.

"Light the lamp," Uto said in the ghoul tongue.

I heard the striking of steel on flint, and by the showers of sparks that fell into the tinderbox I saw two young male ghouls of the White Skull Clan standing on either side of one of the nameless ones, who was bound with his arms above him to a wooden post that supported whatever structure was above us. The glowing tinder was applied to the wick of a crude stone oil lamp on a table, and a dull red glow spread from its feeble flame.

"Where are we?"

"The cellar of an abandoned warehouse. It is boarded up. No one comes here."

Approaching the bound ghoul with caution, I studied him. No necklaces or other jewellery such as ghouls often wear adorned his black skin. He was almost as tall as I am, and that was more than a head above the tallest ghoul of Uto's clan. The tendons and muscles of his lean body sprang into relief each time he strained against his bindings. He glared at me with black eyes and curled back his lips to show his sharp teeth.

"How did you capture him?"

"He was lurking in the Place of Skulls, spying on us. The fool thought he could hide from us. We took him from behind. They have thick skulls – this one should be dead."

The black skin was broken on the upper side of the ghoul's round head, and the surrounding tissue had swollen.

"Has he spoken to you?"

"Not yet. But we have prepared instruments that may help loosen his tongue."

Uto gestured toward the table, on which rested a razor, a long needle, a hammer and a chisel.

"What do you intend?"

"We will begin by breaking his bones. If he does not talk to us, we will flay his skin."

The methods of torture used by ghouls were crude and direct, but they were usually effective.

"Before you begin, let me try to reason with him."

"I don't think he's very reasonable."

Approaching the bound ghoul, I stood facing him and stared into his black eyes. His body flexed, but his legs were tied to the post by the ankles.

"What is your name?" I asked in the ghoul language, which is universal throughout the world.

No response.

"What is the name of your clan?"

Nothing.

"He may not be able to speak," I suggested to Uto in my own language.

"I can speak," he said in a croaking voice.

"You know the language of men?" I said in surprise.

He nodded.

"But not the language of ghouls?"

He shook his head.

"Are you a ghoul?"

He turned his head to one side and spat toward Uto's feet.

"He is not a ghoul," I told Uto.

Uto relayed this information to the young ghouls in their own language. They responded with excited chattering.

"He must be a ghoul," Uto said. "Look at his skin, his teeth, his claws."

"We are not carrion eaters," the bound one told him with contempt. "We hunt the living."

"Do you eat fresh meat?" I asked.

"We eat only fresh meat."

I noticed a wound on the side of his belly that looked as though it had been made by a sword.

"Were you among those who attacked me in the street a week ago?"

He smiled at the memory. "We would have had you, but the other was too quick with his sword, and then this one came." He glared murderously at Uto.

"Yet you learned to stay away from the Lane of Scholars."

"We hunt for meat, not for battle."

I paused in thought for a few moments.

"Can you eat any other meat than human meat?"

He shook his head.

"I asked you once what your name is. Will you tell me now?"

He hesitated, then shook his head.

"There is no reason to be afraid. We will work no magic against your name. My own name is Alhazred."

He considered this, and at last said in a low tone, "Kolak."

"Kolak," I repeated. "A strong name."

"A warrior's name," he said with pride.

"Kolak, you must realize that the ghouls cannot allow your clan to stay in Damascus. In time the residents of the city will turn against them and hunt them down."

"My people care nothing for what these tunnel rats want."

"Even so, your people will be hunted down and killed unless you can reach some accord with Uto's clan."

"What accord could there be between my people and this vermin?"

The younger ghouls did not understand his words, which were spoken in Arabic, but Uto could not restrain his fury. He struck Kolak across the face with the back of his hand. Kolak merely laughed, and spat the blood from his split lip at Uto.

"I don't know what accord can be reached," I admitted. "Maybe if your people took only beggars and orphans from the streets, who would not be missed. In time the householders of the city might come to look upon your people as a blessing rather than a curse."

"They must leave Damascus," Uto told me firmly. "There can be no debate about this."

"Kolak, will you take us to your leader, so that we can talk and try to reach some agreement? Your clan must be made to realize that you cannot go on snatching humans from the streets at random. You will be hunted down, wherever you hide."

"Alhazred speaks the truth about this," Uto told Kolak, who ignored him.

"I will take you to our leader, so that you may talk," he said to me. "But only you, Alhazred. Not these tunnel rats."

Uto started toward Kolak, but I caught his arm and held him.

"Very well, I agree. I will go with you and talk to your leader."

Uto turned to me.

"You can't trust this monster," he said in the ghoul tongue. "To him, you are nothing but meat."

"I know that. But if I can reason with the leader of their clan, maybe I can convince them to leave Damascus without the need for warfare."

"It is too dangerous. I will not allow it."

"Uto, it may save the lives of young ghouls, like these two who stand listening."

He looked at his young warriors with fondness.

"They will kill you."

"No, I don't think so. First their leader will want to talk to me. I can be very persuasive."

He frowned and looked up at Kolak's face. The bound creature could not understand our words, but he was watching us with intense interest.

"This one wants to kill you," he said at last. "I can feel it."

"So can I, but that is not important."

Uto shook his head until his pointed ears flapped against the sides of his bare skull.

"All humans are crazy."

"I'm not human, I'm a ghoul," I reminded him. "I will offer nothing unless it is in the best interest of your clan."

"I know that, Alhazred," he said with a trace of weariness. "I don't want to lose you."

Gripping Uto's arms, I turned to Kolak.

"It is agreed. The ghouls will release you if you guide me to your leader."

"I will take you there, Alhazred," he said, rolling his black lips away from his teeth. "But you may wish I had killed you in the street."

4.

We emerged from the abandoned warehouse onto the dark street, leaving the ghouls behind us in the cellar. Kolak led the way with confidence, moving with the stealth of a true ghoul, and I did my best to imitate him. At times I followed no more than the reflected gleam of starlight in his black eyes as he glanced over his shoulder, or a whiff of his body scent. It was more by instinct than skill that I stayed close behind him.

He could have left me behind, had he wished to do so, but he stayed true to his word, leading me to some unknown place where he would reunite with his own kind. What would happen then, I could not predict. As Uto had pointed out, I was no more than meat to these creatures, who had none of the hospitality or honour of ghouls.

I felt him stop in front of me, and realized we stood before an ancient abandoned Christian church. The outline could be dimly seen against the stars. I often passed it, walking from my house to the marketplace. The priests who once inhabited it were long gone, driven from Damascus by the army of Khalid ibn al-Walid half a century ago.

Kolak led me around the back of the building, which was a thicket of untrimmed dead stalks that had once been a garden. Descending a small flight of stone steps, I felt with my fingertips the outline of a little door, the top of which was rounded to fill an arch in the stone. Kolak pulled it open and pushed me through, then closed it behind him.

We went down more steps into a series of tunnels and low rooms with arched ceilings. I felt bones and skulls in niches in the walls as I brushed my hand across them, and realized it was the burial place of the old church. The air was thick with the musty scent of bone dust, and overlying it the sharper smell of unwashed living bodies.

Ahead I glimpsed a faint yellow glimmer of lamp light on the edge of an entranceway. As we went forward, the light grew stronger, and I realized that I was not following a single creature, but surrounded by four of them. So quiet were their steps, I had not heard their approach.

We came into a long room where the clan lay sleeping on the bare stone floor, or sat on their naked haunches eating raw, bloody meat. They were all young males. I looked around for children or the aged, and for females, but saw none. This meant that I had not been taken to their true lair, unless the females and young were hidden away in some adjoining chamber.

When the creatures saw me, they stood and watched with hungry eyes. Kolak muttered a few words in a language I did not recognize, and they allowed me to pass between their ranks, but they came so close that they almost brushed my shoulders.

"Leave your weapons here," Kolak ordered.

I took my sword and knife from their sheaths and laid them on the stones.

"Where are you taking me?" I asked him.

"To talk to our leader."

I followed another tunnel into a larger chamber that was more brightly illuminated. The roof was composed of a series of Roman arches supported by substantial pillars. Between them glimmered the black surface of a great cistern that was filled to its brim with water. The Christians had kept their secret well. No one in Damascus knew of the existence of this reservoir. I wondered how the deformed ghouls had learned about it.

Bending to one knee at the edge, I cupped my hand and dipped it into the chill liquid, then put it to my lips. It was fresh, with no trace of salt or minerals to the taste.

"Go forward," Kolak ordered.

I saw that a narrow walkway of stones led to the center of the cistern, where there was a round island build of massive stone blocks. Someone sat alone in the center of the island on a kind of white throne. As I drew nearer, I saw that it was a woman, and that the throne was made of bleached bones joined together with pegs of bone driven through holes. It was a crude yet oddly impressive construction.

My attention was held by the countenance of the woman. The throne rested on an elevated platform of stone, so that she sat gazing down at me with an expression of serene indifference, in which was mingled just a trace of disdain. Her long gown, which completely covered her lower body and draped wide across the stone steps, was of cloth of gold. Upon her head she wore a golden crown crafted to resemble bones. Her skin was black with no trace of coloring, her eyes black as jet. The shape of her bald head had some of the qualities of a ghoul's skull, but it was rounder, and her jaw was not as massive as that of a true ghoul.

She motioned me forward with a hand, and I saw that the nails on her fingers were black and hooked to tear flesh. For a time she studied me in silence. Gor's skull seemed to fascinate her. She stared at it, then studied my face, which was overlaid by its usual mask of glamour. She spoke a few words in the strange language of the creatures, and Kolak, who stood behind me, responded at greater length, no doubt relating the events of his capture and release.

"She wants you to speak your name," he told me.

"Alhazred."

She touched her throat with one hand.

"Halakindra."

Something moved beneath the skirts of her robes. I gave no sign of having noticed. Stepping away from Kolak, I addressed her directly.

"Halakindra, I have come to you to help you save the lives of your clan."

She frowned, and Kolak quietly translated my words. What he said made her laugh. It was a surprisingly youthful sound.

"Do you understand the tongue of the Romans?" I asked her in Latin. She stared at me. "Maybe you are familiar with the language of the Greeks," I said in Greek.

At this, she nodded. "The Greek speech is known to me," she said, in a style of Greek that was so ancient I could barely comprehend it.

"I have come to you to say that your clan must leave Damascus. If you do not, both the people of the city and the ghouls who dwell outside its walls will rise up and destroy you."

She stared into the distance above my head, contemplating my words.

"Many have tried to destroy us. We live, they died."

Again, something squirmed beneath the shimmering gold fabric of her gown, and I heard a kind of murmuring.

"This is not like other cities. The Caliph has his palace here. If he begins to hunt your warriors, he will not stop until all of you are dead."

She made a humming noise in her throat.

"The Caliph is only a man. My warriors have walked in the dark halls of his palace."

If true, and the Caliph learned of it, he would double his efforts. Moawiya was not vindictive, but he had the strongest survival sense of any man I knew.

"It is not merely the men of the city who will hunt you. The ghouls of the White Skull Clan will not cease until you have been driven forth or slaughtered."

Her face hardened. She looked older this way. I wondered how old she was.

"It was ever thus. Ghouls hate us for having their skills and weapons, but not their scent, not their look, not their reverence for ancient customs."

"The righteous ever walk in the shadow of the law," I quoted, translating from the ghoul tongue. The saying did not have the same force in Greek.

"Law," she said with disdain. "What use have we for laws? We are our own law. Where we choose to dig our burrows, there we take our meat, and no one can oppose us."

"That may be your usual experience, but it will not be so in Damascus," I assured her.

"So little you know, Alhazred. When last we dwelt in this city, a thousand years ago, we took what we wanted and none dared defy us."

"This time the laws of ghouls and men will oppose you."

"I am the only law," she went on without hearing me. "I am the beginning and the end."

"Yet your numbers are few."

"Soon we will be many. The more meat that is available, the more numerous my children."

"Your women will be slaughtered in their sleep by ghouls. How will your children fare without mothers to protect them?"

She cocked her head to the side like a puzzled dog.

"My what?"

"Your women. The mothers of your warriors. They are vulnerable. Once the ghouls find their nest they will show no mercy."

She grinned at me, showing an array of needle-sharp teeth.

"You know nothing of our ways. I am the mother of all. I will show you. Come close and look upon my children."

Bending forward, she grasped her skirt and gathered it up in her hands, raising it by degrees to reveal her feet, her ankles, her calves.

The power of speech died in my throat. Her legs were covered in blood. Six or seven naked creatures clung to them with their teeth, sucking blood with their throats and writhing their arms and legs. They were of different sizes but all were male. Two of them were as large as youths ready for the hunt. Their bodies were intertwined into a solid, wriggling clump that reminded me of a ball of serpents. As I watched, her hairless vulva opened, and an infant slid forth into the sticky, blood-covered mass of the others. It groped around for several seconds, then smelled the blood and fastened its sharp little teeth into the flesh of her thigh.

She laughed at my reaction and dropped her dress to veil the horror.

"What manner of creature are you?" I did not even try to keep the revulsion from my dry throat.

"My mother was human, my father a ghoul. Ages ago, too many now to count, he raped her and left her to nurture his child. In the fullness of time she brought forth a baby girl. When I was born I was not as you see me now. I appeared human. That is the only reason she did not dash my brains out on a rock, or so she told me shortly before I killed and ate her. As I grew older, I changed. My skin darkened, my teeth lengthened, and my fingernails became claws. All the hair fell from my head. You would never know it, Alhazred, but when I was a child I had beautiful golden hair."

She stopped talking and gazed into the distance, as though listening to some inner voice.

"I have always been told that ghouls and humans cannot breed together," I said quietly.

"So it is universally believed. I am a freak of nature. There has never been one such as I and never will be again. When I reached the age of maturity, instead of bleeding between my thighs like any normal girl, I became pregnant. It was brief, and I brought forth my first son. He did not want my milk but drank my blood, and within weeks he was old enough to fight for me. All of my children are sons, all fine warriors who fight to defend me. My children grow with unnatural quickness, as you have seen."

I turned to Kolak, who watched us from some distance, his face without emotion.

"How old are you?"

"This is my second year."

"How long will you live?"

His jaw muscles flexed. "None of my people ever lived past the sixth year."

"Except for me," Halakindra said. "I seem to be deathless. Age after age I live, I eat, I give birth, over and over again. Where the meat is plentiful, my children are many. Is it not a rare joke the old one has played on me?"

"To which old one do you refer?" I asked.

"To Shub-Niggurath, or course. She fashioned me in her own image, self-engendering and self-begetting."

"Even Shub-Niggurath requires the song of Azathoth," I pointed out.

"It is the seed of my father that re-creates itself in my womb. That is why my children resemble ghouls more than humans."

A tremor ran through her body. She lifted her head and arched her back, pulling her lips away from her teeth.

"You have received your answer, messenger. Now cower away out of my sight before my hunger overcomes my self-restraint."

"You mean to let me go?"

She tittered, a sound that was disturbingly ghoul-like.

"I will not stop you. As for my children, they have their own hunger and may not be as generous. Leave me, cringing human. We will not speak again."

What I would have done had she not voiced her final words, which condemned me to death at the hands of her sons, I can never know.

What I did was run forward and leap upward toward her throne. The pulpy mass of her children beneath my boots sank and moved as I stepped upon them, climbing upward. My attack surprised her. Before she could raise her hooked claws to defend herself, I slid behind her and took her head in both my arms. The golden crown of bones fell off her bald skull. Her long neck was not thick. I heard it snap like a dry twig.

My next leap carried me off her throne to the far side of the little stone island, where I immediately dove into the black water of the cistern.

Close behind me, just before my head entered the water, I heard Kolak's mad howl of fury. It is a peculiarity of ghoul nature that ghouls cannot swim. I have considered the matter, and believe it has to do with the density of their bones. I had no way of knowing that the children of Halakindra shared this limitation with true ghouls, but when my rising head broke the surface, Kolak yet stood on the edge of the island of stone, howling at me in impotent rage.

Still I would have been dead had no tunnels existed on the far side of the cistern. Luck was on my side. I found a passage that led upward to the cellar of an ancient building, and escaped onto the street just as the sun was rising above the rooftops.

5.

Nealayna was delighted to greet me when I returned to my house. Sometime during the night Martala had discovered me gone and roused Altrus from sleep. The two were still out searching for me. When they returned, they found us in the dining room, enjoying a breakfast of boiled eggs and flat bread, with cheese and pastries. I made them sit down beside the Persian and told the cook to bring more food. As I ate, I related the events of the night.

"Can you be certain the monster is dead?" Altrus asked.

"Her neck was broken. Of that I am sure. She may have been immortal, but she was not invulnerable."

Martala nibbled a bit of bread covered in green mint jelly.

"If these creatures live no longer than six years, and there are no more being born, that means we have only to wait for the plague of Damascus to cure itself."

"Six years is a long time," Nealayna pointed out. "Many would die in six years."

"I don't think it will come to that," I told her. "When I see Uto, I will tell him how to find the passages under the old church.

His ghouls will hunt them every night until there are no more of them."

"They will probably flee Damascus," Altrus said. "That would be the wisest course."

"Where would they go?" I asked. "Their living mother goddess is dead. What would give them purpose?"

"Hate," Martala said.

"That is a poor reason to live."

She clutched my arm. Her large gray eyes were serious as they stared into mine.

"You must stay out of the shadows. Don't ever go out at night alone. We must always lock our doors from this day forward, at least for several years."

"You are being too emotional," I told her as I gently removed her fingers from my flesh. I was thankful she had ceased to sharpen her fingernails to points, after the manner of the worshippers of Bast.

"No, I'm not. Think about it, Alhazred. You gave this clan a purpose when you killed their goddess, the only purpose they can possibly still pursue with passion. That purpose is your death."

"The girl has a point," Altrus said as he chewed his boiled egg.

"It was foolish for you to attack Halakindra alone, in the midst of her clan," Martala told me with anger in her voice. "You could have waited to tell Uto where they were."

"Haven't you been listening? They had no intention of ever allowing me to leave their tunnels." I frowned, remembering my emotions just before I broke Halakindra's neck. "Anyway, she made a fatal mistake."

"What was that?" Altrus asked.

"She called me human."

The table fell silent. I looked around at my companions, but their eyes were on their food, not on me.

After breakfast, I went into the cellar and closed the iron grate in the corner of the little room, then moved three heavy barrels on top of it. Martala's words were still with me, and the more I thought about them, the more probable they seemed.

Only one small corner of the grate remained exposed. I was certain no ghoul or half-ghoul could possibly lift it from its place. Even so, I stood for a time, staring down at the darkness below the slots in the grate, wondering if there were eyes below, looking up at me.

I could not resist leaning down to sniff the damp air that rose through the grate from below. There was no trace of the foul animal stench of the clan of half-ghouls.

Laughing at my own foolishness, I left the little room and locked the door. Better to be safe. I thought I heard something through the wooden planks, a faint scratching sound, but when I laid my ear-hole against the door, the sound was gone. The temptation came to me to unlock the door and open it, just to verify that there was nothing beneath the grate, but I firmly squared my shoulders and forced myself to climb up the cellar steps into the sunlit house above.

Six years, I thought to myself. After all, what are six years?

Anisah

1.

"**I** will take your knight," Martala said.

"Such conceit angers the gods," I murmured as I stared down at the chess board.

"Nonetheless, I will take your knight, and there is nothing you can do to stop me."

We lounged on cushions in the formal sitting room with the chess board on the floor tiles between us. The air was cooler near the floor. I had acquired a taste for the game while a youth in the royal court of King Huban at Sana'a, before my rude expulsion from his service, and having no one to play with in my household, some months ago I had taught the girl.

She proved such an apt pupil, that at present she was besting me two games in three. Her style of play was aggressive and unpredictable, much like her own personality. My own style was more methodical and tended to be defensive.

"Does Nealayna play this game?" I asked.

"She does."

"Maybe I should play her instead of you."

"She's much better than I am. You wouldn't stand a chance against her."

"You've played her?"

"I've tried to play her. The games were over so quickly, I wasn't sure what happened."

"They must teach their women chess in Persia."

"She told me the game is very popular."

"It's originated in India, you know. The game, I mean."

"Alhazred," she said in a tone of exasperation.

"I'm trying to teach you something, girl. You could at least have the patience to listen to me."

"The sand runs through the hourglass."

"Indeed it does, for all of us."

"The budding flower blooms, then wilts."

"So I have observed."

"When are you going to move?" she demanded.

"Where did Altrus and Nealayna go in such a rush?"

"She took him to try on clothing that arrived from the east by caravan the other day."

"If he's not careful, she'll have the monthly wage I pay him spent in the first week."

"He's the best bodyguard in Damascus. You should pay him twice as much as you do."

"I know. Never say that to Altrus."

"Have you decided on your move?"

"When I decide, you will be the first to know."

The bell on the front gate jangled. A minute later, my manservant Borka entered the sitting room and stood over me.

"What is it, Borka?"

"A note from Harkanos."

I took it and saw with surprise that it had been hastily scribbled in pen on a torn scrap of papyrus. The note read: "I need your help. Come at once." It was not even signed.

I jumped to my feet, overturning the chess board in my haste.

"That's an old trick," Martala said in disgust.

"Harkanos needs me. I must go at once."

Her expression changed from annoyance to concern.

"I'll come with you."

"No, wait here until I find out what the trouble is. If I need you, I'll summon you."

I touched the ghoul's skull on my belt to reassure myself it was still there. It was an habitual gesture. Gor's bleached skull seldom left me. It was the custom among ghouls to wear the skull of their best friend as a token of admiration. Humans did not understand it, and I had ceased trying to explain it to them. I had been born a man, but my ordeal in the Empty Space and the period I lived as a member of the Black Spring Clan of desert ghouls had made me more ghoul than human.

My sword and dagger were where I had left them, on a table in the entrance hall. I attached them to my belt with haste and left the house. The distance was not great. Harkanos lived next door to me in the Lane of Scholars. His brown gate was open when I reached it. A servant shut it behind me and ushered me into the library.

Harkanos sat before his desk, intently studying a yellowed scroll. He was twenty years my senior, but no strand of grey sullied the chestnut brown of his hair, which he wore cut short to expose the tops of his ears. He also went about with a clean-shaven chin, as I do, in defiance of the prevailing fashion.

He glanced up at me, and I saw relief in his eyes. This worried me. Of all the magicians and necromancers who lived in the Lane, Harkanos was the most dignified and self-contained. He was also reputed to be the most potent in the arts of magic. When there was trouble, the residents of the Lane looked to him for guidance. Yet here he was, seeking reassurance from me.

"My daughter has been abducted," he said without preamble.

I looked around the library and realized that the golden-haired little girl who usually sat naked on the floor near where he worked, playing with her ball, was nowhere to be seen.

"When was she taken?"

"This morning. They must have come into the back garden over the rear wall. When she didn't come into the house at her usual time, I went into the garden and searched for her. Then I searched the house. She is not here."

"If she is being held for ransom, those who took her will contact you with their price."

He nodded, but his worried expression did not change.

"I fear they don't want money."

"If not money, then what?"

"I fear they want the girl herself."

This was a sickening thought. I thrust the images that arose in my mind away before they showed on the mask of glamour I wore to conceal my disfigured face. I should have known I could hide nothing from Harkanos.

"It would almost be a relief, if it were as you think," he said grimly. "At least it would be natural, although perverted and base. But it is my belief that they want the child for other reasons that are more complex, and in some ways more sinister."

"If you want my help, you must tell me what you know."

"Of course, Alhazred, of course." He face took on a haggard cast, and for the first time since I have known him, he looked old. He waved me toward a chair. "Sit down."

I sat facing him across his desk.

"Six years ago, I went to the northern isle of Albion, which the Romans called Britannia, to search for a magical stone. It was my custom then to travel the world to acquire magical objects that would enhance my power. While there, I became acquainted with the race of spiritual beings that inhabits the island. They are like our own djinn, but less malicious. The people who live in Albion call them the Shee. They dwell in caverns beneath enchanted hills. One of their queens, a very beautiful Shee with golden hair, became infatuated with me. She claimed to know the location of the magic stone I sought, so I encouraged her interest in the hope that she would tell me where the stone lay hidden."

He cleared his throat and lowered his eyes.

"It is not easy to speak of these things. I behaved with dishonour and deceit. Eventually she realized my true interest, and her heart turned cold to me. She went away, but many months later she returned and handed me a bundle of cloth in the midst of which lay my infant daughter. She said she had no use for the child, but that her name was Anisah and that I might do as I wished with her. I brought the child home with me to Damascus, and raised her in this house as my own. This is the first time I have spoken to anyone about her true nature, which is sure to offend or even terrify the good citizens of this city."

"It is not so unusual a union as you may believe," I said.

In a few words, I told him of my recent meeting with my true father, a djinn of the Ninth Circle. He did not seem surprised.

"I knew there was something more than human in you. I sensed it the first day we met."

"If your daughter is Shee, then she must be more spirit than flesh."

"The Shee themselves are flesh, of a sort. They are eternal and do not grow old. They are all of unearthly beauty – slender of body, graceful, cunning in speech."

"Yet your daughter hardly speaks," I said.

"I know," he said with a frown. "That is something that worries me. Unless I am gravely mistaken, the first thing her abductors will wish to learn from her is her name."

"Now that I think on it, you almost never call her by name."

"There is a reason for it. Her name is bound up with her very substance, and is charged with a great potency. Those who speak her name in invocation gain access to that force and can then use it to empower their magic."

"Do you think that is why they took her? For her to act as a kind of magical reservoir to draw upon in their works?"

"I fear it may be so, but I do not yet know who took her."

"I can go to the Caliph, and ask him to use his palace guard to search Damascus by day. At night, the ghouls of the White Skull Clan will search."

"That is a generous offer, but that is not why I called you here."

"Why, then?"

"I need the assistance of one I can trust. I intend to scry for the girl. You will have to guide me. When I scry, I must rely on pure intuition and my faculty of reason becomes inert. I want you to ask questions that relate to the visions I see, and write down my responses.

"Of course I will do so, but wouldn't a professional seer, such as Chigaru el-Masri, be more effective?"

He made a noise of disgust in his throat.

"I don't wish to involve the Hound. I've never trusted that Egyptian juggler. The less he knows about my daughter, the better for all of us."

He picked up a globe of polished rock crystal that rested on some of the papers on his desk. It was about the size of an orange and flattened on both sides. Until then I had assumed it was merely a paperweight. Realization struck my mind.

"That is the magic stone you went to Albion to find."

Nodding, he held it in a beam of sunlight from one of his window screens and turned it over between his long fingers. It was cloudy in the center.

"This stone was used by a great mage of Albion who lived a century ago. His name was Myrddin, or as the Romans would have styled it, Merlinus. With it he was able to foretell the future. I confess, it has not been reliable in its working for me, but then, I make no claim to be a seer. However, because of its connection with me, the girl, and the girl's mother, I believe it may yield results in the matter of her abduction."

"I could summon Martala. While she lived in Bubastis, she made some of her living by scrying into ink."

"Yes, but she was younger then," he said with a shake of his head. "She has become a woman. The power leaves most child seers when they become adults."

He gripped the stone tightly in his fist, and I saw his fingers go white. He was fighting to control his emotions.

"I will scry for my daughter. I cannot explain it, but I have a sense that it will speak to me today."

"By all means, let us try the stone."

2.

He closed all the screens on his windows to darken the room and lit a table lamp, which he placed in the center of his desk. First he spoke an invocation to Yog-Sothoth, in which he humbly asked the Old One for passage through his gates. Then he sat with his elbows on the top of the desk and peered at the flame of the lamp through the flattened crystal globe, rotating it slowly as he did so.

I had found a sheet of parchment and his pen set while he was closing the screens. The ink was already mixed in the ink well. I sat on the opposite side of the desk with quill poised over parchment.

For many minutes he said nothing. Then his eyes lost their focus and his face became slack. He ceased to rotate the crystal, but merely stared into, or rather, through its depths. When he began to speak, I jotted down what he said.

"The sun ... at my back ... the road is rocky and poor ... mountains on the horizon ... I fly above the road ... now I walk."

"What do you hear?" I asked.

"Only the wind ... no, there is something more ... water flowing ... to the left of the road is a small spring and a mill ... the water turns its wheel ... I fly again, and the ground rushes beneath me ... before me on a hilltop there is a keep ... walls of stone ... corner towers for defense."

I had a sudden inspiration.

"Call to your daughter."

"Little one, can you hear me?" he murmured.

"Call her by name. Draw upon the power of her name."

"Anisah. Anisah, my child."

He groaned and leaned forward as though struck in the stomach.

"Forward I fly through the stones of the keep ... I see her ... tied by the neck to an iron ring in the wall of a cell in the foundations of that wretched place ... darkness ... rats ... she is weeping ... wrapped only in a dirty blanket ... three men approach her."

"What do they look like?"

"They have their backs to me, but they wear long black robes with their hoods up, like Christian monks. The robe of one man is trimmed with red. Wait, he turns as though sensing my presence ... he stares at me but cannot see me ... he is old and terrible of aspect, his face gaunt, his great nose thrusting from his cheeks, his eyebrows covered with bristling gray hair ... his eyes are an intense black ... cold and hard, like the eyes of a serpent. Wait, now he speaks ... his lips move but I cannot hear what he says ... he says it again, staring at me. Now his two companions rush forward and grasp the arms of my little child ... he draws forth a dagger and holds it to her throat, and speaks again."

"What does he say?"

"He says, 'Leave us, or I will cut her throat.' He pulls her head back with his other hand to expose her throat. She is screaming with terror ... she calls out to me again and again."

Quickly, I reached forward and knocked the crystal out of his hands. It clattered over the desk and rolled across the rug on the floor. Harkanos fell back in his chair with a cry, as though having a seizure, then went limp.

I pulled his head back and slapped him gently on the cheek. The pulse in his neck was rapid but weak. While I was wondering whether to have his servants call a physician, he roused himself and opened his eyes, then blinked up at me. It was a few moments before he knew who I was. Then he remembered the scrying and clutched my arm.

"They have my daughter in that keep in the mountains."

"I had to force you out of your trance. They would have killed the girl."

"I understand. You did well. I could not have broken contact with her by myself. The attraction was too powerful."

Picking up the crystal, I examined it. There was no damage, but it was unnaturally hot. Rock crystal is usually cold to the touch. That is what led the ancients to believe it was petrified ice. This was almost hot enough to be painful. I handled it like a piece of roasted meat pulled straight from the cooking spit until it began to cool. Then I passed it to Harkanos.

He set it on his desk and stared at it moodily.

"Do you know these black monks?"

"I have had dealings with their order, but not for many years. They are what the Christians call a Gnostic sect, and degenerates of the worst kind. There is no crime they will not commit with enthusiasm. They believe that liberation from the bonds of the flesh is to be had through intense physical sensation."

"A strange belief, but not in itself criminal."

"They use their knowledge of the black arts to extort money from wealthy merchants and men of high position. Those who do not pay what they demand die mysterious and horrible deaths. I see why they want Anisah. They mean to use her to enhance the efficacy of their deadly spells."

"What were your dealings with them?"

"The abbot of a monastery of black monks wanted me to teach him some of my magic, so that he could protect himself from his own ambitious brethren, or so he told me. When I learned how he really intended to use the knowledge, I refused. He sent an entity to kill me. I caused it to rebound upon him. It killed them all, and the monastery itself was reduced to a heap of broken and blasted stones."

"All this happened before you got Anisah?"

"Yes, years before." He tilted his head in thought. "It took place ten years ago, before I came to live in Damascus."

"Why would they trouble you now, after the passage of a decade?"

He shook his head. "That I don't know, unless they somehow learned about Anisah's origin and how she might be exploited."

"Did you tell anyone in Damascus about the girl's mother?"

"No, of course not. Why would I?"

"Even so, somebody discovered the girl's secret and passed the information on to the black monks."

"So it appears," he said, nodding. "If the monks were merely seeking revenge upon me, they would have killed the girl and left her corpse for me to find. To abduct her and carry her so far away, they must have known about her special nature."

"That raises another question – how could her abductors have carried her to the mountains in so short a span of hours?"

His clear, grey eyes widened.

"That's right, they could never have done so, unless they had wings." He looked at the crystal. "It may be this stone opened a window upon the future, and showed me what is yet to occur."

"That is my way of thinking. If so, we may be able to surprise these black monks and take back the girl."

"Your words give me hope," Harkanos said. "But I confess, I do not understand what you intend."

I picked up the crystal. It had cooled, and now felt like any other rock crystal globe.

"Lend Merlinus's stone to me for a few hours."

"Take it. I have no further use for it at this time."

3.

Martala was waiting for me in the sitting room when I returned to my house.

"I have set up the chess board exactly as it was before you knocked it over. What did Harkanos want with you? Or was that just a ruse to escape from losing another game to me?"

Before she could begin to ask her questions, I laid a finger against her lips.

"Has Altrus returned from shopping?"

"They got home just a minute ago. They're upstairs."

I listened, and heard their footsteps and laughter.

"Tell him to come into the library." I caught her arm as she turned to go. "And tell him to wear his sword."

This sobered her playful mood.

"Am I to come with him?"

"What could I do without you?"

She smiled with a quirk of her lips and went up the stairs while I entered the library and laid the stone on my reading table, and beside it the parchment on which I had written down the visions Harkanos had glimpsed in it. Seating myself, I picked up the crystal globe between the fingers of both hands.

Altrus and the girl entered without speaking and stood on the other side of the table, watching me.

"Shut the door."

The girl did as told and returned without comment.

"I don't know if this will work or not," I admitted. "The daughter of Harkanos was taken from his garden this morning and carried outside the city. I have reason to believe she is being carried north into the mountains. Harkanos scried into this crystal and was able to derive some information from it."

Turning the parchment around, I pushed it forward so they could read it.

"Why was the girl taken?" Altrus asked.

"She is a special child. Her mother was a kind of djinn. Her name is a name of power. There may also be an element of revenge involved."

In a few words I told them about the black monks, the

entity they sent to kill Harkanos, and the way he had caused the malevolent spell to rebound on its source.

"The monks will try to learn the child's name. If she speaks it to them, they will use it to draw upon her innate potency and use it against us, or Harkanos, or anyone they consider their enemy."

"That poor little girl," Martala said. "She must be terrified."

"I might have guessed there was something not right about the girl," Altrus said. "Never wearing any clothing, singing to herself, talking when there was no one close enough to hear."

"I always assumed she was simple-minded," I admitted.

"What are we doing here? Are you going to scry for her in the crystal?"

"Not exactly."

Holding the crystal up so that it caught the light from a window, I turned it slowly and stared through its depths into infinite distance, at the same time letting my mind empty. Then I sent my focused will through the heart of the crystal, like an arrow through a window.

"Salaymorlaynah, hear me," I said silently in my mind. "Your son needs to speak to you."

There was a shift in reality that I felt in my bones. I found myself standing in darkness and emptiness. In all directions, even the floor, the black was shot with thousands of bright stars. It was like having the night sky both above and below me at the same time and made me dizzy. I stumbled and had to catch myself before I fell to my knees.

A short distance away stood my father, Salaymorlaynah, a djinn of the Ninth Circle. He was dressed in the white robe of a Roman senator, of a kind that had not been worn for centuries. Like me, his hair was cut short and his chin clean-shaven.

He held the crystal and was examining it with a smile of amusement.

"A pretty toy," he said, tossing it back to me.

"Where are we?"

"Inside the crystal, of course. What was so important that you felt the need to summon me in this uncouth manner?"

I told him about the abduction of Harkanos's daughter, and his attempt to scry her location in the crystal. My words interested him.

"So they have taken one of the Shee. That is something they may come to regret."

"I need you to spirit the girl away and carry her back to her house and father."

"No, that I cannot do."

"Cannot, or will not?"

"Will not. I will not interfere in the working of human destiny in such an overt and obvious manner."

"I thought djinn were free to kill humans whenever they wished."

"That may be true for some, but it is against my moral code to interfere with your race in ways that affect their term of days."

The djinn had their own set of laws. As strange as some of them seemed, they would not break them. I thought quickly.

"Then do something less intrusive. Carry my companions and I to this mountain keep to what Harkanos saw in the crystal, so that we can rescue the girl when the monks arrive with her."

"Harkanos is nothing to me. Why should I do this?"

The tone of indifference in his words angered me, but I struggled not to show it. That he had not immediately rejected my request gave me encouragement.

"Because I am your son, and of your blood."

"That is true beyond dispute, Alhazred, but you ask me to involve myself in human affairs. That is something a djinn of my circle is loath to do."

"You weren't loath to involve yourself when you raped my mother."

He frowned.

"It was not rape, of that I assure you. Your mother was both eager and willing to lie beneath me."

"If you won't do this for your son, then do it in repayment of the debt of honour you owe me. When I fought the duel with Xhalarhinni, you told me you were in my debt."

His face was expressionless as he looked at me, but in his jade-green eyes I saw what I took to be a glimmer of admiration.

"It is true, I owe you a debt. You have the right to ask that it be repaid. But know this, my son, this is the only debt I owe to you. I will not involve myself in the affairs of men again."

Abruptly, I was back in my library, seated at my desk. The crystal fell from my fingers to the desktop with a clatter. I stared at Martala.

"How much time has passed?"

"What?" She glanced at Altrus. "No time has passed."

The air stirred in the corner of the room. Altrus whirled on his heel and drew his sword. There stood my father, in all his mock senatorial splendour. He moved his hand, and the point of Altrus's sword was forced against his will to the floor.

"Put away your sword, mercenary," Salaymorlaynah said in a bored voice.

"What manner of unnatural creature are you?" Altrus demanded.

"This is my father." I said.

Standing from my chair, I came forward and made a formal introduction between them.

"I always thought your father was a goat-herder," Martala said, staring at the djinn with wondering eyes.

"So did I, until recently."

Altrus looked back and forth from my face to my father's.

"You are just like the little girl," he said, an astute observation.

"Not quite. My mother was flesh and blood, and my name holds no power."

I told them what Salaymorlaynah was here to do. When neither of them expressed an objection, I went to stand between them.

"Cling to each other tightly lest you be separated," the djinn said.

I clasped both of them with my arms and felt their arms around my back.

"Do not be alarmed. I have traveled this way before. There is a great whirling of the air and a rushing wind –"

I stopped talking and looked around. We were standing in front of the ruin of an ancient fortification built to guard a mountain road that appeared to have fallen into disuse. The road was overgrown and the roof of the keep had collapsed. We separated awkwardly.

"Is this where the child is being held?" Altrus asked.

"This is where she will be held, if my father has carried us to the right place."

"How long until she gets here?"

"Without knowing where we are, it is impossible to say, but I would estimate that we are at least three days removed from Damascus, at a normal riding pace."

"How can you guess that?" the girl asked.

"The appearance of the hills around us."

"We have no provisions for a long journey, and no horses," the mercenary pointed out.

"We'll climb that dune when we reach it."

With caution we went through the gaping, empty gateway to investigate the keep. The doors had either been torn off or rotted off many years ago. It was not a particularly large fortification. The floors of the upper levels had fallen in, resulting in stone staircases that led up only to empty space. We found an opening in the floor on a flight of stone steps that went down into cellar.

The air below was dank and thick with the cloying odors of mud, mould, and rat droppings. One room had been turned into a kind of barracks. Sleeping mats and blankets were spread on the dirt floor. I counted fourteen of them.

"Fourteen armed men, at the least," Altrus said beside me. "Those are not good odds."

"We have the element of surprise," I reminded him.

"Only for the first instant."

"Then we must make that instant count," Martala said.

In a small alcove in the cellar wall the monks had placed a store of water, lard, bread, cheese, dried goat meat, and wine. The rats had only managed to spoil a small portion of it.

"We won't starve while we're waiting," the girl said around the piece of cheese she had broken from the block.

"This can't be where the monk's live," Altrus observed.

"Obviously," I agreed.

"Then why are they bringing the girl here?"

"They probably believe it to be a secure place of concealment. They must fear the power of Harkanos, if he destroyed one of their monasteries."

We made a meal from the monks' larder, and while we ate, we began to plan how we would free the child from her captors.

4.

"Do you think your father would really let you die rather than help you?"

The girl's question had been on my mind over the past three days while we had waited inside the keep for the arrival of the monks.

"He told me he would not help me again. Djinn are nothing if not true to their word."

"Those are the words of a cold heart. He did not look cold to me."

"He's a djinn. He can look whatever way he wants to look."

Altrus climbed down from atop the broken wall where he had been sitting.

"Riders approach along the road."

I peered through a crack in one of the walls. They were still some distance away from the keep. Silently, I counted them, and whatever optimism I had been trying to nourish in my breast died. There were nineteen men in black robes, most mounted on Arabian horses. One drove a small enclosed wagon pulled by two draft horses. I was amazed they had managed to get the wagon along the road in one piece, it was so rough a track. The girl must be inside it, because she was nowhere else. Two monks walked on each side of the wagon. They were armed with swords that hung at their waists and wore bows slung over their shoulders.

"I thought Christians were men of peace," Altrus said.

"These are heretical Christians. Whatever they believe, it is condemned by the bishops of Byzantium.

"They look more like a band of outlaws than an order of monks," Martala said, and neither of us could disagree with her.

We had made good use of our two days by placing a spell upon a corner of one of the cellar chambers where a portion of the floor above had caved in, and hung down at an angle. The dust on the cellar floor indicated that the monks did not walk there, probably fearing the rest of the roof might collapse on their heads. The spell was not difficult, but it was subtle. It caused anything within the corner to vanish from sight and merge with the shadows that lay behind the slanting beam of sunlight shining through the rent above.

I was fairly confident that when we stood in that place, none of the monks would see or hear us. Nervousness remained in the pit of my stomach, because I had never actually worked this spell before. The girl and I had discovered it in one of my books and had practiced it together at my house, in a mock sort of way. Now we would learn whether we had truly comprehended its making.

Altrus has spent his time rigging a series of deadfalls in the ruin of the keep. When triggered, they would rain blocks of stone and wooden beams on the heads of those below. He had disguised them with utmost cunning, but they were a risk. Should one of them be spotted by a monk, our presence at the keep would surely be suspected.

I was worried about the food and drink we had taken from the monks' rat-nibbled larder, so much so that I had taken the trouble to add water to return the wine in its vessel to its former level. I could not replace the flatbread and dried meat we had consumed, but its absence was not obvious at a glance, and if noticed would probably be blamed on rats.

When the column of riders drew near enough that we could hear the footfalls of their horses and the creak of the wagon's axle, the three of us withdrew to the ensorcelled corner to wait and watch for an opportunity to rescue the child. It was my hope that we could manage it while most of the monks were either absent from the keep, or asleep. I would have drugged the wine had I possessed a drug that was tasteless, but anything I could compound from the herbs growing around the keep would have been detected.

The horses were tied up outside, and the monks descended to the cellar to get water for them. There was a well in the middle of the cellar that held good water. Some of the monks carried it out in wooden buckets. They did not talk much among themselves, but merely grunted or muttered a few words. As they passed our corner, unaware of our presence, I saw that their faces were not the faces of scholars or youths. They were hard-visaged and grim.

The little girl was carried down the stone stairs into the cellar bound and hooded. Her body dangled limp, and at first sight I assumed she was dead. But they set her on her feet and slapped her head until she found the strength to stand upright without her knees buckling. One of them pulled off her hood. She gasped for air, her face slick with sweat and her golden hair plastered flat on her cheeks. She had been crying. Tracks of dirt ran down from her eyes and from under her nose.

She was pulled into another room, where we could not see her. As she passed our corner, she glanced at me, and I felt a thrill of alarm along my nerves. She seemed to see me clearly, although she gave no sign of it to her captors.

Martala shook her head. There was pain in her eyes as she

caught my glance. Altrus did not react, but his jaw was set tight and hard.

I will not detail the hours we sat in the corner and waited for a chance to grab the girl and flee with her. It was in my mind to try to take three of the horses, and frighten the rest into scattering over the hillside. I could ride bareback well enough not to fall off the horse. Altrus and the girl were expert at it. Altrus was the best person to hold the child due to his horsemanship, I reasoned; then I changed my mind and decided that we needed his sword arm free. I would take the child on my horse, assuming we were able to get horses.

All these things ran through my mind for hours. We did not dare to sleep. The monks came and went, passing back and forth in front of our hidden corner. I wondered how long the spell would last? It was not likely it was eternal. Most spells had a duration of effectiveness, after which they failed, either slowly over time, or all at once. My own spell of glamour that I use to hide my mutilated face had dropped away like a fallen mask, and I had not bothered renewing it. Both the mercenary and the girl were well-accustomed to seeing my true features. It occurred to me that the horrifying effect of seeing me for the first time might give me some advantage in a battle with the monks, if only the advantage of a moment.

The monks ate and later retired to sleep, but throughout the night armed guards walked the length of the cellar or stood in front of the room where they had put the child. I heard her whimper from time to time. The temperature drops quickly in the mountains after sunset, and all of us were cold and shivering before morning.

When the monks were roused to their prayers and their morning meal by a bell, the corner in which we cowered began to look more like a trap than a clever plan. We were tired, cold, and hungry. Water was one problem we did not face. I had possessed the forethought to draw a bucket of water from the well and place it in the corner with us.

When all but two of the chanting monks were in the large chamber where they slept, fulfilling whatever hellish morning prayers they offered to their serpent gods, Altrus leaned close to me and put his lips against my ear-hole.

"We can't wait forever."

"We must wait," I whispered back. "There are too many of them. They would cut us down before we could carry the child up the stairs. She is probably bound to the wall or floor."

"We are not going to get stronger," he whispered.

He didn't need to say more than this. I took his point. The longer we crouched in the corner, without food or sleep, the weaker we would become. However, I did not think this would be a problem. I firmly believed that the spell that concealed us could not last more than another day, at most.

One of the monks wore a robe that was trimmed in red, with some kind of red emblem sewn onto its breast. He was older than the others and had a face like chipped flint. The way the other monks bowed to him and backed away with their heads lowered left no doubt about his leadership. When the sun had climbed high enough to send down beams through the rents in the floor above our heads, he entered the chamber where the girl had been placed, with two younger monks following him.

I wondered when the child had last been given food and water. This was an ordeal that could unhinge the reason of a mature woman. Was the child sane to begin with? Even in her happy condition in her father's house she had not behaved like a normal six year old. I estimated her age at six, although she might have been a year older or younger.

The harsh voice of the leader of the monks came to us through the open doorway of the child's prison, but because of the angle, we could see nothing of what transpired within the room. He began quietly enough.

"What is your name, child?"

Silence.

"If you speak your name we will bring you water. What is your name?"

I heard a faint voice. "I want my papa."

"He is here, child. He wants to see you, but first he wants you to tell us your true name."

"Papa is here?"

"He is right outside the door. Speak your name."

"Forbidden," she said, and some other words I could not distinguish.

"Nonsense. Your papa wants you to tell us your name."

"Papa! Papa!"

The sound of slaps came to us clearly from the room. The child began to shriek.

"Tell me your name, you little slut," the leader of the monks roared. It was a practiced voice pitched to frighten grown men and enforce immediate obedience. The child said nothing.

"Who watches?" the grey-faced monk demanded. "Who is there?" There was a pause. "Leave us, or I will cut her throat."

These were the words Harkanos had heard while scrying into the stone.

"He has withdrawn," the voice said with satisfaction.

For the next hour we listened while they tortured the little girl. Martala touched my arm while it was going on and nodded her head toward the doorway. Her grey eyes were grim. I looked at Altrus and was surprised to see him nod his head in affirmation. Silently I shook my head and held up my hands.

Both of them were maddened by the sounds of torture and the child's screams, and ready to charge out and fight regardless of the consequences. I felt much the same fury, but I knew that the monks would not torture the child to death. They needed her for their magic. As much as she was suffering at their hands, she would live.

What astonished me was her strength of will. Her father must have told her never to speak her name to strangers, and she kept that promise no matter what the monks did to her.

In the afternoon a party of five younger monks with bows slung over their shoulders went outside the keep. We heard them take horses and ride away. I assumed they were a hunting party, gone to look for fresh meat. There were deer in the mountains.

The number of monks inside the keep was now fourteen – the same number Harkanos had scried in the crystal.

5.

We had to wait until dark, or the monks with bows would have cut us down from the walls of the keep as we tried to escape across the open land around it. This necessity I tried to convey to my companions, but neither was in a mood to listen. They both wanted to attack at once. Somehow I held them in check.

Darkness fell, and the hunting party did not return. This was good news, for it reduced their number. I had a plan of sorts, and when the keep was quiet, I explained it to Altrus.

"I will leave the corner and try to get a bow and a quiver of arrows for Martala. She will then keep watch over the entrance to the child's prison while you and I take the child out. Then the three of us will run for the stairs and make for the horses. Take the first three you see and cut the others loose. If we're lucky, and can get out of this ruin without disturbing the monks, we may even have time to saddle them. If not, we ride bareback."

They made no argument. Both merely wanted to act. They knew I could move in darkness like a ghoul, without making a sound, and both I and Altrus trusted the archery skills of the girl, which were extraordinary for one of her age and sex.

The keep was not well illuminated. A single oil lamp burned in the long room where the monks slept. Some small light filtered out the door to illuminate the space before us. I could distinguish the vague outlines of doorways. Every so often a single guard walked over and stood for a few moments, listening at the doorway of the child's prison. He was probably listening for her breathing.

When the way was clear, I emerged from the corner and moved around the room close to the wall, making for a doorway opposite to that of the long room where the monks slept. I was pleased to note that my ghoulish skills had not left me. While I was near the wall, one of the monks walked past, but he did not see or hear me, even though I could have reached out and tapped him on the shoulder.

I was disappointed to discover that the weapons of the monks were not stored in the darker half of the cellar. Against my will, I was forced to enter the long chamber, after waiting for the pacing sentry to vacate it. The weapons were stacked midway in the chamber. Wasting no time, I picked my way over the snoring monks and took up the first bow and quiver of arrows that came to hand.

When I glanced down, I found myself looking at the sleeping leader of the monks, whose face was no more gentle in slumber than in wakefulness. For just an instant I contemplated trying to cut his throat without arousing the others, but I knew that any strange noise would wake them. I dared not take the risk, for the child's sake. On the balls of my feet I returned to the dark corner in which Altrus and Martala hid.

Altrus stepped out of the spell into my sight, his sword already drawn, and a ghostly slender hand and arm reached out from the nothingness to receive the bow and quiver I carried, then withdrew again into the void.

The mercenary moved as quietly as he could toward the child's prison. I cringed beside him at the racket he made, and thanked the Old Ones that the monks did not keep a dog.

As I anticipated, the poor girl was tied to a ring of iron set in the stones of the wall behind her. The monks had left her enough slack in the rope to lie down on the bare floor. She was naked, and I saw her shiver in her sleep.

Altrus used his sword to cut her free near her neck, as I reached down to pick her up. She chose that moment to open her eyes.

The light in the cell was so dim, she could see no more than vague shadows.

"I am Alhazred," I whispered into her ear. "I have come to take you home to your father."

"Papa," she said before I could cover her mouth with my hand.

We froze in place, but no alarm was raised. If any monk heard the child, he must have assumed she was talking in her sleep.

I carried her out of the cell and into the open area that held our bespelled corner. The stairs that led up and out of the cellar were just across the floor, but they were near the entrance to the barracks of the monks, where the light from the single lamp was stronger.

No blame should be fixed on the child for shrieking in terror. I have heard grown men cry out upon seeing my true face. I cursed myself for not renewing my mask of glamour before carrying her into the light, but of course it was too late.

Voices sounded from the barracks. A bow string twanged, and I saw an arrow magically appear through the neck of the sentry monk, who had been trying to creep upon us from behind.

I looked at the shadowed corner. "Get up the stairs," I told Martala.

She materialized in the air as she passed through the spell and ran for the stairs. Altrus was already engaged with the monks, who had not been too befuddled by sleep to snatch up their swords and daggers. He held them in the doorway to the long chamber as I ran past him and up the stairs. Above me, Martala's bow sang again and again as she sent feathered shafts past Altrus into the barracks. At least two struck home, to judge by the bellows of pain.

Once out of the cellar, I ran to the place where Altrus had set up one of the deadfalls and stopped with my hand on the trigger.

"Altrus, come out of there. Cover him, girl."

He did not need to be told twice. As good a swordsman as he was, the monks were overwhelming him with sheer fanaticism. He jumped up out of the stairwell, and a dozen monks poured up after him, driving him and the girl back toward me. Some of the monks had bows, and other arrows began to fly through the darkness that did not come from Martala.

I waited as long as I dared to trigger the deadfall. Under the starlight I had the satisfaction of watching a cascade of broken stone fall upon the densest cluster of monks. Several went down under it and did not stir.

"The horses!" I yelled.

The three of us found where the horses were tethered. There was no time to saddle them. Martala grabbed three sets of reins, and Altrus cut the other beasts loose.

As the arrows hissed around us, I handed him the little girl and jumped onto the first horse I could grab by the mane. He passed the child back to me and I cradled her close to my chest as I kicked the frightened beast in the flanks. It leapt into darkness, causing me to hope that its eyes were better than mine, or at least that it knew the road. I heard the pounding of hooves behind me, but could see next to nothing when I turned my head. A bowstring twanged as Martala fired an arrow behind her from horseback, but I could not see her target.

6.

The return to Damascus required two days of hard riding. We stopped only to rest the horses, and did not sleep. If the monks followed us, they never managed to draw near enough for me to catch a glimpse of them, although I cast frequent glances over my shoulder. Once inside the city, I rode my exhausted mount directly to the brown gate of Harkanos. His servant answered the bell. I carried the child in my arms through his front door.

His face did not change when he saw her. He motioned for me to carry her into his study and place her on his desk. This I did without speaking. What was there to say?

With gentle fingers, he unwrapped the undershirt I had wound about her tiny body. The stub of an arrow projected from her chest, just under her heart. I had broken the arrow off, but not attempted to pull it out. There was surprisingly little blood. Her face, although grimed with dust and dried tears, was angelic in its tranquility. For a time he merely stroked her hair, brushing it away from her forehead and cheeks.

His sorrow was so deep, yet so silent, I found it difficult to speak. Even so, I forced myself to tell him the events of our ill-conceived rescue mission. He listened without even looking at me.

"I did not realize the child had been shot until I felt her growing cold in my grasp. Then I felt the arrow. We stopped at once and examined her, but it was obvious that she had died at the keep. Altrus said the placement of the arrow was instantly fatal."

At last he looked at me, and his eyes were haunted with an agony too deep to express.

"Thank you, my friend, for trying to save my child."

My heart withered inside my chest at his few words, so free of all recrimination.

"I am a fool," I said bitterly, spitting out the words like poison. "My arrogance caused the death of your child. Blame me for her death. I was so sure that I could find a way to save her."

"I do not blame you."

"I blame myself. The monks tortured her, but they would never have killed her. We could have taken the time to gather a hundred mercenaries and stormed that keep by force. Maybe the monks would have given the child up rather than be slaughtered."

"You do not know them as I do," he said, shaking his head, his eyes still on his dead daughter. "They would have murdered her in front of me out of spite, and gone happily to their deaths. They are fanatics."

"Not that it matters, but Martala killed several of them with her bow, and Altrus cut down at least as many with his sword. The deadfall I released took the lives of two or three more."

"Did you see their leader die?"

I shook my head.

"If ever a man was evil, it is that man."

He gathered his child up into his arms with such tenderness, tears started from my eyes. I did not know that I could still weep.

"Go home, Alhazred. You are exhausted. Eat and sleep. We will talk more on this once you have rested."

"There is a way," I murmured to him.

He stopped and nodded.

"It is not unknown to me," I said, "and Martala is even more skilled in its use than I am."

He did not move, and I knew that he was considering the possibilities.

"She is not wholly human," he said.

"I am not wholly human, either, but the process of the essential salts worked on my corpse."

He looked at me, and into the gray wasteland of his eyes, a glimmer of hope stirred.

"Are you the same man you were, before you were raised?"

Shrugging my shoulders like a ghoul, I said, "How can any man know that? I do not feel different today than I felt before my death. It was a painful ordeal, but I survived it."

"I have heard it said that some come back mad."

"This is true. I will not lie to you, Harkanos. The strain upon the sanity is severe. There is physical agony, but the pain in the mind is much, much worse."

"Yet you survived."

"As you see." I spread my hands.

He nodded, and cast a tender glance down at the face of his daughter, which apart from its pallor might have only been asleep.

"At least the first part of the process should be done," I advised. "Once the body is rendered down to its essential salts, they can be stored for years, even for centuries, before a resurrection is attempted."

"We will talk more of this matter once you have rested."

I returned to my house. Martala was not yet back with Altrus from disposing of the horses. Nealayna heard me enter and came rushing down the stairs. I was too weary and filled with remorse to talk to her, but told her that Altrus was unhurt and would return home shortly. Leaving her, I went into my library and closed the door.

The stone was where I had left it. I sat at my desk and focused my will upon it. Deep inside me a fury seethed, but I kept it contained so that it did not disorder my thoughts.

"Salaymorlaynah," I called out in my mind.

There was no answer.

"I know you can hear me, father. There is one thing I need to learn."

Again I waited, but either he chose not to response, or he truly did not know I sought to reach him.

"Tell me one thing. Did you alter the flight of the arrow?"

The glistening crystal mocked me with its silence.

"Was the arrow destined for me? Father? Tell me, damn you!"

The Caliph's Garden Party

1.

I approached the Caliph's entourage of advisors and nobles along the avenue of cypresses that extended across the breadth of the walled gardens behind the royal palace. The landscape rose in the distance, giving the illusion that the gardens stretched all the way to the horizon. They were not quite so extensive as this, but large enough that their far side was softened by a haze that hung in the morning air.

Near the center of the gardens, an enormous marble fountain composed of ranks of carved figures occupied a broad lawn. Elsewhere, beds of flowers alternated with small groves of fruit trees that were bordered by orderly pathways and roads, all covered in the same pink beach pebbles. Where the stones had originated, I could not imagine, for there were no beaches near Damascus.

The dozen brightly garbed men standing behind the Caliph as he conversed with one of his gardeners seemed to be trying to outdo the peacocks that strutted around them with expanded tails. The rich fabrics of their clothing shimmered and glittered like jewels in the sunlight. These days, such cloths came by caravan from Persia and lands further east, even from distant Chin. They were outrageously expensive, yet there was no shortage of those eager to buy them.

It was apparent to me that the sartorial laws of the Prophet were to be obeyed only by the lower classes of humanity, such as myself, not by the great lords of the Caliphate. Their robes brushed the pebbles of the walk, whereas Mohammed had instructed that no robe should hang below the ankles. They were largely composed of silks and cloth of gold, both fabrics explicitly prohibited to men by the Prophet.

My own tightly-fitted tunic was of the Persian cut, and might have been criticized by the mullahs as a vain affectation, but at least it was white, the color most approved by the Prophet for men's garments. Nor was it encrusted with jewels or pearls.

Stepping with care between the peacocks, I approached Moawiya ibn Yazid, the supreme leader of the civilized world. He was a young man about my own age, but the cares of empire rested heavily on his somewhat narrow shoulders. Every time I saw him he looked a few years older. Streaks of gray had appeared in his beard, and beneath his lustrous eyes were dark rings from lack of sleep.

Moawiya noticed me and motioned me close. His advisors looked on with unconcealed distaste. They were suspicious of anyone who obtained the confidence of the Caliph, but even more so when they knew the man to be a necromancer who conversed with the dead and had dealings with strange gods.

"It is good to see you again, my friend," Moawiya said. "We have not spoken since you gave me a report about the affair in Dumatul Jandal."

I nodded with a smile, remembering the unsatisfactory conclusion to my mission in that city. The Caliph had sent me there to suppress the worship of a pagan idol, and I had failed. The local people had hidden their idol, and presumably continued to worship it. Moawiya was still speaking.

"As you probably know, in three weeks it will be my birthday. I have decided to mark the day by hosting a party in these gardens. Naturally, you and your friends in the Lane of Scholars are invited."

"We will attend with great joy."

He leaned toward me and spoke in a lower voice.

"This is more than just a vain display on my part, Alhazred. I have been advised that I need to make a show of my wealth and authority, as a way of emphasizing the stability of my rule. I have invited all the highborn families across the lands of the Caliphate, as well as the nobles and wealthy merchants who reside here in Damascus."

"It is sure to be a most auspicious celebration."

"It will be a chance for the merchants and tradesmen of Damascus to show their hospitality to the rest of the empire. All the craft guilds will contribute. The bakers will make rich and elaborate pastries for the tables that will be erected on the walks. The wagoners will decorate their best wagons for a parade I have planned that will wind around the garden. The stablers will provide horses to draw the wagons. The tailors will make strange and beautiful costumes for the dancers and jugglers. The metal workers will display their best wares. And so on for all the crafts."

"A glorious time will be had by all," I said, for the sake of saying anything.

"I called you here to make certain the leading mages who dwell along the Lane of Scholars make their special contributions to the entertainment. As you know, in the past they have been slighted, even condemned and driven out of the city, but those dark days are no more. I am inviting them to take their place in the higher ranks of society, and want them to signal their return with a display of their arts."

"I glanced over at the cluster of human peacocks, who strained their necks to hear what we were saying.

"You want us to put on displays of our magic?" I whispered, scarcely able to believe what I was saying.

"That is exactly what I want." He smiled broadly. "Nothing too obscure or scholarly, mind you, but displays the common people will appreciate and talk about with wonder."

"Fireworks, jugglers, that sort of thing?"

"We will have jugglers, but a fireworks display just after sunset would be delightful. I want the mages of Damascus to demonstrate their loyalty to me and to the Caliphate, in a way that all will marvel at and remember."

I glanced again at the advisors and drew him a few paces further away.

"You really should be talking to Harkanos. He is the leader of our community."

"I find you easier to talk to," he said, patting me on the shoulder. "It may be because we are of the same age. Or perhaps it is that you grew up in the palace at Sana'a and understand the requirements of sovereignty."

King Huban of Sana'a, in Yemen, had cut off my nose and ears, and castrated me, for deflowering his daughter, then cast me out naked upon the desert sands to die. I wondered if that had been one of the requirements of sovereignty. But I merely nodded and smiled through the mask of glamour that concealed my disfigured face. Few people in Damascus knew that I was a monster, and Moawiya was not among them. I had a strong suspicion that were he to ever see my true features, he would no longer welcome me in his palace.

It is the nature of men to conceal the truth from other men. I had my secrets, and no doubt the Caliph had his own. Some truths are better left unspoken, even between men of trust. I liked Moawiya as a man, but I knew that he was a weak leader, and that sooner rather than later another man would sit in his throne.

"Will Marwan ibn al-Hakam be attending the celebrations?"

Marwan had been governor of Madina during the reign of Moawiya's grandfather. Recently he had changed his residence to Damascus. He was generally mistrusted and disliked for his brutality and arrogance, and was known among the common people as the "thread of falsehood."

Moawiya made a sound of disgust in his throat and nodded.

"Part of the reason I am hosting this party is to show Marwan that no weakness exists in my rule of the Caliphate."

Marwan had come to Damascus for the same reason a vulture circles a dying camel in the desert. He was awaiting his opportunity to act, and seize the throne for himself, and for his son. Marwan was a fanatic on matters of religious orthodoxy, which did not bode well for the mages in the Lane of Scholars. Under a stricter application of the laws of the Prophet, all of us would have been executed. Fortunately, Moawiya was not a fanatic but a pragmatist.

"I will convey your instructions to the members of our community," I told him with a bow, and backed my way out of the glory of his presence.

2.

"What a magnificent sight," Martala said.

"Where you see magnificence, I see only waste," I admitted.

"It's not your gold being spent," Altrus said.

"It's like something from Babylon before its fall," Nealayna said. The delight was obvious in her voice.

So each of us, in his or her own way, responded to the vision spread before us.

We stood together on a low hill, gazing across the heads of thousands of assembled men and women at a procession of beasts that wound its way along the paths of the palace gardens. Moawiya had managed to gather almost every beast in the world that was capable of walking on four legs, or two. Pairs of tigers marched behind pairs of male lions, and were followed by leopards, baboons, gorillas, elephants, zebras, hippos, giraffes and ostriches, and so on for thousands of paces. Not all these animals walked willingly, but they were prodded along by black-skinned handlers who had ropes and long metal forks to enforce their will. At intervals, groups of musicians walked between the beasts playing on horns, flutes and drums. The forlorn lowing and vexed roars of the animals rose above the music.

Prior to this walking bestiary, we had viewed the passing of a procession composed of all the various tribes and peoples of the world, dressed in their native costumes. Pygmies and giants from Africa, wild men in skirts from the Celtic nations, little men with yellow skin from far to the east, and various Bedouin tribes with the facial tattooing of their women exposed.

Before that there had been a procession of brightly decked wagons and carts depicting various tableaus from history and myth. Some of the figures in the wagons were dressed as pagan gods. I had expected the crowds gathered on either side of the road to be shocked by this, but they only laughed and pointed at the impropriety.

On the open lawn beside the splashing marble fountain, tents had been erected to shelter each delegation from a different part of the Caliphate. The Caliph had his own private tent, larger than any of the others, colored a dark mustard. Beside them were long tables heaped with all manner of foods and drinks. Awnings protected their contents from the sun, and small boys armed with fans ran up and down their lengths to frighten away the flies. There were other smaller tents before which various performers held their demonstrations.

The savory smells of roast meat reached us every time the breeze changed its direction.

"I'm hungry," Altrus said. "I'm going to get something to eat and drink."

"Don't get drunk. I may need you later."

He looked at me with offended dignity.

"I never get drunk during the day."

This was not strictly true, but I let it pass. He made his way after the procession of beasts with Nealayna on his arm, picking his steps with care between the mounds of excrement that dotted the pebbled road.

"I had better talk to Harkanos about our displays."

"I'll come with you," Martala said.

The mages from the Lane of Scholars were due to entertain the people in the latter part of the afternoon, and the sun was already well in decline.

Harkanos stood in front of his little black tent, wearing a beautifully gold-embroidered red robe and a black turban. He looked both impressive and a bit silly, like a child's impression of a Persian magus. Appearances were deceptive. He was the most powerful magician of us all.

"What we're doing is fraught with peril," he said to me when he saw us walking toward his tent. "If we fail, the Caliph will be unhappy with us, but if we succeed, what we do may be used against us at some future time when circumstances in Damascus have changed."

"I understand your meaning. Moawiya's days are numbered."

His eyes widened in alarm. Glancing from side to side, he pulled me close.

"Never say that aloud, Alhazred. Never."

At the moment, I was feeling more irritation at the way we were being used than alarm about what might or might not come in the future. We were to be the final entertainments of the day, the grand conclusion to Moawiya's birthday party. He wanted to send his enemies a message – I control the mages of Damascus, see them dance and perform at my bidding.

"Haven't you cast a recent horoscope for the Caliph?"

"Officially, no. I did not dare." He bent his head near mine. "Unofficially, he has very little time left."

Looking around, I noticed that a nearby striped red and blue tent appeared unoccupied. In front of it a circle of the art and beside that a triangle of evocation were marked on the ground with powdered white chalk.

"Where is the Hound? Didn't he agree to conjure a spirit to visible appearance in the triangle?"

"He hasn't shown his face here. I believe he decided it was too dangerous."

It was like Chigaru el-Masri to take care of his own skin before all other considerations. Unfortunately, the rest of us could not do the same or there would have been no performance.

"Who is to go first?"

"I am," Harkanos said.

People were starting to gather around the double row of our tents, which had been set up in imitation of our houses in the Lane of Scholars, with a broad walkway between the two rows. A group of musicians hired by Harkanos for the demonstration began to play a sinuous, dreaming melody. I wondered if it was his own composition. The girl and I moved away from him to allow him to present himself to the onlookers.

Some distance away, in front of a blue tent, I saw Mahibah, a gray-haired woman of more than sixty years of age, calling out to the crowd, inviting them into her tent to have their palms read. A line began to form at the entrance that was composed mostly of younger women. The young are always eager to learn their future – the old are wise enough not to ask.

Across from her before a white tent, a young woman named Kalila Salib, who had once earned her living as a prostitute, offered to enable the audience to ask questions of their dead friends, neighbours, parents and children. Her expanding line was predominantly older men. I suspected many of them were more interested in a few intimate moments inside the tent with Kalila than with talking to the dead. I felt no concern for her safety – her former work had given her the skills to handle any lecherous advances, be they from man or woman.

Harkanos began to speak, and his sonorous voice carried far across the lawn.

"Friends, visitors, fellow residents of Damascus, it is my honour to allow you a glimpse of the art of glamour. What its origins may be, no man can conceive, but it has existed in all lands from the dawn of time. The priests of Egypt were expert at its use, but no more skilled than the mage cast of ancient Persia. What is this art? It is the art of causing appearances that have no substance or reality. Watch, and I will show you."

Raising his arm, he extended his index finger and drew in the air in front of him an upright circle. Its line appeared as red fire where his fingers traced. The circle continued to float and burn in the air after he lowered his hand.

"Behold! A simple glamour. Is it there, or is it only an illusion?"

He beckoned for an older man to come closer. The man was dressed as a merchant, and at first refused, but when Harkanos persisted, he reluctantly approached the flaming circle.

"Pass your hand through it," Harkanos ordered.

The merchant extended his hand, then hesitated.

"Won't it burn me?"

"Touch it and find out."

The crowd began to urge him to touch the circle. Finally, he passed his fingers quickly through the ring. When he felt no burn, he held out his hand and let the fire curl around it. The crowd applauded his courage as the flaming circle faded to nothingness.

"Not all that is seen is real, and not all that is real is seen." Harkanos put his hands together, palm to palm, and extended his arms toward the audience, which had inched nearer. Slowly, he opened his hands like the two halves of a book. Upon them perched a white dove. It had every aspect of life. In the shocked silence I could hear it coo softly.

"Is it alive, or is it only an image in the mind?"

He threw up his hands. The bird leapt into the air and fluttered higher and higher while the audience craned back their necks to watch. From the blueness appeared a tiny black dot. It became larger, and suddenly it was a black hawk. The hawk struck the terrified dove with its talons in a burst of white feathers and opened its broad wings to glide toward the ground in lazy circles, the dying dove clutched in its claws. But just as the bird was about to touch the ground, it vanished.

"This ancient art can be refined and delicate, or it can be expanded for more impressive effects. Look, all of you, up at the sky. Look to the east, and see the city of Babylon before its fall."

The gasps were loud and many. Even knowing what was to come, I could not help but be impressed by the vision that lay upon a line of golden-edged clouds in the eastern sky. The towering walls of Babylon and the even higher great ziggurat within their bounds rose to the heavens, and the men who walked upon them looked no larger than ants. One part of the city was alive with greenery. I realized it must be the fabled hanging gardens of legend.

As the image in the sky faded, Harkanos received an enthusiastic applause. He bowed to the onlookers with a serene expression and entered his tent to signify that the entertainment was ended.

"Who's next?" Martala asked, her eyes wide with delight.

"We are."

"I hope this ritual works."

"If it doesn't, we will look like fools. But it won't be the first time for me." "Nor for me," she said with a broad grin.

We went to our tent, which by coincidence was a green color much the same as the green on my front gate. Inside, we pulled on matching black robes and cinched them around our waists.

In the open area before the tent, a large circle was drawn with chalk. Inside it were two piles of bones, and two swords. The girl and I entered smaller circles on either side of the large circle and closed the chalk lines behind us.

"Citizens, visitors, friends," I said loudly in my most theatrical voice, waving my hand vaguely in the air. "Prepare to witness the ancient art of necromancy. From the most ancient times men have spoken to the dead, and the dead have answered them, not in the forms of ghosts or airy spirits, but in the resurrected body."

From the corner of my eye I saw that Altrus and Nealayna had returned from their feast, and stood watching with the crowd that surrounded us. Altrus grinned and winked at me. I did not need his mockery to know that I looked like a petty juggler in the marketplace.

"When the blood has ceased to flow, and the flesh has putrefied and been eaten by white worms and black beetles, only the bones remain to show that a man once walked and lived."

I gestured grandly at the circle.

"Here we have the bones of the two most noble heroes who ever drew breath, the Greek Achilles and the Trojan Hector."

In reality, the bones were those of two unknown residents of Damascus that Uto, leader of the White Skull Clan of ghouls, had dug out of the Place of Skulls for my demonstration.

The crowd parted to allow Moawiya and his nobles to reach the front. I saw that Marwan was with him, along with a group of mullahs who were clustered around a holy man with a long white beard.

"Their great battle before the gates of Troy is known to all. It was immortalized in poetry by Homer and will endure for all eternity, even when these bones have turned to dust. But while their bones still exist, with the art of necromancy they can be made to hold the spirits of these great heroes, and assume their former shapes. Let us discover if the enmity between these warriors has faded with time, or still burns hot in the soul of each."

Martala and I both put up the hoods of our robes and raised our arms, facing each other across the circle. We began to chant the words of power written in an ancient scroll in my library where the girl had discovered the bone-raising spell. After a time, the piles of bones began to stir, and the buried skulls emerged.

From the crowd of onlookers there came gasps of wonder.

Slowly, the skulls rose upward, and as they did so, the skeletons formed themselves beneath to support them. I watched the little round pieces of backbone roll across the grass and join up in perfect order. In minutes two complete articulated skeletons stood swaying and staring at each other with hollow eye sockets.

The girl and I chanted the words that would set them at enmity to each other. They were in a forgotten language, which was just as well, for it had nothing to do with the Trojan War. The posture of the skeletons became aggressive. All at once, they snatched up the swords that lay beside them and began to hack at each other.

The murmuring in the crowd intensified. Looking around from the corners of my eyes, I realized that some of the nobles were not happy with what they were seeing. They appeared frightened, and angry at themselves for being afraid. Moreover, the white-bearded holy man and his followers were casting daggers at me from their eyes. I began to think I had not chosen the most auspicious demonstration of my art.

One of the skeletons, whether Hector or Achilles I neither knew nor cared, cut off the head of his foe with a sweep of his sword, and the other skeleton collapsed into a pile of lifeless bones.

"Thus mighty Achilles triumphs again, as he did in ancient times, for the destiny chosen for men by Allah cannot be denied."

The skeleton looked around at the audience and saluted them with his sword, then slowly crumbled back to a heap of disconnected bones.

The applause was loud, but not loud enough to drown out the mutter of angry voices from the Caliph's entourage. Most of the muttering came from the group of mullahs, who did not appear pleased to see necromancy worked beneath the sun and in open sight in Damascus.

To my great surprise, I caught a glimpse of the Egyptian seer, Chigaru el-Masri, bowing his shaved head close to that of

Marwan. Something passed from the old administrator to the Hound, but before I could see what it was, the milling crowd concealed both men.

3.

The girl and I entered our tent to take off our costumes. Her large grey eyes sparkled with delight.

"It went perfectly," she said. "Everything worked, even the salute with the sword at the end."

"The spell worked," I agreed. I refrained from voicing my misgivings.

"What's next? The fireworks?"

Glancing out the slit in the front of the tent at the sky, I shook my head.

"It's not dark enough yet for Abdul-Basir to set off his fireworks. In any case, Dannu the Celt is going to put on a show of elemental magic just before the rockets are lit. I think the next demonstration is by Jacob Hazan."

"The Kabbalist," Martala said in a strained voice.

I looked at her. "You sound nervous."

"I can't help it. For some reason he frightens me."

"So speaks the girl who resurrected me from the dead."

She made a noise of dismissal. "That was different. I had no choice."

"You could have left me dead," I said playfully.

She stared at me for a moment, and said in a softer voice, "No, I could not."

I wondered what was going on in her mind, then decided I did not need to know.

"Let's go out together and see what the Jew has decided to conjure up to entertain the good citizens of Damascus."

Altrus and his woman awaited us outside the tent. The Caliph's group, and the crowd with it, had moved onward to the white and blue striped tent of Jacob Hazan.

"It went well," Altrus said.

"I'm glad you think so."

"The Caliph was delighted. I was watching him. When one bone-man knocked off the skull of the other, he applauded like a little boy."

"He is demonstrating to Marwan and the mullahs that he controls the mages in the Lane of Scholars."

"He should know better than that."

"Perhaps he does. It's all petty posturing, like most of politics."

We made our way along the lines of tents to the ring of spectators. They were disinclined to part for us, but Altrus opened the way with his elbow and his curses.

Hazan was a short man with broad shoulders and a deep chest. He wore a kind of blue coat covered with silver and gold stars that buttoned down the front and hung to his feet. On its right breast was the full, smiling face of the golden sun, and on its left breast the pensive face of the moon in profile. A tall, conical hat of the same color, also decorated with stars, topped his head. His well-brushed gray beard, which hung almost to his waist, was divided into three tails by three golden rings. It gave him a scholarly appearance.

Since my coming to Damascus I had only seen him a few times, when the counsel of mages gathered to deal with some problem. I knew that he dwelt on the Lane in the house behind the black and white gate, and that he had an adult daughter named Judith. In other respects he was a mystery to me.

I studied the faces of the crowd. Some were amused, some nervous, others excited. Moawiya stood on the far side of the circle flanked by his advisors, and gazed around with an expression of contentment. Everything was proceeding as he wished.

Hazan raised his arms for attention. The murmuring of the onlookers quieted.

"What nation does not delight in dance?" he asked in his booming voice, which was one of the deepest voices I have ever heard. He paused a moment as though waiting for an answer.

"What tribe has not its own tradition of dance, that has been handed down from father to son, and from mother to daughter, since the beginning of time?"

Some of the men nodded. I wondered where he was going with his words.

"Today I propose to entertain you with a dance that comes from a land far to the west near the Pillars of Hercules, as they are called by the Greeks."

He smiled at the scattered laughter that greeted his announcement.

"No, my friends, it is not I who will dance." He fixed his black eyes on a young merchant at the front of the audience. "You, good sir, come forward and prove to your neighbours that you are not afraid."

The man looked nervously around. One of his companions laughed and pushed him forward. Hazan pointed at the second man.

"And you, his friend, come forward with him."

The jeering of the crowd finally shamed the two young men into advancing into the open circle.

"Do not be afraid," Hazan said, smiling at them. "This is a joyous magic that you will remember all your days."

He murmured under his breath in Hebrew with his eyes shut, then advanced and put his hands on the foreheads of both men.

The effect was immediate. The men flinched back from his touch, as from the spark that comes from amber when it is rubbed with silk, and began to dance with each other with their hands joined. The amazed expressions on their faces, coupled with the wild and athletic movements of their bodies, caused the audience to applaud and roar with laughter. They leapt into the air, spun on their heels, capered and flexed their knees, waved their arms, swayed from side to side, and bent over backwards until their heads almost touched the grass.

"They cannot dance alone," Hazan cried, his deep voice

carrying over the noise of the crowd. "Which fine woman will join them?"

This remark drew sounds of disapproval. It was considered improper for women to dance with men. Hazan did not heed them. He made a gesture, and one of the dancing men reached out and touched a woman who stood near him on the forehead.

The woman took his hand and began to leap and caper with the two men in spite of the hindrance of her long garment. The crowd was shocked, but also amused.

"One man has a companion but not the other. We cannot let him dance alone," Hazan said.

At once the second merchant touched a woman's head, and she, too, came forward and began to dance.

"Who among you is bold enough to dance with them?" Hazan asked.

The crowd saw where the entertainment was headed and laughed with excitement. A few men and one women stepped forward and were touched on the head. They joined the sinuous line of entranced dancers, who maintained contact with each other by holding hands. The greater number formed a circle and danced with hands clasped while facing inward, then turned themselves and danced while facing out. The dancers broke into spinning groups. The expressions on their faces as they flashed past looked ecstatic. A few began to stumble from fatigue but still they kept dancing. They reached out and touched others in the crowd as they danced past, and spectators became performers against their will.

Martala laughed beside me in disbelief.

"Where will this end?"

Hazan, moving forward to stand in the midst of the dancers, raised his arms.

"It is time to end our revels."

He touched a passing man on the head. Nothing happened. The man continued to leap and caper like an acrobat. Frowning, he brushed his fingers across the forehead of a woman who had lost her headscarf, murmuring as he did so. She danced past him and out of his reach with her long dark hair flying in all directions.

Now the dancers were moaning and crying out with fatigue, which was not to be wondered. Some of them were older, or corpulent of body. It was astonishing they could dance at all. Even so, they continued to touch people, until the audience realized what was happening and panicked. My companions and I were fortunate to be at the inside of the circle, for the crowd turned and ran in all direction, having no regard for the men, women, and even children trampled underfoot. I glimpsed Moawiya being hurried away by his advisors, but of Marwan, who had haunted him all afternoon like a dark shadow, there was no sight.

"Back away," Altrus cried above the screams and shouts. "Do not let them touch you."

The dancers seemed determined to touch as many as they could reach. They followed at the heels of the terrified citizens of Damascus.

"Guard your heads," I said. "Don't let them touch you on the head."

Altrus drew his sword and protected Nealayna with the flat of its blade, using it as a club to beat down the extended arms of the possessed. I used my elbow and shoulder to shield Martala, who clung close to my side. As I suspected, the touch was powerless unless delivered to the bare face.

In minutes the screaming partygoers and the ensorcelled dancers had dispersed to all parts of the walled gardens. The dancers chased after the others like hunting dogs, all the while spinning and leaping as they went. It was a vision of nightmare.

Jacob Hazan stood alone before his tent, an expression of incomprehension on his broad face. He did not even look at me when I approached.

"What went wrong?" I asked.

"I don't know, I don't understand it. This was a simple spell. I have seen it used in the marketplace. I made no mistake, of that I am certain."

I patted him on the shoulder. "Never mind, I think I may have the answer."

He turned to me, and hope lit up his face.

"Can you stop it, Alhazred?"

"No, but I think I know the man who can."

With this enigmatic utterance I left him and went back to the others, who were watching the mayhem all around them with wondering eyes.

"Help me to find Chigaru el-Masri."

"I thought the Hound left the gardens before the demonstrations began," Altrus said.

"No, he's still here. I saw him a while ago standing beside Marwan."

"What dealings would the Hound have with Marwan?" Martala asked.

"That is the question I mean to put to him."

4.

The Caliph, along with his advisors, mullahs, and closest nobles, had retreated to the long mustard-coloured tent that served as his audience chamber and personal quarters during the hours of his birthday party. When we stepped under the shadow of the awning that extended out from the tent entrance, a lone palace guard advanced with his poleaxe held at the ready. He was a young man who could not conceal his dismay at what was happening all across the gardens. His face bore a stunned expression.

"I have business with the Caliph," I told him.

"No one is to enter," he said, blinking at me nervously.

"Where are all the other guards?"

"They are – dancing."

"Has someone been sent to the palace for reinforcements?" Altrus demanded harshly.

The guard nodded.

"I'm going into the tent, alone." I fixed the guard with my gaze. "You won't stop me, if you value your sanity."

He hesitated, but when I stepped around him he allowed it. Which was just as well for him. Altrus would have killed him had he tried to use his weapon against me.

Inside the tent, men milled about in confusion, or sat staring bleakly across the infinite gulf of their fears. I was relieved to see Harkanos with Moawiya. Marwan stood with his own people some distance away, watching everything with his dark eyes. When the young Caliph saw me, he gestured for me to approach.

"What is happening, Alhazred? Do you know what is going on?"

I glanced at Harkanos.

"Haven't you told him?"

"I was in my tent and did not see the beginnings of the madness," he explained.

"The demonstration of Jacob Hazan went wrong."

"Wrong how so?" Moawiya demanded in alarm.

"You saw how he made the people dance for your amusement. It is a spell of contagion. One who is touched touches another, and that person touches another, and so on."

"Do you think this Jacob intended this to happen?"

"Absolutely not. He intended to unmake the spell by the touch of his own hands on the heads of the dancers, but for some reason his touch had no effect. The contagion spread out of his control."

Moawiya was overcome with emotion. Harkanos caught him and steadied him while his aged advisors looked on with grim faces. It was evident to me from their expressions that having no one yet to blame, they were prepared to blame all of us.

"What have I done?" Moawiya said. " Marwan was right. It was foolish to bring forbidden magic into the grounds of the royal palace. What will happen to those poor people?"

"They will dance until they can no longer lift their limbs, and then they will fall to the ground and lie twitching."

"Will they die?"

I looked at Harkanos.

"Many will die, if the spell is not taken from them," he said. "Some from failure of the heart and others from burst blood vessels inside the skull."

"Do you know any way to end this spell?"

He shook his head gravely. "It is a spell unknown to me."

"I have read about it, but don't know how to work it," I confessed. "From my reading, this is not the first time it has been perverted to malicious purposes."

Moawiya grabbed my arm. "What do you mean, perverted? Is this more than an accident?"

I looked across the tent at Marwan, who was drinking in every word. He smiled at me with his thin lips.

"I fear so."

"In the name of the Prophet, who would do such a monstrous thing?"

To speak Marwan's name with no evidence would be a perilous course indeed. I needed to find the Hound and confront him.

"I do not know who did this," I answered. "But I may be able to find out."

Marwan chose this moment to intrude himself.

"Isn't the most likely explanation that the Jew who made this ill-conceived demonstration was incompetent of his craft, and lost control of his magic?"

"Jacob Hazan is far from unskilled," Harkanos told him coldly. "He is also my friend. Have a care how you speak about him."

"Do you hear?" Marwan said to the Caliph. "Do you hear how they threaten me? The arrogance of these conjurers passes all belief. Why should we not assume this was done deliberately, to embarrass and humiliate you? It may even be an attempt on your life."

Outside the tent, the frenzied cries of the dancers were coming nearer. They sounded from all sides.

"I do not believe the residents of the Lane of Scholars would do that," Moawiya told him, but his voice was uncertain.

"What more effective way of reaching you, than to turn your own defenses against you? Half your royal guard are dancing like maniacs across the green."

"Stay here," I told Moawiya. "My companions will help your solitary guard prevent the entrance of any of the dancers."

"How will they do that?"

"With sword and dagger, if necessary."

"But Alhazred, you cannot kill these dancers. They are blameless."

"Your compassion is known throughout the Caliphate," I told him. "However, they cannot be permitted to infect you with this dancing mania. Some may have to be killed to prevent it."

He looked at his silent advisors. Two of them nodded in agreement, though their expressions did not soften.

"Very well. Do what you can to stop this madness before it spreads outside the palace walls and infects the entire city."

I turned to Marwan.

"Do you know where Chigaru el-Masri may be?"

Marwan blinked once slowly.

"That name is not familiar to me."

"Are you sure? Think again. I saw you standing beside him on the lawn."

"The lawn was crowded with all manner of party guests. How am I to know them all?"

"You gave him a package."

He laughed lightly.

"Your eyes must have deceived you. I gave no one a package."

I met the gaze of Harkanos, and an understanding passed between us.

"What is this talk of packages?" Moawiya asked in bewilderment.

"It is of no importance. I will go now, and try to stop the mania."

A cry of challenge came from outside the tent. I recognized Altrus's voice. Nealayna stumbled in through the door flap.

"He would not let me stay outside," she said to me in apology.

The crazed grunts and squeaks and yells of the dancers were very close.

"Can you protect the Caliph?" I murmured to Harkanos when Moawiya's head was turned.

"I don't know."

I looked from him to Moawiya in frustration. I wanted to stay here and fight for them but knew the only hope was to find the person who had interfered with Jacob Hazan's spell. It is a curious truth of magic that when a spell is placed by one magician, another magician cannot easily lift it.

When I squeezed through the flap on the door of the tent, I stepped into a scene of utter madness. Men, women and children, many of them naked or nearly so, jumped and capered all around, their faces distorted into masks of horror. Some of them lay writhing and kicking on the grass, having exhausted the vital forces of their bodies. Others scratched at themselves and tore out their own hair in their extremity of frustration, so that their bodies streamed with fresh blood.

Altrus and Martala were kicking them away from the entrance, and the young guard used the butt end of his poleaxe to push them off, but it was obvious that they were losing ground. Soon they would have to start killing these unfortunate dancers, and even that might not be enough to stop them. The dancers seemed to come in waves and swirls of gyrating bodies, as though impelled by some collective intelligence.

"Hold them as long as you can," I shouted to Altrus, who nodded in my direction.

I ran through a gap in the whirling blood-stained bodies toward an open space on the grass, where I could survey the gardens. The dancers were everywhere, but not evenly spread. They danced in groups that joined and broke apart, the way a flock of sparrows will do. It was a fascinating sight, but I did not allow myself to be distracted by it.

The Hound must still be somewhere in the gardens, for the guards had locked the gates, and were presently absent from their posts and could not open them. It was appalling to see how many of the Caliph's palace guards had been turned into dancers. There were only a scattered few who retained their wits.

I looked at the rows of small tents that had once belonged to the mages, thinking that perhaps he had returned to his own tent, but they were all collapsed in on themselves and trampled by dancing feet, not being sturdy enough to withstand the press of bodies. I scanned the gardens. The larger tents of the nobles were still up. I recognized the grey tent of Marwan ibn al-Hakam, and began to pick my way through the groups of dancers with short darting runs. One gyrating man with blood streaming from his nose, no doubt broken by a flailing hand or elbow, almost infected me, but I managed to turn my shoulder to him. The touch of his palm on my tunic did nothing, to my great relief.

Marwan's tent stood unguarded and appeared abandoned. Its pennants fluttered forlornly in the breeze. The dancers had not yet surrounded it, but they were moving mindlessly toward it across the sweep of grass.

Drawing my sword, I ducked into the tent. The light that found its way through the walls was dim. Lamps burned in various places to liven the gloom, but their flames had little effect.

The Hound sat at a table, drinking red wine from a silver goblet. He did not stand, but lifted a silver pitcher and extended it toward me.

"Have some wine, Alhazred. Whatever Marwan's faults, he has good taste in wine."

5.

I looked around for confederates. Apart from we two, the tent was empty. Sheathing my sword, I went to the table and calmly poured a goblet of wine, then drank as I stood looking down at him. There was always something vaguely repellent about the Hound. His bald head and fat cheeks were shiny, as though coated with a thin layer of oil. The folds of fat on his neck made ridges like fingers beneath his chin when he bent to sip from his goblet.

"It's a pity that the demonstration of the Jew failed so badly," he said. "It will not reflect well on Moawiya."

"It does appear to be to Marwan's advantage."

"Politics is such a cynical, dirty business. Necromancy is so much cleaner, don't you agree?"

I set down my goblet.

"What was it that Marwan gave you while you were watching my demonstration?"

"I don't know what you are talking about."

"The small brown package. Gems, perhaps? Pearls? Some precious document?"

His eyes narrowed slightly as I spoke the last words.

"It was the original copy of the spell Jacob Hazan used, wasn't it? One of Marwan's agents stole it for you from Hazan's tent before he put on his demonstration."

"You are speaking in riddles, my friend."

"You needed the original spell in order to change it, didn't you? What did you do, remove the spell's limits?"

Cocking his bald head to one side, he cupped a hand behind his ear.

"I believe the dancers are coming closer."

"What happens to me happens to you."

"Does it indeed," he asked with a smirk.

He was enjoying his taunts. How it must have galled him to speak politely to me in the past. I tried another approach.

"Chigaru, this must be stopped. It has gone beyond any possible political motive. People are dying. The entire city of Damascus may become infected."

"Only the city?" He smiled as he sipped his wine. "You always were an optimist."

"You want it to spread beyond the city," I said, staring at him. "But why? What possible purpose could so much misery serve?"

"It serves the purpose of the one I serve. That is enough reason."

"Marwan? Why would Marwan want this catastrophe to befall the land?"

He smiled again and said nothing. There was something almost womanly about his round face and smooth cheeks. It disgusted me.

"The one I serve is not opposed to chaos," he said.

A coldness ran up my back to the roots of my hair on centipede legs.

"He delights to watch the gods of earth dance for his amusement," the Hound continued. "He told me he would enjoy watching you dance."

"You are insane. The one you serve cannot be trusted. He will betray you." I did not dare speak his name.

"Nyarlathotep has been watching you, Alhazred," he said.

I shuddered at the utterance. "Do not say that again, if you value your life."

"You think you escaped him? His power is beyond your comprehension. He plays with you the way a cat toys with a mouse before swallowing it."

"Enough of this useless banter." I drew my sword. "Give me the paper with the charm."

He spread his fat hands. "I have no paper."

"Enough!" I roared. "Give it to me now or I will gut you and search your corpse."

Outside the tent, the dancers began to press their bodies against the gray cotton fabric. I could see their shadows moving across the walls as they spun and rolled.

The Hound stood up, and his eyes narrowed until they disappeared into slits. His lack of eyebrows gave his face a pig-like appearance. His hand strayed to the dagger at his belt. He had no sword, but I did not deceive myself. The rumour in the Lane was that he was quick to draw his envenomed dagger, and skilled in its use. I pulled forth my own curved dagger in my left hand and waited.

He relaxed and chuckled.

"A jest, my friend, merely a jest. Of course you may have the charm. I have no further use for it."

From a pocket in his richly jewelled robes he drew forth a folded brown parchment and tossed it onto the table. Sheathing my weapons, and watching him the way a mongoose watches a rearing cobra, I took up the parchment and opened it. Upon it were written instructions in Hebrew and words of power in Greek. In the middle of the sheet a charm had been drawn that was in the shape of two squares laid over each other to produce a star of eight points. Various arcane symbols were drawn in the points of the star.

What interested me more was the addition of certain symbols to this diagram in blood red ink. The additions were recent, for the ink was still fresh and bright, whereas the ink of the original spell had faded from black to brown. Some of the symbols were astrological. Some were geomantic. At least one was numerological. Taken together, they conveyed to me absolutely nothing. This was not a spell I had studied or encountered in my studies, other than a single reference to its effects and malicious use that I remembered reading in an ancient chronicle.

"Suppose I burn this parchment."

He spread his fat white hands, so like two clusters of white grave worms.

"By all means, burn it."

The pressure against the sides of the tent was becoming alarming. I wondered why the dancers had not found their way in through the open entrance? Could it be that something was keeping them out? I looked at the parchment with sudden determination.

"No, I won't burn it. I will keep it on my person."

Folding it carefully, I put it into a pocket in my tunic. Then I went around the table and grabbed the Hound by his collar. His hand went to his dagger. I plucked it from its sheath and tossed it into a corner of the tent.

"What are you doing?" he blustered as I dragged him to his feet. "This is so unseemly. It is beneath your dignity, Alhazred. I thought you were better than this, I really did."

"What I am going to do is cast you out of the tent, so that you can enjoy the chaos you have caused at first hand. Who knows? Perhaps you will dance for me as I watch from the entrance."

"No!" he cried, and the note of distress in his voice was genuine. All of the posturing deserted his manner. "For the love of Allah, don't put me out of this tent."

"So the charm protects the tent. I wondered if it was the tent, or only the person holding it."

"No, it's the tent, the entire tent. As long as the charm is inside, no dancer can enter."

I spun his fat body around and grabbed him by the shoulders. They were surprisingly muscular under their layer of fat. I wondered how well I would fare should he decide to wrestle with me, and wished that Altrus was beside me.

"Enough games, Chigaru. Enough taunts and smooth words. Can you end this dancing mania or not?"

He hesitated, but finally said, "I can end it."

I pushed him away from me and let my hand rest on my dagger hilt.

"Then end it."

"I will need the charm."

It was my turn to hesitate. Was this a trick? Shrugging with the fatalism of a ghoul, I took out the charm and tossed it to him. He unfolded and studied it, then laid his palm on it and looked at me. His eyes rolled back in his head, so that only the whites showed, and he began to chant in a rhythmic way words from a language unknown to me. His body swayed back and forth. Clutching the parchment to his breast, he cried out.

A kind of ring of light expanded from him. I felt nothing as it passed through my body, but when it went through the walls of the tent, the twisting and leaping shadow shapes on the other side all fell down to the grass as though struck with a hammer. The insane yips and shouts that came from distant parts of the gardens gradually died away. Within a few moments there was silence.

I went cautiously to the tent entrance and pulled back the flap to peer out. Men and women lay across the grass as far as I could see. They were naked or nearly so, and smeared with blood and dirt. They looked like the morning after some gigantic drunken orgy.

The odor of smoke made me turn. I darted back to the table, but it was too late. The last of the parchment blazed up merrily from where the Hound had touched its corner to the flame of an oil lamp. He let the ash fall in a cascade of sparks.

"Now you have no evidence to use against me."

"That may be so," I agreed. "But you have given me something far more precious than evidence."

"And what would that be?"

I stared at him with withering contempt, and the smile slowly left his face.

"You have shown me who you truly are, and who you serve. I will never be deceived by you again."

Turning my back on him, I left the tent.

The Redeemer of

Blood

1.

We sat waiting in a small sitting room with a low ceiling. The windows were narrow, but the half-open screens let in enough daylight to read by. It was cooler than outside, thanks to the thick walls of mud bricks, which prevented the heat of noon from penetrating. I wondered how it would be in the evening, when the walls and roof radiated their stored heat inward.

A silent female servant brought a carafe of wine on a silver tray, then withdrew herself and shut the inner door. We sipped the wine from small silver cups.

"I thought Jacob Hazan was a man of wealth," Altrus said in a low voice.

"What gave you that impression?" I asked.

"I don't know. He was always well dressed. He had the bearing of a wealthy man."

"The cost of renting a house in the Khaybar Oasis may be greater than you think, particularly if you are a Jew. Most landholders here are Muslims."

We still wore our white desert thaubs, which were dusty after many days of hard riding by camel. I longed for a bath and a decent meal, but we had paused at the inn only long enough to rent our rooms before coming to Hazan's house.

"I wonder why he sent for you," Martala murmured. We were all talking in hushed tones as though we were in a house of the dead.

"His letter said only that he had uncovered a crime at Katiba, in the Khaybar Oasis, having delicate repercussions for his people, but could not resolve it on his own. He asked me to come at once, if I could find the time to help him."

"When Jacob and his daughter shut up their house and fled Damascus, I never expected to see them again," she said.

"He should have stayed and confronted his accusers," Altrus said. "It wasn't his fault that the spell he worked at the Caliph's garden party was corrupted by the Hound."

"People died," I reminded him. "Feelings were inflamed. There was no proof that the Hound interfered with his dancing spell. The people blamed Jacob."

Two months earlier Moawiya had hosted a grand garden party to celebrate his birthday. The mages who lived in the Lane of Scholars had been invited to put on demonstrations of their magic. Jacob Hazan had chosen to work an obscure spell that caused men and women to dance with uncontrolled abandon, and this dancing mania was spread by touch, so that the hand of a dancer on the face of a man or woman caused them to dance. The Egyptian seer and necromancer Chigaru el-Masri had been paid by the Caliph's enemy, Marwan ibn al-Hakam, to corrupt this spell so that Hazan was unable to stop the contagion, and the dancing spread out of control across the royal gardens. More than a dozen people died, most of them older men with weak hearts.

The inner door opened, and Judith Hazan entered silently. She wore a black dress that hung to her ankles, and a small black cap trimmed with white lace on her head. Her attractive face was set in lines of sorrow. Dark shadows haunted her brown eyes.

"My father is asleep. He sleeps so little these days, I do not like to wake him."

"Let him rest a while," I told her. "Can you tell us why he sent for me?"

"It must be me that tells you, for he cannot speak."

"This is sad news," I said with surprise. "What afflicts him?"

She sat in a chair facing me and folded her white hands in her lap.

"A month or so ago he had a fit and fell to the floor. His left side is paralyzed."

I remembered the strong man with the broad chest I had known in Damascus, a man with a booming voice and ready laughter who had seemed in perfect health. So quickly could our fortunes change.

"What do the physicians say?"

"Our physician thinks his diet was too rich, but I don't believe he really knows the cause of the fit."

This put a different complexion on matters. I had come to the oasis expecting to assist Hazan, and now realized that whatever needed to be done would have to be done without his help.

"Why did your father summon me?"

"He has always had a high regard for your abilities as a necromancer. When you ended the dancing spell it only enhanced his opinion of you."

"Yes, but why did he want me to come to Katiba?"

Judith met my eyes solemnly.

"Because he needs help, and believed you were the only mage in Damascus who would come to his aid."

I glanced at my companions, who sat watching our conversation in silence.

"I barely know your father."

"Yet you came," she said. "You came in answer to his plea for help."

"That can't be denied," I said. "What is the matter that concerns him so deeply?"

She glanced out through the window screen, as if to assure herself that no one stood listening. The houses at Katiba had no front courtyards, as they did in Damascus, but opened directly to the streets. I wondered why she had chosen a front room for our conversation, then realized that a backroom would have disturbed her father.

"There have been murders in the oasis. Men have been killed in the most violent and grotesque ways, their bodies smashed as though crushed by massive stones, their skulls shattered, their ribs pushed through their hearts."

"What is the motive for these murders?"

"Most people believe it is robbery, but my father became convinced that it was political."

"Political? In what way?"

She lowered her voice, causing me to instinctively lean toward her.

"He came to believe they were assassinations."

"For what motive?"

"Vengeance. He believed that old family scores were being settled. How much do you know about the history of Khaybar Oasis?"

"Not a great deal."

"Did you know that the Jews of the Banu Nadir tribe who inhabited the oasis came here because they were driven out of Madina by the army of Mohammed? They fled to this oasis as a refuge. Three years later Mohammed followed them to Khaybar and put heads of prominent Jewish families of the Banu Nadir tribe to the sword. He tortured their leader, a man named Kinana al Rabi, until he revealed the places where the Jews had hidden their treasure, then cut off his head and took his wife, Saffiya, for one of his own wives. The Jews were made to give him half the value of their yearly harvests as a kind of tribute."

"When did this happen?" Martala asked.

Judith turned to her. "It was fifty-six years ago."

"Most of those who suffered must be dead by now," I said.

"That was not the only persecution. Just thirty-eight years ago, the Caliph Umar expelled many prominent Jews from Khaybar, sending them northward to the lands around Damascus. My father's grandfather was one of those expelled."

"Your father thinks the assassinated men were descendants of the Muslims responsible for the expulsion?"

"Some of them. Others belonged to Jewish families that collaborated with the Caliphate and betrayed their fellow Jews. For this they were allowed to remain in Katiba."

"Both Muslims and Jews have been killed?"

She nodded.

"Why would your father believe they were assassinated?"

"Those killed were all older men who would have been young men at the time Umar drove the Jews out of the oasis and forced them to settle in the north. He recognized several of their names as men his grandfather had said were responsible for the expulsion. His grandfather used to tell him stories of the persecution when he was a boy so that he would remember the names as a man."

"Does your father know who is doing the killing?" Altrus asked her.

She shook her head.

"When I was a girl, my father told me the same stories his grandfather told him. You must understand, Alhazred, the Khaybar Oasis was like the land of milk and honey to them, from which Umar drove them out into the wilderness."

"It is indeed one of the greenest places I have ever seen," I said. "The date palms stretch on forever, and the water bubbles up out of the ground in springs."

"I like it here," Judith said. "I could live here in happiness if my father's health were good, but the puzzle of the murders has become a kind of obsession for him. I think it may be what brought on his fit."

The young Jewish servant who had admitted us into the house came from the rear of the house and bent to whisper into the ear of her mistress.

"My father is awake," Judith told us with a smile. "He wants to see you, Alhazred."

Martala and Altrus stood when I did.

"No, just Alhazred. You understand, he is so weak."

They resumed their seats. I allowed Judith to lead me down a dim hallway to a spacious room that received a pleasant breeze from its open windows, which faced a grove of date palms. The soft rustle of their fronds could be heard each time the breeze blew.

Jacob Hazan lay in bed beneath a white cotton sheet, his great brown beard spread across his broad chest. Pillows behind his back and head elevated him to a half-sitting position. His face had a grey cast and the left side sagged as if made of wax that had melted and run in the heat of a fire, but his brown eyes were alive with intelligence. He raised his trembling right hand off the blanket in greeting when he saw me. I stood at the foot of the bed where he could look at me without effort.

"I was distressed to learn of your illness. I wish you a rapid and complete return to health."

He made a noise in his throat, but I could not understand what he said.

"Don't try to talk, father," Judith told him. "The physician said it was too soon for you to talk."

Frustration rippled across the right side of his face. The left side remained slack and lifeless.

"Your daughter has told me about the killings here at the Khaybar Oasis," I said. "She also told me that you believe the killer may be someone seeking revenge upon the men who aided Umar during the expulsion of the Jews."

He tried to nod, and the effort made pearls of sweat spring forth on his forehead. With his right hand he motioned for his daughter to bring him a wax slate and a stylus. She carried them to the bed and held the slate steady while he wrote upon it, then turned it so that I could read it. The wax bore three names of men.

"Are these men who have been killed?"

Hazan made a kind of dismissive grunt that could be interpreted as negative.

"I recognize these names from our family stories," Judith said. "These are three of the men who aided Caliph Umar. Two of them are Muslims and the other is a Jew."

"Do you mean they are still alive?"

She nodded. I looked at Hazan.

"Do you believe these men will be targeted by the assassin?"

He wagged his finger at me, his eyes glittering with awareness.

I stood in silent thought for a dozen seconds. This was not my battle. Never in my life have I felt a deep stirring in my heart to right every injustice I encounter. Yet Hazan was part of the Council of Mages, and I had a professional obligation to help him. In any case, the mystery of these assassinations, if that is what they were, intrigued me.

"My companions and I will stay in Katiba and search for the killer."

A deep sigh of satisfaction escaped his lips and he sank back into his pillows.

"My father is tired now," Judith said. "We must let him sleep."

She ushered me from the room and shut the door behind us.

2.

"There are three names, and three of us," I told Martala and Altrus when I returned to the front room of the house with Judith. "Jacob believes that they will be targeted by the assassin."

"Who will be attacked first?" Altrus asked.

"He doesn't know. He doesn't even know when they will be attacked."

"The assassinations usually happen during the dark phase of the moon," Judith said.

"This is the dark phase of the moon," Martala said.

"Where do these men live?" I asked Judith.

"Two of them live here in Katiba beside the date palm groves. They are both Muslims. The Jew lives up in the fortress, on top of the high place that overlooks the town."

"You mean that big stone prominence with the sheer sides we saw when we rode into Katiba?"

"There are several of them in the oasis, each overlooking its own community. When the Jews came from Medina, their leaders occupied the fortresses on top of each mount to rule over the laborers and craftsmen who dwelt below among the date palms. The wealthy Jewish families still live there. The fortresses are almost invulnerable to attack."

A pebble ticked on a stone just outside one of the windows. I turned my head in time to see a man's face slide past the partly opened window screen. Altrus was on his feet and moving before I could speak. He went out the front door, and I heard his pounding footsteps fade down the street. Martala glanced at me with wide eyes, then ran after him.

"Are you being watched?" I asked Judith.

"I don't know. There has been a strange man loitering on the street. At times he follows me when I leave the house. I have wondered what he was doing, but I did not have the courage to confront him."

"You may be in danger. Be sure to lock your doors and shutters when we are gone."

In a few minutes the mercenary and the girl both returned out of breath.

"I lost him amid the trees," Altrus said.

"Did you get a good look at him?"

"Not at his face."

"Maybe you should stay here with Judith," I said to Martala.

"That isn't necessary," Judith said. "I will ask one of my cousins to stay in the house with us for the next few nights."

"You have relatives here?"

"Of course. That's why we came here from Damascus."

In spite of my misgivings, we left her alone in the house with her ailing father and separated to locate the houses of the names on Hazan's list. Judith did not know their exact locations. While Altrus and Martala went to the marketplace to ask about the two Muslims, I followed the winding road up the hill toward the towering wedge of rock that supported a walled fortress on its flat top. The prominence was almost vertical, but I saw that a pathway had been cut in its side.

All around me stretched the strange landscape of the oasis, which has the curious property of being arid and wet at the same time. The surface of the ground was bare rock and dirt, but just below the surface water flowed, allowing the tall date palms to grow thickly over the gentle slope. I passed a public spring where pure, cool water bubbled up from under the ground into a small square catch basin that had been made for it from pieces of cut stone. It had an ancient look. The oasis must have been inhabited long before the Jews came to it from Madina seeking refuge. I wondered how the original inhabitants had reacted to their sudden appearance?

The massive promontory that supported the fortress seemed to loom higher as I approached its base. It was composed of layers of different types of stone that had originally been beneath the surface of the ground at some period in the immemorial past, before an unimaginably vast flood had washed everything else away, leaving only this elevation and the few others that rose from the oasis like brooding sentinels.

At the base of the path that wound its way up the side was a hut of mud bricks roofed with palm fronds. Two guards in light military armor lounged outside its open door, leaning on their poleaxes. They looked bored and half asleep.

When I started past them, they suddenly sprang awake and crossed their weapons in my path.

"What is your business at the fortress?" the older man demanded.

"I have an appointment to see Yehudah Halevi," I said without hesitation, meeting his glare squarely with my mild gaze.

It was the name of the Jew on Hazan's list. I saw by their faces that both men recognized it.

"I wasn't given any order to admit you," the older guard said. The younger man merely stared at me. "What is your business with him?"

"It is a personal matter, family business. Not something I can discuss on the open road."

He hesitated. I saw that he was weighing the pleasure of telling me I could not pass against the unpleasantness of being cursed at by his superior. To help him decide, I took up my purse and dug into it for a pair of silver coins.

"Your service is always appreciated," I said, holding out the coins. "The Prophet alone knows what the oasis would be like were it not for men like you to keep order."

The older man glanced at his companion, then took the coins. "Go on up."

Climbing the path cut into the side of the cliff face was an ordeal. I wondered how goods of any size were carried up it. Donkeys could probably make the climb with packs on their backs, but not horses or camels. Those who lived on the top must seldom descend. Why would they want to, when they had their own private city in the sky?

When I reached the top, I was relieved to find that the gates of the fortress stood open. The guard at the gates made no objection when I told him I was there to see Yehudah Halevi on personal business, so I walked past him.

Inside was like any prosperous walled community. The houses were three and four levels high, the roads narrow but paved with flat stones like Roman roads. The people paid little attention to me, but continued on with their business, whatever it might be. I found my way to a small marketplace where vendors were selling vegetables, fruits, fowl and meat from stalls. Wherever people lived, they had to eat. One vendor was selling water from an enormous pot. He ladled it out to servants who came to him with pitchers, took their coins, and watched them carry the water away balanced on their heads.

"Are there no wells inside the walls?" I asked him.

He studied me with a shrewd squint.

"You must be a stranger here."

"I am."

"No, there are no wells. Water is caught on the roofs during rains, or carried up from the springs below on the backs of mules."

"It must be laborious work."

"So it is. I tell my customers that when they complain about my prices. Water is heavy and the way is long."

"May I buy a drink?"

He cheerfully ladled me out a cupful of water and took my silver without comment. The water was pure and good.

"Perhaps you can help me. I'm looking for the house of Yehudah Halevi. Do you know it?"

"Everyone knows Halevi's house. He's a very important man up here, for a Jew I mean."

"Are you not a Jew yourself?"

He shook his head. "I follow the teachings of the Prophet, blessings and peace of Allah be upon him. Most of the vendors and tradesmen within the walls are followers of the Prophet, and a few are Christians. The Jews are all men of wealth."

Following his directions, I made my way to a large house that stood upon an elevation that raised its ground level even with the top of the fortress wall. A paved open plaza lay before it, and behind the house I could see the green tops of trees above a garden wall.

I made my way across the empty plaza to the fortress wall, expecting every moment to be hailed from the house, but no challenge came. Peering over the edge cautiously, I had to pull back until my dizziness passed. It was a sheer drop of many hundreds of cubits. Looking a second time, I was surprised to see a narrow stair of steps carved into the stone, and signs of a path on the gentler slope below it. It was not much of a path, more of a trail for mountain goats, but it was a definite path up the side of the prominence from the date palm groves that grew all around its base. I glanced down at the houses spread out below. Their roofs and the roads that ran between them were tiny. I was able to trace the main road to Hazan's house, and wondered how the old man was doing in his bed.

Some inner sense made the back of my neck prickle. Turning quickly, I saw an old man staring down at me from one of the second-level windows of Halevi's house. He did not draw back, but continued to look at me with hard, cold eyes. His hair was white, and a full grey beard spread down his chest.

It was not my intention to confront Halevi in his own house. What could I do, other than warn him that his life might be in danger? I had no evidence to support the claim. He would dismiss me as an eccentric, or worse, he might conclude that I was trying to defraud him. I merely nodded and withdrew from the plaza, retracing my steps back to the marketplace to wait in some unobtrusive alcove for nightfall.

3.

The night sky was shot with its usual ten thousand glittering stars. Across the middle ran the hazy band that some call the Road of the Hay Merchant, for the way in which a hay wagon will drop a carpet of straw behind it as it jolts along. The elevation of the city magnified both the extent and the brilliance of the heavens. There was no moon, but the Evening Star that blazed in the west was bright enough to cast faint shadows.

I emerged from my hiding place behind a cart and stretched to get the stiffness from my limbs and back, then traced my way through the dark streets to Halevi's house, moving with the stealth I had learned while living with the desert ghouls of the Black Spring Clan. Soldiers, drunks and whores passed me without ever realizing I was there.

Gor, the leader of the clan, would have been pleased. I rubbed his skull where it hung on my belt in a meditative way with my thumb, remembering the sound of his voice and his laughter. He had befriended me and taught me how to survive in the Empty Space. Against the challenge of that vast expanse of sand, all other foes seemed trivial.

It was my intention to watch Halevi's house all night for the approach of an assassin. I positioned myself where I could overlook the sheer side incised with the faint stair. From the look of it, the stair was old and probably long forgotten, but it was just possible a daring killer could climb to the house along it.

The air was mild, the night breeze light. It was not an unpleasant vigil. I had managed to get a few hours of sleep while hiding in the marketplace. I watched the Evening Star set in the west, and the constellations wheel slowly overhead around the celestial pole.

A shadow moved beside the house. I sat up straight and tried to peer through the darkness, wondering how anyone had reached the house without me seeing his approach. After a few moments I saw it again. It was a large man, tall and long of limb. I could just distinguish his outline against the stars. He seemed to be climbing over the lip of the fortress wall, which was level with the plaza, and I realized he was descending the old stair.

Sashi, is it possible this shadow figure came from inside the house? I asked silently in my mind.

The desert djinn that inhabits my body caused her human face to materialize in the darkness. It seemed to float bodiless several feet in front of me, but I knew this was an illusion. Sashi's face was no more real than the mask of glamour I wore to conceal my disfigurement.

I did not see anyone leave the house, my love, but it is very dark, she said in my mind.

When inside me, Sashi was forced to rely on my physical senses to perceive the outer world. She could not see any better than I could, but sometimes the djinn noticed things I missed due to inattention.

If he didn't come from inside the house, where did he come from? I wondered.

I do not know, beloved.

Approaching the house across the plaza, I made my way along the top of the wall to where I had seen the shadow. It was gone by the time I got there. I leaned over the edge and looked down. A hundred cubits or so below, a shadow shape crawled down the side of the rock face. I wondered how it could see the steps cut into the rock in the darkness.

If the shadow had come from the house, it was possible it had already killed Halevi. I debated the wisdom of entering the house to discover the fate of the Jew, then decided it was more important to follow this shadow back to his master.

Help me find the places to put my hands and feet, I told Sashi silently.

Looking up at the stars and wondering if this was the last time I would see them, I swung my legs over the edge of the wall and began to climb down the stair. It would have been perilous even in daylight. The darkness forced me to feel my way. Several times Sashi was able to help me by noticing details on the rock that I missed. How long it took me to descend, I could not have said. It must have been the better part of an hour. In places the path was safer, but there were dangerous places where one slip meant a fall to my death. I forgot about the shadow figure below me. All my awareness was focused on the next jut of rock, the next hollow for the toe of my boot.

Before I fully realized it, I was standing on the ground. I looked around and saw I was alone. Cursing under my breath, I began to run along the road that led into the heart of the city.

Luck was with me. A tall shadow moved along the road ahead of me, walking with long strides that made surprisingly little sound. I could not see him well, but he leaned forward and seemed to slink along. There was something odd about the proportions of his body. His legs and arms were longer than they should have been. I wondered what was creating this curious illusion. He was a giant of a man who must have stood more than a full head and shoulders higher than me, when he straightened his back.

He led me through the sleeping city to a quiet road that bordered the date palms on a gentle slope. I was relieved to find that the way he was going ran nowhere near Jacob Hazan's house. Where the winding road was intersected by another road, I took a wrong turn and lost him. I ran back and down the way I guessed he had gone, taking care to peer into the darker shadows that lay next to the high walls bordering the road. It would have been easy in the darkness to run directly into him.

At last I stopped and stood with my hands clenched in frustration. My fingers and the muscles in my forearms ached from the long climb down from the fortress.

In the silence came the distant sound of wood splintering. I ran toward the sound, heedless of what lay in front of me. Another noise drew me along a crossing road.

In the starlight I saw that a door was missing from its frame. It had been ripped off and lay in the road. Sounds of struggle came from the black rectangle. I drew my dagger and approached with caution.

Inside the house, a man groaned in agony and something snapped, then came the sound of a body crumpling to the floor.

"Die, you mother-whore son of a diseased goat."

I had heard Martala curse often enough to recognize her voice. Steel clashed on stone several times.

"Martala, are you in there?"

"Stay out, Alhazred, it's too dark to see."

Ignoring her advice, I advanced on the doorway, only to be bowled over backwards by a massive form that emerged. It was too large for the door frame and had to straighten up when it was in the street. All I could see of it was an outline, but it had a curious smell, like newly turned earth. Something smaller flew from the doorway and began to attack its hunched back as I scrambled to my feet. The girl continued to curse as she struck at the figure with her knife. I saw sparks where her blade scraped against it.

Before I could use my dagger, the shadow ran to the wall at the side of the road and leapt over it. Its heavy footfalls pounded the earth as it ran through the date tree grove on the other side.

I grabbed the top edge of the wall to pull my head above it. The other side was nothing but a mass of darkness. There was no hope of following the shadow. Reluctantly, I lowered myself back to the road.

"It ripped the door off the house before I could get to it," Martala said, breathing heavily. "By the time I got inside, it had Asad ibn Bakr in its arms. It must be able to see in the dark, and it's as strong as an ox. It broke his back, I think. I stabbed it in the back while it was killing him but my dagger could not penetrate its skin. It's hard, like stone."

"I followed it from Yehudah Halevi's house."

"Did it kill the Jew?"

"I don't know. We'll have to inquire tomorrow."

"Do you suppose it's gone to kill the man Altrus is guarding?"

I looked up at the stars. "I doubt it. It will soon be morning."

We made our weary way to the inn where we had arranged for rooms upon our arrival at the oasis, undressed, and went to bed.

4.

Altrus returned to the inn early the next morning and woke us with

the clatter he made, throwing down his sword and dagger.

"I watched all night. Nothing happened," he said in disgust.

While we relieved ourselves in the chamber pot and dressed, we told him what he had missed.

"It was big," I said. "It walked with a crouch, but when it came out of the house it filled the entire doorframe."

"My dagger couldn't cut it," the girl added. "Its skin is too hard."

"What is it?" he asked. "A giant wearing armor?"

"That is the most reasonable explanation."

In my heart, I did not believe my own words. There was something unnatural about this assassin.

When the hour was more civilized, we took ourselves to Jacob Hazan's house. Judith greeted us and escorted us in. Her father was awake, and was just finishing his breakfast. Judith fed him with a spoon like a baby, wiping his chin with a cloth after each mouthful. When she was done, she told her maid to take away the breakfast tray, and I related the events of the night while Altrus and Martala stood at the back of the room and looked on silently.

Hazan's eyes blazed with awareness. He tried to speak, but only noises came from his lips. He clenched his right fist in frustration and motioned to his daughter with his index finger for her to bring the wax tablet. He wrote in haste, the stylus digging deep into the wax, while he rolled his right eye to see what he had written.

Judith looked at the tablet, then passed it to me. It took me a few moments to make out what was written there, so energetic were the strokes of the stylus. I read it aloud for the others.

"Golem."

Holding up the tablet for Judith to see, I pointed to the word. "What is this?"

She shook her head and glanced down at her father with a pitying expression.

"I fear his fit has injured his brain," she said, leaning close to whisper into my ear.

"But what is it?"

"It is nothing, a fairy story we Jews tell our children. The golem is a man made out of clay who is brought to life by the power of the names of our god. He serves the will of his maker, who sends him forth to slay the enemies of our people."

"What I fought last night was no fairy story," Martala told her.

"But such things are not possible." Judith looked at me. "Are they, Alhazred?"

"With magic, many things are possible. I have not read of this legend in my studies, but I would not say it is beyond the power of magic."

In the bed, Hazan waved his right hand to show his agreement with my words.

"When you and your father fled Damascus, did you carry his library with you?"

She shook her head, smiling at the thought.

"That would have required several wagons. We brought only those books my father considered essential to his work."

"I suppose they are in Hebrew."

"Some in Hebrew, some in Greek."

"Do you read Greek?"

She nodded.

"May I ask you to go through the books and look for any reference to the golem?"

"I will do as you ask, but my father may be able to make my work easier."

She positioned the wax tablet beneath his right hand and put the stylus between his fingers. He wrote several words.

"I know this book," she said, reading it. "I will look through it for references to this creature of clay."

"There is another possibility that has occurred to me," I told her. "If we are facing a worker of black magic, how can we be sure that your father's fit was natural?"

It was obvious this idea had not occurred to her by the sudden expression of alarm in her face. She stared at her father, who met her gaze calmly.

"If your house is being watched, as you suspect, it is not impossible that whoever sent forth the assassin also worked magic against your father to prevent him from investigating the matter."

"If I can catch the spy, we'll know soon enough," Altrus said.

"If the house is being watched, the spy will have reported to his master our arrival, and our appearances," the girl pointed out.

"I agree. We may all be targets." I looked around at the others. "We should not go anywhere alone, particularly at night."

"Can this thing move in the day?" Altrus asked.

I looked at Hazan. He made a hand gesture.

"My father says yes," Judith said.

"It probably stays in hiding during the day to prevent an alarm being raised throughout the oasis," I said.

"What are you going to do?" she asked.

"I want Martala to stay with you at the house. It may be that this creation of magic will not move about during the day, but I don't trust the man who watches you."

"If you wish it," Martala said.

"Altrus and I will climb to the fortress and determine whether Yehudah Halevi is living or dead. Later tonight we will watch over the house of the last man on Jacob's list, Fakhir ibn Hayyan."

5.

"Your concern for my welfare touches my heart, but I assure you, I am in no danger in my own house. My servants have been chosen for their military skill. They can protect me from all who might wish me harm."

Yehudah Halevi was the same elderly man with the flowing grey beard who had watched me from his window yesterday. When informed of our presence at his door by a manservant with a lean face and suspicious eyes, he had admitted us readily enough into his house and given us tea, then listened with admirable patience to our warning that he might be the target of an assassin.

Everything about him proclaimed his wealth – the elegant robes he wore, the gold chains about his neck and glittering rings on his fingers, the rich furnishing of his spacious house. His servants were many, and all men of military age.

"If the creature that broke the back of Asad ibn Bakr comes to you in the darkness, your servants will be of little help to you," I assured him.

He spread his bejewelled hands disarmingly.

"Why would anyone in Katiba want to kill me? I contribute a portion of my income to the upkeep of the city. I speak ill of no man."

"The events of thirty-eight years ago are not so easily forgotten."

"Yes, I remember those times," he said, nodding. "Terrible things were done to my people. Some were driven from their homes and robbed of their possessions, while others were permitted to remain here and tend the date palm groves."

"You were one of those permitted by Umar to remain," Altrus said.

"Yes." Halevi studied the mercenary, but his placid face betrayed none of his thoughts. "I was too valuable to send away. Umar knew that the date crop might fail without me to manage the harvest."

"Someone is killing those who collaborated with Umar's army," I told him bluntly. "The heads of prominent families are being assassinated. Do you have any idea who would be motivated to do such a thing?"

He shook his head.

"It seems like madness after the passage of so many years. What would anyone gain by it?"

"Vengeance, the strongest motive of them all," Altrus said.

I stood and went to a window on the wall of the house that was built above the fortification wall of the city. Opening the screens,

I leaned out. The sheer drop to the green date palm groves so far below made me dizzy, and I found myself gripping the frame of the window harder than necessary.

"Did you know there is a path on this side of your house that leads from the fortress to the groves below?"

"The old stair? Of course I know about it, but it hasn't been used by anyone for decades."

"You're wrong. Last night I watched the assassin of Asad ibn Bakr climb down it."

"You were watching my house?" he asked sharply with a frown.

"Only to keep you safe. A friend of mine, Jacob Hazan, believes that you have been targeted for death."

"Hazen, Hazen, the name is familiar, but I have not heard it for many years."

"His family was one of those forced to travel north by Umar and resettle in the lands near Damascus."

"Your friend is mistaken. I was never a collaborator. Ask any man who lived during the coming of Umar. They will tell you that I resisted, along with my father and grandfather, who both died because of it."

"Maybe the man who hired this assassin doesn't know that you resisted," Altrus said.

"Everyone knows. It is common knowledge here in the fortress."

"Is it so well known in the streets below?"

Halevi shrugged. "Perhaps not. I seldom descend to the groves these days. I have no reason to go down there."

I ran my fingers lightly over the spines of books in a bookcase that stood against a wall.

"You are very well read. Some of these books are quite rare."

"I have much time for leisure and prefer to occupy my mind with study."

"An admirable attitude."

"After all, if we do not strive always to improve ourselves, we are little better than animals, is that not so?"

"Indeed. Where did you get this book on poisons? I've sought it for years but never managed to find a copy."

"It was a fortunate acquisition from a dealer in Alexandria, many years ago."

He stood and came toward me.

"Now, if I have satisfied your concerns and the concerns of your friend – what was his name again?"

"Jacob Hazan."

"If I have satisfied you both that I am safe from any possible harm, perhaps you will leave me. I am weary and wish to sleep an hour before my midday meal."

"Are you sure you don't want me to watch over your house tonight, in case the assassin returns?"

"As I have told you, it would be quite unnecessary. I've enjoyed our chat. You must come again, Alhazred, and bring your friend Hazan with you."

"That won't be possible. Jacob suffered a fit and is bedridden. Half of his body is paralyzed."

"I'm sorry to hear that. Now, if you will excuse me ..."

We left the house and walked across the plaza under the bright sunshine of late morning. I could feel eyes watching my back from more than one window.

"Do you believe him?" Altrus asked.

"I made some inquiries about him in the marketplace yesterday. The common gossip is that his family did resist Umar, and paid a terrible price for it."

"What was the price? He doesn't appear to be suffering to me."

"As he said, his grandfather resisted with a sword and was killed. His father was tortured to force him to reveal the hiding place of the family gold, but he died without speaking. What Halevi didn't say was that his own young wife was also tortured to force Halevi to reveal the location of the treasure, but like his father he also refused. Both his wife and his infant son were killed by Umar as punishment for his stubbornness."

"A heavy price to pay for some gold. Why was Halevi not killed as well?"

"The Caliph needed his skills to oversee the date harvest. He was too valuable to execute. Or so they say in the marketplace."

We continued down a winding street toward the marketplace where we could get something to eat.

"Do you believe Halevi is telling all he knows?"

"On the contrary, I know for certain that he is lying."

Altrus studied the mask of glamour I use to conceal my disfigured face.

"How can you be so sure?"

"Do you remember that manservant with the lean cheeks and long nose who admitted us into Halevi's house?"

"What of him?"

"I'm certain he is the man who has been watching Jacob Hazan's house and following his daughter."

6.

"I'm delighted your cousin has offered to sleep with you in your bed tonight, but I would feel better if it were Martala."

Judith looked at the girl with a faint smile that made Martala bristle.

"Forgive me, Alhazred, but she is such a small girl. What can she possibly do to protect me?"

"Has your cousin ever killed a man?"

"No, of course she has not."

"Martala has killed men. She has a knife and knows how to use it. You and your father will be safer with her than you would be with any of your relatives."

We stood in the sitting room at Jacob Hasan's house. The old man was asleep. The physician had just left, and had reported to Judith that her father appeared to be recovering.

"Are you sure there is danger?" Judith asked.

"I feel it gathering about this house. You are not being watched for no reason. I wonder now if your father's fit was merely a coincidence."

"What do you mean?" she asked in alarm.

"I have no evidence, but I suspect he may have been poisoned."

These words stripped away the carelessness from her manner.

"Of course, if you think it best that Martala sleeps with me, it will be so."

"Have you found time to research the golem in your father's book?"

She nodded.

"What did you discover?"

"The golem is a creature of magic fashioned from clay mixed with human blood."

I considered this information. "That means a sacrifice must have been made to create it."

"The book was not explicit, but I assume so."

"It makes a kind of sense. Every living thing needs a soul. If the clay of the golem is to be animated with life, a soul must be induced to dwell within it."

"The soul of the person who was sacrificed," she said.

"That is the most convenient source."

She frowned and shook her head. "Only imagine how that poor soul must be suffering, as it is made to commit one murder after another. It is a terrible crime to make such an affront to the eyes of the Almighty."

"Remember to always keep your doors bolted and your windows shuttered at night."

"Where will you and Altrus be while I am guarding the house?" Martala asked me.

"Altrus will watch over Fakhir ibn Hayyan again tonight. He is still the most likely target of the assassin, according to your father's researches."

"I've talked to his Jewish neighbors," Altrus said. "They agree that he collaborated with Umar during the expulsion of the Jews from the Khaybar Oasis. He is not a popular man."

"Are you going to warn him?" Judith asked.

"No. We can't risk him fleeing the oasis. We need him to act as a target for the assassin."

"And you?" Martala asked me.

"I am going to keep watch at the base of what Halevi called the old stair, to see if the assassin descends again. If it does, I will follow."

Altrus hefted his latest acquisition, a long-handled mace with a spiked ball on the end. The ball was iron, but filled with lead.

"I hope it comes my way this time. I want to try this on its skin."

"Can you even swing that thing?" I asked with a doubtful smile.

"At least a dozen good, hard strokes. After that, it probably won't matter."

"The moon is starting to show itself," I said. "After tonight the assassin will go into hiding. We cannot stay in the oasis another month. This may be our one chance to stop him."

The night came on, as black as the heart of a forty-year-old harlot. It found me at the base of the prominence that supported the fortress of Katiba. It was a long vigil, and tedious. Fortunately for me, a breeze kept most of the mosquitoes away. One of the disadvantages of the wetness of the oasis were the swamps that bred insects of every kind, but chiefly those that bit and sucked blood. A secondary consequence was that night air was filled with bats. I did not hear their quiet flights, but could see them flashing across above my head by the stars their wings occluded. An occasional sleepy dog barked in the distance.

It must have been shortly after midnight when a shower of pebbles announced the descent of someone on the stair. I drew deeper into my hiding place.

A shadow outline dropped from the sheer wall of rock into a crouch and looked around. Again I was struck by its silence. It was uncanny for such a large body to be so quiet. I could not so much see it as feel its presence. The scent of warm clay filled my nose.

It began to walk with an ungainly loping stride of its long legs with its back bent and head lowered. As it was about to pass me, it stopped and seemed to test the air. I knew it could not see me, but somehow it sensed some trace of my presence. After a few moments, it resumed its progress down the gentle slope to the sleeping town. At what I hoped was a safe distance, I followed as only a ghoul could follow.

For a while the shadow seemed to be heading toward Jacob Hazan's house, but it turned down a side street and I realized it was going neither to the Jew's house nor to the house of Fakhir ibn Hayyan, where Altrus waited, but somewhere else. I had no recourse but to follow it.

It stopped before the door of a house in darkness. Before I could act, the door was torn off its hinges and thrown across the street, making a terrific crash in the silence. Two dogs started to bark from some distance away, and then a third animal joined in. A shriek sounded from inside the house, followed by noises of a struggle.

I hesitated to go into the dark dwelling, where my sword would be useless due to the constricted spaces and I would not be able to see anything.

The sound of breaking furniture came through the open doorway, followed by a crash of pottery. A flame began to flicker inside the house. I realized a hooded but still burning oil lamp had been knocked off a table or shelf to the floor, and shattering, had spilled its oil, which had then ignited.

The shadows of two conjoined figures were thrown onto an interior wall by the flames, one a giant with a malformed head and strangely elongated limbs, the other a woman. The giant lifted the woman by her shoulders and shook her until her neck broke. I heard it crack.

This was too much like the previous night's encounter, but this time I could not depend on Martala at my side. Against my better judgment, I forced myself into the house.

What I saw in the light of the spreading flames was something from nightmare. It was humanlike, but far from human. Sensing my presence, it dropped the dead woman and turned. The face on its wedge-shaped head looked like the face of a child's doll, with two shining black buttons for eyes, a barely formed nose, and a small round hole for a mouth that gave it a perpetual expression of dismay. It had no eyebrows, nor even eyebrow ridges, and its cheeks were flat. It had no ears, only ear holes, a defect we shared in common. King Huban of Sana'a had cut off my ears, along with my nose and prick, for deflowering his daughter. I was able to cover my mutilated face with a spell of glamour, but this monster had no concealment.

Without pausing to think about the mistake I was making, I darted forward and stabbed at where its heart should have been in its elongated, narrow torso. I heard and felt the tip of my dagger snap off. It came at me quickly, its enormous hands reaching forward, but I backed up with the same quickness and found myself on the street.

The neighbours had begun to awaken. Some peered curiously from their windows, while others clustered together in the street. A collective gasp of horror sounded when the monster stepped out of the burning house and straightened its back. It was taller than I had thought, almost six cubits. No hair of any kind grew on its body, a fact that was obvious due to its nakedness. Nothing dangled between its thighs, another detail of anatomy the monster and I shared in common.

I drew my sword and cut at one of its extended arms. Sparks flew up where the steel struck its rock-hard skin, but the blade left no mark. A man ran at it and thrust a kind of hay fork into its face, but the creature batted it aside. Others began to pry up stones from the road and threw them.

The monster turned and ran away with astonishing rapidity on its long legs. In a few steps it was lost in the darkness. The people stared after it in surprise, then realized the danger to their houses and began to try to put out the fire inside the dead woman's house by beating at it with blankets and articles of clothing. Fortunately, the house was mainly composed of mud bricks. The fire did not spread beyond the sitting room in which it had started.

"Whose house was this?" I asked one of the men who had fought the fire.

"Miriam Zebara lived there. She was an old widow. Why would anyone break into her house? She was poor. She owned nothing of value. Why was she killed?"

"Did she collaborate with Umar?"

He stared at me for several seconds, then said, "I will not speak ill of the dead."

I did not press him, but merely nodded and backed away. His eyes had told me all I needed to know. She should have been on Jacob Hazan's list. I wondered how many others there were like her.

Wasting no more time, I hurried after the monster. I had a good sense of where it was going. When I reached the base of the old stair, pebbles falling from above were clicking on the stones.

The climb up in the dark was less difficult than the climb down. I was able to close much of the distance between the monster and myself, so that when I saw it clamber past the top of the fortress wall and up the side of Yehudah Halevi's house, where it disappeared through a dark but open window, I was no more than a dozen body lengths behind.

The handholds and footholds up the side of the house were subtle, but I found them by touch. I realized this was the same window I had peered out from during my visit to the house the previous morning. After listening for any sounds inside, with great care I slid my body through the opening and stood in the darkness.

"Take him," a quiet voice said.

They came at me from three directions, pinning my arms while someone struck me in the head from behind. There was just barely enough light coming through the window for me to make out their outlines when they moved. They were ordinary men. I struggled to free my arms. The one who stood behind me hit me again, harder this time, and I slid into oblivion.

7.

A lamp burned. The light hurt my eyes. Squinting against it, I saw that I was in some sort of work room, tied upright to a wooden pillar. I could feel the grain of the wood with my fingers. My hands were bound behind my back and my knees had also been lashed to the pillar to keep me from collapsing to the floor while I was unconscious. There was a sickening scent in my nose hole that I recognized as drying blood. My neck felt sticky, so I assumed it was probably my own blood I was smelling. Scalp wounds have a tendency to bleed freely.

As my eyes slowly regained their focus, I saw that Yehudah Halevi stood before me, but he was not what I stared at. Behind him stood a figure from nightmare.

Its head almost touched the horizontal logs that supported the floor above. In overall shape it was vaguely human-like, but its proportions were all wrong. I had caught a glimpse of it in the firelight at the house of Miriam Zebara, as it towered over the old woman's corpse, but now I was able to study it in detail.

I shook my head. My eyes lost their focus and everything blurred. I realized that Halevi had been speaking to me. How much time had passed? His words were a kind of droning in my ear holes until I concentrated upon them.

"I thought you were not going to wake up again. In some ways that would have been the simple solution. Since you are still alive I will question you to discover all you know about Hazan and his researches concerning the expulsion."

He said something else but my mind would not separate the

words, and my eyes kept wandering to the monster that stood like a statue behind him. It was too tall, too thin, with legs longer than human legs and arms that ended in enormous hands like blocks of stone. Its little wedge-shaped head with its flat face stared at me from button-like eyes, but I sensed that it was not aware of me. It was asleep, or dormant. Something white projected from the small circular opening that formed its mockery of a mouth. The thing's entire face was like a child's attempt to mould a face in wet clay.

Halevi slapped me hard on the right cheek. I forced my eyes to focus on him.

"Pay attention, Alhazred. Stop drifting off. I want you to see how Joseph works. I'm very proud of my creation. Do you know that it took me more than twenty years of study and failed experiments before I was able to make him from clay? In some ways he is like the son that was taken from me by Umar so many years ago."

"Was your child's name Joseph?" My lips were dry and my tongue felt numb. I wondered how much damage that blow to the head had done to my brain.

"Yes. I took the name of my dead son for my creation, to honour his memory. He was so small, so frail, when one of Umar's officers dashed out his brains on my doorstep."

He put his hand on the inert monster's arm and rubbed it gently.

"Now my Joseph is strong. No one can hurt him."

"It is a very impressive creation," I said in an effort to make the madman talk. "How was it made?"

"That is a secret of my people," he said. "But I will tell you this – the ineffable name of our Lord has an infinite power both to create and to destroy, for what are they but the same thing? When something is created, the pattern from which it was made is destroyed. The two can never be separated. To make one thing is to unmake something else."

"I am a necromancer, as you know. You must have used more

than mere clay to make this assassin. You would have needed a concentrated measure of vital life force."

He nodded, pleased that I was taking an interest in his mania.

"Of course, you are correct. Such magic requires fresh blood. There is no other way."

"So you murdered a man to make a monster."

"Not a man. I wanted the soul of Joseph to be pure, unstained by the violent transformations of life. And the blood of the young is always more potent than the blood of the aged."

"A child," I said with understanding. "You murdered a child to make this abomination."

He frowned at me. "Have a care with your tongue, or I will cut it out."

"Not before you question me."

He snorted a stifled laugh.

"No, not before I question you. Not willingly. But have a care, Alhazred, lest you arouse my anger beyond my ability to control it."

"You were telling me about Joseph."

"Yes, that's right. You will enjoy this part, as a necromancer. It is so beautifully simple."

He went to the figure of hardened clay and plucked from its round mouth a small scroll of parchment, which he unrolled and held up to me. On it were Hebrew letters.

"Can you read this?"

I squinted at the parchment before my face. My vision blurred, then cleared, as I sounded the letters silently.

"It is the name of the old woman who was killed tonight."

"Yes, it is," he said. "You know Hebrew; I am impressed by your scholarship."

He went over to the lamp on his writing desk, which occupied a corner of the room, and held the parchment in the flame until it was consumed to ashes.

"To awaken Joseph is simplicity in itself. It is only necessary to insert the name of his intended target into his mouth, and he comes alive and seeks out the man or woman to whom the name belongs. When he has completed his task, he returns here and falls dormant until the next time."

He came close to my face and smiled.

"You had better answer my questions when I ask them, or I will put your name into Joseph's mouth."

"At least it would be quick."

"That is true," he said. "Joseph is a simple child."

"Before you question me, answer me this – did you poison Jacob Hazan?"

He decided to humour me. He was feeling good about the night's work.

"Yes, but the old fool was stronger than I ever imagined he could be."

"Why not send Joseph after him?"

Halevi shrugged. "He was not a collaborator with Umar. Joseph is an instrument of justice."

"Is it justice to kill old men and women for something that was done so long ago?"

"Yes," he said angrily. "It is the only justice the dead will ever find. It is the only justice for my own dear boy."

"That thing isn't for justice. It's an instrument of vengeance."

He hit me again, this time with his fist. I tasted blood and spat it out. The binding around my wrists were too tight to slip. I had been trying to loosen them since awakening but they gave no indication of stretching, and I could not reach the knots with my fingers, which in any case were becoming numb.

Somewhere behind me a door opened and shut. A household servant came into my field of view. He glanced at me with indifference and leaned close to whisper into Halevi's ear.

"I must leave you for a time. Joseph here will keep you company until I return."

Halevi and the servant walked behind me and I heard the

door open and shut. There was silence. The man of clay stared at me with its button eyes, which must have been made of polished obsidian. Its round little mouth mocked me. I almost expected to see a tongue snake out from it, but the figure remained inert and lifeless.

The door opened and shut behind me.

"That didn't take long," I said.

Something tugged at the bindings around my wrists. I realized the thin loops of rope were being peeled away from my skin, where they had sunk deeply into the swollen flesh. My arms came free from the pillar. I waited patiently until my knees were cut loose from their bindings. When I turned, I saw Martala standing there with her little dagger. Her face bore an expression of concern.

"What's wrong, girl?"

"Alhazred, your head and face are covered with blood."

"It's nothing. How did you get into the house?"

She was looking at Joseph with mingled awe and fear. I had to repeat the question.

"When the assassin struck elsewhere in the city, Altrus knew he was on a fool's errand and returned to Hazan's house. The two of us went to the base of what you call the old stair to look for you. Altrus was afraid to climb it. He's coming up the long way."

"You weren't afraid."

She smiled. "No. You know me, I can climb like a monkey."

"How did you get into the house?"

"I'm coming to that. I reached the top of the stair and found an open window. But I think a servant heard me enter. They are all awake now with the lamps blazing light. I was trying to hide when I found my way here."

"Where are we?"

"In the back of the house on the ground level."

"They must be searching for you now." When I listened I could hear footfalls and the occasional murmur of a voice.

"Altrus won't be long."

"He may not arrive soon enough."

I felt my belt for my sword and dagger with my tingling fingers. Both were missing, but Gor's skull still hung on my belt. Evidently Halevi had not thought it important enough to remove.

"You need a weapon," the girl said. She began searching around the room.

My eyes strayed to Joseph.

"We have a weapon, if I dare use it."

"What do you mean?"

I did not answer, but went to the writing desk and tore a strip of parchment from the bottom edge of a letter. Taking up the quill that rested upright in its pen holder, I opened the lid of the inkwell, dipped the nib, and carefully wrote what I conceived to be the Hebrew letters of Yehudah Halevi's name. My Hebrew was not extensive. I wondered what would happen if I spelled the name wrong.

There was no time to let the ink dry by itself. I blotted it with the desk blotter and blew on it to dry it, then quickly rolled the scrap of parchment into a tight little scroll.

"What are you doing?" Martala asked.

"Making a weapon." I stopped and looked at her. "No, not a weapon – an instrument of justice."

I shoved the scroll into the round mouth of the statue. A kind of dull redness pulsed along its limbs, and I felt heat radiating from it. Slowly, it straightened up and looked down at me.

I pointed at the closed door and tried to keep my voice steady.

"Go and do your task."

It moved with that eerie smoothness and silence that I had noticed in the darkened streets. I expected it to break the door down, but it merely opened it and bent its back to fit its long body through the opening. I went over and closed the door.

"What have you done?" the girl said, staring at me with wide eyes.

"Saved our lives, if we're lucky."

"The servants will fight to protect their master."

"I'm counting on it. There are too many of them for Altrus and we two to handle."

From the forward parts of the house came shouts of alarm and challenge, the clash of steel against stone, and the crashing of furniture. Then the screams began. Gradually, the sounds diminished.

The door opened and Joseph ducked his grotesque head to get through the opening. Now that I knew his name, I could no longer think of him as merely an "it." His stony body was covered in splashes of red blood, and his hands and forearms were red almost up to the elbows. He walked across the floor, ignoring us, and resumed his former place, then ceased to move.

I approached him with caution and laid a hand on his arm. It was cold, merely hardened clay. Reaching up, I plucked the scroll out of his mouth, carried it to the desk, and set it on fire as I had seen Halevi do earlier.

"What happened here?" Altrus demanded.

He entered cautiously with his sword drawn. He eyed the figure of Joseph but did not approach him.

"Is Halevi dead?" I asked.

"Torn into two parts, by the look of it. His servants haven't fared very well, either."

"Are they all dead?"

"Most of them. At least two ran away as I approached the house." He sheathed his sword.

"Shall we get out of here?" Martala asked. "That wound on your head needs tending to."

I looked at Joseph, stroking Gor's skull meditatively with my thumb. Going to the desk, I tore another scrap of parchment and wrote Hebrew letters on it, blotted it, rolled it rightly, and pressed it into the mouth of the clay figure.

When the clay warmed and came to life, Altrus jumped back to the wall and drew his sword. I waved for him to put it away.

"You know what you must do," I told the monster.

He made no response to my words, but began to walk toward the door. We followed him out of the room and through the house. The rooms were brightly lit with lamps. Splashes of wet blood covered the floor tiles, the walls, the overturned furniture, even the ceilings. Corpses, many missing limbs, lay strewn about like discarded dolls.

Following the silent giant to the front door, I stepped between the two halves of Halevi's corpse, taking care not to get his blood on my boots.

"Where is it going?" Altrus asked.

We followed Joseph across the plaza to the top of the fortification wall. He stopped and stood at the edge, staring downward. Dawn had just begun to turn the eastern horizon a pale pink.

The monster looked at me over his shoulder. His face was incapable of expression, but I felt something in his black eyes, or thought I did. Then, with infinite slowness, he allowed himself to topple forward into space. Many seconds later we heard his body shatter against the rocks.

THE SHORTCUT

1.

We were less than a day's camel ride outside of Damascus, returning from our visit to the Khaybar Oasis, when I decided to take a shortcut that would save us more than an hour on the road. For some reason that was not obvious to me, the road made a large loop around a section of terrain that did not appear in any way impassable. I had ridden the road often, and taken the loop without question, as travels usually will, but today I felt an impatience to get home. I was tired of the rolling lurch of the animal under my legs.

Predictably, my companions were less than enthusiastic.

"If the road turns to the side and goes around this place, there must be a good reason," Altrus pointed out.

"The reason is not evident to me."

"Nor to me, but that doesn't mean there's no reason."

"Those who stray from the trodden path wander in thickets and thorns," Martala quoted.

"I'm not interested in your Egyptian proverbs. I'm tired, the bones of my buttocks ache, and I want to get home before darkness falls."

They both became silent, but I saw them look at each other and roll their eyes.

We will see who is right, I thought grimly, and resolved to ride a straight path regardless of what opposed our way.

Like most such resolves, mine was destined to fall by the wayside. After a time we came to an impassable ridge of rock we could not ride around. There was a way through it, but so narrow a way that it was impossible for our camels to follow it.

"He who rides highest falls furthest," Martala quoted with satisfaction.

I made my camel kneel and dismounted in disgust.

"Where are you going?" Altrus asked. "I thought you were in a hurry to get home."

"I'm going to stretch my legs. You may join me, or not, as you wish."

Without waiting for their reply, I slid my body sideways between the rocky outcroppings on either side of the narrow way and pressed through it.

After walking for several minutes, I came to the crest of a gentle downward slope where the terrain opened and allowed me to see that a shallow valley lay before me. At one time a river had flowed through it. The track of the dry riverbed was still discernable on the sand. Beside it stood the remains of an ancient walled city.

"What is this place?" Martala asked behind me. "Have you ever heard of it before?"

I shook my head.

"It's too close to Damascus to be unknown."

"It's unknown to me."

"The city has been a ruin for a long time," Altrus said. "Most of the roofs of the houses have fallen in, and the fortification wall that surrounds the city has collapsed in places as well."

I looked at the two of them. Martala just shrugged.

"So much for reaching Damascus before nightfall," Altrus said with disgust.

We descended toward the dry river course.

The city was little different from most ruins. It had been built from cut stones instead of mud bricks, and so was in a better state of preservation than some abandoned habitations I had seen in my travels. We entered the walls through the arched gateway, which was still standing. It was a Roman arch, if that meant anything. The timber gate itself had long since turned to dust, leaving iron bolts and straps lying in heaps on the sand.

Over the centuries, the capricious winds had kept the streets scoured clean of sand. They might just as easily have buried the entire city. I saw that the streets were wide and well laid out.

"I wonder what happened to the inhabitants?" Martala mused as we wandered along, with the ruined buildings on either side.

"The river ran dry, and the inhabitants moved to a place where they could find water," I speculated. "Of all necessities, water is foremost."

"They must have had wells."

"Why would they have had wells, living beside a river?"

"They could have dug wells," she persisted.

"Who knows?" I said with a shrug. "Maybe they did, and found that the well water was tainted and undrinkable."

"Such speculation is pointless," Altrus said. "We'll never know what happened to them. Nor do I greatly care."

All at once, a dizziness came over me. I clutched at the arms of my companions, who walked on either side, and we stood holding onto each other as the earth seemed to shift and roll beneath our feet.

"Look at the sun," Martala said.

Looking up, I blinked in amazement. The sun was moving across the heavens. I could not stare directly at it, but looked to one side and watched it slide across the zenith and decline in the west. As it touched the rocky hills, the sky paled, then darkened and became filled with stars. Amid them was a waxing moon.

I released my companions and shook my head to clear it, then turned all around. We were still within the ruined city, but it was night.

"What we just saw ..." Altrus said.

"Was impossible," I finished for him. "The sun cannot move at such a pace across the heavens."

"Maybe it was moved by magic."

"There is no magic that can move the sun. It is a vast sphere unimaginably far away from us, and our Earth revolves around it."

"I thought the sun went around the Earth," Altrus said.

"So do many people believe, but it is not true. The Greek philosophers have proved it."

"What are you saying?" the girl demanded. "That what we saw happen did not happen?"

"It could not have happened. No magic I know could cause such a violation of nature."

"Yet is it not written in the holy books of the Jews that the sun stood still in the heavens?"

"Many absurdities are written in holy books."

"Say what you will," Altrus told me. "I will believe what I saw with my own eyes until I have a reason not to."

The silver of the waxing moon lined the silent buildings around us and frosted the paving stones in the street. I shivered in the chill night breeze, and felt a sudden and intense urge to be away from this strange city.

"Let us return to our camels."

We turned and retraced our steps. After walking for some time, we stopped and looked at each other. Altrus said the words we were all thinking.

"We should have reached the gateway long ago."

"Could we have turned the wrong way?" Martala wondered.

"We'll go back and turn the other way," I said.

We retraced our steps to the intersection, and continued through it in the opposite direction. After walking for many minutes, we stopped again.

"This city cannot be so large," Altrus said in disgust. "We should have reached the wall long ago."

"Let us try another direction," I said, trying to keep my voice emotionless.

After walking for long enough to have put us a mile away from the ruins, we were still in the city streets. They seemed to stretch on forever in every direction. Which was both absurd and impossible.

There was no bluster remaining in Altrus's manner.

"What's going on, Alhazred?"

Inside me a clamorous alarm bell was ringing. I had to resist the urge to run wildly down the street. I looked at the windows of the silent ruins that watched us like dead eyes.

"I don't know."

2.

Morning came. We had wandered the streets of the city all night, unable to find a way out or even to reach the wall that surrounded it.

"This is like the great labyrinth we have in Egypt," the girl said.

We were all tired of walking, and weary from lack of sleep. My lips were dry and beginning to crack. I licked them but my tongue was also dry.

"We can climb to the top of the highest building," I suggested. "Now that it is daylight, we may be able to see our way out."

Even as I spoke these words, the rising sun began to move across the heavens. We held onto each other as the ground heaved and slid beneath us. In moments the sun reached the west and declined to the horizon. There was a moment of twilight, and it was night once again.

"I'm getting dry," Altrus said.

I tested my mouth and cursed silently. My tongue was beginning to swell. It was as though we had stood beneath the hot sun for an entire day, instead of for a dozen seconds.

"I should have brought a water skin with me when I left the

camels," I said with difficulty due to the dryness of my tongue, and tasted blood from the cracks in my lips.

"How could you know you would need it?" Martala said.

"Never walk abroad in the desert without water," I recited. It was one of my sayings, which no doubt my companions were tired of hearing me repeat.

I thought about the fat, cool water skins that presently hung over the saddles of our camels, which should have been no more than ten minutes walking from where we stood.

Looking around in the moonlight, I found a way up the side of a building that retained a part of its second level and climbed the wall.

"What do you see?" Altrus asked.

"The gateway is in that direction," I said.

He looked down the street in the direction I pointed.

"I don't see it."

"You should be able to see it. I could almost hit it with a stone."

Climbing back down to the street, I set off in the direction where I had seen the open gateway. They followed me without speaking. We walked for half an hour or so before I stopped in frustration.

"This is not possible. None of it is possible."

"Maybe we are all dreaming and we will wake up," Altrus said with some of his customary sarcasm.

"If so, let it be soon," the girl said. "I need a drink of water."

My thoughts were grim. Unless we got out of this confounding city we would all die of thirst. I chose another high place and climbed to the top. It was as though we had not moved from the previous place I had climbed. There was the arched gateway, mocking me with its nearness, yet no closer than it had been before. I climbed down, jumping the last few cubits to the street.

"This is a haunted place," Martala said.

"Don't talk nonsense, girl," Altrus scolded her.

"It must be cursed. What other explanation can there be?"

Movement caught the corner of my eye.

"Look, down the street. Something is coming this way."

We slowly began to back up. Altrus and I both drew our swords. I saw that it was a column of soldiers marching four abreast, with a single officer in front to lead them. But there was something not right about them. They were completely silent, and I could see the decaying walls of the ruined city through their transparent bodies, which seemed to glow with silver light. Indeed, they almost appeared to be made of moonlight. They were dressed in the armor of ancient Roman soldiers, and many of them had arrows jutting from their bodies. They looked exhausted, as though they had just fought a long, hard battle. There was something else wrong, but I could not place it until the girl spoke.

"Look at their leader."

He wore the armor of a Roman centurion and carried his helmet under his right arm. His head was inside the helmet. The neck between his shoulders ended in a stump. The head opened its mouth as if to speak, and a stream of milky liquid poured forth. It was not vomit, but thicker and heavier, like molten metal.

We tried to back up more quickly, but they were on us before we could react. Then they were passing through us as though we were made of air. I felt a kind of coolness as their transparent bodies slid through my flesh. In seconds the entire column had passed through us. We stood bewildered and watched it diminish in the distance down the street.

"What just happened?" the girl asked.

Altrus said nothing, but merely looked at me.

"Were they ghosts?" she asked.

"Have either of you ever read the story of the Battle of Carrhae?"

They shook their heads.

"A Roman army led by Crassus fought the Parthians just outside the city of Carrhae. Parthian archers, firing their arrows from horseback as they rode, cut the Roman infantry to pieces. It was one of the worst military defeats ever suffered by Rome. When

Crassus tried to negotiate a peace treaty, the Parthians cut off his head. The story goes that they poured molten gold into his mouth as a mockery of his well-known love for that metal. The Roman quaestor Cassius led ten thousand surviving Roman troops from Crassus's army in retreat back to Syria, where he ruled the land as proquaestor for two years. He led them back to this land we're standing on."

"Do you really believe what we saw was the defeated army of Crassus?" Altrus asked.

"I don't know what to believe," I admitted.

We walked onward. What else was there to do? As we moved through the city, we began to see ghostly figures going about mundane tasks. In front of a forge a blacksmith was fashioning horseshoes. A woman carried a board laden with freshly baked loaves of bread. Another woman walked with a pitcher of water balanced on her head. A child ran after another child, chased by a dog. Their clothing was Roman and centuries out of date. All these figures were completely silent, and none of them noticed us as we passed through their midst.

"They are all ghosts," the girl said in wonder. "The entire city is haunted."

"If we don't find water, we'll be joining them," Altrus pointed out.

"Follow the woman with the bread," I said with sudden inspiration.

We ran after her as she was about to round a corner and managed to keep her within sight, although she walked with deceptive quickness, and seemed to glide above the paving stones in the street without quite touching them.

The throng of silent silver people around us thickened. Suddenly we found ourselves standing in a marketplace. In the center of this crowded space, a marble fountain bubbled, sending a stream of water several feet into the air to cascade down on all sides and fill a large circular marble bowl.

Altrus ran to the fountain, then stopped. His shoulders sagged. As I approached at a walking pace behind him, I realized the fountain made no sound. Dipping my hand into the bowl, I drew up a fistful of dry sand.

"I've never heard of a ghost fountain before," Martala said.

All the food and drink that was being sold around us consisted of nothing more than moonlight. The citizens of the city were mere silver shadows.

3.

The coming of the first light of dawn dispelled the ghosts. One moment they were all around us, and the next, we were alone in the empty marketplace. We continued to sit on the lip of the dry fountain, too weary to move. When the sun began to arc its way across the blue vault above, we held tight to the fountain to keep from falling and waited for the dizziness to pass while day became night and the stars filled the sky. The crescent of the waxing moon was a little fatter than it had been the night before.

I tried to lick my lips and cut my tongue on the rough edges of their bloody cracks. My tongue was dry. I could not swallow. No saliva would come into my mouth.

"We need water and sleep, or we will die," Altrus said with a dry croak.

He and the girl must have been suffering great hardship. My father was a djinn of the ninth circle, and his blood gave me more resistance to thirst than that of ordinary human beings.

"If we don't get out of this accursed city this night, you and the girl may not live to see another."

"What about you?" the girl said. "Are you immune to thirst?"

"Not immune, but I can live longer than you can without water."

We continued to sit without speaking. None of us felt any urge to get up. What was the point, when we were doomed anyway?

I cursed out loud and stood, then held onto the fountain until my dizziness passed. Wherever this doomed attitude came from, I wanted no part of it. I would crawl if I had to, but I would not sit and die. I pulled each of my companions roughly up.

"We will try again."

"Why?" Altrus croaked. "We know it is futile."

"No, we don't know that. Put that idea out of your head. Fight it."

I saw lines of concentration in his face, and when his eyes focused on me, they blazed with anger.

"You're right, Alhazred. We can't give up."

The girl nodded agreement but her mouth was too dry to speak.

Something that had troubled my thoughts before came back to me. We were so dry, it was almost as though we had all stood under the blazing sun for three full days, yet the days had passed in seconds. We should not be as dry as we were.

"We will try something different tonight," I told them.

Pointing to a place where the wall of a house had crumbled to within two cubits of the ground, I told them to climb on top of it.

"What are we doing?" Altrus demanded when he was balanced on the wall.

"When I climbed the ruins, I could see the gateway. If we keep moving over the tops of the ruins, maybe the gateway will remain in view, and we will be able to reach it."

"It's worth a try," Martala managed to say huskily in her throat.

I did not like the look of the girl. She swayed, and had trouble climbing up on the wall. Normally she was as nimble as a monkey and could climb anything. I resolved to stay close behind her so that I could catch her if she started to fall.

We climbed the ruins until we found a high place that offered a clear view of the arched opening, no great distant from us. Then we started toward it. For half an hour we clambered over the broken rock walls, always moving in the general direction of the gateway. Finally we stopped. For a long time none of us spoke.

"It isn't getting any nearer," Altrus said at last.

"It's impossible," Martala said. She swayed and I caught her elbow to steady her.

"Let's keep going for a while, to be certain."

They did not argue with me. We continued to climb for the better part of another half hour over the jagged walls of the ruined houses, with loose stones turning and slipping from under our boots to the streets below. When we stopped again, there was no doubt in anyone's mind. We were no nearer the gateway than when we started, and no nearer to any other part of the enclosing fortification wall that wrapped around the nameless city.

Martala giggled. "It's like a trap, and we are caught in it."

"Don't laugh," I cautioned her.

"Why not? Don't you think it's funny?"

"If you start laughing, you may not be able to stop."

This took her smile away. She licked the blood on her lips. Every time we smiled or talked, the cracks in our lips opened and bled.

"I saw a piece of amber once," Altrus said. "It had a fly in it. The fly looked alive, it was so perfect in every way, but it had been trapped in that stone for aeons."

"We are not flies," I said grimly.

We found a low spot on one of the walls and climbed to the street.

"I'm going to search the interiors of the houses and other buildings for a well."

They did not argue with me. For the rest of the night we made a meticulous search through all the houses for a well in their floors. It was not an easy search. The interiors were cluttered with stones fallen from the walls and tiles from the roofs, and we had to bear in mind that any well might be covered over with slates. During the course of the night we managed to work our way back to the marketplace.

"It's coming again," Altrus said as he studied the pale eastern sky of early dawn.

We stood facing each other and joined hands by silent mutual consent. Again the sun sped across the blue vault of the heavens and fell from sight in the west. The stars came into view with the moon in their midst, its waxing body another day fatter.

"I think we are going to die here," Altrus said.

Saying nothing, I led them to the fountain, where they sat. They were almost too weary and weakened from lack of water and lack of sleep to stand. I wondered why none of us had slept? That, too, was unnatural, just another unnatural thing in this unnatural city.

"I am going to look for a way out," I muttered.

Neither of them moved. They sat slumped forward with their heads bowed. I did not repeat myself, but walked out of the marketplace and along a street that ran directly away from it with as brisk a pace as I could manage, determined to reach the outer wall of the city. If sheer determination and force of will could have achieved it, I would certainly have succeeded, but in the end I was forced to give up and turn in defeat. Hopelessness rose from some dark place in my soul and covered my heart like a shadow.

Do not despair, my love, Sashi said in my mind.

Her beautiful human face swam before my eyes, and I saw that there were tears on her cheeks.

I don't know what to do, I told her with my thoughts. Altrus was right. We're caught like flies in amber.

You will find a way. I have faith in you, beloved.

Her words gave me heart. My anger rose up again within me, hot and red. I found the strength to stagger along the street until I reached the marketplace. There was never any difficulty finding the marketplace. It was as though we were intended to remain there.

As I entered, I saw Altrus and Martala stretched face down across the paving stones of the plaza that surrounded the dry fountain. Neither moved when I croaked out their names.

I stumbled toward them and fell to my knees between them, then turned them over and felt for a pulse in their necks. Both were still alive, but near death. I could not hold back the scream of rage and frustration that rose in my throat, so I tilted back my head and released it to the night.

From somewhere high above I heard a chuckle of amusement.

4.

I dropped my head, pretending I had not heard it, and began to think furiously. Someone was watching us, someone we could not see, someone in the sky. The words the girl had spoken earlier returned to me. She had said, "It's like a trap, and we are caught in it." A trap. Yes, it was like a trap, but how had it been constructed? By magic? No, what I had told Altrus days ago still held true. No magic I knew could speed the sun across the heavens. That meant that this trap was not a real thing, but an illusion of some kind.

I marvelled at the thought. To make the spell of glamour that concealed my disfigured face from the sight of others was one thing, but to construct so vast a glamour as to contain an entire city, and to project it into the minds of three different people at the same time, was a truly impressive feat of magic.

Now that I knew what I was facing, it might be possible to fight it. But I would have to do so in such a way that whoever watched was not alerted.

Crawling to Martala, I eased the girl into a sitting position with her head propped up against the side of the fountain. As I did so, I marked a half circle in the dust on the plaza with the toe of my boot. Turning to Altrus, I pulled him up against the fountain, and made a second half circle so that the ends of the two crescents met around me. Now I had a full circle of the art to work within.

The magic would be difficult. I lacked the tools and materials I usually relied on. As though I were too weary to stand, I pulled myself to a kneeling posture and sat back on my heels, then bowed my head and closed my eyes.

Now I was within myself, and the illusion created to trap me lay outside my circle. I silently spoke a cleansing prayer to purge my circle of any lingering traces of hostile magic, concentrating as I did so, on a pure white light that filled both my mind and the circle around me. I felt the shadows of the illusion scatter out from the circle like broken shards of black glass. I made the white light more intense in my imagination, and began to purge the circle using the powers of the four elements, first fire, then water, then air, and finally earth.

When I finished, I knew that no trace of any illusion could hold sway over my mind. Opening my eyes, I searched the sky without raising my head.

A human figure robed in black floated some twenty or thirty cubits above me. It was a young bald monk who watched me with a smile on his lips. Something about the way he was robed pricked at my memory, and suddenly I knew who he was and why he was trying to kill me.

It was one of the monks from the Christian monastery of Saint John the Divine on the Mountain of Shadows, which was located far to the northeast of Damascus. Some of the monks of that place possessed the power to levitate their bodies through the air. The previous year I had gone to the monastery with my companions to steal a relic reputed to possess great powers of magic. In the end the relic had proved too powerful for me to hold onto, but the monks had not been able to recover it, and this had aroused their hatred against me.

I even recognized the face of this flying monk. He was the same young man Martala had bedazzled with her womanly charms. His name came to me – Brother Manasseh. While we had known him, he had not possessed the ability to levitate, but it appeared that over the intervening months he had learned the skill.

I glanced at other parts of the heavens but saw no other flying monks. When I returned my gaze to the marketplace, I realized the city had vanished, along with the fountain behind us. The three of us were on the sand and stones of the open desert, where we had wandered under the monk's spell for the past four days.

An animal grunt drew my attention to the left. There, no great distance away, stood our three camels. I could see the water skins slung over the saddles even in the dim moonlight, so near were the placid beasts.

It was only with great difficulty that I controlled the anger that rose within my breast. How long has this monk studied the spell of glamour he had used against us? Months, probably. The fact that he was alone suggested it was some kind of solitary quest for vengeance on his part. It must have hurt his young pride when the girl cast him aside so easily.

I stood slowly and waited for the blood to begin to flow through my legs once more. When the tingling passed away, I drew my dagger from my sheath. With my head bowed, I brought the curved blade up to my throat and held it there.

As I expected, the monk descended and floated nearer to me. He had no idea that I could see him, so he used no caution in his approach. When he floated no more than ten cubits away, and came no nearer, I lowered the knife and stared directly at him.

"No, Manasseh, this dagger is not for me," I said in Greek, using as powerful a voice as my dry throat could manage. "It is for you."

As I finished speaking, I threw the dagger at him.

I did not expect to kill him with the knife. A thrown knife is seldom an effective weapon. But, as I hoped, the surprise of hearing me speak his name, coupled with the pain when the point of the knife embedding itself in his throat, knocked him out of the sky as effectively as an arrow downs a flying bird. He was unable to maintain the concentration of mind that allowed him to levitate.

Before he could recover his mental balance, or unleash some other weapon of magic against me, I ran to him and threw myself on top of him. Snatching my dagger point from his throat, I turned it and slashed across the shallow wound with its edge. Blood gushed out over my hand.

"The girl always said you were a fool," I told him in Greek, glaring into his eyes. This was a lie – Martala had never spoken words against him.

I had the satisfaction of watching and feeling the life leave his body. After I assured myself that he was dead, I stood and searched the stars for any other floating monks. There were none. This fool had acted alone, and even so had very nearly killed the three of us.

I approached the camels slowly so as not to startle them. They remained where they were. Taking a water skin off my saddle bow, I carried it back to my companions and poured water into their mouths, forcing them to swallow some of it to avoid choking. For a time I thought the girl was too far gone to revive, but eventually she opened her large grey eyes.

When they were both recovered enough to understand what I was saying, I told them what had happened.

"It's always a bad idea to rob a monastery," Altrus said. "Monks clutch their grudges to their hearts like strings of pearls."

"So the entire city was nothing but an illusion," the girl said, staring around the empty desert in wonder.

"Not just the city. The bend in the road does not exist. The idea of taking a shortcut was put into my mind to get us away from the road. The narrow passage through the rocky ridge doesn't exist, either. It was a way of separating us from our camels."

When they were recovered enough to stand up, I supported them as we walked to the camels, and helped them climb upon their backs.

"Everything that happened to us from the time we left the road was false," Martala said, as though having difficulty accepting it.

"The monk had control of our thoughts even before we left the road," I told her. "He must have been floating above us, watching us as we rode along, listening to our words and gloating over his plan to kill us."

"I should have slit his throat that night he lay in my bed at the monastery," she said darkly.

"Don't worry about it. That oversight has been remedied."

"Will the monks send someone else, do you think?" Altrus asked.

"If they do, we'll be ready for them. They won't catch us with the same illusion."

In my own mind I wondered what other plots they might contrive to kill us, but I did not speak my concern to my companions.

The sun was setting at its usual slow pace when at last we rode through the gates of Damascus.

THE HAIRY COMET

1.

I joined Harkanos on the roof of his house at the tenth hour of night by my water clock as he had requested in his terse note. It was the first time I had been with him since delivering the corpse of his young daughter, killed by her kidnappers during an ill-conceived rescue attempt. I was unsure how he would greet me, but I need not have worried. He welcomed me as though nothing unpleasant had occurred between us.

A platform was built on the roof for observing the stars. Harkanos was a renowned astrologer, with many wealthy clients in Damascus, and the only way to cast accurate astrological charts was to take measurements directly from the heavens.

To my surprise, the white-bearded ancient, Abdul-Basir, was also present. He wore a Persian robe of midnight blue silk covered with gold and silver stars, and on his head a conical hat. He was using an enormous set of wooden astrological dividers, each side of which was longer than his leg, to measure the angle between Mars and Jupiter. He nodded to me when I climbed the iron ladder that led to the elevated section of the rooftop.

"I'm glad you could come," Harkanos said. "I need your judgment in a matter of some importance."

Leaning back, I looked almost straight up into the dark sky at the new comet that had appeared the week before. It was larger every night.

"You are much more learned than I in the interpretation of starry portents."

"It is your judgment about earthly matters that I value the most," he said.

He handed me an oval disk of glass.

"View the comet through this."

Shrugging, I raised it to my eye.

"Remarkable."

"It is a kind of filter that intensifies a certain colour usually difficult to see with the eye alone."

Through the disk the comet appeared twice as long, and many fine details were visible. Its tail was hairy, with thin tendrils extending out to the sides, and divided into two parts like the tongue of a serpent.

"You know what this means," Harkanos said darkly.

"The hairy comet with a tail divided is a most ominous portent," I said. "It foretells the fall of a king or the overthrow of an empire."

"It is the single worst astrological portent I have seen in my lifetime," Abdul-Basir said. "As you know, young Alhazred, that is a very long time."

"Can there be any doubt that it pertains to the reign of Moawiya?" Harkanos asked him.

"None at all. I have examined the Caliph's own birth stars in relation to the comet's angle and position, and the significance could not be more clear."

"What significance?" I asked the elderly mage.

"Moawiya will lose his throne. He will be cast down and humiliated."

This alarmed me. Moawiya came as close as anyone in the

world to what I would consider a friend. Over the past year I had grown to admire the brash young Caliph, who was very near my own age.

"Do you foresee assassination?"

Abdul-Basir eyed the heavens and considered, then shook his hoary head.

"No. But it will not be a gracious exit for the young ruler."

"Marwan's malice against him has been steadily growing since Marwan moved to Damascus to live," Harkanos said.

"He wants to found a dynasty with his own bloodline," Abdul-Basir agreed. "Moawiya is a stone in his path."

"If what you say is true, it will not be easy for the mages who dwell in the Lane of Scholars," I said. "Marwan hates us as much as the old Caliph, Yazid, ever did, and he has no mental illness to cloud his judgments against us."

"That is why I asked you to come here tonight," Harkanos said. "We must do what we can to make the transition of power as smooth as possible, lest Marwan should see fit to make examples of us to demonstrate the firmness of his rule."

"What has that to do with me?"

"You know Moawiya better than any of us. It falls to you to warn him of the comet's significance."

"He will take it better from you than he would from us," Abdul-Basir said.

Putting the disk of glass to my eye, I regarded the comet for several minutes in silence while I thought on the matter. Whoever carried the ill news to the Caliph risked arousing his displeasure, and that was not something to do lightly. He had the power to have me executed with a single word of command. I did not believe he would react this way, but I could appreciate why no other necromancer in the Lane of Scholars wanted to bear him bad news.

"I will take the official judgment of the Council of Mages to the Caliph," I said. "As Moawiya's friend, I owe him that much."

"Thank you, Alhazred." Harkanos laid a hand on my shoulder. "I knew we could depend on you."

"There is another matter," Abdul-Basir said.

"What would that be?" I asked.

"I have consulted the oracles about this hairy comet, and have interrogated the spirits of the upper air. They are in agreement that this comet carries with it an evil intelligence from beyond the stars."

"You mean, a passenger?"

He nodded.

"It will soon leap across the gulf of space and descend to our world, if it has not already done so."

"What must we do to stop it?"

"We cannot prevent it from coming to the earth," Harkanos said. "We can only remain vigilant. It is likely to be attracted to the focus of the comet's dark portent."

"Damascus," I said.

"Very likely," Abdul-Basir agreed. "Damascus is the jewelled navel of the world, and the prime seat of earthly power."

"How will we recognize this evil when it arrives?"

Neither mage had an answer.

2.

When I paid a visit to the royal palace the following morning, there was a strange sombreness in the air. I have noticed a similar hush in houses where the family awaits the patriarch to breathe his last breath. It is the solemn acceptance of a profound loss, coupled with a fear of change.

I was made to wait in an antechamber for more than an hour. This was uncharacteristic of the Caliph. He usually admitted me at once. When one of his long-faced advisors finally opened the padded door and ushered me into his private audience chamber, I was shocked at his appearance. His cheeks were hollow beneath sharp cheekbones, and crescents of shadow hung under his bloodshot eyes. Both his hair and beard were unkempt. When he turned to me, his gaze wandered, and his eyes held a wild look, like that of a hunted animal.

"Forgive me for making you wait, my friend," he said. "I had work to finish that could not be delayed."

"Think nothing of it."

His writing desk was covered with letters and parchment scrolls. Balled up scraps of parchment lay scattered around the floor where he had thrown them.

"You have been working hard."

He glanced at his desk. "Yes. There are great pressures of state at this time."

"Perhaps this is the wrong time for my visit."

"Nonsense." He put his arm around my shoulders. "I need a respite to cool my brain. Come into the library. We'll have some wine."

He led me through an archway into his personal library, which was almost as extensive as my own. It is unusual for a caliph to read anything, and unheard of for him to study the difficult historical and philosophical works that Moawiya valued. He was like a single pearl on a necklace of coal. His father had been a drunkard and a pervert, and the man who would replace him was a malicious schemer.

We sat in comfortable padded chairs with a table between us and waited for a servant to pour wine into silver cups. He sipped the wine with appreciation.

"You have a solemn face," he said. "The news you carry cannot be good."

"I have been sent to you by the Council of Mages with information pertaining to the portent of the hairy comet that recently appeared in our night sky."

He smiled bleakly.

"Information, you say. Is not the appearance of a comet always an ill-omen for crowned heads?"

"Not for all rulers. It is the task of the astrologer to determine who is affected by this rare portent."

"And what has the Council of Mages determined about this comet?"

I hesitated, trying to find the best words to use.

"Don't be afraid to speak the truth, Alhazred."

"Very well, I will do so. It has been determined that this comet foreshadows your departure from the seat of power."

He nodded, and did not appear greatly surprised.

"I am to be deposed."

"That is the opinion of our greatest astrologers."

He raised his cup and drained it. When he took it away, his lips had a sour twist of a smile.

"Your news does not come entirely as a surprise. I have considered that this comet may portend my downfall. Tell me, am I to die?"

"No," I said quickly. "Your death is not foreseen, only your removal from the throne."

He closed his eyes and rested his head against the high back of his chair. He looked exhausted, like a man burdened by a heavy load who can only set it down for a few moments before being forced to pick it up again.

Opening his eyes, he smiled at me.

"Do you know what I have been doing all afternoon?"

I shook my head.

"I have been drafting my abdication of the throne of the Caliphate. An exhausting business. There are so many details to be considered."

"But, if you abdicate, who will rule?"

"I have recommended Marwan. Why do you look that way?"

"You hate Marwan, besides which, he has tried to destroy you more than once."

"Do you mean that business in the royal gardens on my birthday?"

"That, and the matter of the red stone of Jubbah."

"How is Jacob Hazan, by the way? Has anyone ever learned of his whereabouts?"

"No," I lied. "It seems that after your garden party, he decided it would be prudent for him to remove himself from Damascus, but where he went, nobody knows."

"You are an excellent liar, Alhazred. It is an admirable quality."

"Thank you, my Caliph."

"Caliph now, but not for much longer," he said. "Marwan has been spinning his spider's web, solidifying his support among the officers of my guard and my advisors. He knows my time is short. I have offended too many men of power and wealth."

"You sought to serve the people."

"Yes, and what did it get me?" He shook his head sadly. "I was never made for the machinations of the throne room. I'm nothing more than a simple scholar."

"The laws you have made will be your legacy to the Caliphate."

"Do you think so? Well, you may be right. Only time will tell how I am remembered."

A great sorrow filled my heart as I looked at him. He had never asked for the burden of rule, but when it was set upon his shoulders he had carried it as well as he could, yet he had received nothing but derision and contempt for his efforts. He was too intelligent to be a ruler. A caliph needed to be hard of heart and ruthless in action. Purely in the matter of holding onto power, his drunken father had been a better ruler than Moawiya.

I made the determination then that I would do all I could to try to preserve his life. I had little doubt that Marwan would try to have him assassinated. Damascus was not large enough for two caliphs.

"Let me stay at your side when you make your announcement."

"No. I have guards I trust. You don't need to be here to protect me."

He was trying to spare me the danger of falling under Marwan's notice. Marwan would make a careful record of everyone who remained loyal to Moawiya, so that he could deal with them at a later time. To remain loyal to Moawiya would be almost the same as suicide. I wondered how many of his trusted friends would fail to desert him? Would anyone stand beside him?

"Have you decided where you will go? What you will do?"

"No." He shrugged. "There's hasn't been time for that."

"Come to my house and stay with me. You should be with those you can trust."

"My wives and servants –"

"They should be safe enough in the palace. Marwan would not dare to harm them. It would look petty and spiteful to the common people."

He hesitated in thought.

"Very well. After I have passed the throne to Marwan, I will come to your house in the Lane of Scholars."

"Good, that's settled." Already I was regretting my hasty words. Having the former caliph under my roof would be the same as painting a target on my back.

He seemed to sense my misgivings.

"Alhazred, are you sure about this? There are noble houses where I could stay."

"Are there any householders you can trust with your life?"

"No, there aren't."

"When are you going to make the announcement?"

"This afternoon. I'll come to your house immediately after, as quickly as I can get away from the palace."

If Marwan allows you to escape, I thought to myself, but held my tongue.

3.

Moawiya abdicated in the late afternoon. Criers were sent running through the streets of Damascus to announce the news. The riots began shortly after nightfall. When I stood in my front courtyard with Martala, Altrus, and his Persian woman, I could smell burning and faintly hear the cries of angry voices. The riots continued and spread from the streets around the royal palace to the marketplace, and then to the rest of the city. There were the red glows of burning houses on all sides.

Around midnight Marwan sent out the palace guard to restore order. We heard a unit of armored soldiers march in lockstep down the Lane of Scholars. They passed just outside my barred green gate.

"Let me go out on the streets to learn what is happening," Altrus demanded.

"No," I told him for the third time. "It is too dangerous. Besides, I want you here to defend the house after Moawiya arrives."

"We're blind behind these walls," he argued. "We need to know what is going on."

"We'll go out in the morning, after the fighting has played itself out."

"Are you sure it will end before morning?" Martala asked.

"No," I admitted. "But riots usually don't last for more than a dozen hours or so."

"I don't want you going out there," Nealayna told Altrus in a quiet voice. She laid her hand on his arm. "I'm frightened for you."

"I've dealt with rioting city populations before," he told her.

"That was when you were part of an army. You're alone now."

"Not entirely alone," Martala said.

"You know what I mean," Nealayna told her. "He might get killed by the mob or by the soldiers."

"We all stay in tonight, and that's my final word," I said firmly.

Looking across at Harkanos's house, I saw movement on the roof and realized he must be watching the riots from his astronomical observatory. I waved, and saw him wave back against the stars. Nobody in the Lane was going out tonight.

I wondered how Moawiya would find his way safely through

the riot-torn streets to my gate? It was quite possible his own soldiers would kill him by accident. Since I didn't know where he was hiding, there was nothing I could do to help him.

"They may burn down all of Damascus," Martala said.

"Doubtful," Altrus said. "There are fewer fires now than an hour ago."

"I'm going upstairs," she said. "I can see what's happening better from the windows."

We all followed Martala back into the house to await the outcome of this night's events. I was surprised that the people of the city had rioted. The way Moawiya had spoken to me the previous morning, I had expected a bloodless transition of power.

Overhead, the hairy comet with the divided tail seemed to glare down on the city. It was the largest comet I had ever seen. How much of the unrest could be attributed to its malign influence, I wondered.

None of us slept that night. I told the others to go to bed, but they ignored me. We sat in my front sitting room in the dark, with only a single lamp burning with a dim flame, the better to see out the windows, and drank wine, and talked. Through the window screens we could hear the ebb and flow of the running battles between the citizens of Damascus and the royal guard.

Altrus grew restless and climbed over my back garden wall into the back garden of Harkanos. He joined the mage on his rooftop observatory and spent an hour or so observing from that vantage the fires in different parts of the city.

When he returned to my house through the back door, he had little to relate, only that the fires were dying down and the noise of battle seemed to be diminishing. Nealayna fell asleep with her head in his lap as he sat on my divan.

I was on the point of going to bed myself when my serving man, Borka, came to tell me that someone was at my gate. Until that moment I had not realized the tension in my body, but upon hearing his words, sweat broke out all over my skin, and the sudden relaxation of my abdomen was almost painful.

"It must be the Caliph," I said. "Show him in, Borka."

My servant ushered in a man wrapped from head to toe in a black cloak. He slid the hood of his cloak off his head, revealing a steel-gray beard and dark, remorseless eyes, and I saw that it was Marwan ibn al-Hakam, the man designated by Moawiya as the next Caliph.

He didn't look like a ruling monarch. His sinister face bore an expression of mingled bewilderment and fear.

"This honour is unexpected," I said, rising to greet him. "Borka, take the Caliph's cloak."

"Caliph?" he repeated. "It sounds strange to be called that."

"Didn't Moawiya abdicate and pass the throne to you?"

He blinked at me, as though repeating my words in his mind. The shock he had suffered must have been significant to put him into such a precarious mental state.

"Yes, I suppose you could say that, in a manner of speaking."

"You talk in riddles," Altrus said harshly. "Say what you mean."

"Moawiya did pass the Caliphate to me earlier this evening. I know this is so, because I watched him do it."

"That's an odd way of phrasing it," I said.

"I watched Moawiya pass his authority on to Marwan, but I watched it from a distance."

"I'm not quite following you."

"The man who became the new Caliph looks like me and answers to my name, but it isn't me." Before I could react, he grabbed my shoulders with sudden passion and shook them. "I swear it isn't me."

Waving Altrus back, I gently removed his hands.

"Calm down, Marwan."

"I am Marwan ibn al-Hakam ibn Abu al-'As ibn Umayyah," he said. "You can see that, can't you? I am Marwan."

"Yes, we can see that. You are Marwan. Compose yourself and tell us exactly what happened."

Nealayna poured him a cup of wine and he drank it without

taking a breath. His hands trembled as he set down the cup.

"I was late getting to the ceremony Moawiya's advisors had improvised for the transition of power. I see now that I was deliberately delayed, but I didn't know that at the time. It seemed like nothing more than an inconvenience. When I reached the throne room I was prevented from entering. I could only watch from the open doorway as Moawiya passed his letter of abdication to a man who looked exactly like me. Exactly. Even the tunic he was wearing was identical to mine. I tried to get into the room to disrupt the ceremony, but the guards prevented me."

"It's strange they did not recognize you as Marwan," Altrus said.

"Yes, that is strange. I have no explanation. They didn't seem to know me."

"A spell of glamour," I said. "Your features were disguised by magic."

"They threw me out of the palace. I wandered the streets, trying to get back to my house, but the crowds were surging all around me, carrying me this way and that. I thought I was going to be knocked over and trampled to death. When I finally reached my house, it was on fire. I didn't know where to go or what to do, so I came here."

I led him to a chair, and we regarded him in silence while he stared down at his hands. His story was incredible, but I did not doubt it. There was no deceit in his voice, nor could I conceive of any reason why he would come to my house to trick me in such a strange manner.

We stayed together in the sitting room until morning lit the sky. Marwan fell asleep in his chair. His terror and confusion had exhausted him. As the sun rose, it became obvious that Moawiya was not going to appear at my gate. I wondered if he had been killed by the rioters. That is the trouble with knowing nothing – the mind is eager to replace its void with all manner of dark fancies.

4.

After breakfast, I sent Borka out to the marketplace to inquire about the state of the city. He returned with the news that the palace guard had quelled the rebellion, which had been inspired by mullahs inciting revolt in the mosques. Something the new Caliph had said to them had angered them, but Borka was not able to tell us what it was. The new Caliph was due to be formally crowned on the front steps of the royal palace before the people of Damascus at noon.

Marwan offered no resistance when I had Martala and Nealayna escort him to a bedroom and prepare him for sleep. He was not a young man, and the affairs of the turbulent night had completely exhausted him, both physically and mentally.

"What do you intend?" Altrus asked me.

"I will view the crowning of the impostor calling himself Marwan at the palace. My status as representative of the Council of Mages should insure my entry through the iron gates."

"I will come with you."

"No, I want your sword guarding Marwan. Also, it's possible that Moawiya may yet appear at our door. I would not wish those two men alone together in the same house."

"You should not go to the palace alone. There is dark treachery here."

"Agreed. I will take the girl with me."

For the ceremony I dressed in my finest Persian garments, which consisted of a black silk tunic above loose cream-colored pants in high leather boots, and a matching long black silk coat. I have always favored Persian styles over those of Arab lands. The girl took care with her disguise as a young scribe, which she had worn so often, it was second nature. Her face was still boyish enough that she could pass as a youth, when she wore no cosmetics and concealed her long dark hair.

An officer of the guard was quick to admit us through the

palace gate when I identified myself as the official representative of the Council of Mages. He asked no questions. There are few men who willingly incur the anger of necromancers.

We stood on the palace grounds before the broad marble steps, in a crowd of several thousand citizens of Damascus, all of them either wealthy or of noble birth. The rabble of the city had been excluded, and milled about just outside the gate. Feelings were still running high, and many voices were raised.

"This is the first time I've been presented as your apprentice at the royal palace," Martala whispered in my ear.

"I had to call you something to get you through the gate."

Marwan came forth from the palace just as the sun reached the zenith, and took his seat upon a portable throne that had been placed at the top of the steps. There was a roar of recognition from the onlookers, which was echoed by another more hostile roar outside the gates. I studied the thin, sour-faced man from a distance. To my eyes, he looked exactly like the Marwan I had concealed behind the walls of my house.

"The likeness is astonishing," the girl said. "Every line in his face, every gesture, every intonation of voice, is perfectly reproduced."

Which raised in my mind an interesting question – was the real Marwan asleep at my house, or was this the real Marwan?

His own son stood not ten feet away from him when the chief mullah of the city placed the crown around his brow, yet even he found no fault in the man we believed to be disguised as his father.

I was well acquainted with the ability of a good spell of glamour to deceive the eye, and indeed, all the other senses. The glamour that concealed my disfigured face from the gaze of others had withstood the closest examination, not only by sight but by touch. While I listened to the droning voice of the holy man with half my attention, I sent the other part of my mind inward.

Sashi, are you able to find fault with the appearance of the man who was just crowned?

After a moment, the lovely almond-eyed face of my lover, a

minor djinn of the great desert known as the Empty Space, formed itself on the air. These were not her actual features, but a human semblance she had adopted for communications with me. Although her face appeared perfectly solid, only I could see it.

I can find no defect in his appearance, she said silently within my mind. *However, there is something else.*

What is that, Sashi?

It is the way he moves.

What is there about his movement?

It is not quite human, my love.

This was an interesting statement. I studied Marwan's posture on the throne. Now that my attention had been drawn to it, I noticed an unusual degree of precision.

The false Marwan abruptly stood up and waved the elderly mullah aside with an impatient gesture of his hand. He began to address the crowd.

"For too long the Caliphate has suffered under the incompetence and laxity of men who had not the wits nor the will to govern it. The timely abdication of Moawiya has given us new hope that the grandeur and militant daring that once existed has returned to us.

"For too long we have been self-indulgent in our decadence, but now we will return to the old ways of our forefathers, the ways that never should have been abandoned. It is my first decree as Caliph that the idols of our forefathers, sacred to our tribes, be re-erected in the holy places of Damascus, and that they be worshipped as they were in ancient times."

An angry murmur arose from the mullahs, who were gathered together on the end of the steps to watch the ceremony. Now I understood what had sparked the riots of the night before. Some rumor of what this Marwan intended had reached their ears.

"With the old gods fighting at our side, we shall extend the boundaries of the empire, as it was in the days of Umar. The Christians will fall beneath our swords. Byzantium will be ours, and in time, Rome."

A lusty cheer went up from the crowd behind us, but whether it was spontaneous, or had been deliberately forced by the supporters of this Marwan, I could not judge.

As though it were a single body, the crowd knelt on the paving stones and began to pray. I realized it was noon, the hour of prayer. Naturally the girl and I knelt and prayed toward Mecca along with them. Was it merely an accident that the crowd bowed toward the steps of the palace, where Marwan stood watching them, an expression of fierce delight on his face? He seemed to absorb the force of their devotion like a potent drug.

As the ceremony came to a close, a royal messenger handed me a folded slip of parchment.

"What is it?" Martala asked as I read the note.

"Marwan, or rather, the one calling himself Marwan, requests an audience with us in the royal audience chamber."

"Now?"

"So it would seem."

"How did he even know we were watching the ceremony?"

"I don't know."

"What do you think he wants?"

"No doubt he will tell us."

There was no question of avoiding the audience, or even delaying it. A request from the Caliph, politely worded though it might be, had the force of a command.

5.

We were escorted, not to the large formal audience chamber where the Caliph received delegations from foreign nations and the provinces, but to the smaller private chamber where it had been the custom of Moawiya to receive me, on those occasions when I was called to the palace.

I recognized only a scattering of the faces of the advisors who were clustered around Marwan when we entered. Those Moawiya had trusted were not present. He waved them out of the room and they filed out the door, casting us sidelong glances of malice as they went. Necromancers were not well liked in the higher circles of power.

He spoke to a serving man, then gestured for us to seat ourselves in a cluster of padded arm chairs that were grouped around a small round table. The girl sat at my left, and Marwan took the chair opposite mine across the table. The servant returned with wine and cups on a silver tray, poured our drinks, then withdrew from the room.

"Alhazred, I asked you here to sound you out as to the disposition of the necromancers in the Lane of Scholars concerning my ascension to the throne."

"That is a matter I can scarcely speak about on their behalf, without consulting them."

"But you know their way of thinking. Tell me, will they approve of my returning the old gods to the temples?"

For a few minutes I considered this question, as I sipped my wine. Marwan's intense dark eyes never left me.

"I believe most of them will approve," I said. "By the nature of our arts, we necromancers are conservative in our beliefs. We resist change. But a change that returns us to a traditional way of worship will be well received."

He nodded as though I had spoken the words he expected to hear.

"What of you yourself? Do you welcome the return of the idols to the places of worship?"

"The objects of my worship are ..." I searched my mind for the correct term "...unconventional. The return of the old gods that were worshipped before Mohammed smashed and burned their idols does not greatly concern me, one way or the other."

"I thought as much. You are an unusual man."

Not knowing how to respond to this, I kept my silence. He leaned forward in his chair.

"I know you were close to Moawiya while he was Caliph. It is my hope that you can serve me in a similar capacity during my reign."

"I'm not sure I know what you mean."

"You have unusual skills. It may be useful for me to employ them from time to time.

"Naturally, I am at your disposal," I said with a slight bow of my head.

"Soon I will make war. The armies of the Caliphate have been turned inward for too long. I may send you forth from Damascus to gather strategic information. Or it may be necessary that you end the life of various men in positions of power who would seek to obstruct my purposes."

I was careful not to allow anger to show in my face.

"You wish me to spy for you, and to act as your assassin."

"Bluntly spoken but accurate. Not all wars are won on the battlefield. A dagger in the dark can do as much as an army."

Glancing at Martala, I saw she had no more liking for these words than I had. Her grey eyes smouldered with fury.

"I would like to think I had the support of the entire Council of Mages. Their arts could prove most useful. With your eloquent persuasion, I am sure we can bring them around to my purposes."

"May I ask you a question?" I said.

"Of course. What do you wish to know?"

"I have not heard anything concerning the fate of Moawiya. Do you know what became of him?"

He sat back in his chair, eyeing me the way a cat eyes a bird.

"You were close to him, were you not?"

"I have come to know him."

"Then set your heart at ease. He is being held under palace arrest in his royal chambers, purely for his own protection. When the people began to riot in the streets, I could not allow him to leave the palace. He is quite safe, I assure you."

"I would like to see him."

He pursed his thin lips and shook his head. "I think it best that he is not disturbed. The events of the past day and night have been difficult for him. I'm sure you understand."

"Indeed, I do."

Moawiya was being held captive in the palace to insure the compliance of those loyal to him by this false Marwan. Evidently he considered me one of the former Caliph's friends and was using his captivity to insure my acquiescence to his will. It was a kind of emotional blackmail in which the blade of the dagger was exposed, but not drawn fully from the sheath.

At no time did Marwan's dark eyes leave me. I had the eerie sense that he could read my thoughts, and deliberately stopped allowing them to echo in my mind. I decided to test him.

"These are strange times."

"How do you mean?"

"The coming of the comet is an evil omen for the Caliphate. In such times, reason and order are turned on their heads, and nothing is what it appears to be on the surface."

"What is considered an evil omen for one man may be an omen of good for his enemy, is that not true?"

"I would say that an omen foretelling disaster to a ruler would be universally evil to those who dwell beneath his laws, with the exception of the usurper who seeks to overthrow those laws."

"I take your point," he said, nodding. "Speaking of deception, that is an uncommonly good glamour you wear on your face."

My placid expression did not betray my surprise. There were very few men who could see through the spell of glamour that concealed my mutilated face. Harkanos, the greatest mage in Damascus, was one of them. In my travels I had encountered only a few others, all of them profound students of the occult arts. To my knowledge, Marwan knew nothing about magic.

"It is an affectation, to be sure. Forgive the vanity of a young man. Here, let me remove it."

I spoke the words and made the gesture that would dissolve the mask from my features. The spell that removed the glamour was a general spell of banishment for such forms of magic.

As my mask fell away, revealing my grotesque features, for just an instant the outline of Marwan's body flickered and changed. It was almost too brief a transformation to register on my eyes, but it remained imprinted in my memory.

"Yes, I see why you wear it," he said with feigned compassion, studying my face. "You were badly mutilated. Who did this?"

"King Huban of Sana'a took offense when I deflowered his only daughter and got her with child. What you see was a portion of his punishment."

"Tragic, most tragic. Have you tried to get the damage repaired?"

I resisted the urge to speak in anger. "It cannot be fixed. My face is lost."

"That is not entirely true, friend Alhazred. There are races of intelligent beings who possess advanced sciences and medical procedures far beyond anything you have encountered in your brief lifetime. Believe me when I assure you that, with the aid of this alien science, it would be a simple matter to restore your lost face."

"I know nothing of this alien science."

"Of course you do not. Very few men have encountered it, and only a few humans have benefited from it. Only those who serve. It is conferred on them as a reward for their faithful service."

With a few words and a gesture I restored my mask of glamour.

"I will consider what you have told me."

"I know you will." He stood up to indicate that the audience was ended. "This is a crucial moment for you, Alhazred, when the lines of your destiny meet and cross, then move in different directions. You must choose your actions wisely. There is great benefit in service, and in defiance only death."

I did not speak to Martala until we passed through the palace gates and were in the streets of Damascus.

"Did you see?"

"I saw something," she murmured, watching the people in the street with suspicion. "It was so quick, I'm not sure what it was."

"The creature that pretends to be Marwan is not human. He was carried to this world on the comet that blazes in the night sky. He wears a glamour to conceal his true shape and make him appear to be Marwan ibn al-Hakam."

"What are you going to do?"

"The Council of Mages must be convened. I will put what we have learned before them, and we will decide what must be done."

The slender fingers of her hand crept into my hand. It was an uncommon gesture of tenderness for her. I let her hand stay in mine as we walked.

"Do you think he spoke the truth?"

"About what?"

"Your face. Do you think he possesses the skills to restore your features and your manhood?"

I thought about it for a time.

"Yes, I believe he spoke the truth."

6.

We sat around the long table beneath the house of Harkanos, in one of his cellar rooms. It was spotlessly clean and free of all dust. Harkanos had decided to call a meeting of the Council here to avoid the chance that any of his servants might overhear our words.

A set of oak shelves was attached to the wall, and on the top shelf amid various other boxes and jugs and receptacles rested a glass bottle with a narrow neck. There was no label. It was filled with something that resembled sifted ashes from the fire. It was not ashes, but the essential salts rendered from the corpse of Harkanos's daughter, Anisah. I had helped him derive the salts by treating and boiling the flesh of the girl in a vat. At a time of Harkanos's own choosing, he would call upon the power of Yog-Sothoth and restore the girl to life. Until that time, there the salts remained. I could not help gazing at them. It was my ill-conceived rescue attempt that had caused the death of the girl.

Most of the Council members were present at the table. Jacob Hazan was still living in the Khaybar Oasis with his daughter, having fled Damascus to avoid the Caliph's wrath. The Egyptian Chigaru el-Masri, called the Hound, had been excluded from the meeting at my insistence. After the events of Moawiya's birthday celebration, I no longer trusted him.

Seated at the head of the table was Harkanos, our leader. I sat at the opposite end. On my left were Abdul-Basir, called the Elder due to his extreme age; the grey-haired soothsayer Mahibah; and beside her the beautiful necromancer Kalila Salib, who in her youth had been a renowned courtesan. On my right sat the wild-haired and tattooed Celt, Dannu, who was expert in elemental magic; Fayyad al-Majid, called the Merchant due to his vast wealth, most of which had been made through trading; and the handsome Baligh ibn Nazari, called the Younger, who dabbled in necromancy and astrology, but spent most of his time gambling and whoring.

"Describe this creature for us," Abdul-Basir demanded when I had finished my account of my meeting with the new Caliph.

I took a moment to summon the brief glimpse I had obtained of the creature back into my mind.

"It was naked and had a kind of head covered with antennae that hung down on the end of a long, wrinkled neck. Its hands were like the claws of a crab. I saw two sets of claws, a larger set and above it a smaller set, but there may have been more. Its feet resembled the talons of a hawk, with three toes on each foot that were spread wide to make a kind of supporting tripod. A naked tail of wrinkled skin, like the skin of a lizard, trailed between its legs, and on its hunched back were what looked like drooping wings of soft leather, somewhat like the wings of a bat."

"Has anyone read of such a monster?" Harkanos asked.

"I believe I know what it is," Abdul-Basir said, stroking his long white beard, which hung down below the tabletop. He pushed himself to his feet. "It is a race that inhabits a cold and dark world beyond the outermost sphere of the planets, as we know them. It is not visible in the night sky to our eyes, but there are mystics who possess the ability to see it with their third eye. The planet is called Yuggoth."

"What are these creatures called?" Baligh asked.

"They have no name, or if they do it has not come before me. They are said to be a race of scientists and warriors who first came to this world seeking to mine its minerals. This was long before the creation of our race. They were driven away by other Old Ones, but they have never completely abandoned an interest in our world. It is said that they are eloquent and persuasive, when their surgeons render it possible for them to speak our languages, and that they possess the ability to cloak their true appearance and to walk among us in the guise of human beings."

"What do you know of their skill in surgery?" I asked.

"It is said to be very great," Abdul-Basir said, looking at me curiously. "They can shape living flesh the way a sculptor shapes stone."

"How dangerous are these creatures?" Dannu asked.

"Their ability to wage war is said to be unparalleled in all the worlds of creation."

"Why would this one ride the comet to our world?" Mahibah asked. "What does he want?"

"As to that, I can only conjecture," Abdul-Basir told her. "It is written that they sometimes make slaves of human beings. It may be that this one intends to enslave the entire Caliphate, perhaps even the entire world."

Having spoken all he knew about the creature, he sat down. There were several minutes of silence at the table. Fayyad finally spoke the question in all of our minds.

"What do we do to stop him?"

"We have an opportunity," I said, standing. "The real Marwan is in our keeping. The false Marwan probably has agents searching for him, but as yet they have not discovered his hiding place. If we can remove this false Marwan from the palace, we can insert the true Marwan, and the people of Damascus will be none the wiser."

"The palace has hundreds of bedchambers," Baligh pointed out. "How will you know where this false Marwan sleeps?"

I considered the matter.

"As I told you, Moawiya is being held under palace arrest in the royal chambers. I can find my way there. We will go to him and ask him where this false Marwan lies sleeping."

"If such a thing sleeps," Mahibah said.

"Moawiya may not know where the false Marwan sleeps," Baligh said.

"It is a starting place," I told him. "If he does not know, we can at the very least try to get him out of the palace to a place of safety."

"It is a task that requires stealth," Harkanos said. "We cannot allow this creature the opportunity to turn his sciences against us."

"I am prepared to undertake the risk, with the aid of my companions," I said.

"Forgive me for raising the point, Alhazred," Fayyad said with an apologetic wave of his many-ringed hand. "But you are the only one at this table who has spoken face-to-face with this creature. How are we to be certain you have not bartered your loyalty to him?"

"Alhazred is not the Hound," Dannu said hotly.

"Of course, you are correct," Fayyad told him. "Even so, I thought the matter should be raised."

"I have promised this creature nothing," I said, which was the truth. I decided it best not to speak about what the creature had promised me.

"Then it is decided," Harkanos said. "Alhazred and his companions shall use stealth to convey Marwan into the palace, and shall remove the alien creature by whatever means are necessary."

"And, if possible, rescue Moawiya," I added.

"How are they to get past the palace guards?" Kalila asked.

It was a good question that had been revolving in my own mind for some minutes.

No one at the table spoke.

7.

"I hope this spell of yours works," Marwan whispered sourly as we approached the front gates of the royal palace. "If it fails, we are all dead men."

"Not all of us," Martala told him with a grin.

"We are all dead," he repeated. "Man or woman."

"The spell will work on the palace guards and servants," I told him in a low voice.

I wished that I felt as confident as I sounded. The spell should work. It had been well constructed, so it would probably work. That is the way with magic – nothing is certain.

We approached the gates. I had been trained on how to walk through the night like a ghoul, and was completely silent. To my ears the others seemed like an appalling clatter on the paving stones. It set my teeth on edge. In truth, it was only the occasional scuff of a boot, and not likely to be noticed.

One armored guard stood at attention beside the iron gates with a poleaxe held vertically in his right hand, its butt resting on the paving stones. Three others were inside their small shelter to the left of the entrance. Their voices drifted out to us as we drew nearer. From the rattle of ivory dice in a tin cup, it was obvious they were gambling.

He looked from side to side, as though suspecting a trick were being played on him. Even though I stood watching him from less than three paces inside the gate, he did not see me. He took hold of the gate and pulled it shut, then refastened the latch. After another furtive look around, he resumed his post.

We made our way across the open square toward the front

doors of the palace. Above our heads, the comet blazed amid the stars. In the space of days it had grown remarkably.

"The spell holds," Martala whispered to me.

"But for how long?" I said.

"Do not invite failure with your lips. It is bad luck."

The front doors were bolted from the inside, which was not unexpected. I knew there had to be some entrance for the guards who patrolled the palace grounds and the royal garden beyond. We worked our way around the enormous building, trying each service door as we passed it. Eventually we found one that opened, and slipped inside. The hallway was narrow and lit by a single oil lamp in a bracket on the wall. We hurried along it.

"Mustafa, is that you?"

A guard came into the hall through a side doorway we had already passed and squinted at the outer door, which I had left ajar. He approached it slowly with his dagger drawn as we watched from behind him. Peering into the darkness, he shook his head, latched the door, and returned to the room he had occupied.

It took me a while to find my way from the servant level to the royal chambers of the palace. Once there, I knew how to get to Moawiya's bedchamber. The toes of our boots made scarcely any sound on the carpets that covered the floors of the broad hallways. The palace was as silent as a crypt of the dead.

Two armored members of the Caliph's guard stood on either side of the bedroom door with their backs to the wall. They both looked bored and sleepy beneath the rims of their steel helmets.

We had already decided to avoid killing the guards wherever possible. It was not their fault they had taken orders from a creature from beyond the seventh celestial sphere. I motioned for Martala to distract them.

She went around a corner and banged on the wall. The guards looked at each other, but did not move. After a while, she banged three times in succession. This brought them slowly away from the door and around the corner. Altrus, Marwan and I slipped into the bedchamber. After a dozen seconds the girl came in behind us and shut the door.

Soft snores from the curtained poster bed indicated that its occupant was asleep. The room was so dark, it was impossible to distinguish more than gray shapes of furniture. I drew the bed curtains softly open on their rail and sat on the side of the bed.

It was vital that Moawiya did not cry out in surprise. Gently, I covered his mouth with my left hand and pressed his chest down with my right. He jerked, and began to struggle and grunt.

"It is Alhazred," I whispered through the darkness close to his ear. "Stop struggling. You must keep quiet."

I felt him nod against my hand and removed it from his face, then took out my tinder box and used it to light the candle stub I carried in my pocket. This I stuck to the bed table with a drop of hot wax.

Moawiya watched this operation with wide eyes, as though watching a conjuring trick. I realized that to his sight, the candle seemed to float upon the air.

"Where are you, Alhazred? I cannot see you."

"We are here with you. A spell conceals us from sight, except to each other."

"Who is with you?"

"My companions, Altrus and Martala. Marwan is also here."

"Marwan is here?"

"I am here, Moawiya," he said.

"Why are you doing this? Haven't you gained everything you ever coveted? I gave you the Caliphate. What more do you want from me?"

I realized Moawiya thought we had come to assassinate him.

"As of yet, I have gained nothing," Marwan said with a trace of bitterness.

"You have the throne."

"The throne is not held by me, but by a thing of evil that fell from the stars."

As concisely as possible, I explained how the creature from Yuggoth had ridden the comet from the outer reaches of space to this world, and had taken on the face and voice of Marwan to deceive us all.

"Are you saying that the man who was crowned on the palace steps is not Marwan?"

"It is not a man, but a monster," I explained patiently. "It wears a cloak of glamour to conceal its true appearance."

"Then Marwan did not order the return of the pagan idols to the holy places of the city?"

"I would never give such an order," Marwan said harshly. "I follow the teachings of the Prophet, may the blessings and peace of Allah be upon him."

"Then the world has not gone mad," Moawiya said.

"The evil being who seized the Caliphate intends to fill the world with war," I said. "There will be madness enough unless we can stop it."

"What do you intend to do?"

"We are here to kill the monster, if such a thing as it can be killed," Marwan told him. "Then we will hide the corpse, and I will take its place, order your release you from your chambers, and revoke the command of the monster regarding the restoration of the pagan idols."

"Do you know where the shape-shifter sleeps?" I asked.

"I know where he is. I can show you."

"No, you must not leave this room. You're safe here."

"I can show you without leaving this room." His voice had a curious hollowness.
A whistling note came from his lips.

Immediately the bedroom door was thrust open, and two creatures of nightmare entered with swords in their claws. They appeared identical to the monster I had glimpsed when the false Marwan's glamour dropped for an instant. I had a moment to wonder why we had all assumed that the comet carried only one passenger.

They shut the door behind them and pressed against it with their drooping leathern wings, swaying from side to side on their thick legs and tripod-like talons.

I turned to Moawiya in time to see his body waver and transform into a third monster from Yuggoth. It looked absurd sitting in the bed.

"I think it is best for us all to dispense without masks," it said in a perfectly enunciated but emotionless voice that no longer resembled the voice of Moawiya.

8.

The spell of invisibility fell away from us. I felt naked without it, and saw the dismay in the faces of my companions. The antennae-covered head of the thing on the bed began to change colours rapidly, and the heads of the two monsters at the door changed colour in response. I realized it was a silent kind of language.

"I knew you would try to use your magic to rescue Moawiya," the false Marwan said. "I could not resist the amusement of toying with you."

"Is Moawiya still alive?"

"Why would I kill him? His knowledge may be useful to me. He resides in one of the dungeons beneath the palace."

"How many of you are in the palace?"

"Only the three you see here. For reasons you would not comprehend, the comet would not accommodate more passengers."

"What will you do with us?" Marwan asked fearfully. The sight of the monsters had shaken him.

"I was going to just have you killed," the monster said. "But I've changed my mind."

Relief made Marwan's narrow shoulders sag.

"I have a fancy to try the flesh of your species on my dining table."

"They may be alien, but they are armed only with swords," I said. "We can fight them."

"Alas, I could not bring any of the potent weapons of war invented by my race with me on the comet. But you will find our skin to be impervious to your primitive steel blades."

The head of the monster flashed several bright colors, and the two at the door advanced in a menacing manner. Altrus and Martala stood their ground to meet them. The girl had drawn her little dagger from its hiding place and held it low at the ready. They engaged the monsters with the clash of steel on steel.

I turned to the bed, intending to use my sword to strike through the wrinkled serpentine neck of the false Marwan. The monster drew a sword from somewhere beneath the bedcovers and stood up on the mattress. Marwan seemed dazed.

"Help me," I snapped at him. "We need your sword."

He shook the terror from his mind and stumbled forward with his sword half-raised.

I cut at the monster on the bed and managed to hit one of its lesser arms. It was like slashing at tough horn. The sword barely left a mark. The monster was quick. I danced out of the way and avoided a thrust of its sword point.

"We cannot pierce their damned hides," Altrus yelled out.

I did not dare turn my head to look at him, but parried the blade of the monster and thrust at its leg. It was like striking a tree trunk.

"This is madness," Marwan said, backing away from the bed. "We cannot kill them. We are all doomed."

He stumbled backward, and his flailing left arm knocked the flaming candle stub into the bed curtains where they trailed on the floor. In seconds a sheet of yellow flame shot up to the curtain rail.

The monster on the bed gave forth a kind of whistling shriek as a fragment of burning cloth fell on it. I saw that the fire did not go out on its skin, but continued to burn vigorously.

The other two creatures ceased to battle Altrus and Martala. Heedless of their own danger, they rushed to the bed to rescue their leader, who seemed paralysed with sheer terror.

Glancing around the room, I saw an oil lamp on a small table. I grabbed it up and threw its oil across the bodies of the two rescuers.

"They are vulnerable to fire," I cried.

Altrus needed no other instruction. He caught the burning bed curtain, ripped it off the rail, and cast it over the three monsters. The lamp oil burst into flame on the wings of the two guards, who had forgotten their swords in their futile effort to rescue their burning leader. In moments the other side of the bed curtains burst into flames and sent cascades of fire down on the three struggling alien creatures. Then the feather mattress of the bed itself took flame.

I had to step back from the blazing bed and shield my face against the heat. Screams that were unlike any I had ever heard from men or beasts mingled and filled the air.

"Summon aid to put out the fire, before the whole palace goes up," I told Martala, who ran out the door. The rest of us began to beat at the flames on the burning bed with whatever we could find.

I noticed Marwan staring at me with an expression of horror and realized that the alien monster had not only cast down the concealment of the invisibility spell, but my mask of glamour as well. I turned my back on him and restored it, then continued fighting the fire.

We were able to drag the flaming mattress to the center of the floor. By that time the bed curtains had burned themselves out, leaving black patches of soot on the ceiling. The three interlocked burning bodies of the aliens were strangely light. They continued to nourish a kind of blue flame that did not cease to burn until every trace of the bodies was consumed. Not even bone or ash remained. The corpses of the monsters seemed to pass through the fire into the air.

At Marwan's direction, several palace guards began to beat at the dying flames on the mattress with their cloaks. Altrus managed to light the oil lamp with what little oil remained in its bottom, and the girl brought in another lamp from some other room. The screens on the windows were opened wide to air the room, which stank of soot and smoke and something foul that sat at the back of my throat and made me gag. Even this stench soon dissipated in the night breeze.

9.

"You must release Moawiya," I told Marwan, who had regained his air of command along with his courage.

"There's no hurry. He is safe enough where he is."

"Remember your promise."

He glared at me spitefully, but nodded, and gave an order to a nearby guard.

We had retired to a sitting room, where awakened servants brought us basins of water and towels with which to wash off the worst of the soot from our faces and arms. Altrus had blisters on his palms from the flaming bed curtain, but the damage was not serious.

When Moawiya was escorted into the room, he blinked against the lamp light as though unaccustomed to its brightness and looked around nervously.

"I could not get away from the palace," he said to me.

"Do not be concerned. Everything has been put right."

While the others listened in silence, I told him what had occurred while he sat in darkness in his dungeon chamber.

"Truly, the comet was a portent of great evil," he said.

"As far as the people of Damascus and the rest of the Caliphate are aware, Marwan was crowned Caliph on the palace steps. It is best that only we know the truth of this strange affair."

"Do you mean to rescind the command that the pagan idols be restored?" he asked Marwan.

"Naturally. I am obedient to the teachings of the Prophet, blessings and peace of Allah be upon him."

Moawiya nodded. His hair was disordered and his eyes rimmed by shadows, but the habitual mildness of his nature had not left him.

"What of my own laws," he asked.

"Which laws do you refer to?"

"The laws I had enacted regarding the rights of women, the prohibition of the death penalty, and the imposition of a charity tax."

Marwan smiled his sour smile and shook his head.

"Are you really so simple-minded? Those laws are an outrage to custom. The only reason you were not dragged out of this palace and torn limb from limb in the street is because you never tried to enforce them. Even if I wanted to keep them, the people would not permit it. The mullahs would not permit it. The noble families would not permit it."

Moawiya nodded with weariness, as though these were the words he had expected to hear. He turned to me.

"So you see, Alhazred, all I have tried to do as ruler has come to nothing. Such is the vanity of human wishes. Think upon this example when you remember me."

"Have you decided where you will go to retire?"

He shook his head.

"It doesn't matter. I think my time of retirement will be brief."

I felt the insane temptation to offer him my house as his refuge, not merely for a few days but for the remainder of his life. But I realized that it would be inappropriate and held my tongue. It was better that he leave Damascus. He would find some remote palace or keep in which to live with his servants and close family members.

Marwan approached me. Wine had made him bolder. When he smiled, it was almost with an honest warmth. He put his hand on my shoulder.

"I will not forget what you have done for me this night. I am a man who remembers his friends, and his enemies. You have proven yourself a friend."

"Remember also the Council of Mages, who aided us in our work," I said.

"Yes, yes," he shrugged. "Of course their help will also be rewarded."

His voice held a vagueness that caused me to wonder how long he would remember his pledge.

"We need to get home," Altrus said. "Nealayna will be worried."

"Tamed by a woman," Martala said with a smile. "Who would ever have believed it could happen?"

"No one has tamed me," he said hotly. "I am my own man."

"Of course you are, sweet little boy," she said, as though talking to a small child.

They continued to fence with words when we left the palace. I had many things to consider, and kept my own counsel.

I glanced up at the stars, and saw that the hairy comet had vanished. This was unnatural, but scarcely more so than the strange freight it had carried to our world. I wondered if any other monsters from Yuggoth would come to our sphere. Could they travel here without a comet to ride? Or were they here already, disguised as human beings, watching us and waiting?

I shook my head at the night and smiled to myself. There were some realities it was best not to brood upon. Let Moawiya spend his days and his nights reckoning up what might have been, and what might yet come. That was not my way. When my head touched my bolster, I would sleep deeply for what remained of the night, and when I awoke it would be a new day. The past could bury itself. I had too many other things to do.

THE LAST 12 DAYS
OF ALHAZRED

Day One

I entered the old man's library with trepidation. My head was filled with the stories told about his youthful exploits that I had heard from my earliest childhood. He was widely recognized as the greatest necromancer in Damascus, a title of dubious honour he had enjoyed for many decades. His prohibited book was whispered about in tones of dread and loathing. Everyone had an opinion about it, or knew someone who had gone mad after reading it, but no one I talked to had actually seen or read the book they called *Al Azif*, which Alhazred himself denied having written. I had my doubts that it even existed.

According to the stories, he had collected the arcane knowledge that composed the book while wandering the Empty Space as a young man. He had seen things in that great desert that no other man had seen, and had spoken with inhuman creatures beneath its sands about the ages of the world before the creation of mankind.

What they whispered to him through cracks in the darkness, Abdul Alhazred wrote down in his book, which was not so much famous as infamous. A mad book written by a madman that drove its readers mad.

For a long while I stood inside the doorway. He did not even glance in my direction. I worked up enough courage to inch my way closer to his reading table.

His shoulders had become slightly hunched beneath the burden of years, and his hair was as white as cotton bleached by the sun, but his lean and shaven face was less lined than I expected. Indeed, it had a strange youthful quality that was almost uncanny.

"So you are Khaled's first born son," he said without looking up from the page he was reading. For so old a man, his voice was surprisingly strong.

"Yes sir, my father is Khaled ibn Umar. My name is Hassid."

"I owe your father a consideration for a service he did me many years ago. Did you know that?"

I shook my head.

"Speak up, boy," he said in annoyance.

"No, sir."

"Call me Alhazred."

"I did not know this, Alhazred."

He grunted to himself, and raised his eyes to look at me. They were a startling gray-green color, like faded jade. I trembled beneath his scrutiny. His gaze held an inhuman quality that intensified my fear. I think it was the complete lack of any emotion. He might have been examining a bit of lint or a grain of salt. I remembered hearing an old rumour that his father was a djinn of the desert.

"They say in the marketplace that I am mad. Do you believe this?"

"No, Alhazred."

"Then you are a fool. No man could see what I have seen and retain his sanity."

I gathered my threads of courage together. "You do not talk like a madman."

This caused him to smile ever so slightly with just the corners of his pale lips.

"There are many kinds of madness."

He shut the book before him and returned it to its place on one of the shelves.

"So you want to learn the true nature of this world, and mankind's place in it?"

"I wish to become a necromancer, like you."

"Even if that knowledge should blast your mind and burn it to cinders?"

"Yes," I said without hesitation.

"Then today will be your first lesson."

Reaching above his head, he pulled from the shelf a large book bound in black leather, with silver hinges and silver corners. It was sealed with five silver hasps, all of them locked into place. Taking a small key that hung around his neck on a silver chain, he inserted it into the five keyholes in succession. The hasps clanked against the table as each fell open.

"Is this the book they call *Al Azif?*" I could not keep my voice from trembling with excitement.

Alhazred smiled, but whether it was to me or to himself, I could not determine. He crooked his long index finger.

"Come and read."

Old Ones

Our race has had the astonishing good fortune to inhabit a small island in a tranquil backwater of the universe, during an epoch when the warring factions that once spanned its strife-torn surface have been rendered impotent by the very aethyr through which it drifts on its endless night. The heavens revolved in their eternal cycles, the rays sent down upon the earth conspired in their angles, and the very colors of the stars became poisonous, forcing the ancient invaders to cease their battles and withdraw themselves from the fierce lights in the sky for their own preservation.

This tranquil moment in eternity has encompassed the entire known progress of human history, so that all the chronicles writ in past ages by scribes recount the same placidity. True, they record human battles, human wars, but such conflicts of man against man are as the quarrels of small children, brief and of no lasting consequence.

The history of our world does not begin with the recorded history of our race. The world is much older than most scholars imagine. Its past ages saw the rise and fall of great civilizations before men descended from the trees or learned the use of fire.

The song of Azathoth impregnated the endlessly fertile womb of Shub-Niggurath, and through the gates of Yog-Sothoth were brought forth monsters in the ocean deeps. The first of the races from the stars descended into the seas and built their cities. They began to shape the things that swam and slithered in the lightless chill of the ocean floor, for they possessed the art of carving living flesh the way a mason carves stone. In this way the diversity of life multiplied and spread to the dry lands, which became green with plants.

Other races came from the stars and fought with the first race. Their endless wars raged across the dry lands and into the ocean depths, even into the air itself as monstrous flying things contested for the heights. And then the stars shifted, their colors changed, and it became prudent for the Old Ones to withdraw themselves from beneath their rays to sanctuaries where they could lie as the dead lie in their tombs, and in their sleep of death, to dream of their coming forth by day, once again to rule beneath the stars.

How could our naked, hairy ancestors have guessed the blessing that the capricious fates bestowed upon them? The knowledge of what walked the fertile plains and straddled the teaming rivers before their coming would have sent them gibbering and shrieking back to the forests, to cower in their madness beneath trembling leaves and await their deaths.

Ignorance is our shield, arrogance our sword. The Old Ones lie sleeping under the roots of the mountains, below the waves of the seas, amid the airy, sun-drenched clouds, and between the glittering stars the very lights of which hold them fixed and impotent, the way amber traps a fly. Men sing and dance on their immemorial thresholds like happy children, careless of disturbing their slumbers. It were more prudent to beat a drum before the den of a sleeping bear, or thrust a hand into a nest of dreaming vipers, for the Old Ones wait, and watch, and remember.

Even you who read these words penned by the Poet, and dismiss them in your conceits as no more than mere fables, even you stand on the brink of annihilation. One thunderbolt from the heavens could remake the face of this world and wipe away all traces of our race as the traveler wipes the sweat from his brow with a single careless gesture.

This awareness of the fragility of our continuance caused the Poet to pen the following couplet, as he wandered the Rub' al Khali in his youth:

> *Squeezed by the fingers of fate, man is a thing of clay;*
> *The winds of time dry his tears, and as dust bear*
> *him away.*

When the world was young, in waves of war they fell from the sky, streaks of burning flame, intent only on conquest. They took joy in battle, found glory in conquest, and derived cruel pleasure from the domination of the vanquished. For untold ages they contested the rule of this realm, while the first hairy men cowered in holes in the earth.

We were beneath their notice, beneath their contempt, not fit to even be their slaves, or their food, but fit perhaps to be the food for their slaves. Then, without explanation, they were gone, and our race found the courage to walk upright beneath the sun, and to dream its dreams while awake.

But echoes of their presence remain to remind us of their power, concealed in the deeps of the earth, on the bottom of the seas, in jungle-grown ancient stone ruins so blasted by time that their very forms are blurred. These stones of history were not engraved by human hands, but by the Old Ones themselves, or the servants of the Old Ones, for even their meanest slaves were as gods to our race.

In wave after wave they fell from the stars to conquer and lay waste to their foes, and build their great cities which now lie in ruins beneath the sands, or buried under ice, or swallowed by the seas. Some Old Ones were of flesh, but so strange in its substance that our race knows nothing of its kind; neither bird nor beast nor fish nor creeping thing, neither meat nor wood nor stone. Others were stranger still, their bodies not formed of anything to be found on this world; and when they die their flesh shrinks and passes into the air, the way water dries to nothingness on sunlit stone.

Why did they come? Why did they contest with each other for the rule of this spinning globe? Why did they stay and build their cities here? There is a secret whispered in darkness by creatures not human that is known to few. Think hard before you seek to find it written upon these pages. Once it has entered your mind, it cannot be purged, and never again will your thoughts be innocent like those of a child.

Better for you if you shut this book and never open it again; better for you if you burn it and scatter the ashes in darkness across the sands; better for you that you do not speak of it until the angel of death shall seal up your lips and tear your soul from its clay.

Day Two

Alhazred's stone-faced manservant admitted me through the green gate from the Lane of Scholars and led me without speaking between the pagan statues of gods and goddesses that decorated the courtyard. I realized he must have been informed by his master that I would be a regular afternoon visitor. He had a stealthy, guarded expression and a way of glancing at me from the corners of his eyes that I did not like.

We entered under a kind of porch formed by the overhang of the upper story of the house, which was supported by pillars of rose-colored marble. The massive front door was sheathed in brass and decorated with brass nails in a floral pattern. The servant opened it and held it wide for me, then gestured silently toward the library.

I went into the room where the old man had received me the last time, but it was empty and as silent as a crypt. Dust motes danced in beams of sunlight that found their way through gaps in the carved wooden screens over the windows. For a short while I stood and waited, but I became restless and went to look for someone.

I wanted to hear a human voice. The silent house made me nervous. It is impossible to define why this was, but I felt a kind of watchfulness that was more pronounced when I was alone within its walls. It was clean and orderly. There were no occult objects on the ground floor other than the books in the library. Yet I had the feeling that the house had its own sentience, that it was aware of my intrusion and barely tolerated my presence.

Wandering slowly down the main hall toward the rear, I heard soft splashes of water and followed the sounds into a washroom off the kitchen. There was Alhazred, dressed in a long black robe that was tied at the waist with a sash of braided golden threads.

His back was to me as I entered. I saw that he was bent over a wooden wash tub, laving water over his hands and arms, which were covered with blood almost up to the elbows. The metallic odor of fresh blood made me grimace in disgust.

He heard me, or in some other way sensed my presence, and turned his head with a sardonic smile, yet I had the sense that his mockery was not directed at me, but rather toward himself.

"I'll be with you shortly, young Hassid. Go and wait for me in the library."

I stood staring stupidly at the blood in the water-filled basin as he continued to cup it over his forearms.

"This?" he said, holding up his red-stained hands. "Necromancy is not always a tidy occupation. If the sight of a little blood offends your noble sensibilities, I suggest you forego your lesson and return to your home."

At this rebuff, I found that I could move my legs and walked stiffly back to the long hall. My mind was shocked on a level below words by what I had seen, so I cannot say what my thoughts might have been as I made my way toward the front door. Perhaps I intended to leave the house. Whatever my purpose, when I came to the archway that led to the library, I turned and passed through it.

This was not bravery. It was not even a conscious decision. Something deep in my nature refused to allow me to be sent away like a frightened child.

The large black book lay unlocked and open on the reading table. This was odd, because earlier while I had stood waiting in the room, the table had been bare. I assumed the silent manservant had lifted it from the shelf and opened it according to Alhazred's prior instruction while I was with the old man in the washroom. If he had not taken the book down, then it must have been done by someone in the house I had yet to encounter.

Staring nervously at the book, I half expected its pages to flutter and turn by themselves, but its inertness disappointed my fears. Was it truly the dread tome known as *Al Azif*, or was it another of

Alhazred's writings? It was scarcely to be imagined that a scholar of Alhazred's years and eminence would only pen a single work. There was no title page and no signature of an author to introduce its contents, as I discovered when I turned to the front of the book.

Half a dozen ribbons of different colors were sewn into its spine at the top to use as registers. As was the case in my previous lesson, the few leaves intended for my eyes lay between the white ribbon and the black – the others trailed off the edge of the table.

I listened for the old man's approaching step on the tiles in the hall but heard nothing. The day before he had sat watching me all the while I read, and then had questioned me about the reading to determine how much of it I understood and remembered. No doubt he intended to do the same today after I absorbed the text set forth for me.

The silence pressed like an invisible hand upon the top of my head. It was really quite unsettling. I thought about sitting in a side chair to wait for his arrival, but in the end my curiosity overcame my timidity, and I sat in the chair before the open book.

Fallen Earth

It is whispered in the lightless caverns deep beneath the ground, by things that are so ancient they have no memory of their beginnings, but always were, and are, and mayhap always will be, that this world of sea and stone is a great goddess who has fallen from a higher and more noble estate to her present humble condition of forgetfulness. When she fell, there was no life upon her surface, no life in her seas, no life in her deep caverns. For long aeons she slept, barren and solitary, but pure of essence in her lifelessness.

To the Old Ones of the heights, who worship the goddess Earth and seek to rouse her from her long sleep so that she may ascend once more to her throne amid the stars, all life upon her surface is a disease, all growing things an infection, all creatures that swim and walk and fly no more than crawling vermin to be exterminated with cleansing fire and sulphurous blasts of lightning.

These Old Ones are the blight of life and the bane of man, though few men know of their existence. They wait and watch us on the other side of the shadows, envious of our freedom to walk unhindered beneath the stars. Their whole purpose is the cleansing of the world and the resurrection of their most sacred goddess. They never cease their efforts to break through the gates of Yog-Sothoth, as legend states they broke through of old.

Should they succeed in their purpose – and their success may come at any moment – the continuance of humankind, and indeed of all things that live on the land or in the seas or in the air, will end. The Earth shall become silent and barren, as she was at the beginning of time.

Only ancient creatures whose origins are not of this world, who dwell deep beneath its surface in the nethermost bowels of forgotten caverns and tortuous tunnels, may survive this harrowing of the Old Ones. What their fate will be when the goddess awakens, no man can predict, nor will any man witness it, for our entire race will be dead.

The Old Ones came from the spaces between the stars and frolicked on this world during the long ages before the stars went wrong. After the stars turned poisonous, they continued to lurk on the edges of our reality, where the hateful stellar rays could not reach them, watching and waiting for a form of life to arise that was intelligent enough to serve as their mortal agents. While they waited, mountains were worn smooth, the waters of the seas rose and fell, massive sheets of ice covered the poles and retreated before the returning sun, and the very masses of the land itself slid and shifted from their places.

The things of this world changed, new kinds of life springing forth as older kinds died away. The early creatures that walked the steaming fern forests were monstrous and crude, lumbering masses of flesh and bone that were savage in strife, but with tiny brains useless to the work of the Old Ones. And so they waited with the patience of serpents for the coming forth of our race.

It is the purpose of these alien priests of the goddess Earth to open a vast gate in time and space. Through this gate they will raise the fallen Earth once again to her former glory in the higher spheres. But before she can sit upon her throne, she must be cleansed of all forms of earthly life, for to the Old Ones life itself is a kind of foulness that stains her face. She cannot be passed up through the gate of Yog-Sothoth unless she is made sterile.

The harrowers of our world stand waiting in rank and file for the opening of the gate that will admit them to our sphere. The gate cannot be opened from their side, but must be opened by ritual magic from our side by men who serve the Old Ones as their agents.

In this purpose the Old Ones face a conundrum. How can they use their chosen agents among mankind to aid in cleansing the world of all ordinary forms of life, when those agents themselves would be annihilated by the cleansing? Men of healthy minds and flesh cannot do this work, but only men who have arisen from the breeding of the Old Ones upon the wombs of mortal women. The half-breed children of the Old Ones shall be strange in their flesh, and stranger still in their minds, and this strangeness shall be a shield of protection from the harrowers.

These Old Ones are strange beyond the outer limits of the minds of men to fathom. They float upon the aethyr, forever invisible to our eyes. From the other side of the shadows that hide them from the hateful colors of the stars, they cannot affect our world directly, but they have the power to engender offspring within the wombs of living things.

In the ages before the rise of human kind, the more ancient races not of our world defied their power, for they needed to preserve the life of this world for their own use. With their passing away, of all the forms of life that remain in this sphere, only humanity has the intelligence to serve these Old Ones. To those who heed their calls, which come in dreams, they teach a magic that allows them to pass through the gate of Yog-Sothoth and to endure the venomous stars long enough to impregnate mortal women with their alien seed.

From the wombs of these brood mares arise monsters too varied in their atrocities to describe. Some resemble men in portions of their parts, and possess the ability to reason and speak, while others are so alien to all we know that our minds cannot grasp the very colors that paint them, but turn away oblivious to their presence, so that they walk among us, invisible.

There are some that squirm from the womb with serpentine motions and vanish into cracks in the ground, and others that glisten with black shells and sprout transparent wings to fly away with buzzing sounds. This endless fecundity of the Black Goat caused the Poet to compose the following couplet:

> *In the belly of the beast, abortions shun the light;*
> *Seeds of madness engender the children of the night.*

Sometimes one is born of these cross-matings sane enough to serve them. Through the occult works of these rare sons and daughters of nightmare, they seek to open wide the portal of Yog-Sothoth to all their race, so that the world may be scoured clean of all normal, healthy forms of life. Only then can they lift her out of her present orbit and raise her beyond the spheres of the wandering stars, through the great gate of Yog-Sothoth to the higher spiritual estate from which she fell so many aeons ago.

Because they are not normal in their birth, not healthy in their growth, they believe in their conceit that they shall be spared the harrowing, and shall ascend with the goddess and her priests to her high throne above the stars. The Old Ones nurture this fond hope in their servants since it ensures their loyalty.

The ascent of the goddess is a labor of ages not yet perfected, but the Old Ones have the patience of stone idols. They will never cease the making of monsters in the wombs of mortal women until a half-breed is born with the precise qualities needed to realize their ambitions.

Then will the harrowing of the world begin, a hint of which is foreshadowed in the book of the Christian prophet John. In those final days none will be spared from death, not the sucking babe in arms nor the whimpering schoolboy, not the farmer in the field nor the aged grandfather seated by the hearth, nor yet horse or dog or fish or bird or any other thing that has the breath of life. Then all the world will be made as the Rub' al Khali is today – dry, barren, and empty.

Day Three

An elegantly dressed woman escorted me through the house of the necromancer to a walled back garden, where grew many varieties of flowers and several types of fruit trees. I guessed that she was Egyptian from her profile, but she said nothing and did not answer when I spoke. I wondered if she might be deaf. Her steel-grey hair, bound securely behind her head with tortoise-shell combs, accentuated the length of her neck. Slender and slight of body, she moved with a grace that defied her advanced years.

She left me in the sunlight with the sounds of bees and songbirds. I followed a white pebble path between flower beds until I found Alhazred, in earnest conversation with a man who, from his leather apron and rough manner, I took to be his gardener.

He saw me and motioned me to his side.

"As I become older, the tending of plants holds greater delight for me. There is comfort in watching the slow vigor of the natural world unfold itself in its timely and predictable way through out the year."

He plucked a lemon from the tree beside the path and cut it into two parts with his dagger, then passed me one of the pieces.

"When I bought this house decades ago, this tree was almost dead, but with care and attention it now bears the finest fruit in Damascus. Try it."

At his urging I bit into the yellow pulp and tried to prevent the shrivelling of my face at the intense sourness. He smiled at me and nodded.

"It is the true nature of a lemon to be sour. Perfection lies in remaining true to one's own nature."

"A delightful flavor," I said, my words distorted somewhat by my puckered lips.

He put his hand on my back.

"Come with me to my rose bower. I will sit in the shade while you read the lesson I have marked out for you. Then we will discuss it together."

The book lay open on a table beneath a flowering trellis of rose stems. Bees hummed lazily overhead amid the pink blooms, indifferent to our presence.

"If I say to you that everything has a center, what is your response?"

Instead of speaking at once, I thought about his words.

"I would say you are correct."

"The universe all around us is what the Greeks call the macrocosm, or greater world, and our own bodies in conjunction with our souls they refer to as the microcosm, or lesser world. It is a truism for them that everything in the microcosm has its correspondence in the macrocosm, and conversely everything in the macrocosm has its correspondence in the microcosm. Would you concur?"

"I confess I have never considered the matter."

"So the Greek philosophers tell us. I speak now of the Greeks who dwelt in Egypt during the reigns of the Ptolemys. More recently the Persians have adopted this theory, and it is said it has even made its way into the distant eastern kingdom of Chin. Let me put another question to you before you begin to read. If the beating heart is the center of a man, what then is the corresponding center of the universe?"

These questions were beyond me. I had not come prepared to answer them, and so was at a loss for words. I did not wish to appear a complete fool, so I forced myself to say something.

"The sun?"

He chuckled and nodded.

"A credible answer that any well-instructed young scholar might make who had read an account of the works of Seleucus, who was a student of Aristarcus of Samos, but completely false. Philolaus the Pythagorean was nearer to the truth when he asserted that the earth, the sun and all the planets revolve around a central fire, but even he could not begin to imagine the vastness of the cosmos or the truth of what lies at its heart."

"I have never heard the name of this Philolaus."

"Few men have in this decadent age. What if I tell you that each star in the night sky is itself a sun, and that around it circle innumerable worlds, some of which are so alien to ours that we cannot even conceive their shapes?"

I shook my head, bewildered at this audacious statement, the like of which I had never before heard expressed. No wonder the men of Damascus called him mad.

"Have you nothing to say in response?"

"Th-then I would say," I stammered in my nervousness, "that the center of anything is what that thing turns upon, as a wheel turns upon an axle, and therefore the center of the universe is the thing the universe turns upon."

He looked at me in silence, his face impassive. I thought he was angry with me and began to apologize for my hasty words, but he stopped my mouth with a gesture.

"I confess, you surprise me. There may be some hope for you, young Hassid."

While he sat some distance away and watched me, I opened the book to the place he had marked with ribbons and began to read.

Throne of Chaos

In his dreams the Poet has glimpsed what sits upon the black throne at the eye of the chaotic vortex that turns in the heart of all the universes. Fat, gross, naked and soiled with his own feces, his long black hair dangles across his broad face, matted with filth. Drool drips from his blubbery lips when he makes incoherent noises, for he is an idiot and cannot speak. His eyes are covered with white caps that render him completely blind, and he is deaf to all sounds. His name is Azathoth.

Between his enormously bloated hands he holds a slender reed that is carved into a flute. With astonishing dexterity, his fingertips touch the holes in the sides of this instrument, dancing from one to the next as he fills its length with the breath of frantic life. From the flute there drifts up toward the stars a whining melody that constantly changes, never ceasing for even an instant. Up and down in cadence it drifts like a sinuous serpent, or like the white line of smoke that rises from burning incense. It bends, it curls back upon itself, it darts forward daringly, then coils itself coyly around and knots its length, all the while moving, shifting, sliding onward into infinity.

The Poet has seen the other gods who dance naked in the heavens around the black throne of chaos, moving against their will to the notes of the blind god's melody. Some say they are twelve in number but he has counted thirteen. Their bloated, malformed shapes are ill-made for dancing, and they stumble and jerk in a great circle, all moving in the same direction, against the course of the sun were any sun to shine in this unearthly vault of stars, and streaming chaotic bands of unnameable colors.

The awkward skip and stumble of these other gods to Azathoth's flute caused the Poet to compose the following couplet:

> *Silence, framed by reedy shrills, spirals forth across the night,*
> *Turns the stars to madmen's eyes that fear to wink and miss the sight.*

It is said by some of our philosophers that the song of Azathoth creates not only our world, but countless other worlds that are ranked above and below ours from moment to moment, like nesting crystal bowls, so that if the music of his flute were to cease for even an instant, all the worlds would crash into each other and be destroyed. Everything that has existence arises from his flute. All thoughts, all dreams, all births and deaths, all purposes, are notes in his endless song, which never repeats itself but pours forth forever varied and renewed, as it has done from the first moment of time.

There is a secret teaching which I set here so that it will not be lost. Some assert that when Azathoth sounded the first note on his flute, when the universe was newly formed, so pure and powerful was that note that the flute could not contain it, but split from the force of it. Since that first pure note, the music of the blind idiot god has been imperfect. Nothing that arises from his song is without defect. As the flute is cracked, and the notes it plays imperfect, so all that has its root in those notes is stained with impurity, and harbours within itself the seeds of its own destruction.

By this dark teaching, which is not spoken openly but only whispered mouth to ear, we are all of us fallen creatures, incapable of perfection, and therefore destined never to attain our high seats upon the stars that the Greek philosophers in Egypt under the reign of the Ptolomys promised us.

It may be conjectured that the purpose of the Old Ones is to cleanse the goddess Earth of all her living things, and is driven by the desire that the creations arising from Azathoth's cracked flute, which are inherently flawed, may be burned away, so that the essential purity and perfection of the naked goddess shall be fit to be elevated through the great gate of Yog-Sothoth back to the higher realm from which she is said to have fallen.

A shadow figure stands behind the black throne as Azathoth plays his flute. His face is veiled in darkness, but those who have glimpsed it in a drugged trance claim it is a skull bleached white, with redly blazing eyes in the sockets. Some have called him the Crawling Chaos, but the wise know him as the Messenger of Azathoth, for it is by his primary function that he may be best understood.

Just as it is the part of the idiot god in the scheme of things to pour forth his song of creation unchecked and unexamined, so it is the place of his Messenger to restrict the consequence of that melody, so that a degree of order may be maintained across the worlds. Were Azathoth's song not restrained, it would result in ungovernable chaos. His Messenger is like a judicious gardener who moves from bush to bush, plucking a flower here and snipping off a branch there, to insure that the growth in the garden does not become so wild that it cannot be contained.

The Messenger has another name that men fear to speak aloud, and it is Nyarlathotep. In this guise he walks the caravan roads beneath the moon and stars. Sometimes he wears the ancient garb of a king of Egypt. At other times he goes cloaked in a long gray robe, and is mistaken for a wandering hermit.

It is the essence of Azathoth to never stray from his black throne for even an instant, and it is the nature of his Messenger to walk up and down upon the worlds of creation, restricting at his pleasure the consequences of the idiot god's wild melody. The song of Azathoth brings forth life, but the hand of Nyarlathotep is death.

Day Four

I sent word by messenger to Alhazred that I would be delayed by pressing personal affairs, but was unable to wait for his reply. My father had entrusted me to secure the financing for a caravan he was assembling, and the young nobleman who was his chief backer had chosen the night before to go on a drunken whoring spree. It took me hours to locate him in the wine house where he lay unconscious, make him sober enough to comprehend what I was saying, and secure his name and seal on the contract.

By the time I reached Alhazred's house, night had draped its velvet cloak over the city. The gate was unlatched and the door unlocked. I entered the front hall with hesitation, listening for the sound of a servant's footfall so that I could ask if the master was still prepared to receive me, but the house appeared empty. It was too early an hour for the servants to be in bed. I debated with myself whether I should continue or retreat, but in the end made my way slowly along the hall toward the back of the house.

Faintly, I heard the screams of what sounded like an animal in torment. At first I assumed they must come from outside the house, but as I drew nearer to a closed door, the screams became louder, and I realized they emanated from somewhere below my feet. It came to my mind that the door led to the cellars beneath the house. I put my hand on the latch and hesitated, listening. The screams had ceased as suddenly as they had begun.

Before I could depress the latch, the door opened and Alhazred appeared framed in the shadows, a brass oil lamp flaming in his hand. His Egyptian house mistress ascended the steps behind him, her slender body swaying gracefully. With horror, I saw that she carried in her hands a blood-stained, severed arm.

In the uncertain light of the lamp, my first surmise was that the arm was human, but when they both emerged into the rear hall where the light was better, I realized that it was the limb of some type of humanoid ape the likes of which I had never seen. The skin was black, the hair like the bristles of a pig, and the fingers elongated to a grotesque degree, so that the splayed hand had the appearance of some great black spider. On the tip of each finger was a hooked black claw.

"Take it to my preparation table," he said to the woman. "Have a care for the blood. It is a deadly poison."

"This I know as well as you," she murmured as she glided past me toward the entrance to the kitchen.

"So you came at last," he said to me. "I had ceased to expect you."

"Did you not receive my letter?"

"No. I was working below, and my servants have orders never to disturb me while I am working."

"At least they left the gate and the door unlocked for me."

"Did they indeed?" He did not appear happy.

He made his way down the hall toward his library, and I followed a pace behind him.

"Surely no necromancer of Damascus needs to lock his door?"

He glanced at me, as though considering whether to speak.

"It is true, there is no danger from the thieves of the city, who know better than to trouble this house, but there are other entities far more dangerous, and some of them would delight in my death. No man can live as long as I have lived without making enemies."

I hesitated, but could not resist asking the question.

"The arm you carried from your cellar – may I ask what it will be used for?"

"That is not something you need concern yourself with," he said sternly.

"Forgive me, it is none of my business –"

"Nevertheless, I will tell you. It will be used to construct the sign of Koth, which will protect this house from intruders, whether they be human or other than human."

"Have you need for such occult protection?"

"I believe that I do." He eyed me keenly. "For you see, my young student, the door of this house is never left unlocked."

As much as I wanted to ask more questions, I did not dare speak again. Yet Alhazred himself continued his discourse.

"Among the Old Ones who came to this world before there were men are those who traveled, not through the air or on the ground or across the sea as we do, but through the layers of reality that are defined and distinguished by certain vibrations. Yog-Sothoth opened the way, and through his gates they came. For understand this, young Hassid, Azathoth created all things out of the harmonies and rhythms of his flute. Music is a vibration on the air, yet it is not merely sound that vibrates, but all things. There are higher vibrations that we cannot hear or see or touch, and from these some of the Old Ones descended.

"They do not have fixed forms as we understand the nature of matter. They are able to put on various shapes as we put on masks when they communicate with us, but none of these are their true shapes, which are beyond our comprehension. The greatest danger arises when we see them, for when we perceive their masks, they become aware of our existence. Most men are protected by a cloak of ignorance. They know nothing about what walks beside them unseen and unheard. It is those of us who seek to throw off this cloak who are in peril, for the more clearly we see these Old Ones, the nearer our minds stray to the center of the chaotic vortex of Azathoth, and there lies madness."

While speaking these strange matters, he took down his black book and opened it, then sat watching while I read the passage he had exposed for me.

Concerning the Dead

Of dealings with the dead, there are several kinds. It may be that a rich merchant dies without revealing the hiding place of his gold and silver. His widow and children are naturally anxious that this information should not be lost to the world, and ask the necromancer to raise his shade that it may speak the secret, or lead the grieving spouse to the place where the wealth lies buried.

Some men, maddened with grief over the loss of their beloved, will have their shades animated so that they may lie with them and sport with them in love play. Widows may seek the return of their husbands for the purpose of conceiving a child by them after their death. In this they invariably suffer disappointment, for the seed of a shade is without physical substance and unsuited to engender a normal, healthy offspring. What grows in the widow's womb is a horror of malformed tissues that mercifully aborts before its full-term is reached.

The touch of these risen shades is soft and cool, like the brush of silk against the skin. Their fleshless bodies can penetrate into the bodies of the living, so that at times the touch of the shade is felt not on the skin, but within the organs and in the bones. This caress draws vital warmth from the living, and leaves them with a pleasant lassitude that is not unlike that caused by the juice of the poppy. An excess of intercourse with shades will weaken the body, resulting in illness, and in extreme indulgence, even death.

If the flesh of the corpse is not too much rotted or riddled with white worms and black beetles, the shade of the dead man may be called back into his corpse to animate it and make it walk. This is sometimes done for revenge, if an enemy seeks to kill a member of the dead man's family in a horrifying way. For know that a corpse can always find the place where its spouse and children reside, no matter how far removed they may be. The risen dead are hungry for fresh blood and living flesh, and no meat will satisfy them so well as the flesh and blood of those who loved them in life.

This reflection caused the Poet to compose the following couplet:

Dead arise and seek out those they loved,
Returning not for kisses, but for blood.

The dead are sometimes reanimated to guard sacred places and prevent the entry of the profane, or to guard buried treasure. This they will do with faithful service for so long as their sinews remain fixed to their bones and their muscles have not turned to black water. They guard by day and by night, but their strength and their hunger are more in darkness, and especially beneath the rays of the waxing moon.

The bald priests of Egypt who dwell beneath the Sphinx have a magic that enables them to render down any corpse to its essential salts, and then to reconstitute those vital salts into the living man or woman from whom they were derived. This great act of necromancy is enabled by the indulgence of Yog-Sothoth, who is induced to open his gate between the land of the living and the domain of the dead. So perfectly is the body remade that no friend or relation who know the resurrected corpse in life could detect any flaw.

If left to his own devices, the resurrected man will live out the remainder of a normal span of life, and then die a normal death. It is not possible to resurrect a corpse that has expired at the very last instant of the full-term of life allotted to him by fate, for there is no remaining vital energy bound up with the essential salts, but it is rare indeed that a man dies at the last instant of his natural span of days.

It is an easy matter to attract a shade. They remain in the vicinity of their corpse until decay of the body is well advanced. They are forever weak with hunger. Warm milk will bring them to you with great eagerness. They feast on the essence of the milk and are made stronger by it, though not for very long.

If milk fails to bring them, freshly-spilled, hot blood may be used. Blood contains much larger amounts of vital force than milk, and no shade can resist it. Have a care to clear the space where you work from other corpses, or parts of corpses, lest your blood of sacrifice attract the wrong shade, for if you spill your blood in a graveyard, you will soon be surrounded by countless shades maddened with hunger.

The blood of a cock that is all black in feather from its crown to its feet is suitable for sacrifice, to draw forth the shade of the dead. The neck of the bird should be cut over a bowl and the blood allowed to fill the bowl. More potent is the blood of a goat. In extreme necessity the necromancer may cut himself and fill the bowl with his own blood. It would, of course, be a serious crime to take the life of another living human being to draw forth the blood of sacrifice, and indeed, it is seldom necessary to do so.

The dead carry two kinds of secrets of value to the living. The first kind are the secrets known during life, such as the hiding places of treasure, valuable legal documents, precious objects, and so on. Also, secrets having to do with the affairs of men that may be turned to purposes of social advancement or extortion.

The second kind of secrets are those acquired by the shade of the dead after death. The dead know matters pertaining to the salvation of the soul and the avoidance of damnation that are eagerly sought by men who have lived immoral and criminal lives. Such men seek, after their deaths, a freedom from punishment or remorse. They seek a great estate with many slaves in the land of the dead similar to the estate they enjoyed during life.

The Egyptians of old taught the way of this salvation to their kings and nobles. It was written in a book call the *Going Forth by Day*. With its guidance the newly dead was assured an afterlife of wealth and ease similar to the life he had enjoyed in this realm of the living. Examples of this Egyptian book survive, but alas! no living man can read them.

DAY FIVE

At my customary time of two hours in the afternoon I came to Alhazred's house and was admitted by the Egyptian woman with the steel-grey hair.

"He is expecting you," she said.

It was a surprise to see her at the gate. Always before the impassive manservant had opened it for me.

"If I may be permitted to ask, where is the man who usually admits me to the house?"

She regarded me without expression for several seconds, and I feared that I had unknowingly committed some impropriety, but at last she spoke.

"He is no longer with us."

With this ambiguous comment, so potent with possible meanings, I was forced to satisfy myself. She escorted me through the house to the library and there left me.

Alhazred sat hunched over his reading table, a drafting compass in one hand and a reed pen in the other. On the side of the table rested his celestial globe, which showed on its tarnished copper surface the constellations of the heavens. He marked certain astrological symbols on the parchment before him, and I realized he was constructing a horoscope. He did not look up but continued his work. I sat in a chair and waited in silence.

After the better part of an hour had passed, he laid down his pen and rubbed the inner corners of his eyes with both his thumbs, then seemed to notice my presence for the first time.

"I apologize for keeping you waiting, Hassid. It was not arrogance that caused me to do so, but perplexity. As you see, I have cast a horoscope, and I find unexpected difficulty in its interpretation."

"I did not mind the wait. May I ask whose horoscope it is?"

"It is my own, which I have cast for the coming month. It is my custom to read my own fate in the stars for each month of the year, that I may be thus forewarned of impending dangers or difficulties. But this chart –"

He raised it in his hands and looked at it by the light that filtered through the carved screen over one of the library windows. For a few moments he seemed to forget my presence, and an expression of puzzlement set lines in his face. At last he blinked and laid the parchment down.

"I confess this chart has me perplexed."

"Would it help your understanding to describe it to me?"

"It is strangely incomplete. In any horoscope there is a certain fullness, a sense of totality that encompasses the period or matter under examination, but this chart –" He shook his head. "This chart has a beginning but no conclusion."

The obvious surmise came to my mind. He must have seen it in my expression for he smiled sourly.

"It is not death. That is the first thing I suspected, but the indicators are not of death. Rather, they seem to show a termination or a cessation of some kind that I do not understand."

He shivered as though from some cold draft and rolled up the parchment, slid an ivory ring over it, and laid it aside.

"Have you given thought to what I told you the last time we spoke?"

"You asked me to reconsider my decision to study necromancy," I said.

"It is my judgment that your constitution is ill-suited to this art."

"So you told me, but my interest has not diminished," I protested. "Indeed, the lessons you have taught me have only reinforced my desire to learn."

He shook his white head sadly.

"You are too much a part of this world to cast it away and devote yourself to the world of the dead. The life-force is strong in you."

"All the better to study the dead, and dead things," I argued. "The vitality of my nature will guard me against terror and despair, which you have said are common pitfalls to those who seek the necromantic art."

"It is true, a strong will to live is needed," he said. "But you have something else – you have a lust for living. You are a creature of the day, not the night."

"You are wrong, and I will prove it to you. Do not send me away. Let me continue as your student."

He raised a hand and made a negligent gesture. I saw that his fingers trembled slightly. Despite the roundness of his voice, his body had grown frail with age.

"It was not my intention to send you away. I only meant to caution you. The choice is yours what you will devote your life to, and how you will live it."

He cleared away his astrological instruments from the table and took down his black book, unlocked it with his key, then opened it to a page he had marked with the white ribbon. I sat in the chair and read.

Necromancy

Most men are content to worship the gods they are commanded to worship, in the ways they are told to worship them. They accept what they are told by the priests or mullahs without question, and compete with each other to be a better servant or slave to those gods. The penalty for an inquiring mind is usually execution, preceded by torture.

But why the torture, if execution is sure to follow? Because men are fearful of torture and will do or say anything to avoid it. The heretic is tortured both so that he himself shall confess to having committed sin, and so that common men who hear of his torture in craven terror will avoid doing or saying anything that can in any way be construed as heresy.

Even so, there are always a few men, and some women also, who refuse to embrace orthodoxy in their speculations about the gods. They seek a deeper wisdom than that of the devout worshipper, deeper even than that of the robed priest in his mystical observances. They search for wisdom in the hidden byways of the occult, in the forbidden, the veiled and concealed, and they find it in the writings of other heretics who lived before them and wrote the truth about the gods, and our place in this world.

The priests cast of the Magi of Persia were the wisest men who ever walked on this earth. They studied the stars and their rays, the lines on the hand and the bumps on the head, the flights of birds, the patterns made by frost, the fall of white beans on a grid of squares, the glass roots formed by bolts of lightning in sand, and pictures that appeared to them in bowls of water and in polished gems. They did not receive their wisdom from other priests, but sought enlightenment from the gods themselves as to the ways of the natural world, both those ways that are exposed to common view and those ways that lie concealed.

All those of us who presume to follow their path call ourselves Magi, to honor them and to preserve their memory. The path of the magician is not an easy path to walk, for it is rough and wild. Few feet have trodden it, and only at infrequent intervals. The eye has trouble even finding it, so well is it hidden in open sight beneath the moon and sun. The path of the magician winds and twists in a way that bewilders the minds of common men and discourages them from its pursuit. It is a path for the few, not for the many; a path for the man of courage, not for the coward.

This is just as well for the common herd of humanity, for their minds could not withstand the truths of this world or its gods. These truths would drive them insane, and cause them to slay their families, yea, even their own children, and then themselves. For truth burns like the hottest fire of the blacksmith's forge, and few minds are pure enough to withstand its consuming heat. This cleansing fire melts the images in the minds of common men like figures made of wax, but what emerges from the fire is purest gold.

When considering the difference between the common worshipper of the gods and the magician, the Poet was moved to write the following couplet:

> *The faithful ask, "Which is true? The gods of our fathers or the One who is new?"*
> *The Magus seals his lips with a touch, and veils his smile from vulgar view.*

So great is the gulf between common men and wizards that we who walk the crooked path cease to think of ourselves as human. We have no more in common with the milling herd of humanity than they have in common with the apes in the trees. This has led some fools to state that magicians are an alien race fallen from the stars in ancient times, but this is a false teaching. Alien we are, but in mind only – our bodies remain mortal flesh and bone.

It is only within the memory of living men that the Prophet Mohammed conquered the civilized world and imposed upon it the worship of Allah, the One God who cast down all the gods and goddesses of the tribes of our forefathers. The gods our people worshipped for centuries were shattered and thrown out of their shrines to be trampled underfoot. Broken were their blood-stained altars, and razed to the ground their temples and monuments. How quickly the people have forgotten them, those ancient gods who brought comfort to our tribes for a hundred generations.

But it is all one to the magician and the necromancer, who understand the truth behind the facade of our tribal gods and view their passing without regret. For there exist other gods, Old Ones more ancient than our race, older than time itself, who came to our world from beyond the stars through the cascading gates of Yog-Sothoth, and these Old Ones are not so weak that a prophet and a conqueror can cast them aside like so many images of stone and wood and clay.

The Old Ones have no true images, only masks. Their forms are beyond our comprehension. They watch and wait at the boundaries of reality, between the real and unreal, between waking and dreams, and they whisper to us promises of rewards for our faithful service to them. The shattered gods of our tribes are no more than the playthings of children when compared with their greatness, which was, and is not, but which shall be again.

Those who serve them with their whole minds and souls receive teachings of wisdom unknown to any scholar, unwritten in any book, save it may be in this book and others penned by the Poet when he took strong drugs and dreamed of the time before the coming of the gods of our fathers.

And what of the One God of the Prophet that drove out the many gods of the tribes from their houses of worship? Is he not greater than the Old Ones? The Magi laugh at the mullahs. The One God, the Allah of the Prophet, is no more than the fantasy of the Prophet imposed by the strength of his sword upon the tribes of the sands. The prayers that echo from the minarets are never answered, for there is no god to answer them, and those who kneel at prayer and bow to Mecca worship themselves in a mirror of their own conceits.

The Old Ones are real, the Old Ones endure. They were here before life moved from the seas to the land, before birds flew in the sky, before our ancestors put on skins to cover their shame and stood upright, or spoke their first words, or learned the making of fire.

The Old Ones persist, waiting for the time when the stars align and come aright once again in the heavens, so that they can emerge from their places of refuge and make war for sport, as they did so long ago. The Old Ones can never perish, for they do not live as we understand life. They lurk, they watch and wait, and will do so until the end of time if need be, for they have the patience of the very stars.

We who give them our service know these truths, which must

never be spoken aloud or written in any common book or scroll, for they are a confession of heresy and a sentence of death to any man who utters them. Keep this wisdom close and keep it safe. As the gods of our fathers were swept away and scattered like so many bits of stone and clay by the Prophet with his avenging sword, so the god of the Prophet, the One God that drove out the many, will be swept away like a single blade of chaff in the winds of time when the Old Ones walk again.

Day Six

"Alhazred is not in the library. You will have to wait."

I looked at the Egyptian woman with some impatience, for I had hurried through the crush of traffic in the streets of Damascus to reach the house at the hour specified for my lesson, and found irritation stirring within me that again my teacher had not managed to be ready, when he had only to walk down his hall and enter his study.

"Where is he? Has he left the house?"

The sharpness in my voice made the corner of her mouth quirk with amusement, although she allowed no other feature on her face to betray her feeling.

"Perhaps the young necromancer would prefer to go to him?"

"Indeed, yes, that would be my preference."

"Follow me."

She led me to the back of the house, and the door that opened into the cellar. She gestured with her hand.

"Descend, if you wish. You will find him occupied below."

I hesitated and stared at her.

"You want me to go into the cellar?"

"It is a matter of indifference to me what you do," she said as she moved away from me on gliding steps that made no sound on the marble tiles.

For a full minute I stood alone in the empty rear hall and peered into the darkness of the open cellar entrance. Far below I could glimpse an occasional flicker of flame reflected from a wall. I knew there must be a lamp burning. Even so, it was only with great effort that I was able to force my feet to descend the stone steps.

The air was chill. An odor of mustiness filled my nostrils. Barely enough light reached my eyes for me to avoid walking into the walls of the narrow passage. As I continued along, trailing my fingertips against the bricks on either side, I heard the murmur of voices ahead. I stopped and stood with my breath held to listen.

"It is not as fresh as you promised." I recognized the voice of Alhazred.

"Times are hard," said a guttural voice that sounded like coughing in the throat. "The plague is over. The price of food is low. There are not so many cutthroats in Damascus as there once were."

"What you say is true," Alhazred admitted. "I will pay your price."

I heard the clink of coins, and the other voice chuckled.

"The young one is listening to us. I can smell him around the corner. Do you want me to rip out his throat?"

My heart quailed in my breast, and I looked behind but did not dare to move for fear of making a sound.

"Leave him," Alhazred said. "He is my student."

"If he is your student, you should teach him how to walk in darkness," the other voice said, and chuckled again.

There was a period of silence. I had almost worked up enough courage to flee when Alhazred stepped around the corner with a lamp in his hand.

"Help me with this."

He did not wait but returned the way he had come, leaving me to follow him. At the end of the passage was an empty room. I looked around at the bare brick walls in amazement.

"There was someone with you. I heard him speak."

"Perhaps you imagined it."

"I heard a voice," I said more firmly, and swallowed. "It was clear and distinct, only –"

He waited for me to continue with a slight smile on his lips.

" – only it did not sound quite human."

"Help me with this burden," he said, bending over a bundle on the floor. It was tied up in a sheet of dirty linen with hemp cord. As soon as I touched it, I knew it was a corpse, and that the linen was its shroud.

"You wanted to be a necromancer," Alhazred said. "Well, this is part of what we do."

"I – I've never touched a corpse before."

"You'll get used to it. Help me carry it into the workroom."

I forced myself to bend and wrap my arms about its bound legs. As I did so, I looked around the room. There was no other doorway, only a square iron grate set in the flagstone floor. Was it possible the other man, if indeed he was a man, had come up through the sewers?

Alhazred was stronger than I imagined. He held the oil lamp between his teeth and lifted the torso of the corpse as though its weight were of no importance. I held onto its ankles, my insides squirming with disgust. I half expected the feet to kick.

"If you feel yourself about to vomit, leave it and return upstairs. I don't want you to foul my workplace." His words were distorted because he could not move his jaw without dropping the lamp.

I swallowed the bile that rose from my stomach and helped him bear the dead body along the passage and into one of the rooms that branched off from it. A light was already burning within it when we opened the door. We laid the corpse on a low table. On the wall I saw a rack of saws and knives. There was a set of shelves filled with bottles and jars and tin boxes. The scent of spices hung heavy in the air, overpowering the mustiness of the cellar and the faint odor of decay.

Taking the lamp into his hand, he smiled at me.

"This can remain here while we finish your lesson for today."

"Finish? But we haven't started."

"Are you so sure of that?" he said without turning.

I followed him from the workroom and out of the cellar. He blew out the lamp and left it in the kitchen. We made our way to the library, where the black book lay on the table, waiting for me.

Dreamlands

All men live two separate lives, one while they are awake and another while they sleep and dream. Those of common minds prize the waking life alone, and seek in it all that is of value, but philosophers and poets seek inspiration in their dreams and look upon waking existence as a drab and tiresome drudgery.

Two parts of life for waking, one part of life for sleep. So it was apportioned by Azathoth who piped the pattern of man on his cracked flute, ages before life arose from the slime. Two parts for flesh and one part for mind, so the mother of chaos, Shub-Niggurath, shaped us in her womb. Two parts for toil and one part for mingled terror and delight, so the gates of Yog-Sothoth are measured and opened and shut. It is only through Yog-Sothoth that the threshold of sleep is crossed and the door to the palace of dreams thrown wide.

To the necromancer, the land of dreams is where the souls of the dead may be sought out and questioned. For dreams exist in a kind of middle state between waking reality and the underworld. As we pass from under the gold of the sun into the silver vale of the moon, where all things are white and black and nothing has color, we mingle with the dead who wander in their dreams in a condition of distress and confusion, uncertain whether they live or lie lifeless beneath the earth.

Thus do mothers meet their children, wives their husbands, and lovers meet one another, on the middle ground where all is contradiction. Who can know whether he walks in the dream of his dead forefather, or whether the ghost of his ancestor walks in his dream? It is a place of mist and illusion, where the shapes of things change from moment to moment, and dimensions shift from large to small, or far to near.

> In the land of dreams, the living greet the dead,
> Then waking, forget what they have seen or said.

Why do we forget our dreams so swiftly when we wake from sleep? It is to prevent our waking mind from dwelling on the land of dreams and going mad. Dreams and waking life cannot be reconciled. They are separate, with unique experiences in each state that never cross the threshold of Yog-Sothoth. Some shadows persist upon waking of what was done during dreams, but unless it is spoken aloud to another or written down on parchment, these fragments of memory are soon forgotten.

It is the way of the necromancer to remember the waking purpose during dreams, and to remember the events of dreams after waking. Through long months and years of training, the barrier between waking and dreams can be made passable by our awareness, so that we walk through dreams with perfect waking consciousness. Such training allows the mage not only to remember dreams, but to shape events within the dream. Truly, they may be called the masters of sleep.

Through the land of dreams lies the way to the land of the dead. At times it becomes necessary for a necromancer who cannot summon the dead into his dreams to go to the dead in the halls of Hades. This, the prophet Jesus, who was a great necromancer, is said to have done. Indeed, it may be argued that Jesus is a greater prophet than either Moses or Mohammed, since Jesus descended to hell while alive and they did not.

In dreams the ages of man that have long since passed away from the waking world are preserved. There we may find ancient cities or palaces that have rested beneath the sands of the desert for centuries. We walk their streets, pass from room to room, and if we wish, we speak to those who were once living, but who died long ago. For the ghosts of the dead haunt such lost cities, conducting their affairs as they did in life, passing to and fro, buying in the marketplaces, gathering in the plazas. They ape the living, but their eyes are dull and unfocused, their faces drawn with lines of sorrow, their voices dolorous, like the ringing of a bell beneath the waves.

In these cities and in other secret places in the land of dreams may be discovered books of arcane wisdom that have been lost to the waking world. An accomplished necromancer has the skill to study these forgotten tomes during sleep, and to retain the knowledge gained after returning to the waking world.

It is said that in the land of dreams there is a great library that contains copies of all the books ever penned by men since the beginning of the world. It is a tall building of gray stone upon a hill, with a sharply pitched roof of split slates. Monks tend to the needs of those dreamers who come to study there. These students pay for their services with the coins of the dead.

In secret rooms within this library, kept under lock and key behind closed panels, are books that were written by things not of our race, but older and wiser in the ways of war. Few can read the inhuman languages carved upon their stone leaves, or impressed into their golden scrolls. They are books not of our world, and some of them are more ancient than the very stars that shine in the heavens. You will find them nowhere on this earth, but only in the library of dreams.

Day Seven

The elderly Egyptian woman with the graceful posture and haughty bearing admitted me through the necromancer's gate at the usual hour. She did not speak. I followed her into the equally silent house and through it to the library, where the black book lay unlocked and open.

"Alhazred has marked the passage you are to read," she said. "When you have finished, we will discuss its meaning."

I frowned at her.

"Where is Alhazred?"

"He is otherwise engaged. He directed me to take his place."

This was not to my liking. My father had made arrangements with Alhazred that he should be my personal teacher, and had paid the necromancer a large sum in gold.

"I am not accustomed to being ordered about by a servant."

"I am not a servant."

"What are you, then?"

She hesitated, then decided to answer.

"Alhazred's companion in life."

"Companion? Do you mean his mistress?"

"I mean exactly what I say, and say exactly what I mean."

"You speak in riddles to provoke me." Anger flared in my heart. "I came to this house to be taught necromancy from a true necromancer, not to be taunted by a mere woman."

"A mere woman, you say?" She laughed. "Child, I knew more necromancy at your age than you will ever learn in your lifetime, no matter who your teachers may be."

"You are wrong," I said hotly. "I will become a great mage, and a master of the necromantic arts. It is my destiny. I have foreseen it in my dreams."

This revelation did not seem to impress her.

"Are you prepared to stand before a mage of ancient Egypt who has been reconstituted from his essential salts?"

"I am, once I have learned how to protect myself."

She shook her head with a pitying expression.

"Foolish boy. There is no defense against such a mage, except to kill him at once before he can utter a word or make a gesture with his hands."

"You speak as one who knows."

"Necromancy is not called the black art for nothing. It blackens the soul, blackens the heart, as blood blackens after it bubbles forth into the air. Make no mistake in your mind, child. Those who follow this path are damned for eternity. There are entities dwelling in the aethyr who stalk our kind, and things that hide beneath the earth who neither forget nor forgive."

"You are trying to frighten me. Why?"

She studied me coolly.

"Perhaps I want to spare one human soul an eternity of sorrow and despair."

"Yet you did not spare yourself."

"No, I did not spare myself."

"Are you not fearful about your own fate?"

"I fear only one thing in this world."

I thought she would name some entity, perhaps one of the Old Ones written about in Alhazred's black book, but she surprised me.

"I fear only that in his hour of need, I will fail his trust."

For some reason these simple words touched my heart. I was annoyed at my weakness and put a scowl on my face.

"Enough of this talk," I told her. "If Alhazred has ordered that you should teach me, so let it be."

Sitting at the table, I began to read.

Dragons of the Abyss

Concerning the most secret and hidden places of the earth, some are to be found atop the highest mountains in remote northern regions of snow and ice, and can be accessed for only a short period of the year when the weather is favorable; others are located on the distant Plateau of Leng, which lies far to the east and is so high in elevation, that the breath comes only with difficulty into the lungs. But the most secret places of all are located deep below the surface of the ground, in caves and caverns.

There dwell creatures that have not looked upon the sun since the Old Ones ruled our world. In some strange way the darkness and depth preserve their flesh and lengthen the spans of their lives until they become almost immortal. Many are reptilian or serpentine, for the serpent by his nature is great of years, and this natural inclination is enhanced by their deep abodes. It may be that they are forgotten by the gods, who have neglected to send Death to harvest them. Even Death would have difficulty finding them in the maze of tortuous passages where they dwell.

When they speak, it is with a hissing sibilance. Their mouths are not made to shape the words of our tongues. Those not driven insane by ages of solitude know the languages of the Old Ones, and for payment of knowledge or blood will teach their wisdom to any man bold enough to descend to their dwelling places. Have a care should you seek to question them, for their hunger is great and their honour scant or wholly forgotten.

Some say the dragons that once darkened our skies did not pass away, as most believe, but retreated to tunnels beneath the ground, where they burrow like great scaled worms. True it is, for the Poet has seen it, that some parts of the underworld are hot, so that the air sears the lungs and the rocks burn the fingers that touch them. Even the waters of these deep places boil like great cauldrons over a fire. But whether this heat comes from the fire of dragons or from some other source is for philosophers to debate.

Another danger, more stealthful and insidious, arises from the air within these deep tunnels. In places it will not sustain life. The man who tries to breathe it is left gasping and weak, and a candle thrust into it flickers and dies on the wick. When they find such bad air, it is the trick of miners to take small birds down in cages. By observing the birds they are forewarned of danger, for the foulness of the air affects the rapid pulses of the little birds more quickly than the slower pulse of men.

Those who venture into the deeps seeking knowledge of inhuman things have need of much light to guide their way. The passages are treacherous, twisting as they do not only from side to side, but up and down. Many the man has fallen off a precipice when deep beneath the ground, only for lack of a candle or an oil lamp. Also, there are stretches of tunnels that are completely submerged in water, so that they must be traversed by touch of the hand, in complete darkness, with the breath held.

For these and other reasons, the wise necromancer will take with him an assistant when he descends into the depths. Such a servant is useful when passing through more difficult tunnels. Also, when the time comes to bargain with the creatures of the caverns, it is convenient to have a living companion to offer as a blood sacrifice. Such offerings are seldom refused, and are apt to make the receiver of the gift more forthcoming.

The depths of the earth contain wonders so marvellous, they will scarcely be believed by readers of these words. With his own eyes the Poet has seen great pillars of faceted crystal, more transparent than the finest glass, yet of such a size that the pillars at Karnak, in Egypt, can scarcely equal them. The walls of some caverns glitter like ten thousand jewels, or are painted with a rainbow of colors that shimmer and dance in the lamp light. In contemplation of this the Poet was moved to pen the following couplet:

The modest bride hides her face from sight,
But parts her lips beneath the veil of night.

Verily, there is no church in Christendom nor mosque in the Caliphate that can match the lofty roofs of these great caverns, which rise far beyond the limit of any lamp to show. In yet another way they resemble places of worship, for in some there are recumbent stones of vast size that are flat on their tops, like altars. The remnants of offerings of beasts and men may be observed on a few of them, where at some period in the distant past, barbaric tribes of men made of those chambers their feast halls. Their charcoal drawings of buffalo, tigers, and other fierce beasts remain still on the walls.

Those who venture deepest will come upon vast caverns. These great voids in the earth contain salt seas that team with their own unique creatures. The fish are all blind, having no use for eyes in a realm of perpetual darkness. It is not possible to explore the extent of these seas, for there is no wood with which to build boats. It is said that strange things dwell beneath their surfaces, stranger even than the Old Ones, for the subterranean seas were here before the Old Ones filtered down from the stars, and what was bred in their depths was ancient when the Old Ones were young.

Day Eight

I arrived at Alhazred's house at the usual hour in the afternoon and found the necromancer seated in his library, writing what appeared to be a letter. He looked up as I entered and nodded to me, then continued to write for several minutes. I went to the window that overlooked a patch of garden at the side of the house and amused myself by watching his gardener weed a flower bed.

He finished writing and put his pen and ink away, then sealed his letter shut with red wax and impressed the wax with his ring. After waiting a few moments for the wax to cool, he transferred the letter to a cabinet that stood against the wall.

For the first time I noticed that his left arm was bandaged. The bandage was not obvious because the hem on the sleeve of his robe almost covered it, but when he moved his arm, the edge of the white linen wrapping became visible midway down his forearm, and I saw that it was stained with the brown of dried blood.

"Forgive me for not being here to oversee your lesson yesterday. A circumstance arose that could not be delayed."

"You are injured."

He glanced at his arm and shrugged.

"This is nothing. The result of my own carelessness."

"Were you attacked?"

"You are a most inquisitive boy," he said, but there was no real anger in his voice.

"Forgive me, my teacher. I am concerned for your well-being."

"I appreciate your concern, Hassid. Let me tell you this much, which must suffice. I was forced to speak with a creature that has no love for human beings, and I was careless. I could blame it on old age but that would not be honest. My attention wandered for an instant."

"Were you badly hurt?"

"Not when you consider the alternatives. The creature with which I held converse could have ripped off my arm at the shoulder with no more effort than you use to peel a grape. There are things in this world, ancient things, that have powers unconceived by human imaginations. They came here when men were mere apes, and here they stay, well hidden in the secret places of the earth, or beneath the seas, or in the space between the airy realm and the celestial fires."

"Why in the name of the Prophet would you seek out such a monster, if it is so dangerous and so malevolent?"

He gazed at me seriously, considering whether or not to speak.

"My remaining days on this earth are few in number. Forces have been set in motion that intend to remove me to a higher sphere where I will be judged."

"I do not understand. Have you committed some crime?"

He grunted and shrugged with a smile.

"In the eyes of some who watch our race, I committed the worst crime imaginable. I wrote the truth about their history and their natures. That is a transgression they will never forgive. They have been conspiring against me for years. I fear their time has almost come."

This revelation put me at a loss for words. My heart went out to this strange, enigmatic man. Although he had never shown me affection, I felt a bond for him because he was my teacher, and because I held his attainments in such high regard. It seemed wrong to me that so great a scholar should be hounded by inhuman things.

"My father has wealth. Is there anything he can do to keep you safe?"

He waved his hand in dismissal.

"Swords cannot save me. What will come for me will come in no ordinary way, but through one of the higher gates of Yog-Sothoth, and against Yog-Sothoth there is no defense."

He got down his book and opened it to the place marked by a

black ribbon. My heart was filled with emotion, but I could find no other words to speak that would not have sounded impertinent, so I sat at the table and read from the book.

Children of Dagon

It is a truth seldom contemplated that more water covers our world than there is dry ground to walk upon. These oceans existed long before living things crawled forth from them, gasping to breathe the air. What yet dwells in their abysmal depths is more ancient than anything that walks beneath the sun. Deep below the waves the water is cold and lightless. There dwell creatures that bide their time and wait for the stars in the overarching heavens to be purged of their poisonous colors, so that they may ascend into the air and rule above as they rule below.

Where they came from, no man can say. Did they fall from between the stars, as we are told some of the Old Ones fell, or did the ever fertile womb of Shub-Niggurath spew them forth in the dim first age of the universe? The monsters themselves do not remember.

Most of these Deep Ones have no interest in the surface of our world, which as yet remains unhealthful to their kind. A few have found commerce with the upper realm through their offspring. For the younger ones born on this world in more recent ages can bear the rays of the stars more readily than the great ancients, who remain in the abysses, protected by leagues of salt water.

These young are said to be conceived of the mating of the god Dagon with the monster Hydra. They have the likeness of their father, but they are much diminished. Indeed, when adult they are no larger than men, although they differ in their shape from the human form.

Their bodies are adapted to subsist below the waves. Their toes and fingers are webbed for swimming and their eyes large to see in darkness. In the sides of their necks are gills like those of a fish, although they also have lungs with which to breathe the air when they walk upon the surface. Their skin is moist, like the skin of a frog, and a ridge of spines runs down the middle of their backs. They are squat and awkward on the land, for their short legs are ill adapted to walking. They move by means of hops, like frogs, or prop themselves up on sticks, which they strap to their long and powerful arms.

In ancient times, before history records the event, these Deep Ones began to trade with the tribes of men. They came to islanders and gave them abundant catches of fish in return for the products of the upper world.

They began to marry with the daughters of men, for their males can breed offspring in the wombs of women, and men can engender offspring in the wombs of the females of their kind. Here an ancient mystery is revealed, for why should it be that men and the Deep Ones, so unlike in appearance and abode, are able to procreate? It can only be that the origins of Deep Ones and mankind are interwoven and connected. But this mystery remains veiled, and no sage is able to tell what this link, if indeed it exists, may be.

> *Out of the waves, to wed the daughters of men,*
> *They climb with seaweed clinging to their skin.*

It has been observed, by those who have dwelt among the islanders where the crossbreeds are engendered, that at birth those that come forth from the wombs of women are completely human in appearance and manner, so much so that they cannot be distinguished from normal human children. As they age, they progressively acquire the physical qualities of the Deep Ones.

Their noses become broad and flatten, their eyes protrude from their sockets and seem to have no lids, and their mouths widen even as their colorless lips thin. Gill slots develop in their necks, which shorten and thicken until their heads stand directly up from their shoulders. Their chests deepen and their legs bow. Webbing develops between their fingers and toes. In the later stages of transformation, these crossbreeds put forth a spiny ridge down their backs and find it difficult to walk upright. On land they are clumsy, but in the sea they are as swift and graceful of movement as seals.

They begin to spend more and more of their time beneath the waves, breathing not with nose and mouth but through their neck slits. When they are mature, they remain in the sea and dwell in the ancient underwater cities of the Deep Ones, seldom returning to the land except when it is time for them to mate with a human female of the island tribes.

Of the numbers of these children of Dagon, no final account is given, but all authorities agree that there must be many myriads upon myriads of them, for their cities are to be found all around the world in the deepest crevasses of the ocean depths. When the seas are calm, the lights of these cities may sometimes be glimpsed by mariners who pass over them in their ships.

Our race is able to share this world with the Deep Ones without strife only because we have no use for the bottom of the seas, and they have no use for the dry ground. Should this change, it is certain that the underwater race would expunge humankind from the face of the world, for their crafts and artifices of war are subtle and terrible.

They possess crystal weapons that spit out rays of death. In this way the great empire of Atlantis met its demise, when war was fought thousands of years ago between the warlords of Atlantis and the armies of the Deep Ones. So complete was their victory that today there is no trace of Atlantis to be found above the waves.

Day Nine

A man I had not seen before admitted me to Alhazred's house for my customary lesson.

"Who are you?" I asked him with a directness that was lacking in courtesy. What Alhazred had confided to me about his perilous existence had given me concern for the old man's security.

If he was offended, no trace of it betrayed itself on his impartial features.

"My name is Brunni. I have been employed in this household as manservant to its master."

I wanted to apologize for my abrupt speech, but felt foolish and said nothing.

"Alhazred instructed me to tell you to wait for him in the library. You know the way, I believe?"

"Indeed, I do."

"Then I will leave you, for I have other duties."

He turned and made his way up the staircase to the second floor of the house. I started toward the library, when the sound of music attracted me from the other side of entrance hall. It was a melody played on softly-plucked strings. I followed it through chambers of the house I had not entered during my previous visits, and found myself in a pleasant room where Alhazred sat facing his house mistress. Both held stringed instruments in their hands, which they played upon with obvious pleasure.

The music was more beautiful than any other I had ever heard. I listened in wonder. Despite the manifold accomplishments of Alhazred, I had not expected to learn that he was a musician.

The woman played on her *mizafah* with as much skill as her master. So precise was their playing that they seemed to be the right and left hand of a single mind.

There was love in the melody, and a haunting sadness, but also paradoxically a deep joy. From time to time their eyes met as they played, and when the woman smiled, Alhazred smiled as well, but faintly so that his lips barely moved and the smile was more seen in the corners of his eyes. The woman began to sing in the style *al-ghina' al-mutqan* in a sweet, clear voice. It was a story of passion and loss and regret.

I was enraptured and would have stood in the doorway for hours, but after a few minutes they brought the song to a close and sat for a moment in silence, unmoving. Alhazred noticed my presence.

"Did you enjoy the music?"

"It was astonishing. Beautiful. Who is the composer?"

He did not reply, but the woman said, "It is a song of Alhazred's own composition."

"I did not know you were a composer," I told him. Was there anything this man could not do?

He shrugged with indifference.

"In happier times I wrote music, as well as poetry. But I am an old man and poetry is for the young."

The Egyptian woman took his *'ud* and carried it to the wall racks where hung other instruments.

"Come with me and I will give you your lesson," he said.

I followed him into the library.

"I see you have acquired a new manservant," I said, merely to have something to say.

"Yes. This is a large house that requires many servants."

"Was there any news concerning the whereabouts of your former manservant?"

"I sincerely hope not." He noticed my expression. "By that I mean, I have put him so completely from my thoughts that I do not even wish to ever hear his name."

He unlocked and opened the black book that rested on the reading table.

"Read this passage, and then we will discuss its meaning."

Gods of Earth

Every race, every kingdom, every city, every tribe, every clan, every family has its gods. The gods of one region of this world are nothing like the gods of other regions. It has been said of the gods that they are innumerable, and it is true that no scholar has ever possessed the audacity to count them.

The gods of one village differ completely from the gods of another village only a few miles away, and as they are varied by distance so they are diversified by the passage of time, for the gods of our forefathers are not always the gods we worship in the present. They are like the rulers of men. They arise, they gather strength and for a duration they rule, and then they decline even as warlords decline in their old age.

Priests and holy men assert that the gods made men, but there is a secret wisdom held by the priests of Egypt that asserts the opposite – it boldly states that men made the gods, and empowered them by worship and sacrifices. By this, the Egyptians mean that men made the statues and images through which they converse with the gods, which the vulgar mistake for the gods themselves. But the deeper Egyptian wisdom teaches that the statues themselves are not gods, only houses or receptacles in which the gods reside.

By ritual practices and the utterance of words of power, the gods are induced to descend from the stars and take up habitation in the statues fashioned by artisans for this purpose. Once dwelling within a statue, a god is then nourished and made strong by the prayers, offerings and sacrifices of its worshippers. It will answer the prayers it chooses to answer by means of small movements in its facial features, its posture, or the fingers of its hands.

Understand the deeper, secret wisdom in these teachings. The gods do not truly inhabit the statues. They send down to the earth messengers to act as intermediaries between themselves and mankind, and it is these lesser messengers who reside within the images of the gods. The serving spirits pass on the prayers of men to the gods, who remain in the vault of the heavens, and according to their judgment and mercy, the gods sends down rewards or punishments upon those who worship them.

As men need the gods to receive their prayers, so the gods of this earth need men to supply them with worship, for without worship they whither and grow pale and cold. They do not die. As long as a single image of a god remains, or a single man remembers that god's name, the god endures. However, without the daily active worship of many men and women, the gods of earth remain impotent either to help or harm.

In this, the gods of earth differ from the elder gods, who care little or nothing about the affairs of mankind, and are not weakened when we fail to worship them. They have their own purposes, which they pursued before our race arose from the rocks, and they shall continue to pursue it long after we have fallen to dust.

At times it may chance that the purposes of the Old Ones will require the service of men, and then they will condescend to receive our worship, for our submission better allows them to command and control our actions. Before the Old Ones can accomplish their purpose of raising the goddess Earth from her fallen state to her former throne among the stars, they must breed children on the daughters of men to serve them in this great work.

But know this, you who think to adore them and gain thereby wisdom unobtainable from any book, there is nothing of gratitude or mercy in their natures. They will reward you only for so long as it serves their ends, and when you are no longer of service, they will discard you like an empty husk.

The gods of earth speak about the elder gods in whispers, and refrain from naming them aloud, for they are terrified of their vast wisdom and power. When the gods meet together atop mountains in the dreamlands to dance and rejoice in their existence, they wonder about the dangers of the elder gods and debate their fell purposes in fearful tones.

Above all the others they fear Nyarlathotep, the soul and messenger of Azathoth, the blind idiot god who is the source and spark of all creation. It is said that Nyarlathotep hates the gods of earth for their weakness and their dependence on the worship of mankind. He finds amusement in tormenting them, by forcing them to dance for his own pleasure, and bow their heads when he is present. The gods of earth obey, for they are terrified of awakening his wrath.

Heads bowed, they dance, afraid to raise their eyes
To look upon the face that all their works despise.

Since the coming of the Prophet, the uncountable gods of the desert tribes have been replaced by Allah, the One God, who we are told is the same as the god of the Jews and the Christians. This change from many gods to one happened within the memory of living men. There are still remote cities and villages that cling to their many god-vessels of wood and clay and stone, refusing to abandon the deities they represent. But the heel of Islam is heavy on the necks of infidels, and no doubt all these many gods will be discarded in favor of Allah within a generation or two.

Few are the scholars bold enough to write of the place of Allah among the gods of this world. It is considered a blasphemy punishable by death. If a ranking were to be made among the gods, then Allah would surely be placed above the gods of our forefathers because did he not drive them out of their places of worship and destroy their images? Yet it would be foolhardy to assert that this One God is greater than the elder gods, for Allah is certainly a god of men. Does he not receive our prayers and answer them? The Old Ones care nothing for our prayers, nor do they require them. In this they are above the One God, as they are above the many gods of earth.

Day Ten

I entered Alhazred's house with the determination to confront the old man and ask him when he intended to teach me the practices of necromancy. It was all very well to learn about the Old Ones who had inhabited our world before the coming of humanity, but I was growing impatient to study the magic that had first attracted me to necromancy. I longed to converse with the dead and to acquire the secrets that lie beyond the grave.

He must have heard the door when I was admitted, for he motioned for me to come quickly.

"You arrive at a most opportune moment, Hassid. I need you as a witness to a contract I have just drawn up and am about to sign."

I followed him into the library, somewhat deflated of my purpose by my curiosity. The Egyptian woman was there, graceful and poised as always, but there was a redness around her eyes that made me think she must have recently been weeping. A parchment lay across the table. Beside it were Alhazred's pen and his personal seal.

"This document states that in the event of my death or disappearance from Damascus for a period longer than one lunar month, this house and all of my money and possessions shall pass to my house mistress, Martala, who stands before you. Here, read it with care."

I held the parchment so that it caught the light from the window and read his precise handwriting, which was almost as perfect as that of a professional scribe.

"This is your will," I said.

"Indeed, that is so. Have you read it?"

"Yes."

"Do you agree that I have written it without duress, in a sane condition of mind and in good physical health?"

"Yes, of course."

He took the parchment and laid it on the table once again. The woman stepped forward and took the reed pen from its holder, dipped its point in ink, then hesitated.

"Are you certain this is necessary?" she asked him.

"I am certain."

A tremor of distress ran through her body.

"Remember your strength," he said to her with a sternness I had never before heard him use.

She collected herself and bent to sign her name at the bottom of the parchment. He took the pen without ceremony, dipped it, and signed his own name below hers, then held a stick of sealing wax over the flame of a lamp and dripped it beside his name. He took his carnelian desk seal and impressed it into the wax.

"Now you," he said, handing the pen to me.

I wrote my name in full below his, and added the words, "witness to the signing of this document."

"Excellent," he said, and handed the parchment to the woman. "Let this dry, then put it into the strong box."

She took it and left the library without a word to him or a glance at me.

"I am sure you have many years of life remaining," I said. It seemed like a remark appropriate to the circumstances.

"Are you?" he said with his habitual ironic quirk of the lips.

I remembered my original intention and gathered my courage.

"Teacher, I know that our discourses concerning the nature of the Old Ones are important –"

"I'm glad to hear it."

"But I believe it is time for you to teach me some of the actual techniques of the necromantic arts. After all, that it the reason I came to this house, not to learn ancient and forgotten histories."

"Your keenness to move on with your studies does you credit."

"Then you will teach me necromancy?"

"Unfortunately, I must inform you that I can retain you as my student for no longer than the end of this week. You will have to find another teacher to carry forward your studies, in which I have no doubt you will eventually be competent."

This unexpected statement deflated me.

"But why? Have I not been an attentive student?"

"Your punctuality has been admirable."

"Have you heard some gossip about me that has turned your heart against me?"

He looked at me with something that resembled compassion.

"Your character is immaculate, Hassid."

"Then why do you intend to dismiss me?"

"That is not a subject I am prepared to discuss with you. Let us continue with today's lesson."

Taking down the book, he laid it open at the passage he had marked for this day's discussion. I wanted to demand a reason for his refusal to remain my teacher, but I realized by his manner that he would hear no more words on the subject. I sat and read.

Goat with a Thousand Young

All things are formed by a male and a female principle, which unite together to produce a reconciliation of their contrary natures in the generation of offspring. In human society this generative process is sanctified by the marriage of men and women, who together couple and engender children. But as the books of the great mage, Hermes Trismegistus, teach us, what is below is like that which is above. The smaller is replicated and mirrored in the larger, even as a lamp will sometimes cast shadows upon the clouds that are many times greater than the thing that gave them rise.

The secret teachings tell us that the father of the universe is Azathoth, who creates all things from chaos by the song he is forever playing on his cracked flute. The notes of the song fly out to the furthest reaches of his creation in a sequence that never repeats itself, like the numerals that are produced in the squaring of the circle. Yet without a womb in which to plant themselves, these seeds would fall on barren ground and be wasted. It is the ever-open womb of the Old One who is called Shub-Niggurath that receives the musical notes of the all-father and nurtures them in darkness until they are ready to emerge into the light.

Of the true face and shape of this Old One, there is no description, but it is whispered that her womb gapes like the mouth of a great cavern in the earth, forever hungry to swallow whatever may fall within its shadow. From this opening arises an endless groan that is caused by the winds that move in by day and out by night. It is not to be encountered in the waking world, but only in a distant desert waste in the land of dreams.

Within this cave dwell monsters of every description. The mind of man is not clever enough to invent the multitude of misshaped creatures that splash and gibber and howl and scratch in its depths. From time to time, something emerges, and then somewhere in the world a man who lies in sleep shrieks aloud and wakes with the image of the thing still in his mind. This is the source of all nightmares, which few men know.

Not everything born from the womb of Shub-Niggurath is horrifying. The womb gives forth good as well as evil, for it is the source of all generation. As the creatures of nightmare are released in sleep and in dreams, under cover of darkness, so the creatures of our world are brought forth beneath the sun, fully formed and endowed with their souls. The womb pours forth its children without discrimination, for in the eyes of the mother, none is less beautiful than the next.

It is said that Nyarlathotep stands before the cave of the great mother, holding a scythe. As her brood emerges, he exercises his critical judgment. Some he permits to go unmolested, but others he cuts down like ripe wheat in the field. In this way the balance of creation is maintained, and the endless fertility of Shub-Niggurath's womb does not fill the entire world with monsters.

She is worshipped still in distant waste places of the world, where the tribes are barbaric and have never known the gentleness of more humane gods. They adore her in the form of a lustful male goat, black in all parts of its body, and refer to her as the Goat With a Thousand Young. It may seem strange that a goddess of new birth should be adored as a male beast, but the goat signifies lust in all regions of the world, and the overriding principle of Shub-Niggurath is the necessity to breed.

She is beyond male or female, beyond good or evil. Her children define all things that have shape and being. No cry comes to the throat of a man in battle, or moan of pleasure from the reddened lips of a woman in love, except it issues from the womb of this goddess.

Few men seek to approach her carved images with prayers and offerings. She is consumed with her children and has little force remaining for lesser matters. Her joy comes from giving birth. The pain and blood of childbirth both delight her. Every womb of every kind that exists in our world is modeled on the womb of Shub-Niggurath, and every birth, be it perfect in its form or misshapen, be it a birth of flesh or an ideal birth of mind, is the child of this goddess.

> *Horror in darkness, beauty in light,*
> *All are one in the Black Goat's sight.*

Worship of this goddess was the first worship adopted by our race, in its dim beginnings, long before we knew the art of writing, before sailing ships, before the wheel, even before our mastery of fire. Of all wonders, none is more potent and palpable than the wonder of childbirth. For this ability women were worshipped by the men of these ancient tribes, and their goddess was made in the shape of a pregnant woman, with breasts bursting with milk and a round belly. This was the goddess form of Shub-Niggurath, expressing herself through the fertile female principle of our race.

It was only later in our history that a recognition of the necessity for discrimination and selection arose. Those that came forth from the womb that were monstrous and unfit for life were slain. Sometimes they were placed on a high open space where the infant would die of exposure to the elements. Sometimes they were left for wolves to find. Sometimes they were cast into the mouths of deep caves, and in this way given back to the goddess who malformed them. This selection was made by men, who in the exercise of their critical judgement expressed the function of Nyarlathotep.

These are the four great principles of the universe, by which it is sustained: Azathoth, the divine music of creation in all things; Yog-Sothoth, who opens the gates to release the music into the greater world; Shub-Niggurath, the womb that pours forth without ceasing an endless number of children, both those that are monstrous and those that are perfect; Nyarlathotep, who exercises critical judgement over the creatures that stream from the womb of Shub-Niggurath, culling those that are unfit and cannot be permitted to breed.

Day Eleven

"**I** wish I could persuade you to continue as my teacher," I told Alhazred.

He had been waiting in the library at the time of my arrival. His lined face wore a preoccupied expression. He did not seem to hear my words, so I repeated them. He turned to me with a slight smile.

"Your persistence is admirable, but it is simply not possible. However, if you send me the name of your next master, I will write to him and commend your character and intelligence."

"Thank you, but I have no idea who else might be able to teach me."

"As to that, I can recommend several names, all of them competent mages."

He named three names. I found paper and ink, and he repeated the names more slowly while I wrote them down.

"Any of these men has the knowledge to instruct you."

None of them has the knowledge of Alhazred, I thought to myself, but had enough forbearance not to speak the words aloud.

He drew the book from its place on the shelf and set it on the table. As he was unlocking it, he suddenly stopped and stood absolutely still.

"Is something the matter?"

He raised a finger in warning to silence me, his head cocked to the side. I stopped my breath and listened. There was the chirp of birds, the faint rattle of cartwheels in the street, a distant bark of a dog.

"I hear nothing."

"Silence."

Then I heard it, a kind of low hum like a thousand bees in a box, but deeper in pitch. It was not so much in my ears as in the bones of my head and my teeth. My skin prickled and the hairs lifted on the backs of my hands and on my neck. I had felt such a thing only once before when, as a boy, I had traveled into the mountains with my father, and been caught beneath a tempest of thunder and lightning.

"What is happening to the light? It's getting darker."

He did not answer, but turned to look at the window, his mouth set with determination. The humming increased.

At that moment the Egyptian house mistress ran into the library with an expression of alarm.

"Come to me, both of you," Alhazred said. "I need your vital energies."

He made his way around the table to the open center of the floor and stood on the rug that lay there. She went to him immediately. I approached more slowly, my confusion growing. It was now almost as dark as night. Something had occluded the sunlight and prevented it from reaching the window, yet when I looked to the window I saw nothing. The house seemed to have fallen under an invisible yet palpable shadow. I wondered if it could possibly be an eclipse of the sun.

"Give me your hand, Hassid," the old man said harshly.

I hurried over to him and let him grasp my hand in his. The woman took my other hand and Alhazred took her other hand. We stood in a circle, facing each other. Alhazred's features were composed. The woman looked nervous but determined. I can only assume that my face showed the naked terror that was building in my heart as the humming noise continued to increase.

Alhazred began to chant in a language unfamiliar to me. I recognized the name Yog-Sothoth from my readings of his book. He repeated this name several times, and also spoke the name Nyarlathotep, but spat it out as a kind of curse with a grim expression. His strange jade-grey eyes flashed with emotion.

I felt a kind of flowing forth of my strength, and had to catch myself before my knees buckled. Dizziness filled my head. I would have let go of their hands, but they would not release me. It took all of my courage not to cry out in terror.

Alhazred spoke the final words of his chant almost at a shout. I may have imagined it, for I was near to fainting, but I thought I saw a flash of white light strike upward from our circle and pass through the ceiling of the library. It was so brief, I am not certain it even happened.

At that moment, the humming ceased. We all stood like conjoined statues and listened, our faces turned upward to the ceiling, but why this was I cannot say, for there was nothing to see on the ceiling panels.

"It is becoming lighter," the woman whispered.

Indeed, the shadow that had fallen across the window was withdrawing itself. A single bird began to chirp, and it was soon joined by several others. In minutes all trace of the shadow was gone.

Alhazred released my hand. I flexed my fingers and winced. For a man of his years, his grip was unnaturally powerful. The woman also released me. I turned and saw that the new manservant stood in the doorway of the library, trembling and white of face.

"Return to your work, Brunni."

He swallowed with difficulty and nodded several times.

"Yes, Alhazred."

The three of us continued to stand on the rug, listening to the birds.

"What was that shadow?" My own voice sounded strange to me.

"My enemy is determined to end my earthly life," he said. "He is able to use the gates of Yog-Sothoth, but my household defenses served their purpose. He was not able to open a gate within this house."

He went to the table and opened his book, using one of its ribbons to find the page he had marked for my lesson.

The Egyptian nodded to him and left the library without speaking a word to me.

"Sit down and read," he said.

Wondering in my mind at what had just occurred, I sat and read the indicated passage.

Gates of Yog-Sothoth

All gates are one in Yog-Sothoth. He is the lord of transitions, the master of all comings-in and goings-out. None can pass from one place to another without passing through his mouth. When he parts his lips the gateway is formed, and it subsists only so long as his lips are parted. For he has the power to prohibit passage through his gates, and if he will say no, then none may pass, not even the greatest gods or djinn.

By the Romans he was called Janus, the god of portals, and they gave him a head with two faces, one for entering in and the other for going out. But the Romans did not comprehend his greatness or his glory. No god is mightier than Yog-Sothoth. If he forbid the transition of a gate, then no man or god may pass. Not even the Old Ones dare defy him. No art of magic, no alien craft, no primal force of nature can open a gate that Yog-Sothoth seals.

By a spiral vortex the gates are opened, and by a counter spiral they are shut. When a door is opened, the spiral is formed although it may not be seen, and when a door is closed the opposite spiral turns. From a point source the spiral opens the circle, and from the circle to the point the spiral closes.

These spirals are represented in our art by the symbols of the Persian astrologers that express the Head and the Tail of the Dragon. The dance of the moon with the sun is the never-ending ritual dance of Yog-Sothoth. For when the moon intersects the path of the sun in her rising the gate is opened, and when she crosses the path of the sun in her descent the gate is shut. By drawing the symbols of transition and holding them clear in the mind are the gates moved, even the greater gates of birth and death.

Those who pass through the doors of this world and other

worlds pass into the mouth of this god and exit from his anus. This transition has no duration and occupies no dimension. It is not a place in itself, but the space between places, which is the smooth point that some erudite sages among the Hebrews call the White Head, and after another fashion, the Ancient of Days.

Go in at the north and pass forth in the south,
What falls 'neath the tail was consumed by the mouth.

The door to the meanest hovel and the door to the most magnificent palace are alike the gates of Yog-Sothoth. Birth is the coming forth and death is the entering in. Each passage of the threshold is a little birth and a little death, which in truth are no different from the great birth and great death, for is it not written by Thrice-great Hermes that what is above is like to that below; and what is below is like to that above?

It is the office of this Old One to command the higher gates between the stars through which passage is made between the worlds. It is within his power to make a journey of many years take only an instant; or if he wills he may extend a journey of only a brief while to endless years of toil and torment. So was the voyage of the Greek Odysseus lengthened by Yog-Sothoth for the amusement of the gods.

Call him with the nodes of the moon, and with spiral force within the stone circle of art, and with blood freshly spilled and steaming. He comes upon the air to the high places, heralded by warm winds that stir the dust. His face is called the Macroprosopus, the Great Face. It has the form of circles within circles, and wheels within wheels, all of them turning and bright with a thousand colors that flash out like the colors of a serpent that has newly shed its skin.

His voice, when he speaks, rolls across the heavens like thunder, and lightning strikes down from his eyes, which are countless in number and always turning, revolving one inside another. Upon the air above the blood of sacrifice his mouth will open, and the portal will form. Pass through swiftly! If it shall close, no art of man or god can open it again. Each gate opens but once and never thereafter. Other gates may appear similar, and may lead to similar places, but they are never the same gate.

Seize your chance when it is offered and pass through boldly, with courage. Never hesitate. Yog-Sothoth hates the man of lukewarm heart, who knows not whether to go or stay; who will not commit himself to an action, but vacillates like a young child or a woman upon the threshold. It is the boldness of the golden lion to seize the head or the tail of the silver dragon in his jaws and thereby find success in transition. He who hesitates is lost.

Day Twelve

When I arrived at the house of Alhazred for my final lesson from the aged necromancer, I knew something was wrong almost before his newly-hired manservant opened the door. There was a depth of silence in the entrance hall that had not been there before, a kind of funeral pall that descended upon me like an invisible cloak.

Even the manner of the manservant was altered. He was always silent when he answered my ringing of the bell on the gate, but today he was withdrawn, almost vacant, as though his mind engaged itself with remote thoughts and had no inclination to attend to what passed around him.

He left me to make my own way to the library. There I found the Egyptian house mistress seated at the reading table, Alhazred's black book open before her. She stood up and studied me as I approached, her face tranquil.

"I am to teach you the lesson today."

Her words dismayed me. I had hoped to offer my thanks to the old man for his instruction.

"Where is Alhazred?"

Instead of answering me, she smiled and rolled her pale blue eyes upward.

"That is the question everyone is asking."

"I don't understand you."

"Haven't you heard the gossip in the marketplace?" she asked in surprise.

"No. I spent the morning studying at home and came directly from there."

"Ah, that explains your manner. Alhazred has vanished."

I stared at her in silence.

"Vanished?" I repeated stupidly.

"It happened shortly before noon. We were walking between the stalls in the marketplace when he was snatched into the air by some invisible creature and then swallowed by the monster – or so it appeared to those of us who watched from below."

"You saw this? You were there?"

For the first time I perceived the tension in her back and the slight tremor in her hands, but when she spoke her voice was firm.

"I saw it all. I heard his screams. More than a hundred people saw it."

I was at a loss to know what to say. The revelation shocked me so that I could barely stand. I put one hand on the table to steady my legs.

"Your face is white," she said with detachment. "Come and sit down before you fall."

She led me to the chair. I realized my own hands were trembling more than hers.

"Was it some trick of magic? Some form of deception?"

"I was showered with his warm blood. It was no deception."

For a time I sat breathing heavily.

"He is dead, then. The great necromancer is truly dead."

"Yes."

With sudden resolution, I stood.

"There is no reason for me to be here."

She put a hand on my shoulder and gently pressed me back into the chair.

"Before he died, Alhazred told me to give you your final lesson."

"He knew he was about to be killed by an invisible monster?"

"He sensed that his time was short, and the agent of his enemy close at hand."

"How is it that he did not protect himself?"

"I do not believe he tried to protect himself."

I looked at her and realized what a terrible blow this must be for her. She had been with Alhazred for many years. She had studied with him, worked with him, and knew all his secrets. This realization wove a new thread of thought through my mind.

"Will you become my teacher? My father is wealthy. He will pay you well."

She shook her head with the ghost of a smile on her lips. I felt transparent, like an empty crystal cup.

"I cannot become your teacher. I must spend all of my skills and all of my remaining life energies searching for Alhazred."

"But you just told me he is dead."

"Yes, but I must search for his corpse, or what remains of his corpse. If I can find where it has been hidden, no matter what its condition may be, it can be rendered down to its essential salts, and my love can be returned to me."

Her open admission of her affections for her master was embarrassing. I did not know what to say to her. She noticed my expression and her jaw hardened.

"Read your final lesson. It lies open before you. Then we will discuss what you have learned."

With a heavy heart and confusion in my head, I began to read.

Crawling Chaos

It is said that long ago, when the world was young, a man came out of Egypt. He wore the robes of a pharaoh and the crown of a king. His face was soft with youth and beautiful to look upon, his lips red and sensual, but his eyes were as black as obsidian glass. Where he stepped, the grass withered and died in his footprints; the flowers drooped and dropped their petals when the hem of his magnificent golden garments brushed them. When he spoke, in a voice that was like soft music, the birds fell dead from the sky.

He came bearing the gift of strange wisdom that twists and burns the minds of those who seek to learn it. On the palm of his extended right hand he offered hope, and with his clenched left fist he snatched hope away. Mankind has ever been his toy that he plays with like a malicious child. It amuses him to destroy our souls.

Upon the sands of the great desert known as the Empty Space he walks beneath the moon and stars. Travelers who chance to meet him in the silence of the night report that he wears a hood and a long black robe to conceal his finery, seeking to adopt the guise of a simple desert hermit. The hood veils his face with shadow.

Often he walks past the traveler without a word or gesture, but sometimes it amuses him to hold a conversation with men, who tell him of their affairs and their desires. And it may suit this Old One to grant to a man the thing he most desires in all the world, which he can do upon a whim. But more often from the malice in his heart, he takes away the thing the unfortunate traveler most loves. Or if the mood be upon him, with a single touch of his hand he reduces a man to ashes that blow away on the desert wind.

He is called the Crawling Chaos, but his true name, which few men dare write and even fewer speak aloud, is Nyarlathotep. Have a care that you voice it not, nay, not even in the silence of your own thoughts, for it will produce echoes in this world and in other worlds, and the Dark Wanderer may chance to hear, and may regard it as an invocation.

> *Speak not the name upon your breath,*
> *Lest you invoke the crawling death.*

It is said that Nyarlathotep is the soul and the messenger of the blind idiot god, Azathoth, and of those gods who dance around the black throne for eternity to the music of Azathoth's cracked flute. For the thirteen that dance are mere extensions of Azathoth's own substance. As it is the role of Azathoth to bring forth creation with the measures and rhythm of his music, so it is the place of his messenger to tailor that music so that chaos does not overwhelm cosmos, and the balance of the many worlds is maintained.

Nyarlathotep resents the task imposed upon him by his own nature, for he regards himself as the supreme being. Yet for all his arrogance and power, he cannot create, he can only limit and destroy.

It amuses him to keep the gods of earth his captives, and to make them dance for his pleasure, in imitation of the thirteen who dance around the black throne. Upon a high black mountain they are held prisoners, within a vast keep no army may breach. This is why the gods of man have ceased to answer the prayers of their worshippers. They continue to exist only with the sufferance of this Old One, who hates them all.

Across the many worlds, through the gates of Yog-Sothoth, Nyarlathotep walks in shadow, seeking diversion from his endless ennui. Existence holds for him no true pleasure, and the future offers nothing he has not seen before. He puts on countless shapes and faces, searching for respite from his eternal tedium, and it is for this same reason that he plays games with men and other living things. Games of chance afford him a few moments of uncertainty, and this condition of not knowing the outcome is one he relishes.

Yet beware, should you seek to match wits with this Old One. As much as he delights in winning, he is angered when he loses, and is not gracious toward those who best him. Though they think they have won, yet Nyarlathotep will find some way to turn their victory to defeat, and the wine in their mouths to vinegar.

Joyless, loveless, without compassion or involvement, he walks to and fro, and up and down, across the sands, his mind a writhing nest of spiders. It is whispered that he has it in his musings to one day strangle the blind, idiot god and thereby end his ceaseless song. Should he do so, then all creation on all the myriads of worlds within worlds would at once cease, and the entire cosmos would dissolve into a frothing sea of chaos.

Afterword

When I returned home after receiving my final lesson from Alhazred's companion, I found a letter waiting for me. It was from Alhazred. With trembling fingers I broke the wax seal and read the following:

If you are reading this, I am dead, or at least I am assumed to be dead, for I do not believe my corpse will be discovered in Damascus. My enemy knows full well that the body of a man may be reduced to its essential salts and then returned to life and health by the application of an incantation to Yog-Sothoth, who has the power to open all gates, even the gate of death. My companion, Martala, knows the way of this necromancy. It would not be the first time she has used it.

It may seem to you that I have been cold and distant in my manner toward you. Let me tell you now that my feelings for you are not so remote as they seemed. It was my purpose to make necromancy an unattractive subject of study, in order to test the sincerity of your desire, and if possible discourage you from this course of life, which is fraught with danger and sorrow. You remained steadfast in your desire to master the art, and I believe you are sincere.

Therefore, I send you this letter to ask a service of you, which you may freely decline. I know that my companion will seek to find the resting place of my body, so that she may recover it and rend it down to its essential salts. I ask that you help her in this quest.

She is alone in the world. Her determination is iron, her skills and cunning are formidable, but the forces that conspire against her purpose are many and great in power. Become her assistant. She will try to send you away. Do not allow her to do so, but show her this letter and tell her it is my wish that she allow you to help her. It is my belief that your help may prove crucial in the success or failure of her quest.

I will not lie to you, Hassid. I am asking you to leave the security and wealth of your family to venture into forbidden realms where death, and far worse than death, may lurk in every shadow. If you decline, I ask that you burn this letter and say nothing to Martala or anyone else about its contents.

Whatever is your decision, you are a fine young man of good character, with an excellent mind that always seeks the truth. You have my best wishes for your future life, wherever it may lead you.

I folded the letter and held it against my cheek while I thought about what I should do. Despite my high regard for the old man, I had not believed him to feel anything for me other than impatience and contempt.

Even if I showed the Egyptian woman the letter, I doubted she would allow me to accompany her. Did I really want her to say yes? My life was sedate and comfortable. I had everything I could ever wish for, thanks to my father's wealth, and my hours were free to pursue the arcane studies that delighted my heart. Did I want to give it up for a mad quest after the bones of a dead man that might lead me completely out of this earthly realm? Was I ready to face the wrath of the Old Ones?

Viewed in this way, the decision was not difficult to make and took only a moment. I left the house with the letter in my hand and returned to the Lane of Scholars to confront the Egyptian and demand that she let me accompany her as her assistant. After all, it was the will of my teacher, and I was eager that he resume my lessons.

About the Author

Donald Tyson has been writing about strange and uncanny things for four decades, both in the form of fiction and nonfiction. He is the author of the collection of stories, *The Skinless Face and Other Horrors* (Weird House, 2020), as well as the seminal novel *Alhazred* (Llewellyn, 2006), a collection of stories detailing Alhazred's adventures as a young man, *Tales of Alhazred* (Dark Renaissance Books, 2015) and a novel concerning Alhazred's quest for a fabled magic talisman, *The Red Stone of Jubbah* (Weird House, 2020). He lives with his wife, Jenny, in a farm house in rural Cape Breton, on the tip of the province of Nova Scotia, Canada.